07

823-912831

KU-722-251

Longman Study

£2.95

(Parade)

Brave New World

Longman Study Texts   General editor: Richard Adams

Aldous Huxley

Brave New World

edited by
Mark Spencer Ellis

Longman

LONGMAN GROUP UK, LIMITED
Longman House,
Burnt Mill, Harlow, Essex CM20 2JE, England
and Associated Companies throughout the World.

First published by Chatto and Windus Ltd 1932
This edition first published by Longman Group Ltd in
association with Chatto and Windus Ltd 1983

Ninth impression 1989

ISBN 0-582-33099-8

Set in 10/12pt. Linotron 202 Baskerville

Produced by Longman Group (FE) Ltd
Printed in Hong Kong

Contents

Introduction

Ever since its publication in 1932 *Brave New World* has provoked hundreds of essays, reviews and discussions. Such interest is an obvious tribute to the book. But there is, unfortu-
nately, a persistent tendency among many critics to oversim-
plify it. Some assert confidently that a particular point is the
crux of the novel. Others simply reduce it to a clearly defined
attack on a certain set of ideas. Sometimes such claims amount
almost to a rewriting of Huxley's book. Usually they spring
from two sources. The first is the reluctance to accept *Brave
New World* as something unique: instead, people feel the need
to try to place it within a specific pattern, relating it to Huxley's other novels or to 'utopian' or 'distopian' literature in
general. The second is the mistaken assumption that a work
which poses such frightening questions about human nature
and human society ought also to provide some answers. The
damaging social criticism contained in *Brave New World* could
only be valid, it is sometimes claimed, if a 'constructive'
alternative was offered. Such an assumption is unreasonable of
course. 'Don't criticise if you can't suggest anything better'
may sound like common sense. But a guide's warning that you
should not try to walk across a quicksand can hardly be
ignored just because he fails to suggest a different route.

Critics of *Brave New World* have differed about almost everything in the book except its importance and this introduction
will not try to suggest which view is the most convincing. Instead, its first aim will be to illustrate the experience – personal, social and cultural – from which Aldous Huxley was writing
in the summer of 1931.

Huxley's life

The bare facts of Huxley's early life can be stated quite easily.

He was born on 26 July 1894 at Laleham, near Godalming in Surrey, where his father Leonard Huxley was a schoolmaster at Charterhouse. After the publication in 1900 of the *Life and Letters of Thomas Henry Huxley*, Aldous' grandfather, Leonard Huxley left Charterhouse and took up a post with a publishing firm and also became assistant editor of the *Cornhill* magazine. The family moved the short distance to Prior's Field where Julia Huxley, Aldous' mother, started a school. After a year of education there, Huxley moved on to a preparatory school, and then in 1908 to Eton as a scholar.

In 1911 came a major disruption in his apparently conventional upper-middle-class education. After only two and a half years at Eton, Huxley left, following the sudden attack of an eye infection which made him almost blind. The next year there began a very gradual recovery of sight, but he never achieved anything like the full use of his eyes again. During the year of almost total blindness he learned Braille and in 1913 he entered Balliol College, Oxford where he read English. The first class degree which he achieved may not be surprising in someone of his ability, but it is also an indication of the determination with which he undertook all the necessary reading, slowly, with the aid of a powerful magnifying glass. Of course he was unfit for any war work, and between 1917 and 1919 he taught at Eton. But once the regular masters returned after the war there was no place for him. His worries about how he was to earn a living started to resolve themselves, however, as he began to undertake several jobs as a journalist and reviewer in London.

At this time he married Maria Nys, a Belgian whom he had first met during the war when her family had come to Britain. Their son Matthew was born in the following year, 1920. The next three years were an exhausting period of writing hundreds of articles for various London journals, and his first novel, *Crome Yellow*, was published in 1921.

The whole pattern of the Huxleys' life was to change in 1923 after Aldous had signed his first contract with the publishers

Chatto and Windus. Although their requirement of two books every year was demanding, the advances provided the freedom to live and work abroad, first in Italy and later in France, where the light was less of a strain on his eyes and where the cost of living was a fraction of what it was in London. Although the original terms of the contract proved to be too exacting, he established a growing reputation with *Antic Hay*, published in 1923, and *Those Barren Leaves*, in 1925. It was after the experience of a world tour which covered India, the Far East and Huxley's first visit to America, that he achieved real financial reward after the publication of his fourth novel, *Point Counter Point*, in 1928.

What this brief outline cannot indicate is the range of experience Huxley was bringing to his work in 1931. The world in which the young Aldous Huxley grew up was an intensely stimulating one for an intelligent child. The sense of being a Huxley, belonging to the family of one of the foremost nineteenth-century intellectuals, was not intimidating to a boy like Aldous, who was capable of fulfilling the expectation that all Huxleys must be clever and distinguished. Indeed, it is difficult to do justice to the range of a man who was rumoured to have read the entire *Encyclopaedia Britannica*. He was phenomenally well informed, and whatever the topic his mind was always sharply observant.

Before he was twenty-one Huxley underwent three traumatic emotional experiences, the effects of which can be seen in *Brave New World*. The first of these was the death of his mother from cancer in 1908 during his first term at Eton. Julia Huxley had been born into another distinguished family, the Arnolds, and certainly seems to have been a more natural teacher than her husband. Accounts from former pupils of Prior's Field speak of her as inspirational and extremely kind. Mercifully her final illness was not long, but her death must have been a devastating and sudden blow for her fourteen-year-old son.

Six years later, in August 1914, Aldous' brother Trevenan, then aged twenty-four, committed suicide. Of his two older brothers, Julian and Trevenan, Aldous was closer to Trevenan, the nearer to him in age. The suicide may have been related to Trevenan's sense of failure in not having achieved the highest academic successes, but the immediate reason was his falling in love with a girl whom there was no hope of his marrying. These two close experiences of untimely death seem to have filtered into the writing of *Brave New World*. There is a surprising intensity in the Savage's response to his mother Linda's death, and his final suicide by hanging not only uses the method of Trevenan Huxley's death, but also, more poignantly, takes place in the same area of Surrey where Trevenan killed himself. A passage in *Antic Hay* in which the central character reflects on his mother's death prompted Leonard Huxley to accuse his son of 'botanizing on his mother's grave', which is unfair. But it does indicate how Huxley was not afraid to use moments of intensely private emotion as the material of his novels.

Of course the knowledge that a situation has a particular personal significance for the writer does not necessarily help our appreciation of it within a piece of literature. But what it can do here is prevent us from seeing *Brave New World* as a purely intellectual novel in which no feelings or emotions are explored.

The third of these important experiences was the sudden onset of near-blindness, for this had the effect of turning him in on himself. Huxley was already distinguished from his contemporaries by his outstanding intellectual ability. He was also physically very thin and, at sixteen, well on his way to reaching his eventual height of six feet four inches (1.9 m) – another factor which set him apart from others. His new handicap must have increased his strong sense of being different, and certainly provoked the development of a single-minded determination to read as fully and as widely as he possibly could. In 1950, he wrote in a long essay on the philosopher Maine de Biran (whose writing is quoted by Mustapha Mond in *Brave New World*) that:

He was painfully aware that he had not been 'born like the rest of his race', that he was a foreigner, far from home in an environment he did not like and with which he was congenitally unfit to deal.

(*Themes and Variations* by Aldous Huxley)

It is not difficult to see the similarities of temperament which drew Huxley to the writer, of whom he also wrote: 'Few men have lived a life so intensely personal, so constantly introverted and self-conscious.'

Acute self-consciousness and shyness prompt the most moving moments in *Crome Yellow*. Although the book is usually seen as harsh, even cruel, in the treatment of the society it portrays, it is the vulnerable characters, those who do not see the world through self-confident intellectual patterns, who seem most sympathetic and most fully human. There is one particularly well written episode about a pair of dwarfs who are hounded into suicide by the insensitivity of their normal-sized son.

The yearning of men for unattainable or only briefly attainable women is a recurrent theme in these novels. This is also part of Huxley's own emotional experience and there was at least one period after his marriage when he lived in an almost perpetual agony of longing and apprehension after falling under the spell of another woman. Such frustrated longing appears in *Brave New World*, to some extent in Bernard Marx's feelings for Lenina, and even more in the Savage's attitude to her. The Savage's revulsion at what he sees as the sordid and shallow reality of his idol is also familiar ground for Huxley. Francis Chelifer in *Those Barren Leaves* reflected bitterly on the girl whom he had worshipped but who had left him for a rich admirer:

Every hour I spent with Barbara brought fresh evidence of her inability to play the ideal part my imagination had all these years been assigning to her. She was selfish, thirsty for pleasures of the most vulgar sort, liked to bask in an atmosphere of erotic admiration, amused herself by collecting adorers and treating them badly, was stupid and a liar – in other words, was one of the normal types of healthy young womanhood.

(*Those Barren Leaves*)

The self-loathing which Chelifer also feels as a result of his altered view of Barbara finds a parallel in the Savage's behaviour in the final chapter of *Brave New World*.

Moments of emotional stress in *Brave New World* are prefigured in earlier novels, and some have acute personal significance for Huxley. Another preoccupation of his, found both in the earlier novels and in *Brave New World*, is the search for self-knowledge. Self-discovery, perhaps through mysticism, is central to the conclusion of *Those Barren Leaves*, and in *Point Counter Point* Philip Quarles, a figure who shares many characteristics with his creator, does little more than analyze himself throughout the novel.

Brave New World: *background*

One can only suggest the possible relationship between a man's writing and the emotional impact of any crisis in his life; to go further is to risk providing the kind of explanation of novels through certain of their episodes which amounts to critical distortion. In the same way, though the enormous range of Huxley's reading and other interests will not prove a key to *Brave New World*, in itself the attempt to appreciate its extent can still be illuminating. The breadth of his knowledge is indicated by the catalogue of names he chose for the characters. These names, whether used to make significant points or chosen as jokes, refer to many areas of human activity. But Huxley's work was not confined to reading and his own writing.

In the year before he wrote *Brave New World*, Aldous Huxley had collected and edited D H Lawrence's letters for publication. This posthumous tribute to a writer for whom the Huxleys had considerable affection had involved Aldous in a lot of effort as well as travelling to bleak and, to him, unfamiliar parts of England in order to check the letters with Lawrence's relations.

The range of experience from which *Brave New World* came to be written was not confined to impractical knowledge. The title suggests the difficulties which may arise when naive wonder is not tempered, or perhaps blunted, by experience. In Act V, Scene I of Shakespeare's *The Tempest* Miranda, a young girl who has spent almost all her life on a secluded island with her father, Prospero, is having her first sight of a group of other human beings, and exclaims:

> O, wonder!
> How many goodly creatures are there here!
> How beauteous mankind is! O brave new world,
> That has such people in't!

Although Prospero knows that some of these 'goodly creatures' are the very people who plotted twelve years previously to remove him from his dukedom, he does not respond by rebuking Miranda or trying to extinguish her wonder by applying his experience to the situation. His only reply is a reserved: ' 'Tis new to thee.' The old man seems to be acknowledging the young generation's right to this sense of optimistic wonder, however naive it may appear to him, with the implication that true knowledge of the 'brave new world' can only come through experiencing it. To the Savage, in Chapter XV of *Brave New World*, Miranda's words are an inspiration:

> Miranda was proclaiming the possibility of loveliness, the possibility of transforming even the nightmare into something fine and noble. 'O brave new world!' It was a challenge, a command.

Clearly someone who is familiar with the Shakespearean plays most frequently referred to in *Brave New World* has a more immediate understanding of the book. The well-read reader can see, for instance, the way in which the sense of wonder expressed in the Savage's use of the romantic plays, *Romeo and Juliet* and *The Tempest*, dissolves into revulsion against the souring of love as he turns to the more pessimistic *Troilus and Cressida* and *Othello*. The Savage's repeating of Troilus' agonized longing for his idealized vision of Cressida is particularly ominous if it is realized how closely Troilus' attitudes to Cressida parallel those of the Savage to Lenina. The blankness at the end of the novel is underlined by the last two Shakespearean quotations, which echo first the despair and disgust of Othello and then the dismissive crudity of Thersites, the cynic of *Troilus and Cressida*. Elsewhere, less momentously, in quotations from *King John* or *Twelfth Night* for example, knowledge of the plays will allow the reader to see the jokes more quickly.

A similar use of a literary background comes in the echoes of Charles Dickens. For example, the rhythm of Dickens's most self-confident style is imitated in the picture of Henry Foster in the first chapter. For two paragraphs every sentence begins with a brisk verb:

> Told them of the growing embryos... Explained why it had to be stimulated... Showed them the jets... Spoke of those gradually increasing doses... Described the artificial maternal circulation... Referred to the embryo's troublesome tendency to anaemia...

This bold use of syntax in order to ridicule the character makes him a caricature. The self-important Mr Foster becomes a figure of fun, like so many of the objects of Dickens' laughter. More seriously, in alluding to Dickens' *Hard Times*, Huxley reminds us of what happened in that novel. A schoolmaster's ordered vision of humanity was shown to be hopelessly inadequate when applied to human emotion. His ideal school was a failure. So just as the Savage's use of the words of Troilus, a doomed lover, suggests that his own love for Lenina is doomed, the deliberate echoes in *Brave New World* of the ludicrous model school in *Hard Times* make the reader alert to the inadequacies of the system embodied in the brave new world.

There are other, more immediate examples from Huxley's reading which lie behind the book. In a letter of May 1931 he wrote: 'I am writing a novel about the future – on the horror of the Wellsian Utopia and a revolt against it.' The sort of optimism about the future which the writer H G Wells expresses can be illustrated from a book of his which was published in 1928, only three years before Huxley was writing. Wells foresaw an ideal world – a Utopia – where education was capable of solving all the pressing problems of mankind. With what Huxley saw as devastating naivety, Wells wrote

Utopia has no parliament, no politics, no private wealth, no police nor prisons, no lunatics, no defectives nor cripples, and it has none of these things because it has schools and teachers who are all that schools and teachers can be.

(*Men Like Gods* by H G Wells)

Wells seems to have no doubt about man's capacity to benefit from education. And near the end of the book Sungold, an old Utopian, proclaims: 'Before us lies knowledge, endlessly, and we may take and take, and as we take, grow.'

Of course Huxley was not the only articulate person to see that this vision of progress was a false one. There are notable parallels, for instance, between *Brave New World* and a little book called *Daedalus or Science and the Future* by J B S Haldane, published in 1924. Huxley had been a close friend of the Haldane family since his early days at Oxford, and it can be safely assumed that he had read the book. Haldane suggests that it is through applied biology, rather than the other sciences, that the most striking changes to human existence will come about. He foresaw the wholesale adoption of ectogenesis in the way *Brave New World* suggests, and in words that could have come straight out of Huxley's novel remarks that: 'the abolition of disease will make death a physiological event like sleep.' It is only in his conclusion that he differs essentially from Huxley's vision; he does not see these developments reaching their logical conclusion because

> the tendency of applied science is to magnify injustices until they become too intolerable to be borne, and the average man whom all the prophets and poets could not move, turns at last and extinguishes the evil at its source.

Mass production

It is wrong, however, to read *Brave New World* in simplified terms as a denunciation of scientific and technological progress. To see the figure of Henry Ford as a symbol of all that Huxley opposed is a limited and inaccurate version both of the man and of Huxley's view of him. It is interesting, for example, to read Ford's article on *Mass Production* in the 1929 (Fourteenth) edition of the *Encyclopaedia Britannica*. For even while advancing arguments in favour of mass production, he shows nevertheless, a clear understanding of the issues at stake.

> A cardinal principle of mass production is that hard work, in the old physical sense of laborious burden-bearing, is wasteful. The physical load is lifted off men and placed on machines. The recurrent mental load is shifted off men in production to men in designing. As to the contention that machines thus become the masters of men, it may be said the machines have increased men's mastery of their environment, and that a generation which is ceaselessly scrapping its machines exhibits few indications of mechanical subjection.

Henry Ford's aim in this article was not only to show that man could continue to be independent in the machine age; he also went on to consider the more widespread results of mass production, a concern that is absolutely central to *Brave New World*:

> As to the effects of mass production on society, the increasing supply of human needs and the development of new standards of living are the elements to be estimated. The enlargement of leisure, the increase of human contacts, the extension of individual range, are all the results of mass production.
>
> (*Encyclopaedia Britannica, Fourteenth Edition*)

It is a crude oversimplification then, to see the historical Henry Ford as the symbol of indifference to individualism, and it would be wrong to suggest that this is how Huxley thought of him. Indeed, his first response to reading Ford's *My Life and Work* was recorded in *Jesting Pilate* in 1926.

> It was somewhere between the tropic and the equator that I read the book. In these seas, and to one fresh from India and Indian 'spirituality', Indian dirt and religion, Ford seemed a greater man than Buddah. In Europe, on the other hand, and still more, no doubt, in America, the Way of Gautama has all the appearance of the way of Salvation. One is all for religion until one visits a really religious country. There, one is all for drains, machinery and the minimum wage. To travel is to discover that everybody is wrong.
>
> (*Jesting Pilate* by Aldous Huxley)

In the pueblo at Malpais drains have a lot more to be said for them than do ophthalmia, skin diseases, goitre, and whipping. Huxley's response to scientific progress was essentially one of fascination, though he was disturbed about the possible effects on people of scientific technology. He was also fascinated by the idea of hypnotism and sleep teaching; hypnopaedia as practised in *Brave New World* is horrific, but we cannot take this as a total condemnation of all teaching which takes place below the level of waking consciousness. When his four-year-old son was refusing to eat meat, Huxley wrote to his own father:

> However, he gets on all right on a vegetarian diet. I sometimes wonder, though, whether a course of mild hypnotism and suggestion mightn't do good; but I don't know how young that sort of thing can be begun.
>
> (*Letter, 29 April 1924*)

The grim implications of the hypnopaedic lessons for the Beta babies are clear, but there is no overt criticism of the methods through which these lessons are put across.

Approaches to Brave New World

A comfortable straightforward reading of the book as an attack on the Fordian world in all its manifestations cannot be justified. Huxley denies us a glow of indignation at what happens to 'victims' because they are deliberately created as too shallow to provoke the sort of response which can be produced by characters in a realistic novel. It is true that there are moments of emotional crisis and that Huxley has called on his own experiences to emphasize this, but all the bottle-bred, decanted characters are static, incapable of learning, changing and developing in the way real people do.

'Characters remain constant throughout a lifetime,' Mustapha Mond explains in Chapter IV. Their world of crude practical joking and humiliating laughter is not an adult one. Bernard's petulance undermines our attempts to take his emotions seriously. Not that these emotions are necessarily shallow. As Lenina runs away, Bernard is captivated by:

> the retreating twinkle of white stockings, the sunburnt knees vivaciously bending and unbending, again, again, and the

softer rolling of those well-fitted corduroy shorts beneath the
bottle-green jacket.

There is an excitement and liveliness in this description that is
human and appealing, even though the heightened poetic language is slightly ridiculous. Similarly, Helmholtz Watson's
sense of unfulfilment is genuine. But the practical image that
he uses to express it – 'like all the water that goes down the
falls instead of through the turbines' – is a clear indication of
his narrowness. The revolting image of the twins gathered
round the dying Linda like maggots or lice may suit our responses as well as the Savage's, but the first time such an image is used it describes the view from Henry Foster's helicopter
of the parkland being 'maggoty' with people. Here there is no
sense of revulsion, rather it is the reflection of a detached
observer.

Images do not always provoke the same response. Again and
again the point is made that these people have only a limited
number of possible reactions to situations and characters who
engage our sympathy cannot keep it. Thus, however tempting
it may be to base a reading of *Brave New World* on a sympathetic identification with the characters, it would be a distortion of
the novel to do so.

Huxley described his book as a 'Swiftian novel about the future'. It is as misleading to associate his own views with those
of the newcomer to the brave new world, the Savage, as it is to
see Gulliver as Swift's mouthpiece in *Gulliver's Travels*. Gulliver,
who is so attracted to the self-righteous, passionless and static
world of the Houyhnhnms in Part IV, and who reaches a stage
of insane revulsion from humankind, is no more to be
admired than is the Savage whose eventual self-loathing and
primitive need for self-punishment leads to his suicide. *Brave
New World* should not be read as if it presented competing
alternatives: to turn away from the new world it is not necessary to approve of the pueblo life. This can be seen in terms of
the Shakespearean plays through which the Savage expresses

himself. Although the nobility of the tragic heroes cannot be revealed in a world where everybody behaves sensibly, it does not follow that romance, as in *Romeo and Juliet* and *The Tempest*, can only spring from misery and degradation.

Moral lessons

What gives continued life to *Brave New World* is the urgency with which major moral problems are posed, and these problems remain as important today as they were fifty years ago. How would we respond to the technological advances Huxley suggests? Would we happily abandon political responsibility in return for *soma*? Can we be confident that our civilization would unanimously reject the logic of a *Brave New World* caste system, when we remember the sperm bank in San Diego which only accepts Nobel Prize winners as donors? In our world where credit cards 'take the waiting out of wanting' what can there be to disturb us in the motto: 'Never put off till tomorrow the fun you can have today'? How short a step is it to the moral lessons of hypnopaedia from whispered messages in supermarkets? 'I am honest, I will not steal' broadcast continuously in a New Orleans store put an end to $80,000 worth of pilfering a year. It is not so easy to argue when the results seem to justify the means.

In his 1946 *Preface* to the book, Huxley regretted that he had only given the Savage the choice between 'insanity on the one hand and lunacy on the other'. He went on to suggest a theoretical version of the novel in which there would also lie the possibility of sanity. The form this would take is suggested not only in the *Foreword* but also in his stark post-nuclear age fable *Ape and Essence*, published in 1948:

> Eastern mysticism making sure that Western science should be properly used; the Eastern art of living refining Western energy; Western individualism tempering Eastern totalitarianism.

Island, published in the year before his death, 1962, has been hailed as the fruit of Huxley's accumulated wisdom. A good Utopia is put forward as a positive alternative to the brave new world. But in *Island* there are sperm banks for talented fathers. Human nature seems to have changed so much that sexual jealousy has ceased to exist. Babies' responses are systematically conditioned, yet here this condioning is justified to a visitor from the outside world as:

> Pavlov purely for a good purpose. Pavlov for friendliness and trust and compassion. Whereas you prefer to use Pavlov for brainwashing, Pavlov for selling cigarettes and vodka and patriotism. Pavlov for the benefit of dictators, generals, and tycoons.

Brave New World is better without such alternatives. 'Solutions', especially the most straightforward ones, blunt the questions posed by the novel. However, in describing himself at the time of writing the book as a 'Pyrrhonic aesthete' Huxley implies that no glimmer of hope can be seen in the original work. 'And so they died miserably ever after' is put forward as the fable's conclusion. The careful (and unacknowledged) rewording of the passages of Newman and Maine de Biran (see notes to page 190), quoted by Mustapha Mond, removes the inconveniently dogmatic Christian vision of God while retaining the religious sense of some form of deity. The Huxley of 1931 may not have been as despairing of mankind as the Huxley of 1946 would have us believe.

It is because it refuses to jump to single-minded conclusions that *Brave New World* retains its power to disturb and intrigue us. A world with no strong feelings may be vile, but the madness of the Savage is no convincing alternative. In a review of the book, Bertrand Russell pointed out that it is wrong to claim that Huxley is pleading in *Brave New World* for strong feelings:

A few saints and mystics can love without hating, but for the bulk of mankind the only way not to hate is not to have any strong feelings at all.

(New Leader, 11 March 1932)

Unless man, equipped as he is with horrific methods of killing his fellows, can learn not to hate, Russell suggests that it is better for him to live with no strong feelings at all. This is what happens in *Brave New World*; the model character is that of Benito Hoover who:

was notoriously good natured. People said of him that he could have got through life without ever touching *soma*. The malice and bad tempers from which other people had to take holidays never afflicted him. Reality for Benito was always sunny.

Comparisons

Brave New World is a more disturbing novel than George Orwell's *Nineteen Eighty Four* with which it is often compared. Although Orwell's hero, Winston Smith, is savagely broken, his resistance and attempts to reach a degree of freedom reassure us; they make us feel that there is something in human nature which will always try to assert liberty. But in Huxley's book people have willingly given up all their freedom and moral responsibility in return for a world of stimulating sensation. Indeed, they are unable to cope with freedom. The Cyprus experiment, when a whole island of Alphas were left to govern themselves, ended in exactly the same plea for the burden of liberty to be removed as is described by the Grand Inquisitor in Dostoyevsky's *The Brothers Karamazov* (see introductory note to Chapter XVI in the *Notes*).

An illuminating parallel to the book is provided in *A Clockwork Orange* by Anthony Burgess. Here the question is raised whether removing a man's freedom of moral choice can ever be justified, even if it prevents him from choosing to be violently anti-social. Alex, the narrator, a teenage murderer, has been conditioned in a prison of the future to be revolted by violence. The only person to voice doubts is the prison chaplain. He points out that though Alex is no longer a wrong-doer, he has also ceased to be human as he is now incapable of moral choice:

> 'The point is,' this Minister of the Inferior was saying real gromky, 'that it works.'
> 'Oh,' the prison charlie said, like sighing, 'it works all right, God help the lot of us.'
>
> (*A Clockwork Orange*, Part 2)

Many aspects of Huxley's brave new world work all right – hence its continued power to fascinate and disturb us.

Brave New World

Les utopies apparaissent comme bien plus réalisables qu'on ne le croyait autrefois. Et nous nous trouvons actuellement devant une question bien autrement angoissante: Comment éviter leur réalisation définitive? . . . Les utopies sont réalisables. La vie marche vers les utopies. Et peut-être un siècle nouveau commence-t-il, un siècle où les intellectuels et la classe cultivée rêveront aux moyens d'éviter les utopies et de retourner à une société non utopique, moins 'parfaite' et plus libre.

NICOLAS BERDIAEFF

Foreword

CHRONIC remorse, as all the moralists are agreed, is a most undesirable sentiment. If you have behaved badly, repent, make what amends you can and address yourself to the task of behaving better next time. On no account brood over your wrongdoing. Rolling in the muck is not the best way of getting clean.

Art also has its morality, and many of the rules of this morality are the same as, or at least analogous to, the rules of ordinary ethics. Remorse, for example, is as undesirable in relation to our bad art as it is in relation to our bad behaviour. The badness should be hunted out, acknowledged and, if possible, avoided in the future. To pore over the literary short-comings of twenty years ago, to attempt to patch a faulty work into the perfection it missed at its first execution, to spend one's middle age in trying to mend the artistic sins committed and bequeathed by that different person who was oneself in youth—all this is surely vain and futile. And that is why this new *Brave New World* is the same as the old one. Its defects as a work of art are considerable; but in order to correct them I should have to rewrite the book—and in the process of rewriting, as an older, other person, I should probably get rid not only of some of the faults of the story, but also of such merits as it originally possessed. And so, resisting the temptation to wallow in artistic remorse, I prefer to leave both well and ill alone and to think about something else.

In the meantime, however, it seems worth while at least to mention the most serious defect in the story, which is this. The Savage is offered only two alternatives, an insane life in Utopia, or the life of a primitive in an Indian village, a life more human in some respects, but in others hardly less queer and abnormal.

At the time the book was written this idea, that human beings are given free will in order to choose between insanity on the one hand and lunacy on the other, was one that I found amusing and regarded as quite possibly true. For the sake, however, of dramatic effect, the Savage is often permitted to speak more rationally than his upbringing among the practitioners of a religion that is half fertility cult and half *Penitente* ferocity would actually warrant. Even his acquaintance with Shakespeare would not in reality justify such utterances. And at the close, of course, he is made to retreat from sanity; his native *Penitente*-ism reasserts its authority and he ends in maniacal self-torture and despairing suicide. 'And so they died miserably ever after'—much to the reassurance of the amused, Pyrrhonic aesthete who was the author of the fable.

To-day I feel no wish to demonstrate that sanity is impossible. On the contrary, though I remain no less sadly certain than in the past that sanity is a rather rare phenomenon, I am convinced that it can be achieved and would like to see more of it. For having said so in several recent books and, above all, for having compiled an anthology of what the sane have said about sanity and all the means whereby it can be achieved, I have been told by an eminent academic critic that I am a sad symptom of the failure of an intellectual class in time of crisis. The implication being, I suppose, that the professor and his colleagues are hilarious symptoms of success. The benefactors of humanity deserve due honour and commemoration. Let us build a Pantheon for professors. It should be located among the ruins of one of the gutted cities of Europe or Japan, and over the entrance to the ossuary I would inscribe, in letters six or seven feet high, the simple words: SACRED TO THE MEMORY OF THE WORLD'S EDUCATORS. SI MONUMENTUM REQUIRIS CIRCUMSPICE.

But to return to the future . . . If I were now to rewrite the book, I would offer the Savage a third alternative. Between the utopian and the primitive horns of his dilemma would lie the possibility of sanity—a possibility already actualized, to some extent, in a community of exiles and refugees from the Brave New World, living within the borders of the Reservation. In this community economics would be decentralist and Henry-Georgian, politics Kropotkinesque and co-operative. Science and technology would be used as though, like the Sabbath, they had been made for man, not (as at present and still more so in the Brave New World) as though man were to be adapted and enslaved to them. Religion would be the conscious and intelligent pursuit of man's Final End, the unitive knowledge of the immanent Tao or Logos, the transcendent Godhead or Brahman. And the prevailing philosophy of life would be a kind of Higher Utilitarianism, in which the Greatest Happiness principle would be secondary to the Final End principle—the first question to be asked and answered in every contingency of life being: 'How will this thought or action contribute to, or interfere with, the achievement, by me and the greatest possible number of other individuals, of man's Final End?'

Brought up among the primitives, the Savage (in this hypothetical new version of the book) would not be transported to Utopia until he had had an opportunity of learning something at first hand about the nature of a society composed of freely co-operating individuals devoted to the pursuit of sanity. Thus altered, *Brave New World* would possess an artistic and (if it is permissible to use so large a word in connection with a work of fiction) a philosophical completeness, which in its present form it evidently lacks.

But *Brave New World* is a book about the future and, whatever its artistic or philosophical qualities, a book about the future can interest us only if its prophecies look as though they might conceivably come true. From our present vantage point, fifteen years further down the inclined plane of modern history, how plausible do its prognostications seem? What has happened in the painful interval to confirm or invalidate the forecasts of 1931?

One vast and obvious failure of foresight is immediately apparent. *Brave New World* contains no reference to nuclear fission. That it does not is actually rather odd; for the possibilities of atomic energy had been a popular topic of conversation for years before the book was written. My old friend, Robert Nichols, had even written a successful play about the subject, and I recall that I myself had casually mentioned it in a novel published in the late twenties. So it seems, as I say, very odd that the rockets and helicopters of the seventh century of Our Ford should not have been powered by disintegrating nuclei. The oversight may not be excusable; but at least it can be easily explained. The theme of *Brave New World* is not the advancement of science as such; it is the advancement of science as it affects human individuals. The triumphs of physics, chemistry and engineering are tacitly taken for granted. The only scientific advances to be specifically described are those involving the application to human beings of the results of future research in biology, physiology and psychology. It is only by means of the sciences of life that the quality of life can be radically changed. The sciences of matter can be applied in such a way that they will destroy life or make the living of it impossibly complex and uncomfortable; but, unless used as instruments by the biologists and psychologists, they can do nothing to modify the natural forms and expressions of life itself. The release of atomic energy marks a great revolution in human history, but not (unless we blow ourselves to bits and so put an end to history) the final and most searching revolution.

This really revolutionary revolution is to be achieved, not in the external world, but in the souls and flesh of human beings. Living as he did in a revolutionary period, the Marquis de Sade very naturally made use of this theory of revolutions in order to rationalize his peculiar brand of insanity. Robespierre had achieved the most superficial kind of revolution, the political. Going a little deeper, Babeuf had attempted the economic revolution. Sade regarded himself as the apostle of the truly revolutionary revolution, beyond mere politics and economics— the revolution of individual men, women and children, whose bodies were henceforward to become the common sexual property of all and whose minds were to be purged of all the the natural decencies, all the laboriously acquired inhibitions of traditional civilization. Between Sadism and the really revolutionary revolution there is, of course, no necessary or inevitable connection. Sade was a lunatic and the more or less conscious goal of his revolution was universal chaos and destruction. The people who govern the Brave New World may not be sane (in what may be called the absolute sense of that word); but they are not mad men, and their aim is not anarchy but social stability. It is in order to achieve stability that they carry out, by scientific means, the ultimate, personal, really revolutionary revolution.

But meanwhile we are in the first phase of what is perhaps the penultimate revolution. Its next phase may be atomic warfare, in which case we do not have to bother with prophecies about the future. But it is conceivable that we may have enough sense, if not to stop fighting altogether, at least to behave as rationally as did our eighteenth-century ancestors. The unimaginable horrors of the Thirty Years War actually taught men a lesson, and for more than a hundred years the politicians and generals of Europe consciously resisted the temptation to use their military resources to the limits of destructiveness or (in the majority of conflicts) to go on fighting until the enemy was totally annihilated. They were aggressors, of course, greedy for profit and glory; but they were also conservatives, determined at all costs to keep their world intact, as a going concern. For the last thirty years there have been no conservatives; there have only been nationalistic radicals of the right and nationalistic radicals of the left. The last conservative statesman was the fifth Marquess of Lansdowne; and when he wrote a letter to *The Times*, suggesting that the First World

War should be concluded with a compromise, as most of the wars of the eighteenth century had been, the editor of that once conservative journal refused to print it. The nationalistic radicals had their way, with the consequences that we all know—Bolshevism, Fascism, inflation, depression, Hitler, the Second World War, the ruin of Europe and all but universal famine.

Assuming, then, that we are capable of learning as much from Hiroshima as our forefathers learned from Magdeburg, we may look forward to a period, not indeed of peace, but of limited and only partially ruinous warfare. During that period it may be assumed that nuclear energy will be harnessed to industrial uses. The result, pretty obviously, will be a series of economic and social changes unprecedented in rapidity and completeness. All the existing patterns of human life will be disrupted and new patterns will have to be improvised to conform with the nonhuman fact of atomic power. Procrustes in modern dress, the nuclear scientist will prepare the bed on which mankind must lie; and if mankind doesn't fit—well, that will be just too bad for mankind. There will have to be some stretchings and a bit of amputation—the same sort of stretchings and amputations as have been going on ever since applied science really got into its stride, only this time they will be a good deal more drastic than in the past. These far from painless operations will be directed by highly centralized totalitarian governments. Inevitably so; for the immediate future is likely to resemble the immediate past, and in the immediate past rapid technological changes, taking place in a mass-producing economy and among a population predominantly propertyless, have always tended to produce economic and social confusion. To deal with confusion, power has been centralized and government control increased. It is probable that all the world's governments will be more or less completely totalitarian even before the harnessing of atomic energy; that they will be totalitarian during and after the harnessing seems almost certain. Only a large-scale popular movement toward decentralization and self-help can arrest the present tendency toward statism. At present there is no sign that such a movement will take place.

There is, of course, no reason why the new totalitarianisms should resemble the old. Government by clubs and firing squads, by artificial famine, mass imprisonment and mass deportation, is not merely inhumane (nobody cares much about that nowadays); it is demonstrably inefficient—and in an age of advanced technology, inefficiency is the sin against the Holy Ghost. A really efficient totalitarian state would be one in which the all-powerful executive of political bosses and their army of managers control a population of slaves who do not have to be coerced, because they love their servitude. To make them love it is the task assigned, in present-day totalitarian states, to ministries of propaganda, newspaper editors and schoolteachers. But their methods are still crude and unscientific. The old Jesuits' boast that, if they were given the schooling of the child, they could answer for the man's religious opinions, was a product of wishful thinking. And the modern pedagogue is probably rather less efficient at conditioning his pupils' reflexes than were the reverend fathers who educated Voltaire. The greatest triumphs of propaganda have been accomplished, not by doing something, but by refraining from doing. Great is the truth, but still greater, from a practical point of view, is silence about truth. By simply not mentioning certain subjects, by lowering what Mr. Churchill calls an 'iron curtain' between the masses and such facts or arguments as the local political bosses regard as undesirable, totalitarian propagandists have influenced opinion much more effectively than they could have done by the most eloquent denunciations, the most compelling of logical rebuttals. But silence is not enough. If persecution, liquidation and other symptoms of social friction are to be avoided, the positive sides of propaganda must be made as effective as the negative. The most important Manhattan Projects of the future will be vast government-sponsored enquiries into what the politicians and the participating scientists will call 'the problem of happiness'—in other words, the problem of making people love their servitude. Without economic security, the love of servitude cannot possibly come into existence; for the sake of brevity, I assume that the all-powerful executive and its managers will succeed in solving the problem of permanent security. But security tends very quickly to be taken for granted. Its achievement is merely a superficial, external revolution. The love of servitude cannot be established except as the result of a deep, personal revolution in human minds and bodies. To bring about that revolution we require, among others, the following discoveries and inventions. First, a greatly improved technique of suggestion—through infant conditioning and, later, with the aid of drugs, such as scopolamine. Second, a fully developed science of human differences, enabling government managers to assign any given individual to his or her proper place in the social and economic hierarchy. (Round pegs in square holes tend to have dangerous thoughts about the social system and to infect others with their discontents.) Third (since reality, however utopian, is something from which people feel the need of taking pretty frequent holidays), a substitute for alcohol and the other narcotics, something at once less harmful and more pleasure-giving than gin or heroin. And fourth (but this would be a long-term project, which would take generations of totalitarian control to bring to a successful conclusion), a foolproof system of eugenics, designed to standardize the human product and so to facilitate the task of the managers. In *Brave New World* this standardization of the human product has been pushed to fantastic, though not perhaps impossible, extremes. Technically and ideologically we are still a long way from bottled babies and Bokanovsky groups of semi-morons. But by A.F. 600, who knows what may not be happening? Meanwhile the other characteristic features of that happier and more stable world—the equivalents of soma and hypnopaedia and the scientific caste system—are probably not more than three or four generations away. Nor does the sexual promiscuity of *Brave New World* seem so very distant. There are already certain American cities in which the number of divorces is equal to the number of marriages. In a few years, no doubt, marriage licences will be sold like dog licences, good for a period of twelve months, with no law against changing dogs or keeping more than one animal at a time. As political and economic freedom diminishes, sexual freedom tends compensatingly to increase. And the dictator (unless he needs cannon fodder and families with which to colonize empty or conquered territories) will do well to encourage that freedom. In conjunction with the freedom to daydream under the influence of dope and movies and the radio, it will help to reconcile his subjects to the servitude which is their fate.

All things considered, it looks as though Utopia were far closer to us than anyone, only fifteen years ago, could have imagined. Then, I projected it six hundred years into the future. To-day it seems quite possible that the horror may be upon us within a single century. That is, if we refrain from blowing ourselves to smithereens in the interval. Indeed, unless we choose to decentralize and to use applied science, not as the end to which human beings are to be made the means, but as the means to producing a race of free individuals, we have only two alternatives to choose from: either a number of national, militarized totalitarianisms, having as their root the terror of the atomic bomb and as their consequence the destruction of civilization (or, if the warfare is limited, the perpetuation of militarism); or else one supra-national totalitarianism, called into existence by the social chaos resulting from rapid technological progress in general and the atom revolution in particular, and developing, under the need for efficiency and stability, into the welfare-tyranny of Utopia. You pays your money and you takes your choice.

1946

BRAVE NEW WORLD

Chapter I

A SQUAT grey building of only thirty-four stories. Over the main entrance the words, CENTRAL LONDON HATCHERY AND CONDITIONING CENTRE, and, in a shield, the World State's motto, COMMUNITY, IDENTITY, STABILITY.

The enormous room on the ground floor faced towards the north. Cold for all the summer beyond the panes, for all the tropical heat of the room itself, a harsh thin light glared through the windows, hungrily seeking some draped lay figure, some pallid shape of academic goose-flesh, but finding only the glass and nickel and bleakly shining porcelain of a laboratory. Wintriness responded to wintriness. The overalls of the workers were white, their hands gloved with a pale corpse-coloured rubber. The light was frozen, dead, a ghost. Only from the yellow barrels of the microscopes did it borrow a certain rich and living substance, lying along the polished tubes like butter, streak after luscious streak in long recession down the work tables.

'And this,' said the Director opening the door, 'is the Fertilizing Room.'

Bent over their instruments, three hundred Fertilizers were plunged, as the Director of Hatcheries and Conditioning entered the room, in the scarcely breathing silence, the absent-minded, soliloquizing hum or whistle, of absorbed concentration. A troop of newly arrived students, very young, pink and callow, followed nervously, rather abjectly, at the Director's heels. Each of them carried a note-book, in which, whenever the great man spoke, he desperately scribbled. Straight from the horse's mouth. It was a rare privilege. The D.H.C. for Central London always made a point of personally conducting his new students round the various departments.

'Just to give you a general idea,' he would explain to them. For of course some sort of general idea they must have, if they were to do their work intelligently—though as little of one, if they were to be good and happy members of society, as possible. For particulars, as every one knows, make for virtue and happiness; generalities are intellectually necessary evils. Not philosophers, but fret-sawyers and stamp collectors compose the backbone of society.

'To-morrow,' he would add, smiling at them with a slightly menacing geniality, 'you'll be settling down to serious work. You won't have time for generalities. Meanwhile . . .'

Meanwhile, it was a privilege. Straight from the horse's mouth into the note-book. The boys scribbled like mad.

Tall and rather thin but upright, the Director advanced into the room. He had a long chin and big, rather prominent teeth, just covered, when he was not talking, by his full, floridly curved lips. Old, young? Thirty? fifty? fifty-five? It was hard to say. And anyhow the question didn't arise; in this year of stability, A.F. 632, it didn't occur to you to ask it.

'I shall begin at the beginning,' said the D.H.C., and the more zealous students recorded his intention in their note-books: *Begin at the beginning.* 'These,' he waved his hand, 'are the incubators.' And opening an insulated door he showed them racks upon racks of numbered test-tubes. 'The week's supply of ova. Kept,' he explained, 'at blood heat; whereas the male gametes,' and here he opened another door, 'they have to be kept at thirty-five instead of thirty-seven. Full blood heat sterilizes.' Rams wrapped in thermogene beget no lambs.

Still leaning against the incubators he gave them, while the pencils scurried illegibly across the pages, a brief description of the modern fertilizing process; spoke first, of course, of its surgical introduction—'the operation undergone voluntarily for the good of Society, not to mention the fact that it carries a bonus

amounting to six months' salary'; continued with some account
of the technique for preserving the excised ovary alive and
actively developing; passed on to a consideration of optimum
temperature, salinity, viscosity; referred to the liquor in which
the detached and ripened eggs were kept; and, leading his
charges to the work tables, actually showed them how this liquor
was drawn off from the test-tubes; how it was let out drop by
drop on to the specially warmed slides of the microscopes; how
the eggs which it contained were inspected for abnormalities,
counted and transferred to a porous receptacle; how (and he
now took them to watch the operation) this receptacle was immersed in a warm bouillon containing free-swimming spermatozoa—at a minimum concentration of one hundred thousand
per cubic centimetre, he insisted; and how, after ten minutes,
the container was lifted out of the liquor and its contents re-
examined; how, if any of the eggs remained unfertilized, it was
again immersed, and, if necessary, yet again; how the fertilized
ova went back to the incubators; where the Alphas and Betas
remained until definitely bottled; while the Gammas, Deltas
and Epsilons were brought out again, after only thirty-six hours,
to undergo Bokanovsky's Process.

'Bokanovsky's Process,' repeated the Director, and the
students underlined the words in their little note-books.

One egg, one embryo, one adult—normality. But a bokanovskified egg will bud, will proliferate, will divide. From eight to
ninety-six buds, and every bud will grow into a perfectly formed
embryo, and every embryo into a full-sized adult. Making
ninety-six human beings grow where only one grew before.
Progress.

'Essentially,' the D.H.C. concluded, 'bokanovskification con-
sists of a series of arrests of development. We check the normal
growth and, paradoxically enough, the egg responds by budding.'

Responds by budding. The pencils were busy.

He pointed. On a very slowly moving band a rack-full of
test-tubes was entering a large metal box, another rack-full was

emerging. Machinery faintly purred. It took eight minutes for
the tubes to go through, he told them. Eight minutes of hard
X-rays being about as much as an egg can stand. A few died;
of the rest, the least susceptible divided into two; most put out
four buds; some eight; all were returned to the incubators,
where the buds began to develop; then, after two days, were
suddenly chilled, chilled and checked. Two, four, eight, the
buds in their turn budded; and having budded were dosed
almost to death with alcohol; consequently burgeoned again and
having budded—bud out of bud out of bud were thereafter—
further arrest being generally fatal—left to develop in peace. By
which time the original egg was in a fair way to becoming anything from eight to ninety-six embryos—a prodigious improvement, you will agree, on nature. Identical twins—but not in
piddling twos and threes as in the old viviparous days, when an
egg would sometimes accidentally divide; actually by dozens,
by scores at a time.

'Scores,' the Director repeated and flung out his arms, as
though he were distributing largesse. 'Scores.'

But one of the students was fool enough to ask where the
advantage lay.

'My good boy!' The Director wheeled sharply round on
him. 'Can't you see? Can't you *see*?' He raised a hand;
his expression was solemn. 'Bokanovsky's Process is one of the
major instruments of social stability!'

Major instruments of social stability.

Standard men and women; in uniform batches. The whole
of a small factory staffed with the products of a single bokanovskified egg.

'Ninety-six identical twins working ninety-six identical
machines!' The voice was almost tremulous with enthusiasm.
'You really know where you are. For the first time in history.'
He quoted the planetary motto. 'Community, Identity,
Stability.' Grand words. 'If we could bokanovskify indefinitely
the whole problem would be solved.'

Solved by standard Gammas, unvarying Deltas, uniform Epsilons. Millions of identical twins. The principle of mass production at last applied to biology.

'But, alas,' the Director shook his head, 'we *can't* bokanovskify indefinitely.'

Ninety-six seemed to be the limit; seventy-two a good average. From the same ovary and with gametes of the same male to manufacture as many batches of identical twins as possible— that was the best (sadly a second best) that they could do. And even that was difficult.

'For in nature it takes thirty years for two hundred eggs to reach maturity. But our business is to stabilize the population at this moment, here and now. Dribbling out twins over a quarter of a century—what would be the use of that?'

Obviously, no use at all. But Podsnap's Technique had immensely accelerated the process of ripening. They could make sure of at least a hundred and fifty mature eggs within two years. Fertilize and bokanovskify—in other words, multiply by seventy-two—and you get an average of nearly eleven thousand brothers and sisters in a hundred and fifty batches of identical twins, all within two years of the same age.

'And in exceptional cases we can make one ovary yield us over fifteen thousand adult individuals.'

Beckoning to a fair-haired, ruddy young man who happened to be passing at the moment, 'Mr. Foster,' he called. The ruddy young man approached. 'Can you tell us the record for a single ovary, Mr. Foster?'

'Sixteen thousand and twelve in this Centre,' Mr. Foster replied without hesitation. He spoke very quickly, had a vivacious blue eye, and took an evident pleasure in quoting figures. 'Sixteen thousand and twelve; in one hundred and eighty-nine batches of identicals. But of course they've done much better,' he rattled on, 'in some of the tropical Centres. Singapore has often produced over sixteen thousand five hundred; and Mombasa has actually touched the seventeen thousand mark. But then they have unfair advantages. You should see the way a negro ovary responds to pituitary! It's quite astonishing, when you're used to working with European material. Still,' he added, with a laugh (but the light of combat was in his eyes and the lift of his chin was challenging), 'still, we mean to beat them if we can. I'm working on a wonderful Delta-Minus ovary at this moment. Only just eighteen months old. Over twelve thousand seven hundred children already, either decanted or in embryo. And still going strong. We'll beat them yet.'

'That's the spirit I like!' cried the Director, and clapped Mr. Foster on the shoulder. 'Come along with us and give these boys the benefit of your expert knowledge.'

Mr. Foster smiled modestly. 'With pleasure.' They went.

In the Bottling Room all was harmonious bustle and ordered activity. Flaps of fresh sow's peritoneum ready cut to the proper size came shooting up in little lifts from the Organ Store in the sub-basement. Whizz and then, click! the lift-hatches flew open; the Bottle-Liner had only to reach out a hand, take the flap, insert, smooth-down, and before the lined bottle had had time to travel out of reach along the endless band, whizz, click! another flap of peritoneum had shot up from the depths, ready to be slipped into yet another bottle, the next of that slow interminable procession on the band.

Next to the Liners stood the Matriculators. The procession advanced; one by one the eggs were transferred from their test-tubes to the larger containers; deftly the peritoneal lining was slit, the morula dropped into place, the saline solution poured in . . . and already the bottle had passed, and it was the turn of the labellers. Heredity, date of fertilization, membership of Bokan-ovsky Group—details were transferred from test-tube to bottle. No longer anonymous, but named, identified, the procession marched slowly on; on through an opening in the wall, slowly on into the Social Predestination Room.

'Eighty-eight cubic metres of card-index,' said Mr. Foster with relish, as they entered.

'Containing *all* the relevant information,' added the Director.

'Brought up to date every morning.'

'And co-ordinated every afternoon.'

'On the basis of which they make their calculations.'

'So many individuals, of such and such quality,' said Mr. Foster.

'Distributed in such and such quantities.'

'The optimum Decanting Rate at any given moment.'

'Unforeseen wastages promptly made good.'

'Promptly,' repeated Mr. Foster. 'If you knew the amount of overtime I had to put in after the last Japanese earthquake!' He laughed good-humouredly and shook his head.

'The Predestinators send in their figures to the Fertilizers.'

'Who give them the embryos they ask for.'

'And the bottles come in here to be predestined in detail.'

'After which they are sent down to the Embryo Store.'

'Where we now proceed ourselves.'

And opening a door Mr. Foster led the way down a staircase into the basement.

The temperature was still tropical. They descended into a thickening twilight. Two doors and a passage with a double turn ensured the cellar against any possible infiltration of the day.

'Embryos are like photograph film,' said Mr. Foster waggishly, as he pushed open the second door. 'They can only stand red light.'

And in effect the sultry darkness into which the students now followed him was visible and crimson, like the darkness of closed eyes on a summer's afternoon. The bulging flanks of row on receding row and tier above tier of bottles glinted with innumerable rubies, and among the rubies moved the dim red spectres of men and women with purple eyes and all the symptoms of lupus. The hum and rattle of machinery faintly stirred the air.

'Give them a few figures, Mr. Foster,' said the Director, who was tired of talking.

7

Mr. Foster was only too happy to give them a few figures.

Two hundred and twenty metres long, two hundred wide, ten high. He pointed upwards. Like chickens drinking, the students lifted their eyes towards the distant ceiling.

Three tiers of racks: ground-floor level, first gallery, second gallery.

The spidery steelwork of gallery above gallery faded away in all directions into the dark. Near them three red ghosts were busily unloading demijohns from a moving staircase.

The escalator from the Social Predestination Room.

Each bottle could be placed on one of fifteen racks, each rack, though you couldn't see it, was a conveyor travelling at the rate of thirty-three and a third centimetres an hour. Two hundred and sixty-seven days at eight metres a day. Two thousand one hundred and thirty-six metres in all. One circuit of the cellar at ground level, one on the first gallery, half on the second, and on the two hundred and sixty-seventh morning, daylight in the Decanting Room. Independent existence—so called.

'But in the interval,' Mr. Foster concluded, 'we've managed to do a lot to them. Oh, a very great deal.' His laugh was knowing and triumphant.

'That's the spirit I like,' said the Director once more. 'Let's walk round. You tell them everything, Mr. Foster.'

Mr. Foster duly told them.

Told them of the growing embryo on its bed of peritoneum. Made them taste the rich blood-surrogate on which it fed. Explained why it had to be stimulated with placentin and thyroxin. Told them of the *corpus luteum* extract. Showed them the jets through which at every twelfth metre from zero to 2040 it was automatically injected. Spoke of those gradually increasing doses of pituitary administered during the final ninety-six metres of their course. Described the artificial maternal circulation installed on every bottle at metres 112; showed them the reservoir of blood-surrogate, the centrifugal pump that kept the liquid moving over the placenta and drove it through the synthetic lung and waste-product filter. Referred to the embryo's troublesome tendency to anæmia, to the massive doses of hog's stomach extract and fœtal foal's liver with which, in consequence, it had to be supplied.

Showed them the simple mechanism by means of which, during the last two metres out of every eight, all the embryos were simultaneously shaken into familiarity with movement. Hinted at the gravity of the so-called 'trauma of decanting,' and enumerated the precautions taken to minimize, by a suitable training of the bottled embryo, that dangerous shock. Told them of the tests for sex carried out in the neighbourhood of metre 200. Explained the system of labelling—a T for the males, a circle for the females and for those who were destined to become freemartins a question mark, black on a white ground.

'For of course,' said Mr. Foster, 'in the vast majority of cases, fertility is merely a nuisance. One fertile ovary in twelve hundred—that would really be quite sufficient for our purposes. But we want to have a good choice. And of course one must always leave an enormous margin of safety. So we allow as many as thirty per cent. of the female embryos to develop normally. The others get a dose of male sex-hormone every twenty-four metres for the rest of the course. Result: they're decanted as freemartins—structurally quite normal (except,' he had to admit, 'that they *do* have just the slightest tendency to grow beards), but sterile. Guaranteed sterile. Which brings us at last,' continued Mr. Foster, 'out of the realm of mere slavish imitation of nature into the much more interesting world of human invention.'

He rubbed his hands. For, of course, they didn't content themselves with merely hatching out embryos: any cow could do that.

'We also predestine and condition. We decant our babies as socialized human beings, as Alphas or Epsilons, as future sewage workers or future . . .' He was going to say 'future World Controllers,' but correcting himself, said 'future Directors of Hatcheries' instead.

The D.H.C. acknowledged the compliment with a smile.

They were passing Metre 320 on Rack 11. A young Beta-Minus mechanic was busy with screw-driver and spanner on the blood-surrogate pump of a passing bottle. The hum of the electric motor deepened by fractions of a tone as he turned the nuts. Down, down . . . A final twist, a glance at the revolution counter, and he was done. He moved two paces down the line and began the same process on the next pump.

'Reducing the number of revolutions per minute,' Mr. Foster explained. 'The surrogate goes round slower; therefore passes through the lung at longer intervals; therefore gives the embryo less oxygen. Nothing like oxygen-shortage for keeping an embryo below par.' Again he rubbed his hands.

'But why do you want to keep the embryo below par?' asked an ingenuous student.

'Ass!' said the Director, breaking a long silence. 'Hasn't it occurred to you that an Epsilon embryo must have an Epsilon environment as well as an Epsilon heredity?'

It evidently hadn't occurred to him. He was covered with confusion.

'The lower the caste,' said Mr. Foster, 'the shorter the oxygen.' The first organ affected was the brain. After that the skeleton. At seventy per cent. of normal oxygen you got dwarfs. At less than seventy, eyeless monsters.

'Who are no use at all,' concluded Mr. Foster.

Whereas (his voice became confidential and eager), if they could discover a technique for shortening the period of maturation, what a triumph, what a benefaction to Society!

'Consider the horse.'

They considered it.

Mature at six; the elephant at ten. While at thirteen a man is not yet sexually mature; and is only fully grown at twenty.

Hence, of course, that fruit of delayed development, the human intelligence.

'But in Epsilons,' said Mr. Foster very justly, 'we don't need human intelligence.'

Didn't need and didn't get it. But though the Epsilon mind was mature at ten, the Epsilon body was not fit to work till eighteen. Long years of superfluous and wasted immaturity. If the physical development could be speeded up till it was as quick, say, as a cow's, what an enormous saving to the Community!

'Enormous!' murmured the students. Mr. Foster's enthusiasm was infectious.

He became rather technical; spoke of the abnormal endocrine co-ordination which made men grow so slowly; postulated a germinal mutation to account for it. Could the effects of this germinal mutation be undone? Could the individual Epsilon embryo be made to revert, by a suitable technique, to the normality of dogs and cows? That was the problem. And it was all but solved.

Pilkington, at Mombasa, had produced individuals who were sexually mature at four and full grown at six and a half. A scientific triumph. But socially useless. Six-year-old men and women were too stupid to do even Epsilon work. And the process was an all-or-nothing one; either you failed to modify at all, or else you modified the whole way. They were still trying to find the ideal compromise between adults of twenty and adults of six. So far without success. Mr. Foster sighed and shook his head.

Their wanderings through the crimson twilight had brought them to the neighbourhood of Metre 170 on Rack 9. From this point onwards Rack 9 was enclosed and the bottles performed the remainder of their journey in a kind of tunnel, interrupted here and there by openings two or three metres wide.

'Heat conditioning,' said Mr. Foster.

Hot tunnels alternated with cool tunnels. Coolness was

wedded to discomfort in the form of hard X-rays. By the time they were decanted the embryos had a horror of cold. They were predestined to emigrate to the tropics, to be miners and acetate silk spinners and steel workers. Later on their minds would be made to endorse the judgment of their bodies. 'We condition them to thrive on heat,' concluded Mr. Foster. 'Our colleagues upstairs will teach them to love it.'

'And that,' put in the Director sententiously, 'that is the secret of happiness and virtue—liking what you've *got* to do. All conditioning aims at that: making people like their unescapable social destiny.'

In a gap between two tunnels, a nurse was delicately probing with a long fine syringe into the gelatinous contents of a passing bottle. The students and their guides stood watching her for a few moments in silence.

'Well, Lenina,' said Mr. Foster, when at last she withdrew the syringe and straightened herself up.

The girl turned with a start. One could see that, for all the lupus and the purple eyes, she was uncommonly pretty.

'Henry!' Her smile flashed redly at him—a row of coral teeth.

'Charming, charming,' murmured the Director, and, giving her two or three little pats, received in exchange a rather deferential smile for himself.

'What are you giving them?' asked Mr. Foster, making his tone very professional.

'Oh, the usual typhoid and sleeping sickness.'

'Tropical workers start being inoculated at metre 150,' Mr. Foster explained to the students. 'The embryos still have gills. We immunize the fish against the future man's diseases.' Then, turning back to Lenina, 'Ten to five on the roof this afternoon,' he said, 'as usual.'

'Charming,' said the Director once more, and, with a final pat, moved away after the others.

On Rack 10 rows of next generation's chemical workers were

being trained in the toleration of lead, caustic soda, tar, chlorine. The first of a batch of two hundred and fifty embryonic rocket-plane engineers was just passing the eleven hundredth metre mark on Rack 3. A special mechanism kept their containers in constant rotation. 'To improve their sense of balance,' Mr. Foster explained. 'Doing repairs on the outside of a rocket in mid air is a ticklish job. We slacken off the circulation when they're right way up, so that they're half starved, and double the flow of surrogate when they're upside down. They learn to associate topsy-turvydom with well-being; in fact, they're only truly happy when they're standing on their heads.'

'And now,' Mr. Foster went on, 'I'd like to show you some very interesting conditioning for Alpha-Plus Intellectuals. We have a big batch of them on Rack 5. First Gallery level,' he called to two boys who had started to go down to the ground floor.

'They're round about metre 900,' he explained. 'You can't really do any useful intellectual conditioning till the foetuses have lost their tails. Follow me.'

But the Director had looked at his watch. 'Ten to three,' he said. 'No time for the intellectual embryos, I'm afraid. We must go up to the Nurseries before the children have finished their afternoon sleep.'

Mr. Foster was disappointed. 'At least one glance at the Decanting Room,' he pleaded.

'Very well, then.' The Director smiled indulgently. 'Just one glance.'

Chapter II

MR. FOSTER was left in the Decanting Room. The D.H.C. and his students stepped into the nearest lift and were carried up to the fifth floor.

INFANT NURSERIES. NEO-PAVLOVIAN CONDITIONING ROOMS, announced the notice board.

The Director opened a door. They were in a large bare room, very bright and sunny; for the whole of the southern wall was a single window. Half a dozen nurses, trousered and jacketed in the regulation white viscose-linen uniform, their hair aseptically hidden under white caps, were engaged in setting out bowls of roses in a long row across the floor. Big bowls, packed tight with blossom. Thousands of petals, ripe-blown and silkily smooth, like the cheeks of innumerable little cherubs, but of cherubs, in that bright light, not exclusively pink and Aryan, but also luminously Chinese, also Mexican, also apoplectic with too much blowing of celestial trumpets, also pale as death, pale with the posthumous whiteness of marble.

The nurses stiffened to attention as the D.H.C. came in.

'Set out the books,' he said curtly.

In silence the nurses obeyed his command. Between the rose bowls the books were duly set out—a row of nursery quartos opened invitingly each at some gaily coloured image of beast or fish or bird.

'Now bring in the children.'

They hurried out of the room and returned in a minute or two, each pushing a kind of tall dumb-waiter laden, on all its four wire-netted shelves, with eight-month-old babies, all exactly alike (a Bokanovsky Group, it was evident) and all (since their caste was Delta) dressed in khaki.

'Put them down on the floor.'

The infants were unloaded.

'Now turn them so that they can see the flowers and books.'

Turned, the babies at once fell silent, then began to crawl towards those clusters of sleek colours, those shapes so gay and brilliant on the white pages. As they approached, the sun came out of a momentary eclipse behind a cloud. The roses flamed up as though with a sudden passion from within; a new and profound significance seemed to suffuse the shining pages of the books. From the ranks of the crawling babies came little squeals of excitement, gurgles and twitterings of pleasure.

The Director rubbed his hands. 'Excellent!' he said. 'It might almost have been done on purpose.'

The swiftest crawlers were already at their goal. Small hands reached out uncertainly, touched, grasped, unpetaling the transfigured roses, crumpling the illuminated pages of the books. The Director waited until all were happily busy. Then, 'Watch carefully,' he said. And, lifting his hand, he gave the signal.

The Head Nurse, who was standing by a switchboard at the other end of the room, pressed down a little lever.

There was a violent explosion. Shriller and ever shriller, a siren shrieked. Alarm bells maddeningly sounded.

The children started, screamed; their faces were distorted with terror.

'And now,' the Director shouted (for the noise was deafening), 'now we proceed to rub in the lesson with a mild electric shock.'

He waved his hand again, and the Head Nurse pressed a second lever. The screaming of the babies suddenly changed its tone. There was something desperate, almost insane, about the sharp spasmodic yelps to which they now gave utterance. Their little bodies twitched and stiffened; their limbs moved jerkily as if to the tug of unseen wires.

'We can electrify that whole strip of floor,' bawled the Director in explanation. 'But that's enough,' he signalled to the nurse.

The explosions ceased, the bells stopped ringing, the shriek of the siren died down from tone to tone into silence. The stiffly twitching bodies relaxed, and what had become the sob and yelp of infant maniacs broadened out once more into a normal howl of ordinary terror.

'Offer them the flowers and the books again.'

The nurses obeyed; but at the approach of the roses, at the mere sight of those gaily-coloured images of pussy and cock-a-doodle-doo and baa-baa black sheep, the infants shrank away in horror; the volume of their howling suddenly increased.

'Observe,' said the Director triumphantly, 'observe.'

Books and loud noises, flowers and electric shocks—already in the infant mind these couples were compromisingly linked; and after two hundred repetitions of the same or a similar lesson would be wedded indissolubly. What man has joined, nature is powerless to put asunder.

'They'll grow up with what the psychologists used to call an "instinctive" hatred of books and flowers. Reflexes unalterably conditioned. They'll be safe from books and botany all their lives.' The Director turned to his nurses. 'Take them away again.'

Still yelling, the khaki babies were loaded on to their dumb-waiters and wheeled out, leaving behind them the smell of sour milk and a most welcome silence.

One of the students held up his hand; and though he could see quite well why you couldn't have lower-caste people wasting the Community's time over books, and that there was always the risk of their reading something which might undesirably de-condition one of their reflexes, yet . . . well, he couldn't under-stand about the flowers. Why go to the trouble of making it psychologically impossible for Deltas to like flowers?

Patiently the D.H.C. explained. If the children were made to scream at the sight of a rose, that was on grounds of high eco-nomic policy. Not so very long ago (a century or thereabouts), Gammas, Deltas, even Epsilons, had been conditioned to like flowers—flowers in particular and wild nature in general. The idea was to make them want to be going out into the country at every available opportunity, and so compel them to consume transport.

'And didn't they consume transport?' asked the student.

'Quite a lot,' the D.H.C. replied. 'But nothing else.'

Primroses and landscapes, he pointed out, have one grave defect: they are gratuitous. A love of nature keeps no factories busy. It was decided to abolish the love of nature, at any rate among the lower classes; to abolish the love of nature, but *not* the tendency to consume transport. For of course it was essential that they should keep on going to the country, even though they hated it. The problem was to find an economically sounder reason for consuming transport than a mere affection for primroses and landscapes. It was duly found.

'We condition the masses to hate the country,' concluded the Director. 'But simultaneously we condition them to love all country sports. At the same time, we see to it that all country sports shall entail the use of elaborate apparatus. So that they consume manufactured articles as well as transport. Hence those electric shocks.'

'I see,' said the student, and was silent, lost in admiration.

There was a silence; then, clearing his throat, 'Once upon a time,' the Director began, 'while Our Ford was still on earth, there was a little boy called Reuben Rabinovitch. Reuben was the child of Polish-speaking parents.' The Director interrupted himself. 'You know what Polish is, I suppose?'

'A dead language.'

'Like French and German,' added another student, officiously showing off his learning.

'And "parent"?' questioned the D.H.C.

There was an uneasy silence. Several of the boys blushed. They had not yet learned to draw the significant but often very fine distinction between smut and pure science. One, at last, had the courage to raise a hand.

'Human beings used to be . . .' he hesitated; the blood rushed to his cheeks. 'Well, they used to be viviparous.'

'Quite right.' The Director nodded approvingly.

'And when the babies were decanted . . .'

'"Born,"' came the correction.

'Well, then they were the parents—I mean, not the babies, of course; the other ones.' The poor boy was overwhelmed with confusion.

'In brief,' the Director summed up, 'the parents were the father and the mother.' The smut that was really science fell with a crash into the boys' eye-avoiding silence. 'Mother,' he repeated loudly, rubbing in the science; and, leaning back in his chair, 'These,' he said gravely, 'are unpleasant facts; I know it. But, then, most historical facts *are* unpleasant.'

He returned to Little Reuben—to Little Reuben, in whose room, one evening, by an oversight, his father and mother (crash, crash!) happened to leave the radio turned on.

('For you must remember that in those days of gross viviparous reproduction, children were always brought up by their parents and not in State Conditioning Centres.')

While the child was asleep, a broadcast programme from London suddenly started to come through; and the next morning, to the astonishment of his crash and crash (the more daring of the boys ventured to grin at one another), Little Reuben woke up repeating word for word a long lecture by that curious old writer ('one of the very few whose works have been permitted to come down to us'), George Bernard Shaw, who was speaking, according to a well-authenticated tradition, about his own genius. To Little Reuben's wink and snigger, this lecture was, of course, perfectly incomprehensible and, imagining that their child had suddenly gone mad, they sent for a doctor. He, fortunately, understood English, recognized the discourse as that which Shaw had broadcasted the previous evening, realized the significance of what had happened, and sent a letter to the medical press about it.

'The principle of sleep-teaching, or hypnopædia, had been discovered.' The D.H.C. made an impressive pause.

The principle had been discovered; but many, many years were to elapse before that principle was usefully applied.

'The case of Little Reuben occurred only twenty-three years after Our Ford's first T-Model was put on the market.' (Here the Director made a sign of the T on his stomach and all the students reverently followed suit.) 'And yet . . .'

Furiously the students scribbled. '*Hypnopædia, first used officially in A.F.* 214. *Why not before? Two reasons. (a)* . . .'

'These early experimenters,' the D.H.C. was saying, 'were on the wrong track. They thought that hypnopædia could be made an instrument of intellectual education . . .'

(A small boy asleep on his right side, the right arm stuck out, the right hand hanging limply over the edge of the bed. Through a round grating in the side of a box a voice speaks softly.

'The Nile is the longest river in Africa and the second in length of all the rivers of the globe. Although falling short of the length of the Mississippi-Missouri, the Nile is at the head of all rivers as regards the length of its basin, which extends through 35 degrees of latitude . . .'

At breakfast the next morning, 'Tommy,' some one says, 'do you know which is the longest river in Africa?' A shaking of the head. 'But don't you remember something that begins: The Nile is the . . .'

'The-Nile-is-the-longest-river-in-Africa-and-the-second-in-length-of-all-the-rivers-of-the-globe . . .' The words come rushing out. 'Although-falling-short-of . . .'

'Well now, which is the longest river in Africa?'

The eyes are blank. 'I don't know.'

'But the Nile, Tommy.'

'The-Nile-is-the-longest-river-in-Africa-and-second . . .'

'Then which river is the longest, Tommy?'

Tommy bursts into tears. 'I don't know,' he howls.)

That howl, the Director made it plain, discouraged the earliest investigators. The experiments were abandoned. No further attempt was made to teach children the length of the Nile in their sleep. Quite rightly. You can't learn a science unless you know what it's all about.

'Whereas, if they'd only started on *moral* education,' said the Director, leading the way towards the door. The students followed him, desperately scribbling as they walked and all the way up in the lift. 'Moral education, which ought never, in any circumstances, to be rational.'

'Silence, silence,' whispered a loud-speaker as they stepped out at the fourteenth floor, and 'Silence, silence,' the trumpet mouths indefatigably repeated at intervals down every corridor. The students and even the Director himself rose automatically to the tips of their toes. They were Alphas, of course; but even Alphas have been well conditioned. 'Silence, silence.' All the air of the fourteenth floor was sibilant with the categorical imperative.

Fifty yards of tiptoeing brought them to a door which the Director cautiously opened. They stepped over the threshold into the twilight of a shuttered dormitory. Eighty cots stood in a row against the wall. There was a sound of light regular breathing and a continuous murmur, as of very faint voices remotely whispering.

A nurse rose as they entered and came to attention before the Director.

'What's the lesson this afternoon?' he asked.

'We had Elementary Sex for the first forty minutes,' she answered. 'But now it's switched over to Elementary Class Consciousness.'

The Director walked slowly down the long line of cots. Rosy and relaxed with sleep, eighty little boys and girls lay softly breathing. There was a whisper under every pillow. The D.H.C. halted and, bending over one of the little beds, listened attentively.

'Elementary Class Consciousness, did you say? Let's have it repeated a little louder by the trumpet.'

At the end of the room a loud-speaker projected from the wall. The Director walked up to it and pressed a switch.

'. . . all wear green,' said a soft but very distinct voice, beginning in the middle of a sentence, 'and Delta children wear khaki. Oh no, I don't want to play with Delta children. And Epsilons are still worse. They're too stupid to be able to read or write. Besides, they wear black, which is such a beastly colour. I'm *so* glad I'm a Beta.'

There was a pause; then the voice began again.

'Alpha children wear grey. They work much harder than we do, because they're so frightfully clever. I'm really awfully glad I'm a Beta, because I don't work so hard. And then we are much better than the Gammas and Deltas. Gammas are stupid. They all wear green, and Delta children wear khaki. Oh no, I *don't* want to play with Delta children. And Epsilons are still worse. They're too stupid to be able . . .'

The Director pushed back the switch. The voice was silent. Only its thin ghost continued to mutter from beneath the eighty pillows.

'They'll have that repeated forty or fifty times more before they wake; then again on Thursday, and again on Saturday. A hundred and twenty times three times a week for thirty months. After which they go on to a more advanced lesson.'

Roses and electric shocks, the khaki of Deltas and a whiff of asafœtida—wedded indissolubly before the child can speak. But wordless conditioning is crude and wholesale; cannot bring home the finer distinctions, cannot inculcate the more complex courses of behaviour. For that there must be words, but words without reason. In brief, hypnopædia.

'The greatest moralizing and socializing force of all time.'

The students took it down in their little books. Straight from the horse's mouth.

Once more the Director touched the switch.

'. . . so frightfully clever,' the soft, insinuating, indefatigable voice was saying. 'I'm really awfully glad I'm a Beta, because . . .'

Not so much like drops of water, though water, it is true, can wear holes in the hardest granite; rather, drops of liquid sealing-

wax, drops that adhere, incrust, incorporate themselves with
what they fall on, till finally the rock is all one scarlet blob.

'Till at last the child's mind *is* these suggestions, and the sum
of the suggestions *is* the child's mind. And not the child's mind
only. The adult's mind too—all his life long. The mind that
judges and desires and decides—made up of these suggestions.
But all these suggestions are *our* suggestions!' The Director
almost shouted in his triumph. 'Suggestions from the State.'
He banged the nearest table. 'It therefore follows . . .'

A noise made him turn round.

'Oh, Ford!' he said in another tone, 'I've gone and woken
the children.'

Chapter III

OUTSIDE, in the garden, it was playtime. Naked in the warm June sunshine, six or seven hundred little boys and girls were running with shrill yells over the lawns, or playing ball games, or squatting silently in twos and threes among the flowering shrubs. The roses were in bloom, two nightingales soliloquized in the boskage, a cuckoo was just going out of tune among the lime trees. The air was drowsy with the murmur of bees and helicopters.

The Director and his students stood for a short time watching a game of Centrifugal Bumble-puppy. Twenty children were grouped in a circle round a chrome-steel tower. A ball thrown up so as to land on the platform at the top of the tower rolled down into the interior, fell on a rapidly revolving disk, was hurled through one or other of the numerous apertures pierced in the cylindrical casing, and had to be caught.

'Strange,' mused the Director, as they turned away, 'strange to think that even in Our Ford's day most games were played without more apparatus than a ball or two and a few sticks and perhaps a bit of netting. Imagine the folly of allowing people to play elaborate games which do nothing whatever to increase consumption. It's madness. Nowadays the Controllers won't approve of any new game unless it can be shown that it requires at least as much apparatus as the most complicated of existing games.' He interrupted himself.

'That's a charming little group,' he said, pointing.

In a little grassy bay between tall clumps of Mediterranean heather, two children, a little boy of about seven and a little girl who might have been a year older, were playing, very gravely and with all the focussed attention of scientists intent on a labour of discovery, a rudimentary sexual game.

'Charming, charming!' the D.H.C. repeated sentimentally.

23

'Charming,' the boys politely agreed. But their smile was rather patronizing. They had put aside similar childish amusements too recently to be able to watch them now without a touch of contempt. Charming? but it was just a pair of kids fooling about; that was all. Just kids.

'I always think,' the Director was continuing in the same rather maudlin tone, when he was interrupted by a loud boo-hooing.

From a neighbouring shrubbery emerged a nurse, leading by the hand a small boy, who howled as he went. An anxious-looking little girl trotted at her heels.

'What's the matter?' asked the Director.

The nurse shrugged her shoulders. 'Nothing much,' she answered. 'It's just that this little boy seems rather reluctant to join in the ordinary erotic play. I'd noticed it once or twice before. And now again to-day. He started yelling just now ...'

'Honestly,' put in the anxious-looking little girl, 'I didn't mean to hurt him or anything. Honestly.'

'Of course you didn't, dear,' said the nurse reassuringly. 'And so,' she went on, turning back to the Director, 'I'm taking him in to see the Assistant Superintendent of Psychology. Just to see if anything's at all abnormal.'

'Quite right,' said the Director. 'Take him in. You stay here, little girl,' he added, as the nurse moved away with her still howling charge. 'What's your name?'

'Polly Trotsky.'

'And a very good name too,' said the Director. 'Run away now and see if you can find some other little boy to play with.'

The child scampered off into the bushes and was lost to sight.

'Exquisite little creature!' said the Director, looking after her. Then, turning to his students, 'What I'm going to tell you now,' he said, 'may sound incredible. But then, when you're not accustomed to history, most facts about the past *do* sound incredible.'

He let out the amazing truth. For a very long period before the time of Our Ford, and even for some generations afterwards, erotic play between children had been regarded as abnormal (there was a roar of laughter); and not only abnormal, actually immoral (no!): and had therefore been rigorously suppressed.

A look of astonished incredulity appeared on the faces of his listeners. Poor little kids not allowed to amuse themselves? They could not believe it.

'Even adolescents,' the D.H.C. was saying, 'even adolescents like yourselves . . .'

'Not possible!'

'Barring a little surreptitious auto-erotism and homosexuality —absolutely nothing.'

'*Nothing?*'

'In most cases, till they were over twenty years old.'

'Twenty years old?' echoed the students in a chorus of loud disbelief.

'Twenty,' the Director repeated. 'I told you that you'd find it incredible.'

'But what happened?' they asked. 'What were the results?'

'The results were terrible.' A deep resonant voice broke startlingly into the dialogue.

They looked round. On the fringe of the little group stood a stranger—a man of middle height, black-haired, with a hooked nose, full red lips, eyes very piercing and dark. 'Terrible,' he repeated.

The D.H.C. had at that moment sat down on one of the steel and rubber benches conveniently scattered through the gardens; but at the sight of the stranger, he sprang to his feet and darted forward, his hands outstretched, smiling with all his teeth, effusive.

'Controller! What an unexpected pleasure! Boys, what are you thinking of? This is the Controller; this is his fordship, Mustapha Mond.'

In the four thousand rooms of the Centre the four thousand

electric clocks simultaneously struck four. Discarnate voices called from the trumpet mouths.

'Main Day-shift off duty. Second Day-shift take over. Main Day-shift off . . .'

In the lift, on their way up to the changing-rooms, Henry Foster and the Assistant Director of Predestination rather pointedly turned their backs on Bernard Marx from the Psychology Bureau: averted themselves from that unsavoury reputation.

The faint hum and rattle of machinery still stirred the crimson air in the Embryo Store. Shifts might come and go, one lupus-coloured face give place to another; majestically and for ever the conveyors crept forward with their load of future men and women.

Lenina Crowne walked briskly towards the door.

His fordship Mustapha Mond! The eyes of the saluting students almost popped out of their heads. Mustapha Mond! The Resident Controller for Western Europe! One of the Ten World Controllers. One of the Ten . . . and he sat down on the bench with the D.H.C., he was going to stay, to stay, yes, and actually talk to them . . . straight from the horse's mouth. Straight from the mouth of Ford himself.

Two shrimp-brown children emerged from a neighbouring shrubbery, stared at them for a moment with large, astonished eyes, then returned to their amusements among the leaves.

'You all remember,' said the Controller, in his strong deep voice, 'you all remember, I suppose, that beautiful and inspired saying of Our Ford's: History is bunk. History,' he repeated slowly, 'is bunk.'

He waved his hand; and it was as though, with an invisible feather whisk, he had brushed away a little dust, and the dust was Harappa, was Ur of the Chaldees; some spider-webs, and they were Thebes and Babylon and Cnossos and Mycenae. Whisk, whisk—and where was Odysseus, where was Job, where were

Jupiter and Gotama and Jesus? Whisk—and those specks of antique dirt called Athens and Rome, Jerusalem and the Middle Kingdom—all were gone. Whisk—the place where Italy had been was empty. Whisk, the cathedrals; whisk, whisk, King Lear and the Thoughts of Pascal. Whisk, Passion; whisk, Requiem; whisk, Symphony; whisk . . .

'Going to the Feelies this evening, Henry?' enquired the Assistant Predestinator. 'I hear the new one at the Alhambra is first-rate. There's a love scene on a bearskin rug; they say it's marvellous. Every hair of the bear reproduced. The most amazing tactual effects.'

'That's why you're taught no history,' the Controller was saying. 'But now the time has come . . .'

The D.H.C. looked at him nervously. There were those strange rumours of old forbidden books hidden in a safe in the Controller's study. Bibles, poetry—Ford knew what.

Mustapha Mond intercepted his anxious glance and the corners of his red lips twitched ironically.

'It's all right, Director,' he said in a tone of faint derision, 'I won't corrupt them.'

The D.H.C. was overwhelmed with confusion.

Those who feel themselves despised do well to look despising. The smile on Bernard Marx's face was contemptuous. Every hair on the bear indeed!

'I shall make a point of going,' said Henry Foster.

Mustapha Mond leaned forward, shook a finger at them. 'Just try to realize it,' he said, and his voice sent a strange thrill quivering along their diaphragms. 'Try to realize what it was like to have a viviparous mother.'

27

That smutty word again. But none of them dreamed, this time, of smiling.

'Try to imagine what "living with one's family" meant.'

They tried; but obviously without the smallest success.

'And do you know what a "home" was?'

They shook their heads.

From her dim crimson cellar Lenina Crowne shot up seventeen stories, turned to the right as she stepped out of the lift, walked down a long corridor and, opening the door marked GIRLS' DRESSING-ROOM, plunged into a deafening chaos of arms and bosoms and underclothing. Torrents of hot water were splashing into or gurgling out of a hundred baths. Rumbling and hissing, eighty vibro-vacuum massage machines were simultaneously kneading and sucking the firm and sunburnt flesh of eighty superb female specimens. Every one was talking at the top of her voice. A Synthetic Music machine was warbling out a super-cornet solo.

'Hullo, Fanny,' said Lenina to the young woman who had the pegs and locker next to hers.

Fanny worked in the Bottling Room, and her surname was also Crowne. But as the two thousand million inhabitants of the planet had only ten thousand names between them, the co-incidence was not particularly surprising.

Lenina pulled at her zippers—downwards on the jacket, downwards with a double-handed gesture at the two that held trousers, downwards again to loosen her undergarment. Still wearing her shoes and stockings, she walked off towards the bathrooms.

Home, home—a few small rooms, stiflingly over-inhabited by a man, by a periodically teeming woman, by a rabble of boys and girls of all ages. No air, no space; an understerilized prison; darkness, disease, and smells.

(The Controller's evocation was so vivid that one of the boys, more sensitive than the rest, turned pale at the mere description and was on the point of being sick.)

Lenina got out of the bath, towelled herself dry, took hold of a long flexible tube plugged into the wall, presented the nozzle to her breast, as though she meant to commit suicide, pressed down the trigger. A blast of warmed air dusted her with the finest talcum powder. Eight different scents and eau-de-Cologne were laid on in little taps over the wash-basin. She turned on the third from the left, dabbled herself with chypre and, carrying her shoes and stockings in her hand, went out to see if one of the vibro-vacuum machines were free.

And home was as squalid psychically as physically. Psychically, it was a rabbit hole, a midden, hot with the frictions of tightly packed life, reeking with emotion. What suffocating intimacies, what dangerous, insane, obscene relationships between the members of the family group! Maniacally, the mother brooded over her children (*her* children) . . . brooded over them like a cat over its kittens; but a cat that could talk, a cat that could say, 'My baby, my baby,' over and over again. 'My baby, and oh, oh, at my breast, the little hands, the hunger, and that unspeakable agonizing pleasure! Till at last my baby sleeps, my baby sleeps with a bubble of white milk at the corner of his mouth. My little baby sleeps . . .'

'Yes,' said Mustapha Mond, nodding his head, 'you may well shudder.'

'Who are you going out with to-night?' Lenina asked, returning from the vibro-vac like a pearl illuminated from within, pinkly glowing.

'Nobody.'

Lenina raised her eyebrows in astonishment.

'I've been feeling rather out of sorts lately,' Fanny explained. 'Dr. Wells advised me to have a Pregnancy Substitute.'

'But, my dear, you're only nineteen. The first Pregnancy Substitute isn't compulsory till twenty-one.'

'I know, dear. But some people are better if they begin earlier. Dr. Wells told me that brunettes with wide pelvises, like me, ought to have their first Pregnancy Substitute at seventeen. So I'm really two years late, not two years early.' She opened the door of her locker and pointed to the row of boxes and labelled phials on the upper shelf.

'SYRUP OF CORPUS LUTEUM.' Lenina read the names aloud. 'OVARIN, GUARANTEED FRESH: NOT TO BE USED AFTER AUGUST 1ST, A.F. 632. MAMMARY GLAND EXTRACT: TO BE TAKEN THREE TIMES DAILY, BEFORE MEALS, WITH A LITTLE WATER. PLACENTIN: 5CC TO BE INJECTED INTRAVENALLY EVERY THIRD DAY ... Ugh!' Lenina shuddered. 'How I loathe intravenals, don't you?'

'Yes. But when they do one good ...' Fanny was a particularly sensible girl.

Our Ford—or Our Freud, as, for some inscrutable reason, he chose to call himself whenever he spoke of psychological matters —Our Freud had been the first to reveal the appalling dangers of family life. The world was full of fathers—was therefore full of misery; full of mothers—therefore of every kind of perversion from sadism to chastity; full of brothers, sisters, uncles, aunts— full of madness and suicide.

'And yet, among the savages of Samoa, in certain islands off the coast of New Guinea ...'

The tropical sunshine lay like warm honey on the naked bodies of children tumbling promiscuously among the hibiscus blossoms. Home was in any one of twenty palm-thatched houses. In the

Trobriands conception was the work of ancestral ghosts; nobody had ever heard of a father.

'Extremes,' said the Controller, 'meet. For the good reason that they were made to meet.'

'Dr. Wells says that a three months' Pregnancy Substitute now will make all the difference to my health for the next three or four years.'

'Well, I hope he's right,' said Lenina. 'But, Fanny, do you really mean to say that for the next three months you're not supposed to . . .'

'Oh no, dear. Only for a week or two, that's all. I shall spend the evening at the Club playing Musical Bridge. I suppose you're going out?'

Lenina nodded.

'Who with?'

'Henry Foster.'

'Again?' Fanny's kind, rather moon-like face took on an incongruous expression of pained and disapproving astonishment. 'Do you mean to tell me you're *still* going out with Henry Foster?'

Mothers and fathers, brothers and sisters. But there were also husbands, wives, lovers. There were also monogamy and romance.

'Though you probably don't know what those are,' said Mustapha Mond.

They shook their heads.

Family, monogamy, romance. Everywhere exclusiveness, everywhere a focussing of interest, a narrow channelling of impulse and energy.

'But every one belongs to every one else,' he concluded, citing the hypnopædic proverb.

The students nodded, emphatically agreeing with a statement which upwards of sixty-two thousand repetitions in the dark had made them accept, not merely as true, but as axiomatic, self-evident, utterly indisputable.

'But after all,' Lenina was protesting, 'it's only about four months now since I've been having Henry.'

'*Only* four months! I like that. And what's more,' Fanny went on, pointing an accusing finger, 'there's been nobody else except Henry all that time. Has there?'

Lenina blushed scarlet; but her eyes, the tone of her voice remained defiant. 'No, there hasn't been any one else,' she answered almost truculently. 'And I jolly well don't see why there should have been.'

'Oh, she jolly well doesn't see why there should have been,' Fanny repeated, as though to an invisible listener behind Lenina's left shoulder. Then, with a sudden change of tone, 'But seriously,' she said, 'I really do think you ought to be careful. It's such horribly bad form to go on and on like this with one man. At forty, or thirty-five, it wouldn't be so bad. But at *your* age, Lenina! No, it really won't do. And you know how strongly the D.H.C. objects to anything intense or long-drawn. Four months of Henry Foster, without having another man—why, he'd be furious if he knew . . .'

'Think of water under pressure in a pipe.' They thought of it. 'I pierce it once,' said the Controller. 'What a jet!'

He pierced it twenty times. There were twenty piddling little fountains.

'My baby. My baby . . . !'

'Mother!' The madness is infectious.

'My love, my one and only, precious, precious . . .'

Mother, monogamy, romance. High spurts the fountain;

fierce and foamy the wild jet. The urge has but a single outlet. My love, my baby. No wonder those poor pre-moderns were mad and wicked and miserable. Their world didn't allow them to take things easily, didn't allow them to be sane, virtuous, happy. What with mothers and lovers, what with the prohibitions they were not conditioned to obey, what with the temptations and the lonely remorses, what with all the diseases and the endless isolating pain, what with the uncertainties and the poverty —they were forced to feel strongly. And feeling strongly (and strongly, what was more, in solitude, in hopelessly individual isolation), how could they be stable?

'Of course there's no need to give him up. Have somebody else from time to time, that's all. He has other girls, doesn't he?'

Lenina admitted it.

'Of course he does. Trust Henry Foster to be the perfect gentleman—always correct. And then there's the Director to think of. You know what a stickler . . .'

Nodding, 'He patted me on the behind this afternoon,' said Lenina.

'There, you see!' Fanny was triumphant. 'That shows what *he* stands for. The strictest conventionality.'

'Stability,' said the Controller, 'stability. No civilization without social stability. No social stability without individual stability.' His voice was a trumpet. Listening, they felt larger, warmer.

The machine turns, turns and must keep on turning—for ever. It is death if it stands still. A thousand millions scrabbled the crust of the earth. The wheels began to turn. In a hundred and fifty years there were two thousand millions. Stop all the wheels. In a hundred and fifty weeks there are once more only a thousand millions; a thousand thousand thousand men and women have starved to death.

Wheels must turn steadily, but cannot turn untended. There must be men to tend them, men as steady as the wheels upon their axles, sane men, obedient men, stable in contentment.

Crying: My baby, my mother, my only, only love; groaning: My sin, my terrible God; screaming with pain, muttering with fever, bemoaning old age and poverty—how can they tend the wheels? And if they cannot tend the wheels ... The corpses of a thousand thousand thousand men and women would be hard to bury or burn.

'And after all,' Fanny's tone was coaxing, 'it's not as though there were anything painful or disagreeable about having one or two men besides Henry. And seeing that, you *ought* to be a little more promiscuous. . . .'

'Stability,' insisted the Controller, 'stability. The primal and the ultimate need. Stability. Hence all this.'

With a wave of his hand he indicated the gardens, the huge building of the Conditioning Centre, the naked children furtive in the undergrowth or running across the lawns.

Lenina shook her head. 'Somehow,' she mused, 'I hadn't been feeling very keen on promiscuity lately. There are times when one doesn't. Haven't you found that too, Fanny?'

Fanny nodded her sympathy and understanding. 'But one's got to make the effort,' she said sententiously, 'one's got to play the game. After all, every one belongs to every one else.'

'Yes, every one belongs to every one else,' Lenina repeated slowly and, sighing, was silent for a moment; then, taking Fanny's hand, gave it a little squeeze. 'You're quite right, Fanny. As usual. I'll make the effort.'

Impulse arrested spills over, and the flood is feeling, the flood is passion, the flood is even madness: it depends on the force of the current, the height and strength of the barrier. The unchecked stream flows smoothly down its appointed channels into a calm well-being. (The embryo is hungry; day in, day out, the blood-surrogate pump unceasingly turns its eight hundred revolutions a minute. The decanted infant howls; at once a nurse appears with a bottle of external secretion. Feeling lurks in that interval of time between desire and its consummation. Shorten that interval, break down all those old unnecessary barriers.

'Fortunate boys!' said the Controller. 'No pains have been spared to make your lives emotionally easy—to preserve you, so far as that is possible, from having emotions at all.'

'Ford's in his flivver,' murmured the D.H.C. 'All's well with the world.'

'Lenina Crowne?' said Henry Foster, echoing the Assistant Predestinator's question as he zipped up his trousers. 'Oh, she's a splendid girl. Wonderfully pneumatic. I'm surprised you haven't had her.'

'I can't think how it is I haven't,' said the Assistant Predestinator. 'I certainly will. At the first opportunity.'

From his place on the opposite side of the changing-room aisle, Bernard Marx overheard what they were saying and turned pale.

'And to tell the truth,' said Lenina, 'I'm beginning to get just a tiny bit bored with nothing but Henry every day.' She pulled on her left stocking. 'Do you know Bernard Marx?' she asked in a tone whose excessive casualness was evidently forced.

Fanny looked startled. 'You don't mean to say . . .?'

'Why not? Bernard's an Alpha-Plus. Besides, he asked me to go to one of the Savage Reservations with him. I've always wanted to see a Savage Reservation.'

'But his reputation?'

'What do I care about his reputation?'

'They say he doesn't like Obstacle Golf.'

'They say, they say,' mocked Lenina.

'And then he spends most of his time by himself—*alone*.' There was horror in Fanny's voice.

'Well, he won't be alone when he's with me. And anyhow, why are people so beastly to him? I think he's rather sweet.' She smiled to herself; how absurdly shy he had been! Frightened almost—as though she were a World Controller and he a Gamma-Minus machine minder.

'Consider your own lives,' said Mustapha Mond. 'Has any of you ever encountered an insurmountable obstacle?'

The question was answered by a negative silence.

'Has any of you been compelled to live through a long time-interval between the consciousness of a desire and its fulfilment?'

'Well,' began one of the boys, and hesitated.

'Speak up,' said the D.H.C. 'Don't keep his fordship waiting.'

'I once had to wait nearly four weeks before a girl I wanted would let me have her.'

'And you felt a strong emotion in consequence?'

'Horrible!'

'Horrible; precisely,' said the Controller. 'Our ancestors were so stupid and short-sighted that when the first reformers came along and offered to deliver them from those horrible emotions, they wouldn't have anything to do with them.'

'Talking about her as though she were a bit of meat.' Bernard ground his teeth. 'Have her here, have her there. Like mutton. Degrading her to so much mutton. She said she'd think it over, she said she'd give me an answer this week. Oh, Ford, Ford, Ford.' He would have liked to go up to them and hit them in the face—hard, again and again.

'Yes, I really do advise you to try her,' Henry Foster was saying.

'Take Ectogenesis. Pfitzner and Kawaguchi had got the whole technique worked out. But would the Governments look at it? No. There was something called Christianity. Women were forced to go on being viviparous.'

'He's so ugly!' said Fanny.

'But I rather like his looks.'

'And then so *small*.' Fanny made a grimace; smallness was so horribly and typically low-caste.

'I think that's rather sweet,' said Lenina. 'One feels one would like to pet him. You know. Like a cat.'

Fanny was shocked. 'They say somebody made a mistake when he was still in the bottle—thought he was a Gamma and put alcohol into his blood-surrogate. That's why he's so stunted.'

'What nonsense!' Lenina was indignant.

'Sleep teaching was actually prohibited in England. There was something called liberalism. Parliament, if you know what that was, passed a law against it. The records survive. Speeches about liberty of the subject. Liberty to be inefficient and miserable. Freedom to be a round peg in a square hole.'

'But, my dear chap, you're welcome, I assure you. You're welcome.' Henry Foster patted the Assistant Predestinator on the shoulder. 'Every one belongs to every one else, after all.'

37

One hundred repetitions three nights a week for four years, thought Bernard Marx, who was a specialist on hypnopædia. Sixty-two thousand four hundred repetitions make one truth. Idiots!

'Or the Caste System. Constantly proposed, constantly rejected. There was something called democracy. As though men were more than physico-chemically equal.'

'Well, all I can say is that I'm going to accept his invitation.'

Bernard hated them, hated them. But they were two, they were large, they were strong.

'The Nine Years' War began in A.F. 141.'

'Not even if it *were* true about the alcohol in his blood-surrogate.'

'Phosgene, chloropicrin, ethyl iodoacetate, diphenylcyanarsine, trichlormethyl chloroformate, dichlorethyl sulphide. Not to mention hydrocyanic acid.'

'Which I simply don't believe,' Lenina concluded.

'The noise of fourteen thousand aeroplanes advancing in open order. But in the Kurfurstendamm and the Eighth Arrondissement, the explosion of the anthrax bombs is hardly louder than the popping of a paper bag.'

'Because I *do* want to see a Savage Reservation.'

$CH_3C_6H_2(NO_2)_3+Hg(CNO)_2=$ well, what? An enormous hole in the ground, a pile of masonry, some bits of flesh and mucus, a foot, with the boot still on it, flying through the air and landing, flop, in the middle of the geraniums—the scarlet ones; such a splendid show that summer!

'You're hopeless, Lenina, I give you up.'

'The Russian technique for infecting water supplies was particularly ingenious.'

Back turned to back, Fanny and Lenina continued their changing in silence.

'The Nine Years' War, the great Economic Collapse. There was a choice between World Control and destruction. Between stability and . . .'

'Fanny Crowne's a nice girl too,' said the Assistant Pre-destinator.

In the nurseries, the Elementary Class Consciousness lesson was over, the voices were adapting future demand to future industrial supply. 'I do love flying,' they whispered, 'I do love flying, I do love having new clothes, I do love . . .'

'Liberalism, of course, was dead of anthrax, but all the same you couldn't do things by force.'

'Not nearly so pneumatic as Lenina. Oh, not nearly.'

'But old clothes are beastly,' continued the untiring whisper. 'We always throw away old clothes. Ending is better than mending, ending is better than mending, ending is better . . .'

'Government's an affair of sitting, not hitting. You rule with the brains and the buttocks, never with the fists. For example, there was the conscription of consumption.'

'There, I'm ready,' said Lenina; but Fanny remained speechless and averted. 'Let's make peace, Fanny darling.'

'Every man, woman and child compelled to consume so much a year. In the interests of industry. The sole result . . .'

'Ending is better than mending. The more stitches, the less riches; the more stitches . . .'

'One of these days,' said Fanny, with dismal emphasis, 'you'll get into trouble.'

'Conscientious objection on an enormous scale. Anything not to consume. Back to nature.'

'I do love flying, I do love flying.'

'Back to culture. Yes, actually to culture. You can't consume much if you sit still and read books.'

'Do I look all right?' Lenina asked. Her jacket was made of bottle-green acetate cloth with green viscose fur at the cuffs and collar.

'Eight hundred Simple Lifers were mowed down by machine guns at Golders Green.'

'Ending is better than mending, ending is better than mending.'

Green corduroy shorts and white viscose-woollen stockings turned down below the knee.

'Then came the famous British Museum Massacre. Two thousand culture fans gassed with dichlorethyl sulphide.'

A green-and-white jockey cap shaded Lenina's eyes; her shoes were bright green and highly polished.

'In the end,' said Mustapha Mond, 'the Controllers realized

that force was no good. The slower but infinitely surer methods of ectogenesis, neo-Pavlovian conditioning and hypnopædia . . .'

And round her waist she wore a silver-mounted green morocco-surrogate cartridge belt, bulging (for Lenina was not a freemartin) with the regulation supply of contraceptives.

'The discoveries of Pfitzner and Kawaguchi were at last made use of. An intensive propaganda against viviparous reproduction . . .'

'Perfect!' cried Fanny enthusiastically. She could never resist Lenina's charm for long. 'And what a perfectly *sweet* Malthusian belt!'

'Accompanied by a campaign against the Past; by the closing of museums, the blowing up of historical monuments (luckily most of them had already been destroyed during the Nine Years' War); by the suppression of all books published before A.F. 150.'

'I simply must get one like it,' said Fanny.

'There were some things called the pyramids, for example.'

'My old black-patent bandolier . . .'

'And a man called Shakespeare. You've never heard of them, of course.'

'It's an absolute disgrace—that bandolier of mine.'

'Such are the advantages of a really scientific education.'

'The more stitches the less riches; the more stitches the less...'

'The introduction of Our Ford's first T-Model ...'

'I've had it nearly three months.'

'Chosen as the opening date of the new era.'

'Ending is better than mending; ending is better ...'

'There was a thing, as I've said before, called Christianity.'

'Ending is better than mending.'

'The ethics and philosophy of under-consumption ...'

'I love new clothes, I love new clothes, I love ...'

'So essential when there was under-production; but in an age of machines and the fixation of nitrogen—positively a crime against society.'

43

'Henry Foster gave it me.'

'All crosses had their tops cut and became T's. There was also a thing called God.'

'It's real morocco-surrogate.'

'We have the World State now. And Ford's Day celebrations, and Community Sings, and Solidarity Services.'

'Ford, how I hate them!' Bernard Marx was thinking.

'There was a thing called Heaven; but all the same they used to drink enormous quantities of alcohol.'

'Like meat, like so much meat.'

'There was a thing called the soul and a thing called immortality.'

'Do ask Henry where he got it.'

'But they used to take morphia and cocaine.'

'And what makes it worse, she thinks of herself as meat.'

44

'Two thousand pharmacologists and biochemists were subsidized in A.F. 178.'

'He does look glum,' said the Assistant Predestinator, pointing at Bernard Marx.

'Six years later it was being produced commercially. The perfect drug.'

'Let's bait him.'

'Euphoric, narcotic, pleasantly hallucinant.'

'Glum, Marx, glum.' The clap on the shoulder made him start, look up. It was that brute Henry Foster. 'What you need is a gramme of *soma*.'

'All the advantages of Christianity and alcohol; none of their defects.'

'Ford, I should like to kill him!' But all he did was to say, 'No, thank you,' and fend off the proffered tube of tablets.

'Take a holiday from reality whenever you like, and come back without so much as a headache or a mythology.'

'Take it,' insisted Henry Foster, 'take it.'

'Stability was practically assured.'

'One cubic centimetre cures ten gloomy sentiments,' said the Assistant Predestinator, citing a piece of homely hypnopædic wisdom.

'It only remained to conquer old age.'

'Damn you, damn you!' shouted Bernard Marx.

'Hoity-toity.'

'Gonadal hormones, transfusion of young blood, magnesium salts . . .'

'And do remember that a gramme is better than a damn.' They went out, laughing.

'All the physiological stigmata of old age have been abolished. And along with them, of course . . .'

'Don't forget to ask him about that Malthusian belt,' said Fanny.

'Along with them all the old man's mental peculiarities. Characters remain constant throughout a whole lifetime.'

'. . . two rounds of Obstacle Golf to get through before dark. I must fly.'

'Work, play—at sixty our powers and tastes are what they were at seventeen. Old men in the bad old days used to renounce, retire, take to religion, spend their time reading, thinking—*thinking!*'

'Idiots, swine!' Bernard Marx was saying to himself, as he walked down the corridor to the lift.

'Now—such is progress—the old men work, the old men copulate, the old men have no time, no leisure from pleasure, not a moment to sit down and think—or if ever by some unlucky chance such a crevice of time should yawn in the solid substance of their distractions, there is always *soma*, delicious *soma*, half a gramme for a half-holiday, a gramme for a week-end, two grammes for a trip to the gorgeous East, three for a dark eternity on the moon; returning whence they find themselves on the other side of the crevice, safe on the solid ground of daily labour and distraction, scampering from feely to feely, from girl to pneumatic girl, from Electro-magnetic Golf Course to . . .'

'Go away, little girl,' shouted the D.H.C. angrily. 'Go away, little boy! Can't you see that his fordship's busy? Go and do your erotic play somewhere else.'

'Poor little children!' said the Controller.

Slowly, majestically, with a faint humming of machinery, the Conveyors moved forward, thirty-three centimetres an hour. In the red darkness glinted innumerable rubies.

47

Chapter IV

§ 1

THE lift was crowded with men from the Alpha Changing Rooms, and Lenina's entry was greeted by many friendly nods and smiles. She was a popular girl and, at one time or another, had spent a night with almost all of them.

They were dear boys, she thought, as she returned their salutations. Charming boys! Still, she did wish that George Edzel's ears weren't quite so big (perhaps he'd been given just a spot too much parathyroid at metre 328?). And looking at Benito Hoover, she couldn't help remembering that he was really *too* hairy when he took his clothes off.

Turning, with eyes a little saddened by the recollection of Benito's curly blackness, she saw in a corner the small thin body, the melancholy face of Bernard Marx.

'Bernard!' she stepped up to him. 'I was looking for you.' Her voice rang clear above the hum of the mounting lift. The others looked round curiously. 'I wanted to talk to you about our New Mexico plan.' Out of the tail of her eye she could see Benito Hoover gaping with astonishment. The gape annoyed her. 'Surprised I shouldn't be begging to go with *him* again!' she said to herself. Then aloud, and more warmly than ever, 'I'd simply *love* to come with you for a week in July,' she went on. (Anyhow, she was publicly proving her unfaithfulness to Henry. Fanny ought to be pleased, even though it was Bernard.) 'That is,' Lenina gave him her most deliciously significant smile, 'if you still want to have me.'

Bernard's pale face flushed. 'What on earth for?' she wondered, astonished, but at the same time touched by this strange tribute to her power.

'Hadn't we better talk about it somewhere else?' he stammered, looking horribly uncomfortable.

48

'As though I'd been saying something shocking,' thought Lenina. 'He couldn't look more upset if I'd made a dirty joke—asked him who his mother was, or something like that.'

'I mean, with all these people about . . .' He was choked with confusion.

Lenina's laugh was frank and wholly unmalicious. 'How funny you are!' she said; and she quite genuinely did think him funny. 'You'll give me at least a week's warning, won't you,' she went on in another tone. 'I suppose we take the Blue Pacific Rocket? Does it start from the Charing-T Tower? Or is it from Hampstead?'

Before Bernard could answer, the lift came to a standstill.

'Roof!' called a creaking voice.

The liftman was a small simian creature, dressed in the black tunic of an Epsilon-Minus Semi-Moron.

'Roof!'

He flung open the gates. The warm glory of afternoon sunlight made him start and blink his eyes. 'Oh, roof!' he repeated in a voice of rapture. He was as though suddenly and joyfully awakened from a dark annihilating stupor. 'Roof!'

He smiled up with a kind of doggily expectant adoration into the faces of his passengers. Talking and laughing together, they stepped out into the light. The liftman looked after them.

'Roof?' he said once more, questioningly.

Then a bell rang, and from the ceiling of the lift a loud-speaker began, very softly and yet very imperiously, to issue its commands.

'Go down,' it said, 'go down. Floor Eighteen. Go down, go down. Floor Eighteen. Go down, go . . .'

The liftman slammed the gates, touched a button and instantly dropped back into the droning twilight of the well, the twilight of his own habitual stupor.

It was warm and bright on the roof. The summer afternoon was drowsy with the hum of passing helicopters; and the deeper

49

drone of the rocket-planes hastening, invisible, through the bright sky five or six miles overhead was like a caress on the soft air. Bernard Marx drew a deep breath. He looked up into the sky and round the blue horizon and finally down into Lenina's face.

'Isn't it beautiful!' His voice trembled a little.

She smiled at him with an expression of the most sympathetic understanding. 'Simply perfect for Obstacle Golf,' she answered rapturously. 'And now I must fly, Bernard. Henry gets cross if I keep him waiting. Let me know in good time about the date.' And waving her hand, she ran away across the wide flat roof towards the hangars. Bernard stood watching the retreating twinkle of the white stockings, the sunburnt knees vivaciously bending and unbending, again, again, and the softer rolling of those well-fitted corduroy shorts beneath the bottle-green jacket. His face wore an expression of pain.

'I should say she was pretty,' said a loud and cheery voice just behind him.

Bernard started, and looked round. The chubby red face of Benito Hoover was beaming down at him—beaming with manifest cordiality. Benito was notoriously good-natured. People said of him that he could have got through life without ever touching *soma*. The malice and bad tempers from which other people had to take holidays never afflicted him. Reality for Benito was always sunny.

'Pneumatic too. And how!' Then, in another tone, 'But, I say,' he went on, 'you do look glum! What you need is a gramme of *soma*.' Diving into his right-hand trouser-pocket, Benito produced a phial. 'One cubic centimetre cures ten gloomy ... But, I say!'

Bernard had suddenly turned and rushed away.

Benito stared after him. 'What can be the matter with the fellow?' he wondered, and, shaking his head, decided that the story about the alcohol having been put into the poor chap's blood-surrogate must be true. 'Touched his brain, I suppose.'

He put away the *soma* bottle, and taking out a packet of sex-hormone chewing-gum, stuffed a plug into his cheek and walked slowly away towards the hangars, ruminating.

Henry Foster had had his machine wheeled out of its lock-up and, when Lenina arrived, was already seated in the cockpit, waiting.

'Four minutes late,' was all his comment, as she climbed in beside him. He started the engines and threw the helicopter screws into gear. The machine shot vertically into the air. Henry accelerated; the humming of the propeller shrilled from hornet to wasp, from wasp to mosquito; the speedometer showed that they were rising at the best part of two kilometres a minute. London diminished beneath them. The huge table-topped buildings were no more, in a few seconds, than a bed of geometrical mushrooms sprouting from the green of park and garden. In the midst of them, thin-stalked, a taller, slenderer fungus, the Charing-T Tower lifted towards the sky a disk of shining concrete.

Like the vague torsos of fabulous athletes, huge fleshy clouds lolled on the blue air above their heads. Out of one of them suddenly dropped a small scarlet insect, buzzing as it fell.

'There's the Red Rocket,' said Henry, 'just come in from New York.' Looking at his watch, 'Seven minutes behind time,' he added, and shook his head. 'These Atlantic services—they're really scandalously unpunctual.'

He took his foot off the accelerator. The humming of the screws overhead dropped an octave and a half, back through wasp and hornet to bumble-bee, to cockchafer, to stag-beetle. The upward rush of the machine slackened off; a moment later they were hanging motionless in the air. Henry pushed at a lever; there was a click. Slowly at first, then faster and faster, till it was a circular mist before their eyes, the propeller in front of them began to revolve. The wind of a horizontal speed whistled ever more shrilly in the stays. Henry kept his eye on the revolution-counter; when the needle touched the twelve hundred mark, he threw the helicopter screws out of gear. The machine had enough forward momentum to be able to fly on its planes.

Lenina looked down through the window in the floor between her feet. They were flying over the six kilometre zone of parkland that separated Central London from its first ring of satellite suburbs. The green was maggoty with fore-shortened life. Forests of Centrifugal Bumble-puppy towers gleamed between the trees. Near Shepherd's Bush two thousand Beta-Minus mixed doubles were playing Riemann-surface tennis. A double row of Escalator Fives Courts lined the main road from Notting Hill to Willesden. In the Ealing stadium a Delta gymnastic display and community sing was in progress.

'What a hideous colour khaki is,' remarked Lenina, voicing the hypnopædic prejudices of her caste.

The buildings of the Hounslow Feely Studio covered seven and a half hectares. Near them a black and khaki army of labourers was busy revitrifying the surface of the Great West Road. One of the huge travelling crucibles was being tapped as they flew over. The molten stone poured out in a stream of dazzling incandescence across the road; the asbestos rollers came and went; at the tail of an insulated watering-cart the steam rose in white clouds.

At Brentford the Television Corporation's factory was like a small town.

'They must be changing the shift,' said Lenina.

Like aphides and ants, the leaf-green Gamma girls, the black Semi-Morons swarmed round the entrances, or stood in queues to take their places in the monorail tram-cars. Mulberry-coloured Beta-Minuses came and went among the crowd. The roof of the main building was alive with the alighting and departure of helicopters.

'My word,' said Lenina, 'I'm glad I'm not a Gamma.'

Ten minutes later they were at Stoke Poges and had started their first round of Obstacle Golf.

§ 2

With eyes for the most part downcast and, if ever they lighted on a fellow creature, at once and furtively averted, Bernard hastened across the roof. He was like a man pursued, but pursued by enemies he does not wish to see, lest they should seem more hostile even than he had supposed, and he himself be made to feel guiltier and even more helplessly alone.

'That horrible Benito Hoover!' And yet the man had meant well enough. Which only made it, in a way, much worse. Those who meant well behaved in the same way as those who meant badly. Even Lenina was making him suffer. He remembered those weeks of timid indecision, during which he had looked and longed and despaired of ever having the courage to ask her. Dared he face the risk of being humiliated by a contemptuous refusal? But if she were to say yes, what rapture! Well, now she had said it and he was still wretched—wretched that she should have thought it such a perfect afternoon for Obstacle Golf, that she should have trotted away to join Henry Foster, that she should have found him funny for not wanting to talk of their most private affairs in public. Wretched, in a word, because she had behaved as any healthy and virtuous English girl ought to behave and not in some other, abnormal, extraordinary way.

He opened the door of his lock-up and called to a lounging couple of Delta-Minus attendants to come and push his machine out on to the roof. The hangars were staffed by a single Bokanovsky Group, and the men were twins, identically small, black and hideous. Bernard gave his orders in the sharp, rather arrogant and even offensive tone of one who does not feel himself too secure in his superiority. To have dealings with members of the lower castes was always, for Bernard, a most distressing experience. For whatever the cause (and the current gossip about the alcohol in his blood-surrogate may very likely—for accidents will happen—have been true) Bernard's physique was hardly better than the average Gamma. He stood eight centimetres short of the standard Alpha height and was slender in proportion. Contact with members of the lower castes always reminded him painfully of this physical inadequacy. 'I am I, and wish I wasn't'; his self-consciousness was acute and distressing. Each time he found himself looking on the level, instead of downward, into a Delta's face, he felt humiliated. Would the creature treat him with the respect due to his caste? The question haunted him. Not without reason. For Gammas, Deltas and Epsilons had been to some extent conditioned to associate corporeal mass with social superiority. Indeed, a faint hypnopædic prejudice in favour of size was universal. Hence the laughter of the women to whom he made proposals, the practical joking of his equals among the men. The mockery made him feel an outsider; and feeling an outsider he behaved like one, which increased the prejudice against him and intensified the contempt and hostility aroused by his physical defects. Which in turn increased his sense of being alien and alone. A chronic fear of being slighted made him avoid his equals, made him stand, where his inferiors were concerned, self-consciously on his dignity. How bitterly he envied men like Henry Foster and Benito Hoover! Men who never had to shout at an Epsilon to get an order obeyed; men who took their position for granted; men who moved through the caste system as a fish through the water—so utterly at home as to be unaware either of themselves or of the beneficent and comfortable element in which they had their being.

Slackly, it seemed to him, and with reluctance, the twin attendants wheeled his plane out on the roof.

'Hurry up!' said Bernard irritably. One of them glanced at him. Was that a kind of bestial derision that he detected in those blank grey eyes? 'Hurry up!' he shouted more loudly, and there was an ugly rasp in his voice.

He climbed into the plane and, a minute later, was flying southwards, towards the river.

The various Bureaux of Propaganda and the College of

Emotional Engineering were housed in a single sixty-story building in Fleet Street. In the basement and on the lower floors were the presses and offices of the three great London newspapers —*The Hourly Radio*, an upper caste sheet, the pale-green *Gamma Gazette*, and, on khaki paper and in words exclusively of one syllable, *The Delta Mirror*. Then came the Bureaux of Propaganda by Television, by Feeling Picture, and by Synthetic Voice and Music respectively—twenty-two floors of them. Above were the research laboratories and the padded rooms in which the Sound-Track writers and Synthetic Composers did their delicate work. The top eighteen floors were occupied by the College of Emotional Engineering.

Bernard landed on the roof of Propaganda House and stepped out.

'Ring down to Mr. Helmholtz Watson,' he ordered the Gamma-Plus porter, 'and tell him that Mr. Bernard Marx is waiting for him on the roof.'

He sat down and lit a cigarette.

Helmholtz Watson was writing when the message came down.

'Tell him I'm coming at once,' he said and hung up the receiver. Then, turning to his secretary, 'I'll leave you to put my things away,' he went on in the same official and impersonal tone; and, ignoring her lustrous smile, got up and walked briskly to the door.

He was a powerfully built man, deep-chested, broad-shouldered, massive, and yet quick in his movements, springy and agile. The round strong pillar of his neck supported a beautifully shaped head. His hair was dark and curly, his features strongly marked. In a forcible emphatic way, he was handsome and looked, as his secretary was never tired of repeating, every centimetre an Alpha-Plus. By profession he was a lecturer at the College of Emotional Engineering (Department of Writing) and in the intervals of his educational activities, a working Emotional Engineer. He wrote regularly for *The Hourly Radio*, composed feely scenarios, and had the happiest knack for slogans and hypnopædic rhymes.

'Able,' was the verdict of his superiors. 'Perhaps' (and they would shake their heads, would significantly lower their voices) 'a little *too* able.'

Yes, a little too able; they were right. A mental excess had produced in Helmholtz Watson effects very similar to those which, in Bernard Marx, were the result of a physical defect. Too little bone and brawn had isolated Bernard from his fellow men, and the sense of this apartness, being, by all the current standards, a mental excess, became in its turn a cause of wider separation. That which had made Helmholtz so uncomfortably aware of being himself and all alone was too much ability. What the two men shared was the knowledge that they were individuals. But whereas the physically defective Bernard had suffered all his life from the consciousness of being separate, it was only quite recently that, grown aware of his mental excess, Helmholtz Watson had also become aware of his difference from the people who surrounded him. This Escalator-Squash champion, this indefatigable lover (it was said that he had had six hundred and forty different girls in under four years), this admirable committee man and best mixer had realized quite suddenly that sport, women, communal activities were only, so far as he was concerned, second bests. Really, and at the bottom, he was interested in something else. But in what? In what? That was the problem which Bernard had come to discuss with him—or rather, since it was always Helmholtz who did all the talking, to listen to his friend discussing, yet once more.

Three charming girls from the Bureau of Propaganda by Synthetic Voice waylaid him as he stepped out of the lift.

'Oh, Helmholtz darling, *do* come and have a picnic supper with us on Exmoor.' They clung round him imploringly.

He shook his head, he pushed his way through them. 'No, no.'

'We're not inviting any other man.'

But Helmholtz remained unshaken even by this delightful promise. 'No,' he repeated, 'I'm busy.' And he held resolutely on his course. The girls trailed after him. It was not till he had actually climbed into Bernard's plane and slammed the door that they gave up pursuit. Not without reproaches.

'These women!' he said, as the machine rose into the air. 'These women!' And he shook his head, he frowned. 'Too awful.' Bernard hypocritically agreed, wishing, as he spoke the words, that he could have as many girls as Helmholtz did, and with as little trouble. He was seized with a sudden urgent need to boast. 'I'm taking Lenina Crowne to New Mexico with me,' he said in a tone as casual as he could make it.

'Are you?' said Helmholtz, with a total absence of interest. Then after a little pause, 'This last week or two,' he went on, 'I've been cutting all my committees and all my girls. You can't imagine what a hullabaloo they've been making about it at the College. Still, it's been worth it, I think. The effects . . .' He hesitated. 'Well, they're odd, they're very odd.'

A physical shortcoming could produce a kind of mental excess. The process, it seemed, was reversible. Mental excess could produce, for its own purposes, the voluntary blindness and deafness of deliberate solitude, the artificial impotence of asceticism.

The rest of the short flight was accomplished in silence. When they had arrived and were comfortably stretched out on the pneumatic sofas in Bernard's room, Helmholtz began again.

Speaking very slowly, 'Did you ever feel,' he asked, 'as though you had something inside you that was only waiting for you to give it a chance to come out? Some sort of extra power that you aren't using—you know, like all the water that goes down the falls instead of through the turbines?' He looked at Bernard questioningly.

'You mean all the emotions one might be feeling if things were different?'

Helmholtz shook his head. 'Not quite. I'm thinking of a

queer feeling I sometimes get, a feeling that I've got something important to say and the power to say it—only I don't know what it is, and I can't make any use of the power. If there was some different way of writing . . . Or else something else to write about . . .' He was silent; then, 'You see,' he went on at last, 'I'm pretty good at inventing phrases—you know, the sort of words that suddenly make you jump, almost as though you'd sat on a pin, they seem so new and exciting even though they're about something hypnopædically obvious. But that doesn't seem enough. It's not enough for the phrases to be good; what you make with them ought to be good too.'

'But your things are good, Helmholtz.'

'Oh, as far as they go.' Helmholtz shrugged his shoulders. 'But they go such a little way. They aren't important enough, somehow. I feel I could do something much more important. Yes, and more intense, more violent. But what? What is there more important to say? And how can one be violent about the sort of things one's expected to write about? Words can be like X-rays, if you use them properly—they'll go through anything. You read and you're pierced. That's one of the things I try to teach my students—how to write piercingly. But what on earth's the good of being pierced by an article about a Community Sing, or the latest improvement in scent organs? Besides, can you make words really piercing—you know, like the very hardest X-rays—when you're writing about that sort of thing? Can you say something about nothing? That's what it finally boils down to. I try and I try . . .'

'Hush!' said Bernard suddenly, and lifted a warning finger; they listened. 'I believe there's somebody at the door,' he whispered.

Helmholtz got up, tiptoed across the room, and with a sharp quick movement flung the door wide open. There was, of course, nobody there.

'I'm sorry,' said Bernard, feeling and looking uncomfortably foolish. 'I suppose I've got things on my nerves a bit. When people are suspicious with you, you start being suspicious with them.'

He passed his hand across his eyes, he sighed, his voice became plaintive. He was justifying himself. 'If you knew what I'd had to put up with recently,' he said almost tearfully—and the uprush of his self-pity was like a fountain suddenly released. 'If you only knew!'

Helmholtz Watson listened with a certain sense of discomfort. 'Poor little Bernard!' he said to himself. But at the same time he felt rather ashamed for his friend. He wished Bernard would show a little more pride.

Chapter V

§ 1

BY eight o'clock the light was failing. The loud-speakers in the tower of the Stoke Poges Club House began, in a more than human tenor, to announce the closing of the courses. Lenina and Henry abandoned their game and walked back towards the Club. From the grounds of the Internal and External Secretion Trust came the lowing of those thousands of cattle which provided, with their hormones and their milk, the raw materials for the great factory at Farnham Royal.

An incessant buzzing of helicopters filled the twilight. Every two and a half minutes a bell and the screech of whistles announced the departure of one of the light monorail trains which carried the lower-caste golfers back from their separate course to the metropolis.

Lenina and Henry climbed into their machine and started off. At eight hundred feet Henry slowed down the helicopter screws, and they hung for a minute or two poised above the fading landscape. The forest of Burnham Beeches stretched like a great pool of darkness towards the bright shore of the western sky. Crimson at the horizon, the last of the sunset faded, through orange, upwards into yellow and a pale watery green. Northwards, beyond and above the trees, the Internal and External Secretions factory glared with a fierce electric brilliance from every window of its twenty stories. Beneath them lay the buildings of the Golf Club —the huge lower-caste barracks and, on the other side of a dividing wall, the smaller houses reserved for Alpha and Beta members. The approaches to the monorail station were black with the ant-like pullulation of lower-caste activity. From under the glass vault a lighted train shot out into the open. Following its south-easterly course across the dark plain their eyes were drawn to the majestic buildings of the Slough Crematorium. For the safety of night-flying planes, its four tall chimneys were flood-lighted and tipped with crimson danger signals. It was a landmark.

'Why do the smoke-stacks have those things like balconies round them?' enquired Lenina.

'Phosphorus recovery,' exclaimed Henry telegraphically. 'On their way up the chimney the gases go through four separate treatments. P_2O_5 used to go right out of circulation every time they cremated some one. Now they recover over ninety-eight per cent. of it. More than a kilo and a half per adult corpse. Which makes the best part of four hundred tons of phosphorus every year from England alone.' Henry spoke with a happy pride, rejoicing whole-heartedly in the achievement, as though it had been his own. 'Fine to think we can go on being socially useful even after we're dead. Making plants grow.'

Lenina, meanwhile, had turned her eyes away and was looking perpendicularly downwards at the monorail station. 'Fine,' she agreed. 'But queer that Alphas and Betas won't make any more plants grow than those nasty little Gammas and Deltas and Epsilons down there.'

'All men are physico-chemically equal,' said Henry sententiously. 'Besides, even Epsilons perform indispensable services.'

'Even an Epsilon . . .' Lenina suddenly remembered an occasion when, as a little girl at school, she had woken up in the middle of the night and become aware, for the first time, of the whispering that had haunted all her sleeps. She saw again the beam of moonlight, the row of small white beds; heard once more the soft, soft voice that said (the words were there, unforgotten, un-forgettable after so many night-long repetitions): 'Every one works for every one else. We can't do without any one. Even Epsilons are useful. We couldn't do without Epsilons. Every one works for every one else. We can't do without any one . . .' Lenina remembered her first shock of fear and surprise; her specu-lations through half a wakeful hour; and then, under the influence of those endless repetitions, the gradual soothing of her mind, the soothing, the smoothing, the stealthy creeping of sleep. . . .

'I suppose Epsilons don't really mind being Epsilons,' she said aloud.

'Of course they don't. How can they? They don't know what it's like being anything else. We'd mind, of course. But then we've been differently conditioned. Besides, we start with a different heredity.'

'I'm glad I'm not an Epsilon,' said Lenina, with conviction.

'And if you were an Epsilon,' said Henry, 'your conditioning would have made you no less thankful that you weren't a Beta or an Alpha.' He put his forward propeller into gear and headed the machine towards London. Behind them, in the west, the crimson and orange were almost faded; a dark bank of cloud had crept into the zenith. As they flew over the Crematorium, the plane shot upwards on the column of hot air rising from the chimneys, only to fall as suddenly when it passed into the descending chill beyond.

'What a marvellous switchback!' Lenina laughed delightedly.

But Henry's tone was almost, for a moment, melancholy. 'Do you know what that switchback was?' he said. 'It was some human being finally and definitely disappearing. Going up in a squirt of hot gas. It would be curious to know who it was—a man or a woman, an Alpha or an Epsilon. . . .' He sighed. Then, in a resolutely cheerful voice, 'Anyhow,' he concluded, 'there's one thing we can be certain of; whoever he may have been, he was happy when he was alive. Everybody's happy now.'

'Yes, everybody's happy now,' echoed Lenina. They had heard the words repeated a hundred and fifty times ever night for twelve years.

Landing on the roof of Henry's forty-story apartment house in Westminster, they went straight down to the dining-hall. There, in a loud and cheerful company, they ate an excellent meal. *Soma* was served with the coffee. Lenina took two half-gramme tablets and Henry three. At twenty past nine they walked across the street to the newly opened Westminster Abbey Cabaret. It was a night almost without clouds, moonless and

starry; but of this on the whole depressing fact Lenina and
Henry were fortunately unaware. The electric sky-signs effec-
tively shut off the outer darkness. 'CALVIN STOPES AND HIS
SIXTEEN SEXOPHONISTS.' From the facade of the new Abbey
the giant letters invitingly glared. 'LONDON'S FINEST SCENT
AND COLOUR ORGAN. ALL THE LATEST SYNTHETIC MUSIC.'

They entered. The air seemed hot and somehow breathless
with the scent of ambergris and sandalwood. On the domed
ceiling of the hall, the colour organ had momentarily painted a
tropical sunset. The Sixteen Sexophonists were playing an old
favourite: 'There ain't no Bottle in all the world like that dear
little Bottle of mine.' Four hundred couples were five-stepping
round the polished floor. Lenina and Henry were soon the four
hundred and first. The sexophones wailed like melodious cats
under the moon, moaned in the alto and tenor registers as though
the little death were upon them. Rich with a wealth of harmonics, their tremulous chorus mounted towards a climax, louder
and ever louder—until at last, with a wave of his hand, the con-
ductor let loose the final shattering note of ether-music and blew
the sixteen merely human blowers clean out of existence. Thunder
in A flat major. And then, in all but silence, in all but darkness,
there followed a gradual deturgescence, a *diminuendo* sliding gradually, through quarter tones, down, down to a faintly whispered
dominant chord that lingered on (while the five-four rhythms
still pulsed below) charging the darkened seconds with an intense
expectancy. And at last expectancy was fulfilled. There was a
sudden explosive sunrise, and simultaneously, the Sixteen burst
into song:

> Bottle of mine, it's you I've always wanted!
> Bottle of mine, why was I ever decanted?
> Skies are blue inside of you,
> The weather's always fine;
> For
> There ain't no Bottle in all the world
> Like that dear little Bottle of mine.

Five-stepping with the other four hundred round and round Westminster Abbey, Lenina and Henry were yet dancing in another world—the warm, the richly coloured, the infinitely friendly world of *soma*-holiday. How kind, how good-looking, how delightfully amusing every one was! 'Bottle of mine, it's you I've always wanted . . .' But Lenina and Henry had what they wanted . . . They were inside, here and now—safely inside with the fine weather, the perennially blue sky. And when, exhausted, the Sixteen had laid by their sexophones and the Synthetic Music apparatus was producing the very latest in slow Malthusian Blues, they might have been twin embryos gently rocking together on the waves of a bottled ocean of blood-surrogate.

'Good-night, dear friends. Good-night, dear friends.' The loud-speakers veiled their commands in a genial and musical politeness. 'Good-night, dear friends . . .'

Obediently, with all the others, Lenina and Henry left the building. The depressing stars had travelled quite some way across the heavens. But though the separating screen of the sky-signs had now to a great extent dissolved, the two young people still retained their happy ignorance of the night.

Swallowed half an hour before closing time, that second dose of *soma* had raised a quite impenetrable wall between the actual universe and their minds. Bottled, they crossed the street; bottled, they took the lift up to Henry's room on the twenty-eighth floor. And yet, bottled as she was, and in spite of that second gramme of *soma*, Lenina did not forget to take all the contraceptive precautions prescribed by the regulations. Years of intensive hypnopædia and, from twelve to seventeen, Malthusian drill three times a week had made the taking of these precautions almost as automatic and inevitable as blinking.

'Oh, and that reminds me,' she said, as she came back from the bathroom, 'Fanny Crowne wants to know where you found that lovely green morocco-surrogate cartridge belt you gave me.'

§ 2

Alternate Thursdays were Bernard's Solidarity Service days. After an early dinner at the Aphroditæum (to which Helmholtz had recently been elected under Rule Two) he took leave of his friend and, hailing a taxi on the roof, told the man to fly to the Fordson Community Singery. The machine rose a couple of hundred metres, then headed eastwards, and as it turned, there before Bernard's eyes, gigantically beautiful, was the Singery. Flood-lighted, its three hundred and twenty metres of white Carrara-surrogate gleamed with a snowy incandescence over Ludgate Hill; at each of the four corners of its helicopter platform an immense T shone crimson against the night, and from the mouths of twenty-four vast golden trumpets rumbled a solemn synthetic music.

'Damn, I'm late,' Bernard said to himself as he first caught sight of Big Henry, the Singery clock. And sure enough, as he was paying off his cab, Big Henry sounded the hour. 'Ford,' sang out an immense bass voice from all the golden trumpets. 'Ford, Ford, Ford . . .' Nine times. Bernard ran for the lift.

The great auditorium for Ford's Day celebrations and other massed Community Sings was at the bottom of the building. Above it, a hundred to each floor, were the seven thousand rooms used by Solidarity Groups for their fortnightly services. Bernard dropped down to floor thirty-three, hurried along the corridor, stood hesitating for a moment outside Room 3210, then, having wound himself up, opened the door and walked in.

Thank Ford! he was not the last. Three chairs of the twelve arranged round the circular table were still unoccupied. He slipped into the nearest of them as inconspicuously as he could and prepared to frown at the yet later comers whenever they should arrive.

Turning towards him, 'What were you playing this afternoon?' the girl on his left enquired. 'Obstacle, or Electro-magnetic?'

Bernard looked at her (Ford! it was Morgana Rothschild) and blushingly had to admit that he had been playing neither. Morgana stared at him with astonishment. There was an awkward silence.

Then pointedly she turned away and addressed herself to the more sporting man on her left.

'A good beginning for a Solidarity Service,' thought Bernard miserably, and foresaw for himself yet another failure to achieve atonement. If only he had given himself time to look round instead of scuttling for the nearest chair! He could have sat between Fifi Bradlaugh and Joanna Diesel. Instead of which he had gone and blindly planted himself next to Morgana. *Morgana!* Ford! Those black eyebrows of hers—that eyebrow, rather—for they met above the nose. Ford! And on his right was Clara Deterding. True, Clara's eyebrows didn't meet. But she was really *too* pneumatic. Whereas Fifi and Joanna were absolutely right. Plump, blonde, not too large . . . And it was that great lout, Tom Kawaguchi, who now took the seat between them.

The last arrival was Sarojini Engels.

'You're late,' said the President of the Group severely. 'Don't let it happen again.'

Sarojini apologized and slid into her place between Jim Bokanovsky and Herbert Bakunin. The group was now complete, the solidarity circle perfect and without flaw. Man, woman, man, in a ring of endless alternation round the table. Twelve of them ready to be made one, waiting to come together, to be fused, to lose their twelve separate identities in a larger being.

The President stood up, made the sign of the T and, switching on the synthetic music, let loose the soft indefatigable beating of drums and a choir of instruments—near-wind and super-string —that plangently repeated and repeated the brief and unescapably haunting melody of the First Solidarity Hymn. Again, again—and it was not the ear that heard the pulsing rhythm, it was the midriff; the wail and clang of those recurring harmonies haunted, not the mind, but the yearning bowels of compassion.

The President made another sign of the T and sat down. The service had begun. The dedicated *soma* tablets were placed in the centre of the dinner table. The loving cup of strawberry ice-cream *soma* was passed from hand to hand and, with the formula, 'I drink to my annihilation,' twelve times quaffed. Then to the accompaniment of the synthetic orchestra the First Solidarity Hymn was sung.

> Ford, we are twelve; oh, make us one,
> Like drops within the Social River;
> Oh, make us now together run
> As swiftly as thy shining Flivver.

Twelve yearning stanzas. And then the loving cup was passed a second time. 'I drink to the Greater Being' was now the formula. All drank. Tirelessly the music played. The drums beat. The crying and clashing of the harmonies were an obsession in the melted bowels. The Second Solidarity Hymn was sung.

> Come, Greater Being, Social Friend,
> Annihilating Twelve-in-One!
> We long to die, for when we end,
> Our larger life has but begun.

Again twelve stanzas. By this time the *soma* had begun to work. Eyes shone, cheeks were flushed, the inner light of universal benevolence broke out on every face in happy, friendly smiles. Even Bernard felt himself a little melted. When Morgana Rothschild turned and beamed at him, he did his best to beam back. But the eyebrow, that black two-in-one—alas, it was still there; he couldn't ignore it, couldn't, however hard he tried. The melting hadn't gone far enough. Perhaps if he had been sitting between Fifi and Joanna . . . For the third time the loving cup went round. 'I drink to the imminence of His Coming,' said Morgana Rothschild, whose turn it happened to be to initiate the circular rite. Her tone was loud, exultant. She drank and passed the cup to Bernard. 'I drink to the imminence of His Coming,' he repeated, with a sincere attempt to feel that the Coming was imminent; but the eyebrow continued to haunt him, and the Coming, so far as he was concerned, was horribly remote. He drank and handed the cup to Clara Deterding. 'It'll be a failure again,' he said to himself. 'I know it will.' But he went on doing his best to beam.

The loving cup had made its circuit. Lifting his hand, the President gave a signal; the chorus broke out into the Third Solidarity Hymn.

> Feel how the Greater Being comes!
>   Rejoice and, in rejoicings, die!
> Melt in the music of the drums!
>   For I am you and you are I.

As verse succeeded verse the voices thrilled with an ever intenser excitement. The sense of the Coming's imminence was like an electric tension in the air. The President switched off the music and, with the final note of the final stanza, there was absolute silence—the silence of stretched expectancy, quivering and creeping with a galvanic life. The President reached out his hand; and suddenly a Voice, a deep strong Voice, more musical than any merely human voice, richer, warmer, more vibrant with love and yearning and compassion, a wonderful, mysterious, supernatural Voice spoke from above their heads. Very slowly, 'Oh, Ford, Ford, Ford,' it said diminishingly and on a descending scale. A sensation of warmth radiated thrillingly out from the solar plexus to every extremity of the bodies of those who listened; tears came into their eyes; their hearts, their bowels seemed to move within them, as though with an independent life. 'Ford!' they were melting, 'Ford!' dissolved, dissolved. Then, in another tone, suddenly, startlingly. 'Listen!' trumpeted the Voice. 'Listen!' They listened. After a pause, sunk to a whisper, but a whisper, somehow, more penetrating than the loudest cry. 'The feet of the Greater Being,' it went on, and repeated the words: 'The feet of the Greater Being.' The whisper almost expired. 'The feet of the Greater Being are on the stairs.' And once more there was silence; and the expectancy, momentarily relaxed, was stretched again, tauter, tauter, almost to the tearing point. The feet of the Greater Being—oh, they heard them, they heard them, coming softly down the stairs, coming nearer and nearer down the invisible stairs. The feet of the Greater Being. And suddenly the tearing point was reached. Her eyes staring, her lips parted, Morgana Rothschild sprang to her feet.

'I hear him,' she cried. 'I hear him.'

'He's coming,' shouted Sarojini Engels.

'Yes, he's coming, I hear him.' Fifi Bradlaugh and Tom Kawaguchi rose simultaneously to their feet.

'Oh, oh, oh!' Joanna inarticulately testified.

'He's coming!' yelled Jim Bokanovsky.

The President leaned forward and, with a touch, released a delirium of cymbals and blown brass, a fever of tom-tomming.

'Oh, he's coming!' screamed Clara Deterding. 'Aie!' and it was as though she were having her throat cut.

Feeling that it was time for him to do something, Bernard also jumped up and shouted: 'I hear him; he's coming.' But it wasn't true. He heard nothing and, for him, nobody was coming. Nobody—in spite of the music, in spite of the mounting excitement. But he waved his arms, he shouted with the best of them; and when the others began to jig and stamp and shuffle, he also jigged and shuffled.

Round they went, a circular procession of dancers, each with hands on the hips of the dancer preceding, round and round, shouting in unison, stamping to the rhythm of the music with their feet, beating it, beating it out with hands on the buttocks in front; twelve pairs of hands beating as one; as one, twelve buttocks slabbily resounding. Twelve as one, twelve as one. 'I hear him, I hear him coming.' The music quickened; faster beat the feet, faster, faster fell the rhythmic hands. And all at once a great synthetic bass boomed out the words which announced the approaching atonement and final consummation of solidarity, the coming of the Twelve-in-One, the incarnation of the Greater Being. 'Orgy-porgy,' it sang, while the tom-toms continued to beat their feverish tattoo:

> Orgy-porgy, Ford and fun,
> Kiss the girls and make them One.
> Boys at one with girls at peace;
> Orgy-porgy gives release.

'Orgy-porgy,' the dancers caught up the liturgical refrain, 'Orgy-porgy, Ford and fun, kiss the girls . . .' And as they sang, the lights began slowly to fade—to fade and at the same time to grow warmer, richer, redder, until at last they were dancing in the crimson twilight of an Embryo Store. 'Orgy-porgy . . .' In their blood-coloured and fœtal darkness the dancers continued for a while to circulate, to beat and beat out the indefatigable rhythm. 'Orgy-porgy . . .' Then the circle wavered, broke, fell in partial disintegration on the ring of couches which surrounded—circle enclosing circle—the table and its planetary chairs. 'Orgy-porgy . . .' Tenderly the deep Voice crooned and cooed; in the red twilight it was as though some enormous negro dove were hovering benevolently over the now prone or supine dancers.

They were standing on the roof; Big Henry had just sung eleven. The night was calm and warm.

'Wasn't it wonderful?' said Fifi Bradlaugh. 'Wasn't it simply wonderful?' She looked at Bernard with an expression of rapture, but of rapture in which there was no trace of agitation or excitement—for to be excited is still to be unsatisfied. Hers was the calm ecstasy of achieved consummation, the peace, not of mere vacant satiety and nothingness, but of balanced life, of energies at rest and in equilibrium. A rich and living peace. For the Solidarity Service had given as well as taken, drawn off only to replenish. She was full, she was made perfect, she was still more than merely herself. 'Didn't you think it was wonderful?' she insisted, looking into Bernard's face with those supernaturally shining eyes.

'Yes, I thought it was wonderful,' he lied and looked away; the sight of her transfigured face was at once an accusation and an ironical reminder of his own separateness. He was as miserably isolated now as he had been when the service began—more isolated by reason of his unreplenished emptiness, his dead satiety. Separate and unatoned, while the others were being fused into the Greater Being; alone even in Morgana's embrace—much more alone, indeed, more hopelessly himself than he had ever been in his life before. He had emerged from that crimson twilight into the common electric glare with a self-consciousness intensified to the pitch of agony. He was utterly miserable, and perhaps (her shining eyes accused him), perhaps it was his own fault. 'Quite wonderful,' he repeated; but the only thing he could think of was Morgana's eyebrow.

Chapter VI

ODD, odd, *odd*, was Lenina's verdict on Bernard Marx. So odd, indeed, that in the course of the succeeding weeks she had wondered more than once whether she shouldn't change her mind about the New Mexico holiday, and go instead to the North Pole with Benito Hoover. The trouble was that she knew the North Pole, had been there with George Edzel only last summer, and what was more, found it pretty grim. Nothing to do, and the hotel too hopelessly old-fashioned—no television laid on in the bedrooms, no scent organ, only the most putrid synthetic music, and not more than twenty-five Escalator-Squash Courts for over two hundred guests. No, decidedly she couldn't face the North Pole again. Added to which, she had only been to America once before. And even then, how inadequately! A cheap week-end in New York—had it been with Jean-Jacques Habibullah or Bokanovsky Jones? She couldn't remember. Anyhow, it was of absolutely no importance. The prospect of flying West again, and for a whole week, was very inviting. Moreover, for at least three days of that week they would be in the Savage Reservation. Not more than half a dozen people in the whole Centre had ever been inside a Savage Reservation. As an Alpha-Plus psychologist, Bernard was one of the few men she knew entitled to a permit. For Lenina, the opportunity was unique. And yet, so unique also was Bernard's oddness, that she had hesitated to take it, had actually thought of risking the Pole again with funny old Benito. At least Benito was normal. Whereas Bernard . . .

'Alcohol in his blood-surrogate,' was Fanny's explanation of every eccentricity. But Henry, with whom, one evening when they were in bed together, Lenina had rather anxiously discussed her new lover, Henry had compared poor Bernard to a rhinoceros.

'You can't teach a rhinoceros tricks,' he had explained in his brief and vigorous style. 'Some men are almost rhinoceroses; they don't respond properly to conditioning. Poor devils! Bernard's one of them. Luckily for him, he's pretty good at his job. Otherwise the Director would never have kept him. However,' he added consolingly, 'I think he's pretty harmless.'

Pretty harmless, perhaps; but also pretty disquieting. That mania, to start with, for doing things in private. Which meant, in practice, not doing anything at all. For what was there that one *could* do in private. (Apart, of course, from going to bed: but one couldn't do that all the time.) Yes, what *was* there? Precious little. The first afternoon they went out together was particularly fine. Lenina had suggested a swim at the Torquay Country Club followed by dinner at the Oxford Union. But Bernard thought there would be too much of a crowd. Then what about a round of Electro-magnetic Golf at St. Andrews? But again, no: Bernard considered that Electro-magnetic Golf was a waste of time.

'Then what's time for?' asked Lenina in some astonishment.

Apparently, for going walks in the Lake District; for that was what he now proposed. Land on the top of Skiddaw and walk for a couple of hours in the heather. 'Alone with you, Lenina.'

'But, Bernard, we shall be alone all night.'

Bernard blushed and looked away. 'I meant, alone for talking,' he mumbled.

'Talking? But what about?' Walking and talking—that seemed a very odd way of spending an afternoon.

In the end she persuaded him, much against his will, to fly over to Amsterdam to see the Semi-Demi-Finals of the Women's Heavyweight Wrestling Championship.

'In a crowd,' he grumbled. 'As usual.' He remained obstinately gloomy the whole afternoon; wouldn't talk to Lenina's friends (of whom they met dozens in the ice-cream *soma* bar between the wrestling bouts); and in spite of his misery absolutely refused to take the half-gramme raspberry sundae which she pressed upon him. 'I'd rather be myself,' he said. 'Myself and nasty. Not somebody else, however jolly.'

'A gramme in time saves nine,' said Lenina, producing a bright treasure of sleep-taught wisdom.

Bernard pushed away the proffered glass impatiently.

'Now don't lose your temper,' she said. 'Remember, one cubic centimetre cures ten gloomy sentiments.'

'Oh, for Ford's sake, be quiet!' he shouted.

Lenina shrugged her shoulders. 'A gramme is always better than a damn,' she concluded with dignity, and drank the sundae herself.

On their way back across the Channel, Bernard insisted on stopping his propeller and hovering on his helicopter screws within a hundred feet of the waves. The weather had taken a change for the worse; a south-westerly wind had sprung up, the sky was cloudy.

'Look,' he commanded.

'But it's horrible,' said Lenina, shrinking back from the window. She was appalled by the rushing emptiness of the night, by the black foam-flecked water heaving beneath them, by the pale face of the moon, so haggard and distracted among the hastening clouds. 'Let's turn on the radio. Quick!' She reached for the dialling knob on the dashboard and turned it at random.

'. . . skies are blue inside of you,' sang sixteen tremoloing falsettos, 'the weather's always . . .'

Then a hiccough and silence. Bernard had switched off the current.

'I want to look at the sea in peace,' he said. 'One can't even look with that beastly noise going on.'

'But it's lovely. And I don't want to look.'

'But I do,' he insisted. 'It makes me feel as though . . .' he hesitated, searching for words with which to express himself, 'as though I were more *me*, if you see what I mean. More on my own, not so completely a part of something else. Not just a cell in the social body. Doesn't it make you feel like that, Lenina?'

But Lenina was crying. 'It's horrible, it's horrible,' she kept repeating. 'And how can you talk like that about not wanting to be a part of the social body? After all, every one works for every one else. We can't do without any one. Even Epsilons...'

'Yes, I know,' said Bernard derisively. '"Even Epsilons are useful"! So am I. And I damned well wish I weren't!'

Lenina was shocked by his blasphemy. 'Bernard!' she protested in a voice of amazed distress. 'How can you?'

In a different key, 'How can I?' he repeated meditatively. 'No, the real problem is: How is it that I can't, or rather—because, after all, I know quite well why I can't—what would it be like if I could, if I were free—not enslaved by my conditioning.'

'But, Bernard, you're saying the most awful things.'

'Don't you wish you were free, Lenina?'

'I don't know what you mean. I am free. Free to have the most wonderful time. Everybody's happy nowadays.'

He laughed, 'Yes, "Everybody's happy nowadays." We begin giving the children that at five. But wouldn't you like to be free to be happy in some other way, Lenina? In your own way, for example; not in everybody else's way.'

'I don't know what you mean,' she repeated. Then, turning to him, 'Oh, do let's go back, Bernard,' she besought; 'I do so hate it here.'

'Don't you like being with me?'

'But of course, Bernard! It's this horrible place.'

'I thought we'd be more ... more *together* here—with nothing but the sea and moon. More together than in that crowd, or even in my rooms. Don't you understand that?'

'I don't understand anything,' she said with decision, determined to preserve her incomprehension intact. 'Nothing. Least of all,' she continued in another tone, 'why you don't take *soma* when you have these dreadful ideas of yours. You'd forget all about them. And instead of feeling miserable, you'd be jolly. *So* jolly,' she repeated and smiled, for all the puzzled anxiety in her eyes, with what was meant to be an inviting and voluptuous cajolery.

He looked at her in silence, his face unresponsive and very grave—looked at her intently. After a few seconds Lenina's eyes flinched away; she uttered a nervous little laugh, tried to think of something to say and couldn't. The silence prolonged itself.

When Bernard spoke at last, it was in a small tired voice. 'All right, then,' he said, 'we'll go back.' And stepping hard on the accelerator, he sent the machine rocketing up into the sky. At four thousand he started his propeller. They flew in silence for a minute or two. Then, suddenly, Bernard began to laugh. Rather oddly, Lenina thought; but still, it was laughter.

'Feeling better?' she ventured to ask.

For answer, he lifted one hand from the controls and, slipping his arm round her, began to fondle her breasts.

'Thank Ford,' she said to herself, 'he's all right again.'

Half an hour later they were back in his rooms. Bernard swallowed four tablets of *soma* at a gulp, turned on the radio and television and began to undress.

'Well,' Lenina enquired, with significant archness when they met next afternoon on the roof, 'did you think it was fun yesterday?'

Bernard nodded. They climbed into the plane. A little jolt, and they were off.

'Every one says I'm awfully pneumatic,' said Lenina reflectively, patting her own legs.

'Awfully.' But there was an expression of pain in Bernard's eyes. 'Like meat,' he was thinking.

She looked up with a certain anxiety. 'But you don't think I'm *too* plump, do you?'

He shook his head. Like so much meat.

'You think I'm all right.' Another nod. 'In every way?'

'Perfect,' he said aloud. And inwardly, 'She thinks of herself that way. She doesn't mind being meat.'

Lenina smiled triumphantly. But her satisfaction was premature.

'All the same,' he went on, after a little pause, 'I still rather wish it had all ended differently.'

'Differently?' Were there other endings?

'I didn't want it to end with our going to bed,' he specified.

Lenina was astonished.

'Not at once, not the first day'

'But then what . . .?'

He began to talk a lot of incomprehensible and dangerous nonsense. Lenina did her best to stop the ears of her mind; but every now and then a phrase would insist on becoming audible. '. . . to try the effect of arresting my impulses,' she heard him say. The words seemed to touch a spring in her mind.

'Never put off till to-morrow the fun you can have to-day,' she said gravely.

'Two hundred repetitions, twice a week from fourteen to sixteen and a half,' was all his comment. The mad bad talk rambled on. 'I want to know what passion is,' she heard him saying. 'I want to feel something strongly.'

'When the individual feels, the community reels,' Lenina pronounced.

'Well, why shouldn't it reel a bit?'

'Bernard!'

But Bernard remained unabashed.

'Adults intellectually and during working hours,' he went on. 'Infants where feeling and desire are concerned.'

'Our Ford loved infants.'

Ignoring the interruption, 'It suddenly struck me the other day,' continued Bernard, 'that it might be possible to be an adult all the time.'

'I don't understand.' Lenina's tone was firm.

'I know you don't. And that's why we went to bed together yesterday—like infants—instead of being adults and waiting.'

'But it was fun,' Lenina insisted. 'Wasn't it?'

'Oh, the greatest fun,' he answered, but in a voice so mournful, with an expression so profoundly miserable, that Lenina felt all her triumph suddenly evaporate. Perhaps he had found her too plump, after all.

'I told you so,' was all that Fanny said, when Lenina came and made her confidences. 'It's the alcohol they put in his surrogate.'

'All the same,' Lenina insisted, 'I do like him. He has such awfully nice hands. And the way he moves his shoulders—that's very attractive.' She sighed. 'But I wish he weren't so odd.'

§ 2

Halting for a moment outside the door of the Director's room, Bernard drew a deep breath and squared his shoulders, bracing himself to meet the dislike and disapproval which he was certain of finding within. He knocked and entered.

'A permit for you to initial, Director,' he said as airily as possible, and laid the paper on the writing-table.

The Director glanced at him sourly. But the stamp of the World Controller's Office was at the head of the paper and the signature of Mustapha Mond, bold and black, across the bottom. Everything was perfectly in order. The Director had no choice. He pencilled his initials—two small pale letters abject at the feet of Mustapha Mond—and was about to return the paper without a word of comment or genial Ford-speed, when his eye was caught by something written in the body of the permit.

'For the New Mexican Reservation?' he said, and his tone, the face he lifted to Bernard, expressed a kind of agitated astonishment.

Surprised by his surprise, Bernard nodded. There was a silence.

The Director leaned back in his chair, frowning. 'How long ago was it?' he said, speaking more to himself than to Bernard. 'Twenty years, I suppose. Nearer twenty-five. I must have been your age . . .' He sighed and shook his head.

Bernard felt extremely uncomfortable. A man so conventional, so scrupulously correct as the Director—and to commit so gross a solecism! It made him want to hide his face, to run out of the room. Not that he himself saw anything intrinsically objectionable in people talking about the remote past; that was one of those hypnopædic prejudices he had (so he imagined) completely got rid of. What made him feel shy was the knowledge that the Director disapproved—disapproved and yet had been betrayed into doing the forbidden thing. Under what inward compulsion? Through his discomfort Bernard eagerly listened.

'I had the same idea as you,' the Director was saying. 'Wanted to have a look at the savages. Got a permit for New Mexico and went there for my summer holiday. With the girl I was having at the moment. She was a Beta-Minus, and I think' (he shut his eyes), 'I think she had yellow hair. Anyhow, she was pneumatic, particularly pneumatic; I remember that. Well, we went there, and we looked at the savages, and we rode about on horses and all that. And then—it was almost the last day of my leave —then . . . well, she got lost. We'd gone riding up one of those revolting mountains, and it was horribly hot and oppressive, and after lunch we went to sleep. Or at least I did. She must have gone for a walk, alone. At any rate, when I woke up, she wasn't there. And the most frightful thunderstorm I've ever seen was just bursting on us. And it poured and roared and flashed; and the horses broke loose and ran away; and I fell down, trying to catch them, and hurt my knee, so that I could hardly walk. Still, I searched and I shouted and I searched. But there was no sign of her. Then I thought she must have gone back to the rest-house by herself. So I crawled down into the valley by the way we had come. My knee was agonizingly painful, and I'd lost my *soma*. It took me hours. I didn't get back to the rest-house till

79

after midnight. And she wasn't there; she wasn't there,' the Director repeated. There was a silence. 'Well,' he resumed at last, 'the next day there was a search. But we couldn't find her. She must have fallen into a gully somewhere; or been eaten by a mountain lion. Ford knows. Anyhow it was horrible. It upset me very much at the time. More than it ought to have done, I dare say. Because, after all, it's the sort of accident that might have happened to any one; and, of course, the social body persists although the component cells may change.' But this sleep-taught consolation did not seem to be very effective. Shaking his head, 'I actually dream about it sometimes,' the Director went on in a low voice. 'Dream of being woken up by that peal of thunder and finding her gone; dream of searching and searching for her under the trees.' He lapsed into the silence of reminiscence.

'You must have had a terrible shock,' said Bernard, almost enviously.

At the sound of his voice the Director started into a guilty realization of where he was; shot a glance at Bernard, and averting his eyes, blushed darkly; looked at him again with sudden suspicion and, angrily on his dignity, 'Don't imagine,' he said, 'that I'd had any indecorous relation with the girl. Nothing emotional, nothing long-drawn. It was all perfectly healthy and normal.' He handed Bernard the permit. 'I really don't know why I bored you with this trivial anecdote.' Furious with himself for having given away a discreditable secret, he vented his rage on Bernard. The look in his eyes was now frankly malignant. 'And I should like to take this opportunity, Mr. Marx,' he went on, 'of saying that I'm not at all pleased with the reports I receive of your behaviour outside working hours. You may say that this is not my business. But it is. I have the good name of the Centre to think of. My workers must be above suspicion, particularly those of the highest castes. Alphas are so conditioned that they do not *have* to be infantile in their emotional behaviour. But that is all the more reason for their making a special effort to conform. It is their duty to be infantile, even against their inclination. And so, Mr. Marx, I give you fair warning.' The Director's voice vibrated with an indignation that had now become wholly righteous and impersonal—was the expression of the disapproval of Society itself. 'If ever I hear again of any lapse from a proper standard of infantile decorum, I shall ask for your transference to a Sub-Centre—preferably to Iceland. Good morning.' And swivelling round in his chair, he picked up his pen and began to write.

'That'll teach him,' he said to himself. But he was mistaken. For Bernard left the room with a swagger, exulting, as he banged the door behind him, in the thought that he stood alone, embattled against the order of things; elated by the intoxicating consciousness of his individual significance and importance. Even the thought of persecution left him undismayed, was rather tonic than depressing. He felt strong enough to meet and overcome affliction, strong enough to face even Iceland. And this confidence was the greater for his not for a moment really believing that he would be called upon to face anything at all. People simply weren't transferred for things like that. Iceland was just a threat. A most stimulating and life-giving threat. Walking along the corridor, he actually whistled.

Heroic was the account he gave that evening of his interview with the D.H.C. 'Whereupon,' it concluded, 'I simply told him to go to the Bottomless Past and marched out of the room. And that was that.' He looked at Helmholtz Watson expectantly, awaiting his due reward of sympathy, encouragement, admiration. But no word came. Helmholtz sat silent, staring at the floor.

He liked Bernard; he was grateful to him for being the only man of his acquaintance with whom he could talk about the subjects he felt to be important. Nevertheless, there were things in Bernard which he hated. This boasting, for example. And the outbursts of an abject self-pity with which it alternated. And his deplorable habit of being bold after the event, and full, in absence, of the most extraordinary presence of mind. He hated these things—just because he liked Bernard. The seconds passed. Helmholtz continued to stare at the floor. And suddenly Bernard blushed and turned away.

§ 3

The journey was quite uneventful. The Blue Pacific Rocket was two and a half minutes early at New Orleans, lost four minutes in a tornado over Texas, but flew into a favourable air current at Longitude 95 West, and was able to land at Santa Fé less than forty seconds behind schedule time.

'Forty seconds on a six and a half hour flight. Not so bad,' Lenina conceded.

They slept that night at Santa Fé. The hotel was excellent—incomparably better, for example, than that horrible Aurora Bora Palace in which Lenina had suffered so much the previous summer. Liquid air, television, vibro-vacuum massage, radio, boiling caffeine solution, hot contraceptives, and eight different kinds of scent were laid on in every bedroom. The synthetic music plant was working as they entered the hall and left nothing to be desired. A notice in the lift announced that there were sixty Escalator-Squash-Racquet Courts in the hotel, and that Obstacle and Electro-magnetic Golf could both be played in the park.

'But it sounds simply too lovely,' cried Lenina. 'I almost wish we could stay here. Sixty Escalator-Squash Courts . . .'

'There won't be any in the Reservation,' Bernard warned her. 'And no scent, no television, no hot water, even. If you feel you can't stand it, stay here till I come back.'

Lenina was quite offended. 'Of course I can stand it. I only said it was lovely here because . . . well, because progress *is* lovely, isn't it?'

'Five hundred repetitions once a week from thirteen to seventeen,' said Bernard wearily, as though to himself.

'What did you say?'

'I said that progress was lovely. That's why you mustn't come to the Reservation unless you really want to.'

'But I do want to.'

'Very well, then,' said Bernard; and it was almost a threat.

Their permit required the signature of the Warden of the Reservation, at whose office next morning they duly presented themselves. An Epsilon-Plus negro porter took in Bernard's card, and they were admitted almost immediately.

The Warden was a blond and brachycephalic Alpha-Minus, short, red, moon-faced, and broad-shouldered, with a loud booming voice, very well adapted to the utterance of hypno-pædic wisdom. He was a mine of irrelevant information and un-asked-for good advice. Once started, he went on and on—boomingly.

'. . . five hundred and sixty thousand square kilometres, divided into four distinct Sub-Reservations, each surrounded by a high-tension wire fence.'

At this moment, and for no apparent reason, Bernard suddenly remembered that he had left the eau-de-Cologne tap in his bath-room wide open and running.

'. . . supplied with current from the Grand Canyon hydro-electric station.'

'Cost me a fortune by the time I get back.' With his mind's eye, Bernard saw the needle on the scent meter creeping round and round, ant-like, indefatigably. 'Quickly telephone to Helm-holtz Watson.'

'. . . upwards of five thousand kilometres of fencing at sixty thousand volts.'

'You don't say so,' said Lenina politely, not knowing in the least what the Warden had said, but taking her cue from his dramatic pause. When the Warden started booming, she had inconspicuously swallowed half a gramme of *soma*, with the result that she could now sit, serenely not listening, thinking of nothing at all, but with her large blue eyes fixed on the Warden's face in an expression of rapt attention.

'To touch the fence is instant death,' pronounced the Warden solemnly. 'There is no escape from a Savage Reservation.'

The word 'escape' was suggestive. 'Perhaps,' said Bernard, half rising, 'we ought to think of going.' The little black needle was scurrying, an insect, nibbling through time, eating into his money.

'No escape,' repeated the Warden, waving him back into his chair; and as the permit was not yet countersigned, Bernard had no choice but to obey. 'Those who are born in the Reservation —and remember, my dear young lady,' he added, leering obscenely at Lenina, and speaking in an improper whisper, 'remember that, in the Reservation, children still *are* born, yes, actually born, revolting as that may seem . . .' (He hoped that this reference to a shameful subject would make Lenina blush; but she only smiled with simulated intelligence and said, 'You don't say so!' Disappointed, the Warden began again.) 'Those, I repeat, who are born in the Reservation are destined to die there.'

Destined to die . . . A decilitre of eau-de-Cologne every minute. Six litres an hour. Perhaps,' Bernard tried again, 'we ought . . .'

Leaning forward, the Director tapped the table with his forefinger. 'You ask me how many people live in the Reservation. And I reply'—triumphantly—'I reply that we do not know. We can only guess.'

'You don't say so.'

'My dear young lady, I do say so.'

Six times twenty-four—no, it would be nearer six times thirty-six. Bernard was pale and trembling with impatience. But inexorably the booming continued.

'. . . about sixty thousand Indians and half-breeds . . . absolute savages . . . our inspectors occasionally visit . . . otherwise, no communication whatever with the civilized world . . . still preserve their repulsive habits and customs . . . marriage, if you know what that is, my dear young lady; families . . . no conditioning . . . monstrous superstitions . . . Christianity and totem-ism and ancestor worship . . . extinct languages, such as Zuñi and Spanish and Athapascan . . . pumas, porcupines and other fero-cious animals . . . infectious diseases . . . priests . . . venomous lizards . . .'

'You don't say so?'

They got away at last. Bernard dashed to the telephone. Quick, quick; but it took him nearly three minutes to get on to Helmholtz Watson. 'We might be among the savages already,' he complained. 'Damned incompetence!'

'Have a gramme,' suggested Lenina.

He refused, preferring his anger. And at last, thank Ford, he was through and, yes, it was Helmholtz; Helmholtz, to whom he explained what had happened, and who promised to go round at once, at once, and turn off the tap, yes, at once, but took this opportunity to tell him what the D.H.C. had said, in public, yesterday evening . . .

'What? He's looking out for some one to take my place?' Bernard's voice was agonized. 'So it's actually decided? Did he mention Iceland? You say he did? Ford! Iceland . . .' He hung up the receiver and turned back to Lenina. His face was pale, his expression utterly dejected.

'What's the matter?' she asked.

'The matter?' He dropped heavily into a chair. 'I'm going to be sent to Iceland.'

Often in the past he had wondered what it would be like to be subjected (soma-less and with nothing but his own inward re-sources to rely on) to some great trial, some pain, some perse-cution; he had even longed for affliction. As recently as a week ago, in the Director's office, he had imagined himself courage-ously resisting, stoically accepting suffering without a word. The Director's threats had actually elated him, made him feel larger than life. But that, as he now realized, was because he had not taken the threats quite seriously; he had not believed that, when it came to the point, the D.H.C. would ever do anything.

Now that it looked as though the threats were really to be fulfilled, Bernard was appalled. Of that imagined stoicism, that theoretical courage, not a trace was left.

He raged against himself—what a fool!—against the Director—how unfair not to give him that other chance, that other chance which, he now had no doubt at all, he had always intended to take. And Iceland, Iceland . . .

Lenina shook her head. 'Was and will make me ill,' she quoted, 'I take a gramme and only am.'

In the end she persuaded him to swallow four tablets of *soma*. Five minutes later roots and fruits were abolished; the flower of the present rosily blossomed. A message from the porter announced that, at the Warden's orders, a Reservation Guard had come round with a plane and was waiting on the roof of the hotel. They went up at once. An octoroon in Gamma-green uniform saluted and proceeded to recite the morning's programme.

A bird's-eye view of ten or a dozen of the principal pueblos, then a landing for lunch in the valley of Malpais. The rest-house was comfortable there, and up at the pueblo the savages would probably be celebrating their summer festival. It would be the best place to spend the night.

They took their seats in the plane and set off. Ten minutes later they were crossing the frontier that separated civilization from savagery. Uphill and down, across the deserts of salt or sand, through forests, into the violet depth of canyons, over crag and peak and table-topped mesa, the fence marched on and on, irresistibly the straight line, the geometrical symbol of triumphant human purpose. And at its foot, here and there, a mosaic of white bones, a still unrotted carcase dark on the tawny ground marked the place where deer or steer, puma or porcupine or coyote, or the greedy turkey buzzards drawn down by the whiff of carrion and fulminated as though by a poetic justice, had come too close to the destroying wires.

'They never learn,' said the green-uniformed pilot, pointing down at the skeletons on the ground below them. 'And they never will learn,' he added and laughed, as though he had somehow scored a personal triumph over the electrocuted animals.

Bernard also laughed; after two grammes of *soma* the joke seemed, for some reason, good. Laughed and then, almost immediately, dropped off to sleep and, sleeping, was carried over Taos and Tesuque; over Nambe and Picuris and Pojoaque, over Sia and Cochiti, over Laguna and Acoma and the Enchanted Mesa, over Zuñi and Cibola and Ojo Caliente, and woke at last to find the machine standing on the ground, Lenina carrying the suit-cases into a small square house, and the Gamma-green octoroon talking incomprehensibly with a young Indian.

'Malpais,' explained the pilot, as Bernard stepped out. 'This is the rest-house. And there's a dance this afternoon at the pueblo. He'll take you there.' He pointed to the sullen young savage. 'Funny, I expect.' He grinned. 'Everything they do is funny.' And with that he climbed into the plane and started up the engines. 'Back to-morrow. And remember,' he added reassuringly to Lenina, 'they're perfectly tame; savages won't do you any harm. They've got enough experience of gas bombs to know that they mustn't play any tricks.' Still laughing, he threw the helicopter screws into gear, accelerated, and was gone.

Chapter VII

THE mesa was like a ship becalmed in a strait of lion-coloured dust. The channel wound between precipitous banks, and slanting from one wall to the other across the valley ran a streak of green—the river and its fields. On the prow of that stone ship in the centre of the strait, and seemingly a part of it, a shaped and geometrical outcrop of the naked rock, stood the pueblo of Malpais. Block above block, each story smaller than the one below, the tall houses rose like stepped and amputated pyramids into the blue sky. At their feet lay a straggle of low buildings, a criss-cross of walls; and on three sides the precipices fell sheer into the plain. A few columns of smoke mounted perpendicularly into the windless air and were lost.

'Queer,' said Lenina. 'Very queer.' It was her ordinary word of condemnation. 'I don't like it. And I don't like that man. She pointed to the Indian guide who had been appointed to take them up to the pueblo. Her feeling was evidently reciprocated; the very back of the man, as he walked along before them, was hostile, sullenly contemptuous.

'Besides,' she lowered her voice, 'he smells.'

Bernard did not attempt to deny it. They walked on.

Suddenly it was as though the whole air had come alive and were pulsing, pulsing with the indefatigable movement of blood. Up there, in Malpais, the drums were being beaten. Their feet fell in with the rhythm of that mysterious heart; they quickened their pace. Their path led them to the foot of the precipice. The sides of the great mesa ship towered over them, three hundred feet to the gunwale.

'I wish we could have brought the plane,' said Lenina, looking up resentfully at the blank impending rock-face. 'I hate walking. And you feel so small when you're on the ground at the bottom of a hill.'

They walked along for some way in the shadow of the mesa, rounded a projection, and there, in a water-worn ravine, was the way up the companion ladder. They climbed. It was a very steep path that zigzagged from side to side of the gully. Sometimes the pulsing of the drums was all but inaudible, at others they seemed to be beating only just round the corner.

When they were half-way up, an eagle flew past so close to them that the wind of his wings blew chill on their faces. In a crevice of the rock lay a pile of bones. It was all oppressively queer, and the Indian smelt stronger and stronger. They emerged at last from the ravine into the full sunlight. The top of the mesa was a flat deck of stone.

'Like the Charing-T Tower,' was Lenina's comment. But she was not allowed to enjoy her discovery of this reassuring resemblance for long. A padding of soft feet made them turn round. Naked from throat to navel, their dark-brown bodies painted with white lines ('like asphalt tennis courts,' Lenina was later to explain), their faces inhuman with daubings of scarlet, black and ochre, two Indians came running along the path. Their black hair was braided with fox fur and red flannel. Cloaks of turkey feathers fluttered from their shoulders; huge feather diadems exploded gaudily round their heads. With every step they took came the clink and rattle of their silver bracelets, their heavy necklaces of bone and turquoise beads. They came on without a word, running quietly in their deerskin moccasins. One of them was holding a feather brush; the other carried, in either hand, what looked at a distance like three or four pieces of thick rope. One of the ropes writhed uneasily, and suddenly Lenina saw that they were snakes.

The men came nearer and nearer; their dark eyes looked at her, but without giving any sign of recognition, any smallest sign that they had seen her or were aware of her existence. The writhing snake hung limp again with the rest. The men passed.

'I don't like it,' said Lenina. 'I don't like it.'

She liked even less what awaited her at the entrance to the pueblo, where their guide had left them while he went inside for instructions. The dirt, to start with, the piles of rubbish, the dust, the dogs, the flies. Her face wrinkled up into a grimace of disgust. She held her handkerchief to her nose.

'But how can they live like this?' she broke out in a voice of indignant incredulity. (It wasn't possible.)

Bernard shrugged his shoulders philosophically. 'Anyhow,' he said, 'they've been doing it for the last five or six thousand years. So I suppose they must be used to it by now.'

'But cleanliness is next to fordliness,' she insisted.

'Yes, and civilization is sterilization,' Bernard went on, concluding on a tone of irony the second hypnopædic lesson in elementary hygiene. 'But these people have never heard of Our Ford, and they aren't civilized. So there's no point in . . .'

'Oh!' She gripped his arm. 'Look.'

An almost naked Indian was very slowly climbing down the ladder from the first-floor terrace of a neighbouring house— rung after rung, with the tremulous caution of extreme old age. His face was profoundly wrinkled and black, like a mask of obsidian. The toothless mouth had fallen in. At the corners of the lips and on each side of the chin a few long bristles gleamed almost white against the dark skin. The long unbraided hair hung down in grey wisps round his face. His body was bent and emaciated to the bone, almost fleshless. Very slowly he came down, pausing at each rung before he ventured another step.

'What's the matter with him?' whispered Lenina. Her eyes were wide with horror and amazement.

'He's old, that's all,' Bernard answered as carelessly as he could. He too was startled; but he made an effort to seem unmoved.

'Old?' she repeated. 'But the Director's old; lots of people are old; they're not like that.'

'That's because we don't allow them to be like that. We preserve them from diseases. We keep their internal secretions artificially balanced at a youthful equilibrium. We don't permit their magnesium-calcium ratio to fall below what it was at thirty. We give them transfusions of young blood. We keep their metabolism permanently stimulated. So, of course, they don't look like that. Partly,' he added, 'because most of them die long before they reach this old creature's age. Youth almost unimpaired till sixty, and then, crack! the end.'

But Lenina was not listening. She was watching the old man. Slowly, slowly he came down. His feet touched the ground. He turned. In their deep-sunken orbits his eyes were still extraordinarily bright. They looked at her for a long moment expressionlessly, without surprise, as though she had not been there at all. Then slowly, with bent back, the old man hobbled past them and was gone.

'But it's terrible,' Lenina whispered. 'It's awful. We ought not to have come here.' She felt in her pocket for her *soma*— only to discover that, by some unprecedented oversight, she had left the bottle down at the rest-house. Bernard's pockets were also empty.

Lenina was left to face the horrors of Malpais unaided. They came crowding in on her thick and fast. The spectacle of two young women giving the breast to their babies made her blush and turn away her face. She had never seen anything so indecent in her life. And what made it worse was that, instead of tactfully ignoring it, Bernard proceeded to make open comments on this revoltingly viviparous scene. Ashamed, now that the effects of the *soma* had worn off, of the weakness he had displayed that morning in the hotel, he went out of his way to show himself strong and unorthodox.

'What a wonderfully intimate relationship,' he said, deliberately outrageous. 'And what an intensity of feeling it must generate! I often think one may have missed something in not having had a mother. And perhaps you've missed something in not *being* a mother, Lenina. Imagine yourself sitting there with a little baby of your own . . .'

91

'Bernard! How can you?' The passage of an old woman with ophthalmia and a disease of the skin distracted her from her indignation.

'Let's go away,' she begged. 'I don't like it.'

But at this moment their guide came back and, beckoning to them to follow, led the way down the narrow street between the houses. They rounded a corner. A dead dog was lying on a rubbish heap; a woman with a goitre was looking for lice in the hair of a small girl. Their guide halted at the foot of a ladder, raised his hand perpendicularly, then darted it horizontally forward. They did what he mutely commanded—climbed the ladder and walked through the doorway, to which it gave access, into a long narrow room, rather dark and smelling of smoke and cooked grease and long-worn, long-unwashed clothes. At the further end of the room was another doorway, through which came a shaft of sunlight and the noise, very loud and close, of the drums.

They stepped across the threshold and found themselves on a wide terrace. Below them, shut in by the tall houses, was the village square, crowded with Indians. Bright blankets, and feathers in black hair, and the glint of turquoise, and dark skins shining with heat. Lenina put her handkerchief to her nose again. In the open space at the centre of the square were two circular platforms of masonry and trampled clay—the roofs, it was evident, of underground chambers; for in the centre of each platform was an open hatchway, with a ladder emerging from the lower darkness. A sound of subterranean flute-playing came up and was almost lost in the steady remorseless persistence of the drums.

Lenina liked the drums. Shutting her eyes she abandoned herself to their soft repeated thunder, allowed it to invade her consciousness more and more completely, till at last there was nothing left in the world but that one deep pulse of sound. It reminded her reassuringly of the synthetic noises made at Solidarity Services and Ford's Day celebrations. 'Orgy-porgy,' she whispered to herself. These drums beat out just the same rhythms.

There was a sudden startling burst of singing—hundreds of male voices crying out fiercely in harsh metallic unison. A few long notes and silence, the thunderous silence of the drums; then shrill, in a neighing treble, the women's answer. Then again the drums; and once more the men's deep savage affirmation of their manhood.

Queer—yes. The place was queer, so was the music, so were the clothes and the goitres and the skin diseases and the old people. But the performance itself—there seemed to be nothing specially queer about that.

'It reminds me of a lower-caste Community Sing,' she told Bernard.

But a little later it was reminding her a good deal less of that innocuous function. For suddenly there had swarmed up from those round chambers underground a ghastly troop of monsters. Hideously masked or painted out of all semblance of humanity, they had tramped out a strange limping dance round the square; round and again round, singing as they went, round and round—each time a little faster; and the drums had changed and quickened their rhythm, so that it became like the pulsing of fever in the ears; and the crowd had begun to sing with the dancers, louder and louder; and first one woman had shrieked, and then another and another, as though they were being killed; and then suddenly the leader of the dancers broke out of the line, ran to a big wooden chest which was standing at one end of the square, raised the lid and pulled out a pair of black snakes. A great yell went up from the crowd, and all the other dancers ran towards him with outstretched hands. He tossed the snakes to the first-comers, then dipped back into the chest for more. More and more, black snakes and brown and mottled—he flung them out. And then the dance began again on a different rhythm. Round and round they went with their snakes, snakily, with a soft undulating movement at the knees and hips. Round and round.

Then the leader gave a signal, and one after another, all the snakes were flung down in the middle of the square; an old man came up from underground and sprinkled them with corn meal, and from the other hatchway came a woman and sprinkled them with water from a black jar. Then the old man lifted his hand and, startlingly, terrifyingly, there was absolute silence. The drums stopped beating, life seemed to have come to an end. The old man pointed towards the two hatchways that gave entrance to the lower world. And slowly, raised by invisible hands from below, there emerged from the one a painted image of an eagle, from the other that of a man, naked, and nailed to a cross. They hung there, seemingly self-sustained, as though watching. The old man clapped his hands. Naked but for a white cotton breech-cloth, a boy of about eighteen stepped out of the crowd and stood before him, his hands crossed over his chest, his head bowed. The old man made the sign of the cross over him and turned away. Slowly, the boy began to walk round the writhing heap of snakes. He had completed the first circuit and was half-way through the second when, from among the dancers, a tall man wearing the mask of a coyote and holding in his hand a whip of plaited leather, advanced towards him. The boy moved on as though unaware of the other's existence. The coyote-man raised his whip; there was a long moment of expectancy, then a swift movement, the whistle of the lash and its loud flat-sounding impact on the flesh. The boy's body quivered; but he made no sound, he walked on at the same slow, steady pace. The coyote struck again, again; and at every blow at first a gasp and then a deep groan went up from the crowd. The boy walked on. Twice, thrice, four times round he went. The blood was streaming. Five times round, six times round. Suddenly Lenina covered her face with her hands and began to sob. 'Oh, stop them, stop them!' she implored. But the whip fell and fell inexorably. Seven times round. Then all at once the boy staggered and, still without a sound, pitched forward on to his face. Bending over him, the old man touched his back with a long white feather, held it up for a moment, crimson, for the people to see, then shook it thrice over the snakes. A few drops fell, and suddenly the drums broke out again into a panic of hurrying notes; there was a great shout. The dancers rushed forward, picked up the snakes and ran out of the square. Men, women, children, all the crowd ran after them. A minute later the square was empty, only the boy remained, prone where he had fallen, quite still. Three old women came out of one of the houses, and with some difficulty lifted him and carried him in. The eagle and the man on the cross kept guard for a little while over the empty pueblo; then, as though they had seen enough, sank slowly down through their hatchways, out of sight, into the nether world.

Lenina was still sobbing. 'Too awful,' she kept repeating, and all Bernard's consolations were in vain. 'Too awful! That blood!' She shuddered. 'Oh, I wish I had my *soma*.'

There was the sound of feet in the inner room.

Lenina did not move, but sat with her face in her hands, unseeing, apart. Only Bernard turned round.

The dress of the young man who now stepped out on to the terrace was Indian; but his plaited hair was straw-coloured, his eyes a pale blue, and his skin a white skin, bronzed.

'Hullo. Good-morrow,' said the stranger, in faultless but peculiar English. 'You're civilized, aren't you? You come from the Other Place, outside the Reservation?'

'Who on earth . . . ?' Bernard began in astonishment.

The young man sighed and shook his head. 'A most unhappy gentleman.' And, pointing to the bloodstains in the centre of the square, 'Do you see that damned spot?' he asked in a voice that trembled with emotion.

'A gramme is better than a damn,' said Lenina mechanically from behind her hands. 'I wish I had my *soma*!'

'*I* ought to have been there.' The young man went on. 'Why wouldn't they let me be the sacrifice? I'd have gone round ten times—twelve, fifteen. Palowhtiwa only got as far as seven.

They could have had twice as much blood from me. The multitudinous seas incarnadine.' He flung out his arms in a lavish gesture; then, despairingly, let them fall again. 'But they wouldn't let me. They disliked me for my complexion. It's always been like that. Always.' Tears stood in the young man's eyes; he was ashamed and turned away.

Astonishment made Lenina forget the deprivation of *soma*. She uncovered her face and, for the first time, looked at the stranger. 'Do you mean to say that you *wanted* to be hit with that whip?'

Still averted from her, the young man made a sign of affirmation. 'For the sake of the pueblo—to make the rain come and the corn grow. And to please Pookong and Jesus. And then to show that I can bear pain without crying out. Yes,' and his voice suddenly took on a new resonance, he turned with a proud squaring of the shoulders, a proud, defiant lifting of the chin, 'to show that I'm a man . . . Oh!' He gave a gasp and was silent, gaping. He had seen, for the first time in his life, the face of a girl whose cheeks were not the colour of chocolate or dog-skin, whose hair was auburn and permanently waved, and whose expression (amazing novelty!) was one of benevolent interest. Lenina was smiling at him; such a nice-looking boy, she was thinking, and a really beautiful body. The blood rushed up into the young man's face; he dropped his eyes, raised them again for a moment only to find her still smiling at him, and was so much overcome that he had to turn away and pretend to be looking very hard at something on the other side of the square.

Bernard's questions made a diversion. Who? How? When? From where? Keeping his eyes fixed on Bernard's face (for so passionately did he long to see Lenina smiling that he simply dared not look at her), the young man tried to explain himself. Linda and he—Linda was his mother (the word made Lenina look uncomfortable)—were strangers in the Reservation. Linda had come from the Other Place long ago, before he was born, with a man who was his father. (Bernard pricked up his ears.)

She had gone walking alone in those mountains over there to the North, had fallen down a steep place and hurt her head. ('Go on, go on,' said Bernard excitedly.) Some hunters from Malpais had found her and brought her to the pueblo. As for the man who was his father, Linda had never seen him again. His name was Tomakin. (Yes, 'Thomas' was the D.H.C.'s first name.) He must have flown away, back to the Other Place, away without her—a bad, unkind, unnatural man.

'And so I was born in Malpais,' he concluded. 'In Malpais.' And he shook his head.

The squalor of that little house on the outskirts of the pueblo!

A space of dust and rubbish separated it from the village. Two famine-stricken dogs were nosing obscenely in the garbage at its door. Inside, when they entered, the twilight stank and was loud with flies.

'Linda!' the young man called.

From the inner room a rather hoarse female voice said, 'Coming.'

They waited. In bowls on the floor were the remains of a meal, perhaps of several meals.

The door opened. A very stout blonde squaw stepped across the threshold and stood looking at the strangers, staring incredulously, her mouth open. Lenina noticed with disgust that two of the front teeth were missing. And the colour of the ones that remained . . . She shuddered. It was worse than the old man. So fat. And all the lines in her face, the flabbiness, the wrinkles. And the sagging cheeks, with those purplish blotches. And the red veins on her nose, the bloodshot eyes. And that neck—that neck; and the blanket she wore over her head—ragged and filthy. And under the brown sack-shaped tunic those enormous breasts, the bulge of the stomach, the hips. Oh, much worse than the old man, much worse! And suddenly the creature burst out in a torrent of speech, rushed at her with outstretched

arms and—Ford! Ford! it was too revolting, in another moment she'd be sick—pressed her against the bulge, the bosom,
and began to kiss her. Ford! to *kiss*, slobberingly, and smelt
too horrible, obviously never had a bath, and simply reeked of
that beastly stuff that was put into Delta and Epsilon bottles (no,
it wasn't true about Bernard), positively stank of alcohol. She
broke away as quickly as she could.

A blubbered and distorted face confronted her; the creature
was crying.

'Oh, my dear, my dear.' The torrent of words flowed sob-
bingly. 'If you knew how glad—after all these years! A civilized face. Yes, and civilized clothes. Because I thought I
should never see a piece of real acetate silk again.' She fingered
the sleeve of Lenina's shirt. The nails were black. 'And those
adorable viscose velveteen shorts! Do you know, dear, I've still
got my old clothes, the ones I came in, put away in a box. I'll
show them you afterwards. Though, of course, the acetate has
all gone into holes. But such a lovely white bandolier—though
I must say your green morocco is even lovelier. Not that it did
me much good, that bandolier.' Her tears began to flow again.
'I suppose John told you. What I had to suffer—and not a
gramme of *soma* to be had. Only a drink of *mescal* every now
and then, when Popé used to bring it. Popé is a boy I used to
know. But it makes you feel so bad afterwards, the *mescal* does,
and you're sick with the *peyotl*; besides, it always made that
awful feeling of being ashamed much worse the next day. And
I *was* so ashamed. Just think of it: me, a Beta—having a baby:
put yourself in my place.' (The mere suggestion made Lenina
shudder.) 'Though it wasn't my fault, I swear; because I still
don't know how it happened, seeing that I did all the Malthusian
drill—you know, by numbers, One, two, three, four, always, I
swear it; but all the same it happened; and of course there
wasn't anything like an Abortion Centre here. Is it still down in
Chelsea, by the way?' she asked. Lenina nodded. 'And still
flood-lighted on Tuesdays and Fridays?' Lenina nodded again.

'That lovely pink glass tower!' Poor Linda lifted her face and with closed eyes ecstatically contemplated the bright remembered image. 'And the river at night,' she whispered. Great tears oozed slowly out from between her tight-shut eyelids. 'And flying back in the evening from Stoke Poges. And then a hot bath and vibro-vacuum massage ... But there.' She drew a deep breath, shook her head, opened her eyes again, sniffed once or twice, then blew her nose on her fingers and wiped them on the skirt of her tunic. 'Oh, I'm so sorry,' she said in response to Lenina's involuntary grimace of disgust. 'I oughtn't to have done that. I'm sorry. But what *are* you to do when there aren't any handkerchiefs? I remember how it used to upset me, all that dirt, and nothing being aseptic. I had an awful cut on my head when they first brought me here. You can't imagine what they used to put on it. Filth, just filth. "Civilization is Sterilization," I used to say to them. And "Streptocock-Gee to Banbury-T, to see a fine bathroom and W.C." as though they were children. But of course they didn't understand. How should they? And in the end I suppose I got used to it. And anyhow, how *can* you keep things clean when there isn't hot water laid on? And look at these clothes. This beastly wool isn't like acetate. It lasts and lasts. And you're supposed to mend it if it gets torn. But I'm a Beta; I worked in the Fertilizing Room; nobody ever taught me to do anything like that. It wasn't my business. Besides, it never used to be right to mend clothes. Throw them away when they've got holes in them and buy new. "The more stitches, the less riches." Isn't that right? Mending's anti-social. But it's all different here. It's like living with lunatics. Everything they do is mad.' She looked round; saw John and Bernard had left them and were walking up and down in the dust and garbage outside the house; but none the less confidentially lowering her voice, and leaning, while Lenina stiffened and shrank, so close that the blown reek of embryo-poison stirred the hair on her cheek. 'For instance,' she hoarsely whispered, 'take the way they have one another here. Mad, I tell you, absolutely mad.

99

Everybody belongs to every one else—don't they? don't they?'
she insisted, tugging at Lenina's sleeve. Lenina nodded her
averted head, let out the breath she had been holding and managed to draw another one, relatively untainted. 'Well, here,' the
other went on, 'nobody's supposed to belong to more than one
person. And if you have people in the ordinary way, the others
think you're wicked and anti-social. They hate and despise you.
Once a lot of women came and made a scene because their men
came to see me. Well, why not? And then they rushed at me
. . . No, it was too awful. I can't tell you about it.' Linda
covered her face with her hands and shuddered. 'They're so
hateful, the women here. Mad, mad and cruel. And of course
they don't know anything about Malthusian drill, or bottles, or
decanting, or anything of that sort. So they're having children
all the time—like dogs. It's too revolting. And to think that I
. . . Oh, Ford, Ford, Ford! And yet John *was* a great comfort
to me. I don't know what I should have done without him.
Even though he did get so upset whenever a man . . . Quite as a
tiny boy, even. Once (but that was when he was bigger) he tried
to kill poor Waihusiwa—or was it Popé?—just because I used
to have them sometimes. Because I never *could* make him understand that that was what civilized people ought to do. Being
mad's infectious, I believe. Anyhow, John seems to have caught
it from the Indians. Because, of course, he was with them a lot.
Even though they were so beastly to him and wouldn't let him
do all the things the other boys did. Which was a good thing in
a way, because it made it easier for me to condition him a little.
Though you've no idea how difficult that is. There's so much
one doesn't know; it wasn't my business to know. I mean,
when a child asks you how a helicopter works or who made the
world—well, what are you to answer if you're a Beta and have
always worked in the Fertilizing Room? What *are* you to
answer?'

Chapter VIII

OUTSIDE, in the dust and among the garbage (there were four dogs now), Bernard and John were walking slowly up and down.

'So hard for me to realize,' Bernard was saying, 'to reconstruct. As though we were living on different planets, in different centuries. A mother, and all this dirt, and gods, and old age, and disease . . .' He shook his head. 'It's almost inconceivable. I shall never understand unless you explain.'

'Explain what?'

'This.' He indicated the pueblo. 'That.' And it was the little house outside the village. 'Everything. All your life.'

'But what is there to say?'

'From the beginning. As far back as you can remember.'

'As far back as I can remember.' John frowned. There was a long silence.

It was very hot. They had eaten a lot of tortillas and sweet corn. Linda said, 'Come and lie down, Baby.' They lay down together in the big bed. 'Sing,' and Linda sang. Sang 'Streptocock-Gee to Banbury-T' and 'Bye, Baby Banting, soon you'll need decanting.' Her voice got fainter and fainter . . .

There was a loud noise, and he woke with a start. A man was standing by the bed, enormous, frightening. He was saying something to Linda, and Linda was laughing. She had pulled the blanket up to her chin, but the man pulled it down again. His hair was like two black ropes, and round his arm was a lovely silver bracelet with blue stones in it. He liked the bracelet; but all the same he was frightened; he hid his face against Linda's body. Linda put her hand on him and he felt safer. In those other words he did not understand so well, she said to the man,

'Not with John here.' The man looked at him, then again at
Linda, and said a few words in a soft voice. Linda said, 'No.'
But the man bent over the bed towards him and his face was
huge, terrible; the black ropes of hair touched the blanket. 'No,'
Linda said again, and he felt her hand squeezing him more tightly.
'No, no!' But the man took hold of one of his arms, and it hurt.
He screamed. The man put out his other hand and lifted him up.
Linda was still holding him, still saying 'No, no.' The man said
something short and angry, and suddenly her hands were gone.
'Linda, Linda.' He kicked and wriggled; but the man carried
him across to the door, opened it, put him down on the floor in
the middle of the other room, and went away, shutting the door
behind him. He got up, he ran to the door. Standing on tiptoe
he could just reach the big wooden latch. He lifted it and
pushed; but the door wouldn't open. 'Linda,' he shouted.
She didn't answer.

He remembered a huge room, rather dark; and there were
big wooden things with strings fastened to them, and lots of
women standing round them—making blankets, Linda said.
Linda told him to sit in the corner with the other children, while
she went and helped the women. He played with the little boys
for a long time. Suddenly people started talking very loud, and
there were the women pushing Linda away, and Linda was crying. She went to the door and he ran after her. He asked her
why they were angry. 'Because I broke something,' she said.
And then she got angry too. 'How should I know how to do
their beastly weaving?' she said. 'Beastly savages.' He asked
her what savages were. When they got back to their house,
Popé was waiting at the door, and he came in with them. He had
a big gourd full of stuff that looked like water; only it wasn't
water, but something with a bad smell that burnt your mouth
and made you cough. Linda drank some and Popé drank some,
and then Linda laughed a lot and talked very loud; and then she

and Popé went into the other room. When Popé went away, he went into the room. Linda was in bed and so fast asleep that he couldn't wake her.

Popé used to come often. He said the stuff in the gourd was called *mescal*; but Linda said it ought to be called *soma*; only it made you feel ill afterwards. He hated Popé. He hated them all—all the men who came to see Linda. One afternoon, when he had been playing with the other children—it was cold, he remembered, and there was snow on the mountains—he came back to the house and heard angry voices in the bedroom. They were women's voices, and they said words he didn't understand; but he knew they were dreadful words. Then suddenly, crash! something was upset; he heard people moving about quickly, and there was another crash and then a noise like hitting a mule, only not so bony; then Linda screamed. 'Oh, don't, don't, don't!' she said. He ran in. There were three women in dark blankets. Linda was on the bed. One of the women was holding her wrists. Another was lying across her legs, so that she couldn't kick. The third was hitting her with a whip. Once, twice, three times; and each time Linda screamed. Crying, he tugged at the fringe of the woman's blanket. 'Please, please.' With her free hand she held him away. The whip came down again, and again Linda screamed. He caught hold of the woman's enormous brown hand between his own and bit it with all his might. She cried out, wrenched her hand free, and gave him such a push that he fell down. While he was lying on the ground she hit him three times with the whip. It hurt more than anything he had ever felt—like fire. The whip whistled again, fell. But this time it was Linda who screamed.

'But why did they want to hurt you, Linda?' he asked that night. He was crying, because the red marks of the whip on his back still hurt so terribly. But he was also crying because people were so beastly and unfair, and because he was only a little boy and couldn't do anything against them. Linda was crying too. She was grown up, but she wasn't big enough to fight against three of them. It wasn't fair for her either. 'Why did they want to hurt you, Linda?'

'I don't know. How should I know?' It was difficult to hear what she said, because she was lying on her stomach and her face was in the pillow. 'They say those men are *their* men,' she went on; and she did not seem to be talking to him at all; she seemed to be talking with some one inside herself. A long talk which he didn't understand; and in the end she started crying louder than ever.

'Oh, don't cry, Linda. Don't cry.'

He pressed himself against her. He put his arm round her neck. Linda cried out. 'Oh, be careful. My shoulder! Oh!' and she pushed him away, hard. His head banged against the wall. 'Little idiot!' she shouted; and then, suddenly, she began to slap him. Slap, slap . . .

'Linda,' he cried out. 'Oh, mother, don't!'

'I'm not your mother. I won't be your mother.'

'But, Linda . . . Oh!' She slapped him on the cheek.

'Turned into a savage,' she shouted. 'Having young ones like an animal. . . . If it hadn't been for you, I might have gone to the Inspector, I might have got away. But not with a baby. That would have been too shameful.'

He saw that she was going to hit him again, and lifted his arm to guard his face. 'Oh don't, Linda, please don't.'

'Little beast!' She pulled down his arm; his face was uncovered.

'Don't, Linda.' He shut his eyes, expecting the blow.

But she didn't hit him. After a little time, he opened his eyes again and saw that she was looking at him. He tried to smile at her. Suddenly she put her arms round him and kissed him again and again.

Sometimes, for several days, Linda didn't get up at all. She lay in bed and was sad. Or else she drank the stuff that Popé brought and laughed a great deal and went to sleep. Sometimes she was sick. Often she forgot to wash him, and there was nothing to eat except cold tortillas. He remembered the first time she found those little animals in his hair, how she screamed and screamed.

The happiest times were when she told him about the Other Place. 'And you really can go flying, whenever you like?'
'Whenever you like.' And she would tell him about the lovely music that came out of a box, and all the nice games you could play, and the delicious things to eat and drink, and the light that came when you pressed a little thing in the wall, and the pictures that you could hear and feel and smell, as well as see, and another box for making nice smells, and the pink and green and blue and silver houses as high as mountains, and everybody happy and no one ever sad or angry, and every one belonging to every one else, and the boxes where you could see and hear what was happening at the other side of the world, and babies in lovely clean bottles—everything so clean, and no nasty smells, no dirt at all—and people never lonely, but living together and being so jolly and happy, like the summer dances here in Malpais, but much happier, and the happiness being there every day, every day.... He listened by the hour. And sometimes, when he and the other children were tired with too much playing, one of the old men of the pueblo would talk to them, in those other words, of the great Transformer of the World, and of the long fight between Right Hand and Left Hand, between Wet and Dry; of Awonawilona, who made a great fog by thinking in the night, and then made the whole world out of the fog; of Earth Mother and Sky Father; of Ahaiyuta and Marsailema, the twins of War and Chance; of Jesus and Pookong; of Mary and Etsanatlehi, the woman who makes herself young again; of the Black Stone at Laguna and the great Eagle and Our Lady of Acoma. Strange stories, all the more wonderful to him for being told in the other words and so not fully understood. Lying in bed, he would think of Heaven and London and Our Lady of Acoma and the

rows and rows of babies in clean bottles and Jesus flying up and Linda flying up and the great Director of World Hatcheries and Awonawilona.

Lots of men came to see Linda. The boys began to point their fingers at him. In the strange other words they said that Linda was bad; they called her names he did not understand, but that he knew were bad names. One day they sang a song about her, again and again. He threw stones at them. They threw back; a sharp stone cut his cheek. The blood wouldn't stop; he was covered with blood.

Linda taught him to read. With a piece of charcoal she drew pictures on the wall—an animal sitting down, a baby inside a bottle; then she wrote letters. THE CAT IS ON THE MAT. THE TOT IS IN THE POT. He learned quickly and easily. When he knew how to read all the words she wrote on the wall, Linda opened her big wooden box and pulled out from under those funny little red trousers she never wore a thin little book. He had often seen it before. 'When you're bigger,' she had said, 'you can read it.' Well, now he was big enough. He was proud. 'I'm afraid you won't find it very exciting,' she said. 'But it's the only thing I have.' She sighed. 'If only you could see the lovely reading machines we used to have in London!' He began reading. *The Chemical and Bacteriological Conditioning of the Embryo. Practical Instructions for Beta Embryo-Store Workers.* It took him a quarter of an hour to read the title alone. He threw the book on the floor. 'Beastly, beastly book!' he said, and began to cry.

The boys still sang their horrible song about Linda. Sometimes, too, they laughed at him for being so ragged. When he tore his clothes, Linda did not know how to mend them. In the

Other Place, she told him, people threw away clothes with holes in them and got new ones. 'Rags, rags!' the boys used to shout at him. 'But I can read,' he said to himself, 'and they can't They don't even know what reading is.' It was fairly easy, it he thought hard enough about the reading, to pretend that he didn't mind when they made fun of him. He asked Linda to give him the book again.

The more the boys pointed and sang, the harder he read. Soon he could read all the words quite well. Even the longest. But what did they mean? He asked Linda; but even when she could answer it didn't seem to make it very clear. And generally she couldn't answer at all.

'What are chemicals?' he would ask.

'Oh, stuff like magnesium salts, and alcohol for keeping the Deltas and Epsilons small and backward, and calcium carbonate for bones, and all that sort of thing.'

'But how do you make chemicals, Linda? Where do they come from?'

'Well, I don't know. You get them out of bottles. And when the bottles are empty, you send up to the Chemical Store for more. It's the Chemical Store people who make them, I suppose. Or else they send to the factory for them. I don't know. I never did any chemistry. My job was always with the embryos.'

It was the same with everything else he asked about. Linda never seemed to know. The old men of the pueblo had much more definite answers.

'The seed of men and all creatures, the seed of the sun and the seed of earth and the seed of the sky—Awonawilona made them all out of the Fog of Increase. Now the world has four wombs; and he laid the seeds in the lowest of the four wombs. And gradually the seeds began to grow . . .'

One day (John calculated later that it must have been soon after his twelfth birthday) he came home and found a book that he had never seen before lying on the floor in the bedroom. It was a thick book and looked very old. The binding had been eaten by mice; some of its pages were loose and crumpled. He picked it up, looked at the title-page: the book was called *The Complete Works of William Shakespeare*.

Linda was lying on the bed, sipping that horrible stinking *mescal* out of a cup. 'Popé brought it,' she said. Her voice was thick and hoarse like somebody else's voice. 'It was lying in one of the chests of the Antelope Kiva. It's supposed to have been there for hundreds of years. I expect it's true, because I looked at it, and it seemed to be full of nonsense. Uncivilized. Still, it'll be good enough for you to practise your reading on.' She took a last sip, set the cup down on the floor beside the bed, turned over on her side, hiccoughed once or twice and went to sleep.

He opened the book at random.

> Nay, but to live
> In the rank sweat of an enseamed bed,
> Stew'd in corruption, honeying and making love
> Over the nasty sty . . .

The strange words rolled through his mind; rumbled, like talking thunder; like the drums at the summer dances, if the drums could have spoken; like the men singing the Corn Song, beautiful, beautiful, so that you cried; like old Mitsima saying magic over his feathers and his carved sticks and his bits of bone and stone—*kiathla tsilu silokwe silokwe silokwe. Kiai silu silu, tsithl*—but better than Mitsima's magic, because it meant more, because it talked to *him*; talked wonderfully and only half-understandably, a terrible beautiful magic, about Linda; about Linda lying there snoring, with the empty cup on the floor beside the bed; about Linda and Popé, Linda and Popé.

He hated Popé more and more. A man can smile and smile and be a villain. Remorseless, treacherous, lecherous, kindless

villain. What did the words exactly mean? He only half knew.
But their magic was strong and went on rumbling in his head,
and somehow it was as though he had never really hated Popé
before; never really hated him because he had never been able
to say how much he hated him. But now he had these words,
these words like drums and singing and magic. These words
and the strange, strange story out of which they were taken (he
couldn't make head or tail of it, but it was wonderful, wonderful
all the same)—they gave him a reason for hating Popé; and they
made his hatred more real; they even made Popé himself more
real.

One day, when he came in from playing, the door of the inner
room was open, and he saw them lying together on the bed,
asleep—white Linda and Popé almost black beside her, with one
arm under her shoulders and the other dark hand on her breast,
and one of the plaits of his long hair lying across her throat, like
a black snake trying to strangle her. Popé's gourd and a cup
were standing on the floor near the bed. Linda was snoring.

His heart seemed to have disappeared and left a hole. He was
empty. Empty, and cold, and rather sick, and giddy. He leaned
against the wall to steady himself. Remorseless, treacherous,
lecherous . . . Like drums, like the men singing for the corn, like
magic, the words repeated and repeated themselves in his head.
From being cold he was suddenly hot. His cheeks burnt with
the rush of blood, the room swam and darkened before his eyes.
He ground his teeth. 'I'll kill him, I'll kill him, I'll kill him,' he
kept saying. And suddenly there were more words.

When he is drunk asleep, or in his rage
Or in the incestuous pleasure of his bed . . .

The magic was on his side, the magic explained and gave orders.
He stepped back into the outer room. 'When he is drunk asleep
. . .' The knife for the meat was lying on the floor near the fire-
place. He picked it up and tiptoed to the door again. 'When
he is drunk asleep, drunk asleep . . .' He ran across the room and

stabbed—oh, the blood!—stabbed again, as Popé heaved out of his sleep, lifted his hand to stab once more, but found his wrist caught, held and—oh, oh!—twisted. He couldn't move, he was trapped, and there were Popé's small black eyes, very close, staring into his own. He looked away. There were two cuts on Popé's left shoulder. 'Oh, look at the blood!' Linda was crying. 'Look at the blood!' She had never been able to bear the sight of blood. Popé lifted his other hand—to strike him, he thought. He stiffened to receive the blow. But the hand only took him under the chin and turned his face, so that he had to look again into Popé's eyes. For a long time, for hours and hours. And suddenly—he couldn't help it—he began to cry. Popé burst out laughing. 'Go,' he said, in the other Indian words. 'Go, my brave Ahaiyuta.' He ran out into the other room to hide his tears.

'You are fifteen,' said old Mitsima, in the Indian words. 'Now I may teach you to work the clay.'

Squatting by the river, they worked together.

'First of all,' said Mitsima, taking a lump of the wetted clay between his hands, 'we make a little moon.' The old man squeezed the lump into a disk, then bent up the edges; the moon became a shallow cup.

Slowly and unskilfully he imitated the old man's delicate gestures.

'A moon, a cup, and now a snake.' Mitsima rolled out another piece of clay into a long flexible cylinder, hooped it into a circle and pressed it on to the rim of the cup. 'Then another snake. And another. And another.' Round by round, Mitsima built up the sides of the pot; it was narrow, it bulged, it narrowed again towards the neck. Mitsima squeezed and patted, stroked and scraped; and there at last it stood, in shape the familiar water-pot of Malpais, but creamy white instead of black, and still soft to the touch. The crooked parody of Mitsima's, his own stood beside it. Looking at the two pots, he had to laugh.

'But the next one will be better,' he said, and began to moisten another piece of clay.

To fashion, to give form, to feel his fingers gaining in skill and power—this gave him an extraordinary pleasure. 'A, B, C, Vitamin D,' he sang to himself as he worked, 'The fat's in the liver, the cod's in the sea.' And Mitsima also sang—a song about killing a bear. They worked all day, and all day he was filled with an intense, absorbing happiness.

'Next winter,' said old Mitsima, 'I will teach you to make the bow.'

He stood for a long time outside the house; and at last the ceremonies within were finished. The door opened; they came out. Kothlu came first, his right hand outstretched and tightly closed, as though over some precious jewel. Her clenched hand similarly outstretched, Kiakimé followed. They walked in silence, and in silence, behind them, came the brothers and sisters and cousins and all the troop of old people.

They walked out of the pueblo, across the mesa. At the edge of the cliff they halted, facing the early morning sun. Kothlu opened his hand. A pinch of corn meal lay white on the palm; he breathed on it, murmured a few words, then threw it, a handful of white dust, towards the sun. Kiakimé did the same. Then Kiakimé's father stepped forward, and holding up a feathered prayer stick, made a long prayer, then threw the stick after the corn meal.

'It is finished,' said old Mitsima in a loud voice. 'They are married.'

'Well,' said Linda, as they turned away, 'all I can say is, it does seem a lot of fuss to make about so little. In civilized countries, when a boy wants to have a girl, he just . . . But where *are* you going, John?'

He paid no attention to her calling, but ran on, away, away, anywhere to be by himself.

It is finished. Old Mitsima's words repeated themselves in his mind. Finished, finished . . . In silence and from a long way off, but violently, desperately, hopelessly, he had loved Kiakimé. And now it was finished. He was sixteen.

At the full moon, in the Antelope Kiva, secrets would be told, secrets would be done and borne. They would go down, boys, into the kiva and come out again, men. The boys were all afraid and at the same time impatient. And at last it was the day. The sun went down, the moon rose. He went with the others. Men were standing, dark, at the entrance to the kiva; the ladder went down into the red lighted depths. Already the leading boys had begun to climb down. Suddenly one of the men stepped forward, caught him by the arm, and pulled him out of the ranks. He broke free and dodged back into his place among the others. This time the man struck him, pulled his hair. 'Not for you, white-hair!' 'Not for the son of the she-dog,' said one of the other men. The boys laughed. 'Go!' And as he still hovered on the fringes of the group, 'Go!' the men shouted again. One of them bent down, took a stone, threw it. 'Go, go, go!' There was a shower of stones. Bleeding, he ran away into the darkness. From the red-lit kiva came the noise of singing. The last of the boys had climbed down the ladder. He was all alone.

All alone, outside the pueblo, on the bare plain of the mesa. The rock was like bleached bones in the moonlight. Down in the valley, the coyotes were howling at the moon. The bruises hurt him, the cuts were still bleeding; but it was not for pain that he sobbed; it was because he was all alone, because he had been driven out, alone, into this skeleton world of rocks and moonlight. At the edge of the precipice he sat down. The moon was behind him; he looked down into the black shadow of the mesa, into the black shadow of death. He had only to take one step, one little jump. . . . He held out his right hand in the moonlight. From the cut on his wrist the blood was still oozing.

Every few seconds a drop fell, dark, almost colourless in the dead light. Drop, drop, drop. To-morrow and to-morrow and to-morrow . . .

He had discovered Time and Death and God.

'Alone, always alone,' the young man was saying.

The words awoke a plaintive echo in Bernard's mind. Alone, alone . . . 'So am I,' he said, on a gush of confidingness. 'Terribly alone.'

'Are you?' John looked surprised. 'I thought that in the Other Place . . . I mean, Linda always said that nobody was ever alone there.'

Bernard blushed uncomfortably. 'You see,' he said, mumbling and with averted eyes, 'I'm rather different from most people, I suppose. If one happens to be decanted different . . .'

'Yes, that's just it.' The young man nodded. 'If one's different, one's bound to be lonely. They're beastly to one. Do you know, they shut me out of absolutely everything? When the other boys were sent out to spend the night on the mountains—you know, when you have to dream which your sacred animal is—they wouldn't let me go with the others; they wouldn't tell me any of the secrets. I did it by myself, though,' he added. 'Didn't eat anything for five days and then went out one night alone into those mountains there.' He pointed.

Patronizingly, Bernard smiled. 'And did you dream of anything?' he asked.

The other nodded. 'But I mustn't tell you what.' He was silent for a little; then, in a low voice, 'Once,' he went on, 'I did something that none of the others did: I stood against a rock in the middle of the day, in summer, with my arms out, like Jesus on the cross.'

'What on earth for?'

'I wanted to know what it was like being crucified. Hanging there in the sun . . .'

'But why?'

'Why? Well . . .' He hesitated. 'Because I felt I ought to. If Jesus could stand it. And then, if one has done something wrong . . . Besides, I was unhappy; that was another reason.'

'It seems a funny way of curing your unhappiness,' said Bernard. But on second thoughts he decided that there was, after all, some sense in it. Better than taking *soma*. . . .

'I fainted after a time,' said the young man. 'Fell down on my face. Do you see the mark where I cut myself?' He lifted the thick yellow hair from his forehead. The scar showed, pale and puckered, on his right temple.

Bernard looked, and then quickly, with a little shudder, averted his eyes. His conditioning had made him not so much pitiful as profoundly squeamish. The mere suggestion of illness or wounds was to him not only horrifying, but even repulsive and rather disgusting. Like dirt, or deformity, or old age. Hastily he changed the subject.

'I wonder if you'd like to come back to London with us?' he asked, making the first move in a campaign whose strategy he had been secretly elaborating ever since, in the little house, he had realized who the 'father' of this young savage must be. 'Would you like that?'

The young man's face lit up. 'Do you really mean it?'

'Of course; if I can get permission, that is.'

'Linda too?'

'Well . . .' He hesitated doubtfully. That revolting creature! No, it was impossible. Unless, unless . . . It suddenly occurred to Bernard that her very revoltingness might prove an enormous asset. 'But of course!' he cried, making up for his first hesitations with an excess of noisy cordiality.

The young man drew a deep breath. 'To think it should be coming true—what I've dreamt of all my life. Do you remember what Miranda says?'

'Who's Miranda?'

But the young man had evidently not heard the question. 'O

wonder!' he was saying; and his eyes shone, his face was brightly flushed. 'How many goodly creatures are there here! How beauteous mankind is!' The flush suddenly deepened; he was thinking of Lenina, of an angel in bottle-green viscose, lustrous with youth and skin food, plump, benevolently smiling. His voice faltered. 'O brave new world,' he began, then suddenly interrupted himself; the blood had left his cheeks; he was as pale as paper. 'Are you married to her?' he asked.

'Am I what?'

'Married. You know—for ever. They say "for ever" in the Indian words; it can't be broken.'

'Ford, no!' Bernard couldn't help laughing.

John also laughed, but for another reason—laughed for pure joy.

'O brave new world,' he repeated. 'O brave new world that has such people in it. Let's start at once.'

'You have a most peculiar way of talking sometimes,' said Bernard, staring at the young man in perplexed astonishment. 'And, anyhow, hadn't you better wait till you actually see the new world?'

Chapter IX

LENINA felt herself entitled, after this day of queerness and horror, to a complete and absolute holiday. As soon as they got back to the rest-house, she swallowed six half-gramme tablets of *soma*, lay down on her bed, and within ten minutes had embarked for lunar eternity. It would be eighteen hours at the least before she was in time again.

Bernard meanwhile lay pensive and wide-eyed in the dark. It was long after midnight before he fell asleep. Long after midnight; but his insomnia had not been fruitless; he had a plan.

Punctually, on the following morning, at ten o'clock, the green-uniformed octoroon stepped out of his helicopter. Bernard was waiting for him among the agaves.

'Miss Crowne's gone on *soma*-holiday,' he explained. 'Can hardly be back before five. Which leaves us seven hours.'

He could fly to Santa Fé, do all the business he had to do, and be in Malpais again long before she woke up.

'She'll be quite safe here by herself?'

'Safe as helicopters,' the octoroon assured him

They climbed into the machine and started off at once. At ten thirty-four they landed on the roof of the Santa Fé Post Office; at ten thirty-seven Bernard had got through to the World Controller's Office in Whitehall; at ten thirty-nine he was speaking to his fordship's fourth personal secretary; at ten forty-four he was repeating his story to the first secretary, and at ten forty-seven and a half it was the deep, resonant voice of Mustapha Mond himself that sounded in his ears.

'I ventured to think,' stammered Bernard, 'that your fordship might find the matter of sufficient scientific interest . . .'

'Yes, I do find it of sufficient scientific interest,' said the deep voice. 'Bring these two individuals back to London with you.'

'Your fordship is aware that I shall need a special permit . . .'

'The necessary orders,' said Mustapha Mond, 'are being sent to the Warden of the Reservation at this moment. You will proceed at once to the Warden's Office. Good-morning, Mr. Marx.'

There was silence. Bernard hung up the receiver and hurried up to the roof.

'Warden's Office,' he said to the Gamma-green octoroon.

At ten fifty-four Bernard was shaking hands with the Warden.

'Delighted, Mr. Marx, delighted.' His boom was deferential. 'We have just received special orders . . .'

'I know,' said Bernard, interrupting him. 'I was talking to his fordship on the phone a moment ago.' His bored tone implied that he was in the habit of talking to his fordship every day of the week. He dropped into a chair. 'If you'll kindly take all the necessary steps as soon as possible. As soon as possible,' he emphatically repeated. He was thoroughly enjoying himself.

At eleven three he had all the necessary papers in his pocket.

'So long,' he said patronizingly to the Warden, who had accompanied him as far as the lift gates. 'So long.'

He walked across to the hotel, had a bath, a vibro-vac massage, and an electrolytic shave, listened in to the morning's news, looked in for half an hour on the televisor, ate a leisured luncheon, and at half-past two flew back with the octoroon to Malpais.

The young man stood outside the rest-house.

'Bernard,' he called. 'Bernard!' There was no answer.

Noiseless in his deerskin moccasins, he ran up the steps and tried the door. The door was locked.

They were gone! Gone! It was the most terrible thing that had ever happened to him. She had asked him to come and see them, and now they were gone. He sat down on the steps and cried.

Half an hour later it occurred to him to look through the window. The first thing he saw was a green suit-case, with the

initials L. C. painted on the lid. Joy flared up like fire within
him. He picked up a stone. The smashed glass tinkled on the
floor. A moment later he was inside the room. He opened the
green suit-case; and all at once he was breathing Lenina's perfume, filling his lungs with her essential being. His heart beat
wildly; for a moment he was almost faint. Then, bending over
the precious box, he touched, he lifted into the light, he examined.
The zippers on Lenina's spare pair of viscose velveteen shorts
were at first a puzzle, then, solved, a delight. Zip, and then zip;
zip, and then zip; he was enchanted. Her green slippers were
the most beautiful things he had ever seen. He unfolded a pair
of zippi-camiknicks, blushed, put them hastily away again; but
kissed a perfumed acetate handkerchief and wound a scarf round
his neck. Opening a box, he spilt a cloud of scented powder. His
hands were floury with the stuff. He wiped them on his chest, on
his shoulders, on his bare arms. Delicious perfume! He shut his
eyes; he rubbed his cheek against his own powdered arm. Touch
of smooth skin against his face, scent in his nostrils of musky
dust—her real presence. 'Lenina,' he whispered. 'Lenina!'

A noise made him start, made him guiltily turn. He crammed
up his thieveries into the suit-case and shut the lid; then listened
again, looked. Not a sign of life, not a sound. And yet he had
certainly heard something—something like a sigh, something
like the creak of a board. He tiptoed to the door and, cautiously
opening it, found himself looking on to a broad landing. On the
opposite side of the landing was another door, ajar. He stepped
out, pushed, peeped.

There, on a low bed, the sheet flung back, dressed in a pair of
pink one-piece zippyjamas, lay Lenina, fast asleep and so beautiful in the midst of her curls, so touchingly childish with her pink
toes and her grave sleeping face, so trustful in the helplessness of
her limp hands and melted limbs, that the tears came to his eyes.

With an infinity of quite unnecessary precautions—for nothing
short of a pistol shot could have called Lenina back from her
soma-holiday before the appointed time—he entered the room,

he knelt on the floor beside the bed. He gazed, he clasped his hands, his lips moved. 'Her eyes,' he murmured,

> 'Her eyes, her hair, her cheek, her gait, her voice;
> Handlest in thy discourse, O! that her hand,
> In whose comparison all whites are ink
> Writing their own reproach; to whose soft seizure
> The cygnet's down is harsh . . .'

A fly buzzed round her; he waved it away. 'Flies,' he remembered,

> 'may seize
> On the white wonder of dear Juliet's hand,
> And steal immortal blessing from her lips,
> Who, even in pure and vestal modesty,
> Still blush, as thinking their own kisses sin.'

Very slowly, with the hesitating gesture of one who reaches forward to stroke a shy and possibly rather dangerous bird, he put out his hand. It hung there trembling, within an inch of those limp fingers, on the verge of contact. Did he dare? Dare to profane with his unworthiest hand that . . . No, he didn't. The bird was too dangerous. His hand dropped back. How beautiful she was! How beautiful!

Then suddenly he found himself reflecting that he had only to take hold of the zipper at her neck and give one long, strong pull. . . . He shut his eyes, he shook his head with the gesture of a dog shaking its ears as it emerges from the water. Detestable thought! He was ashamed of himself. Pure and vestal modesty . . .

There was a humming in the air. Another fly trying to steal immortal blessings? A wasp? He looked, saw nothing. The humming grew louder and louder, localized itself as being outside the shuttered windows. The plane! In a panic, he scrambled to his feet and ran into the other room, vaulted through the open window, and hurrying along the path between the tall agaves was in time to receive Bernard Marx as he climbed out of the helicopter.

Chapter X

THE hands of all the four thousand electric clocks in all the Bloomsbury Centre's four thousand rooms marked twenty-seven minutes past two. 'This hive of industry,' as the Director was fond of calling it, was in the full buzz of work. Every one was busy, everything in ordered motion. Under the microscopes, their long tails furiously lashing, spermatozoa were burrowing head first into eggs; and, fertilized, the eggs were expanding, dividing, or if bokanovskified, budding and breaking up into whole populations of separate embryos. From the Social Predestination Room the escalators went rumbling down into the basement, and there, in the crimson darkness, stewingly warm on their cushion of peritoneum and gorged with blood-surrogate and hormones, the fœtuses grew and grew or, poisoned, languished into a stunted Epsilonhood. With a faint hum and rattle the moving racks crawled imperceptibly through the weeks and the recapitulated æons to where, in the Decanting Room, the newly-unbottled babes uttered their first yell of horror and amazement.

The dynamos purred in the sub-basement, the lifts rushed up and down. On all the eleven floors of Nurseries it was feeding time. From eighteen hundred bottles eighteen hundred carefully labelled infants were simultaneously sucking down their pint of pasteurized external secretion.

Above them, in ten successive layers of dormitory, the little boys and girls who were still young enough to need an afternoon sleep were as busy as every one else, though they did not know it, listening unconsciously to hypnopædic lessons in hygiene and sociability, in class-consciousness and the toddler's love-life. Above these again were the playrooms where, the weather having turned to rain, nine hundred older children were amusing themselves with bricks and clay modelling, hunt-the-slipper, and erotic play.

Buzz, buzz! the hive was humming, busily, joyfully. Blithe was the singing of the young girls over their test-tubes, the Predestinators whistled as they worked, and in the Decanting Room what glorious jokes were cracked above the empty bottles! But the Director's face, as he entered the Fertilizing Room with Henry Foster, was grave, wooden with severity.

'A public example,' he was saying. 'In this room, because it contains more high-caste workers than any other in the Centre. I have told him to meet me here at half-past two.'

'He does his work very well,' put in Henry, with hypocritical generosity.

'I know. But that's all the more reason for severity. His intellectual eminence carries with it corresponding moral responsibilities. The greater a man's talents, the greater his power to lead astray. It is better that one should suffer than that many should be corrupted. Consider the matter dispassionately, Mr. Foster, and you will see that no offence is so heinous as unorthodoxy of behaviour. Murder kills only the individual—and, after all, what is an individual?' With a sweeping gesture he indicated the rows of microscopes, the test-tubes, the incubators. 'We can make a new one with the greatest ease—as many as we like. Unorthodoxy threatens more than the life of a mere individual; it strikes at Society itself. Yes, at Society itself,' he repeated. 'Ah, but here he comes.'

Bernard had entered the room and was advancing between the rows of fertilizers towards them. A veneer of jaunty self-confidence thinly concealed his nervousness. The voice in which he said, 'Good-morning, Director,' was absurdly too loud; that in which, correcting his mistake, he said, 'You asked me to come and speak to you here,' ridiculously soft, a squeak.

'Yes, Mr. Marx,' said the Director portentously. 'I did ask you to come to me here. You returned from your holiday last night, I understand.'

'Yes,' Bernard answered.

'Yes-s,' repeated the Director, lingering, a serpent, on the 's.' Then, suddenly raising his voice, 'Ladies and gentlemen,' he trumpeted, 'ladies and gentlemen.'

The singing of the girls over their test-tubes, the preoccupied whistling of the Microscopists, suddenly ceased. There was a profound silence; every one looked round.

'Ladies and gentlemen,' the Director repeated once more, 'excuse me for thus interrupting your labours. A painful duty constrains me. The security and stability of Society are in danger. Yes, in danger, ladies and gentlemen. This man,' he pointed accusingly at Bernard, 'this man who stands before you here, this Alpha-Plus to whom so much has been given, and from whom, in consequence, so much must be expected, this colleague of yours—or should I anticipate and say this ex-colleague?—has grossly betrayed the trust imposed in him. By his heretical views on sport and *soma*, by the scandalous unorthodoxy of his sex-life, by his refusal to obey the teachings of Our Ford and behave out of office hours "like a babe in a bottle"' (here the Director made the sign of the T), 'he has proved himself an enemy of Society, a subverter, ladies and gentlemen, of all Order and Stability, a conspirator against Civilization itself. For this reason I propose to dismiss him, to dismiss him with ignominy from the post he has held in this Centre; I propose forthwith to apply for his transference to a Sub-Centre of the lowest order and, that his punishment may serve the best interest of Society, as far as possible removed from any important Centre of population. In Iceland he will have small opportunity to lead others astray by his unfordly example.' The Director paused; then, folding his arms, he turned impressively to Bernard. 'Marx,' he said, 'can you show any reason why I should not now execute the judgment passed upon you?'

'Yes, I can,' Bernard answered in a very loud voice.

Somewhat taken aback, but still majestically, 'Then show it,' said the Director.

'Certainly. But it's in the passage. One moment.' Bernard

hurried to the door and threw it open. 'Come in,' he commanded, and the reason came in and showed itself.

There was a gasp, a murmur of astonishment and horror; a young girl screamed; standing on a chair to get a better view some one upset two test-tubes full of spermatozoa. Bloated, sagging, and among those firm youthful bodies, those undistorted faces, a strange and terrifying monster of middle-agedness, Linda advanced into the room, coquettishly smiling her broken and discoloured smile, and rolling as she walked, with what was meant to be a voluptuous undulation, her enormous haunches. Bernard walked beside her.

'There he is,' he said, pointing at the Director.

'Did you think I didn't recognize him?' Linda asked indignantly; then, turning to the Director, 'Of course I knew you; Tomakin, I should have known you anywhere, among a thousand. But perhaps you've forgotten me. Don't you remember? Don't you remember, Tomakin? Your Linda.' She stood looking at him, her head on one side, still smiling, but with a smile that became progressively, in face of the Director's expression of petrified disgust, less and less self-confident, that wavered and finally went out. 'Don't you remember, Tomakin?' she repeated in a voice that trembled. Her eyes were anxious, agonized. The blotched and sagging face twitched grotesquely into the grimace of extreme grief. 'Tomakin!' She held out her arms. Some one began to titter.

'What's the meaning,' began the Director, 'of this monstrous . . .'

'Tomakin!' She ran forward, her blanket trailing behind her, threw her arms round his neck, hid her face on his chest.

A howl of laughter went up irrepressibly.

'. . . this monstrous practical joke,' the Director shouted.

Red in the face, he tried to disengage himself from her embrace. Desperately she clung. 'But I'm Linda, I'm Linda.' The laughter drowned her voice. 'You made me have a baby,' she screamed above the uproar. There was a sudden and appalling hush; eyes floated uncomfortably, not knowing where to look. The Director went suddenly pale, stopped struggling and stood, his hands on her wrists, staring down at her, horrified. 'Yes, a baby—and I was its mother.' She flung the obscenity like a challenge into the outraged silence; then, suddenly breaking away from him, ashamed, ashamed, covered her face with her hands, sobbing. 'It wasn't my fault, Tomakin. Because I always did my drill, didn't I? Didn't I? Always...I don't know how...If you knew how awful, Tomakin...But he was a comfort to me, all the same.' Turning towards the door, 'John!' she called. 'John!'

He came in at once, paused for a moment just inside the door, looked round, then soft on his moccasined feet strode quickly across the room, fell on his knees in front of the Director, and said in a clear voice: 'My father!'

The word (for 'father' was not so much obscene as—with its connotation of something at one remove from the loathsomeness and moral obliquity of child-bearing—merely gross, a scatological rather than a pornographic impropriety), the comically smutty word relieved what had become a quite intolerable tension. Laughter broke out, enormous, almost hysterical, peal after peal, as though it would never stop. My father—and it was the Director! My *father!* Oh Ford, oh Ford! That was really too good. The whooping and the roaring renewed themselves, faces seemed on the point of disintegration, tears were streaming. Six more test-tubes of spermatozoa were upset. My *father!*

Pale, wild-eyed, the Director glared about him in an agony of bewildered humiliation.

My *father!* The laughter, which had shown signs of dying away, broke out again more loudly than ever. He put his hands over his ears and rushed out of the room.

Chapter XI

AFTER the scene in the Fertilizing Room, all upper-caste London was wild to see this delicious creature who had fallen on his knees before the Director of Hatcheries and Conditioning—or rather the ex-Director, for the poor man had resigned immediately afterwards and never set foot inside the Centre again—had flopped down and called him (the joke was almost too good to be true!) 'my father.' Linda, on the contrary, cut no ice; nobody had the smallest desire to see Linda. To say one was a mother—that was past a joke: it was an obscenity. Moreover, she wasn't a real savage, had been hatched out of a bottle and conditioned like any one else: so couldn't have really quaint ideas. Finally—and this was by far the strongest reason for people's not wanting to see poor Linda—there was her appearance. Fat; having lost her youth; with bad teeth, and a blotched complexion, and that figure (Ford!)—you simply couldn't look at her without feeling sick, yes, positively sick. So the best people were quite determined *not* to see Linda. And Linda, for her part, had no desire to see them. The return to civilization was for her the return to *soma*, was the possibility of lying in bed and taking holiday after holiday, without ever having to come back to a headache or a fit of vomiting, without ever being made to feel as you always felt after *peyotl*, as though you'd done something so shamefully anti-social that you could never hold up your head again. *Soma* played none of these unpleasant tricks. The holiday it gave was perfect and, if the morning after was disagreeable, it was so, not intrinsically, but only by comparison with the joys of the holiday. The remedy was to make the holiday continuous. Greedily she clamoured for ever larger, ever more frequent doses. Dr. Shaw at first demurred; then let her have what she wanted. She took as much as twenty grammes a day.

'Which will finish her off in a month or two,' the doctor confided to Bernard. 'One day the respiratory centre will be paralysed. No more breathing. Finished. And a good thing too. If we could rejuvenate, of course it would be different. But we can't.'

Surprisingly, as every one thought (for on *soma*-holiday Linda was most conveniently out of the way), John raised objections.

'But aren't you shortening her life by giving her so much?'

'In one sense, yes,' Dr. Shaw admitted. 'But in another we're actually lengthening it.' The young man stared, uncomprehending. '*Soma* may make you lose a few years in time,' the doctor went on. 'But think of the enormous, immeasurable durations it can give you out of time. Every *soma*-holiday is a bit of what our ancestors used to call eternity.'

John began to understand. 'Eternity was in our lips and eyes,' he murmured.

'Eh?'

'Nothing.'

'Of course,' Dr. Shaw went on, 'you can't allow people to go popping off into eternity if they've got any serious work to do. But as she hasn't got any serious work . . .'

'All the same,' John persisted, 'I don't believe it's right.'

The doctor shrugged his shoulders. 'Well, of course, if you prefer to have her screaming mad all the time . . .'

In the end John was forced to give in. Linda got her *soma*. Thenceforward she remained in her little room on the thirty-seventh floor of Bernard's apartment house, in bed, with the radio and television always on, and the patchouli tap just dripping, and the *soma* tablets within reach of her hand—there she remained; and yet wasn't there at all, was all the time away, infinitely far away, on holiday; on holiday in some other world, where the music of the radio was a labyrinth of sonorous colours, a sliding, palpitating labyrinth, that led (by what beautifully inevitable windings) to a bright centre of absolute conviction; where the dancing images of the television box were the performers in some indescribably delicious all-singing feely; where the dripping patchouli was more than scent—was the sun, was a million sexo-phones, was Popé making love, only much more so, incomparably more, and without end.

'No, we can't rejuvenate. But I'm very glad' Dr. Shaw had concluded, 'to have had this opportunity to see an example of senility in a human being. Thank you so much for calling me in.' He shook Bernard warmly by the hand.

It was John, then, they were all after. And as it was only through Bernard, his accredited guardian, that John could be seen, Bernard now found himself, for the first time in his life, treated not merely normally, but as a person of outstanding importance. There was no more talk of the alcohol in his blood-surrogate, no gibes at his personal appearance. Henry Foster went out of his way to be friendly; Benito Hoover made him a present of six packets of sex-hormone chewing-gum; the Assistant Predestinator came and cadged almost abjectly for an invitation to one of Bernard's evening parties. As for the women, Bernard had only to hint at the possibility of an invitation, and he could have whichever of them he liked.

'Bernard's asked me to meet the Savage next Wednesday,' Fanny announced triumphantly.

'I'm so glad,' said Lenina. 'And now you must admit that you were wrong about Bernard. Don't you think he's really rather sweet?'

Fanny nodded. 'And I must say,' she said, 'I was quite agreeably surprised.'

The Chief Bottler, the Director of Predestination, three Deputy Assistant Fertilizer-Generals, the Professor of Feelies in the College of Emotional Engineering, the Dean of the Westminster Community Singery, the Supervisor of Bokanovskification—the list of Bernard's notabilities was interminable.

'And I had six girls last week,' he confided to Helmholtz Watson. 'One on Monday, two on Tuesday, two more on Friday, and one on Saturday. And if I'd had the time or the inclination, there were at least a dozen more who were only too anxious . . .'

Helmholtz listened to his boastings in a silence so gloomily disapproving that Bernard was offended.

'You're envious,' he said.

Helmholtz shook his head. 'I'm rather sad, that's all,' he answered.

Bernard went off in a huff. Never, he told himself, never would he speak to Helmholtz again.

The days passed. Success went fizzily to Bernard's head, and in the process completely reconciled him (as any good intoxicant should do) to a world which, up till then, he had found very unsatisfactory. In so far as it recognized him as important, the order of things was good. But, reconciled by his success, he yet refused to forgo the privilege of criticizing this order. For the act of criticizing heightened his sense of importance, made him feel larger. Moreover, he did genuinely believe that there were things to criticize. (At the same time, he genuinely liked being a success and having all the girls he wanted.) Before those who now, for the sake of the Savage, paid their court to him, Bernard would parade a carping unorthodoxy. He was politely listened to. But behind his back people shook their heads. 'That young man will come to a bad end,' they said, prophesying the more confidently in that they themselves would in due course personally see to it that the end was bad. 'He won't find another Savage to help him out a second time,' they said. Meanwhile, however, there was the first Savage; they were polite. And because they were polite, Bernard felt positively gigantic—gigantic and at the same time light with elation, lighter than air.

'Lighter than air,' said Bernard, pointing upwards.

Like a pearl in the sky, high, high above them, the Weather Department's captive balloon shone rosily in the sunshine.

'. . . the said Savage,' so ran Bernard's instructions, 'to be shown civilized life in all its aspects. . . .'

He was being shown a bird's-eye view of it at present, a bird's-

eye view from the platform of the Charing-T Tower. The
Station Master and the Resident Meteorologist were acting as
guides. But it was Bernard who did most of the talking. Intoxicated, he was behaving as though, at the very least, he were a
visiting World Controller. Lighter than air.

The Bombay Green Rocket dropped out of the sky. The
passengers alighted. Eight identical Dravidian twins in khaki
looked out of the eight portholes of the cabin—the stewards.

'Twelve hundred and fifty kilometres an hour,' said the
Station Master impressively. 'What do you think of that, Mr.
Savage?'

John thought it very nice. 'Still,' he said, 'Ariel could put a
girdle round the earth in forty minutes.'

'The Savage,' wrote Bernard in his report to Mustapha Mond,
'shows surprisingly little astonishment at, or awe of, civilized inventions. This is partly due, no doubt, to the fact that he has
heard them talked about by the woman Linda, his m——.'

(Mustapha Mond frowned. 'Does the fool think I'm too
squeamish to see the word written out at full length?')

'Partly on his interest being focussed on what he calls "the
soul," which he persists as regarding as an entity independent of
the physical environment; whereas, as I tried to point out to
him . . .'

The Controller skipped the next sentences and was just about
to turn the page in search of something more interestingly concrete, when his eye was caught by a series of quite extraordinary
phrases. '. . . though I must admit,' he read, 'that I agree with
the Savage in finding civilized infantility too easy or, as he puts
it, not expensive enough; and I would like to take this opportunity of drawing your fordship's attention to . . .'

Mustapha Mond's anger gave place almost at once to mirth.
The idea of this creature solemnly lecturing him—*him*—about
the social order was really too grotesque. The man must have

gone mad. 'I ought to give him a lesson,' he said to himself; then threw back his head and laughed aloud. For the moment, at any rate, the lesson would not be given.

It was a small factory of lighting-sets for helicopters, a branch of the Electrical Equipment Corporation. They were met on the roof itself (for that circular letter of recommendation from the Controller was magical in its effects) by the Chief Technician and the Human Element Manager. They walked downstairs into the factory.

'Each process,' explained the Human Element Manager, 'is carried out, so far as possible, by a single Bokanovsky Group.'

And, in effect, eighty-three almost noseless black brachycephalic Deltas were cold-pressing. The fifty-six four-spindle chucking and turning machines were being manipulated by fifty-six aquiline and ginger Gammas. One hundred and seven heat-conditioned Epsilon Senegalese were working in the foundry. Thirty-three Delta females, long-headed, sandy, with narrow pelvises, and all within 20 millimetres of 1 metre 69 centimetres tall, were cutting screws. In the assembling room, the dynamos were being put together by two sets of Gamma-Plus dwarfs. The two low work-tables faced one another; between them crawled the conveyor with its load of separate parts; forty-seven blond heads were confronted by forty-seven brown ones. Forty-seven snubs by forty-seven hooks; forty-seven receding by forty-seven prognathous chins. The completed mechanisms were inspected by eighteen identical curly auburn girls in Gamma green, packed in crates by thirty-four short-legged, left-handed male Delta-Minuses, and loaded into the waiting trucks and lorries by sixty-three blue-eyed, flaxen and freckled Epsilon Semi-Morons.

'O brave new world . . .' By some malice of his memory the Savage found himself repeating Miranda's words. 'O brave new world that has such people in it.'

'And I assure you,' the Human Element Manager concluded, as they left the factory, 'we hardly ever have any trouble with our workers. We always find . . .'

But the Savage had suddenly broken away from his companions and was violently retching, behind a clump of laurels, as though the solid earth had been a helicopter in an air pocket.

'The Savage,' wrote Bernard, 'refuses to take *soma*, and seems much distressed because the woman Linda, his m——, remains permanently on holiday. It is worthy of note that, in spite of his m——'s senility and the extreme repulsiveness of her appearance, the Savage frequently goes to see her and appears to be much attached to her—an interesting example of the way in which early conditioning can be made to modify and even run counter to natural impulses (in this case, the impulse to recoil from an unpleasant object).'

At Eton they alighted on the roof of Upper School. On the opposite side of School Yard, the fifty-two stories of Lupton's Tower gleamed white in the sunshine. College on their left and, on their right, the School Community Singery reared their venerable piles of ferro-concrete and vita-glass. In the centre of the quadrangle stood the quaint old chrome-steel statue of Our Ford.

Dr. Gaffney, the Provost, and Miss Keate, the Head Mistress, received them as they stepped out of the plane.

'Do you have many twins here?' the Savage asked rather apprehensively, as they set out on their tour of inspection.

'Oh no,' the Provost answered. 'Eton is reserved exclusively for upper-caste boys and girls. One egg, one adult. It makes education more difficult, of course. But as they'll be called upon to take responsibilities and deal with unexpected emergencies, it can't be helped.' He sighed.

Bernard, meanwhile, had taken a strong fancy to Miss Keate. 'If you're free any Monday, Wednesday, or Friday evening,' he was saying. Jerking his thumb towards the Savage, 'He's curious, you know,' Bernard added. 'Quaint.'

Miss Keate smiled (and her smile was really charming, he thought); said Thank you; would be delighted to come to one of his parties. The Provost opened a door.

Five minutes in that Alpha-Double-Plus classroom left John a trifle bewildered.

'What *is* elementary relativity?' he whispered to Bernard. Bernard tried to explain, then thought better of it and suggested that they should go to some other classroom.

From behind a door in the corridor leading to the Beta-Minus geography room, a ringing soprano voice called, 'One, two, three, four,' and then, with a weary impatience, 'As you were.'

'Malthusian Drill,' explained the Head Mistress. 'Most of our girls are freemartins, of course. I'm a freemartin myself.' She smiled at Bernard. 'But we have about eight hundred un-sterilized ones who need constant drilling.'

In the Beta-Minus geography room John learnt that 'a savage reservation is a place which, owing to unfavourable climatic or geological conditions, or poverty of natural resources, has not been worth the expense of civilizing.' A click; the room was darkened; and suddenly, on the screen above the Master's head, there were the *Penitentes* of Acoma prostrating themselves before Our Lady, and wailing as John had heard them wail, confessing their sins before Jesus on the cross, before the eagle image of Pookong. The young Etonians fairly shouted with laughter. Still wailing, the *Penitentes* rose to their feet, stripped off their upper garments and, with knotted whips, began to beat themselves, blow after blow. Redoubled, the laughter drowned even the amplified record of their groans.

'But why do they laugh?' asked the Savage in a pained bewilderment.

'Why?' The Provost turned towards him a still broadly grinning face. '*Why?* But because it's so extraordinarily funny.'

In the cinematographic twilight, Bernard risked a gesture which, in the past, even total darkness would hardly have emboldened him to make. Strong in his new importance, he put his arm round the Head Mistress's waist. It yielded, willowily. He was just about to snatch a kiss or two and perhaps a gentle pinch, when the shutters clicked open again.

'Perhaps we had better go on,' said Miss Keate, and moved towards the door.

'And this,' said the Provost a moment later, 'is the Hypnopædic Control Room.'

Hundreds of synthetic music boxes, one for each dormitory, stood ranged in shelves round three sides of the room; pigeonholed on the fourth were the paper sound-track rolls on which the various hypnopædic lessons were printed.

'You slip the roll in here,' explained Bernard, interrupting Dr. Gaffney, 'press down this switch . . .'

'No, that one,' corrected the Provost, annoyed.

'That one, then. The roll unwinds. The selenium cells transform the light impulses into sound waves, and . . .'

'And there you are,' Dr. Gaffney concluded.

'Do they read Shakespeare?' asked the Savage as they walked, on their way to the Biochemical Laboratories, past the School Library.

'Certainly not,' said the Head Mistress, blushing.

'Our library,' said Dr. Gaffney, 'contains only books of reference. If our young people need distraction, they can get it at the feelies. We don't encourage them to indulge in any solitary amusements.'

Five bus-loads of boys and girls, singing or in a silent embracement, rolled past them over the vitrified highway.

'Just returned,' explained Dr. Gaffney, while Bernard, whispering, made an appointment with the Head Mistress for that very evening, 'from the Slough Crematorium. Death conditioning begins at eighteen months. Every tot spends two mornings a week in a Hospital for the Dying. All the best toys are kept there, and they get chocolate cream on death days. They learn to take dying as a matter of course.'

'Like any other physiological process,' put in the Head Mistress professionally.

Eight o'clock at the Savoy. It was all arranged.

On their way back to London they stopped at the Television Corporation's factory at Brentford.

'Do you mind waiting here a moment while I go and telephone?' asked Bernard.

The Savage waited and watched. The Main Day-Shift was just going off duty. Crowds of lower-caste workers were queued up in front of the monorail station—seven or eight hundred Gamma, Delta and Epsilon men and women, with not more than a dozen faces and statures between them. To each of them, with his or her ticket, the booking clerk pushed over a little cardboard pill-box. The long caterpillar of men and women moved slowly forward.

'What's in those' (remembering *The Merchant of Venice*), 'those caskets?' the Savage enquired when Bernard had rejoined him.

'The day's *soma* ration,' Bernard answered, rather indistinctly, for he was masticating a piece of Benito Hoover's chewing-gum. 'They get it after their work's over. Four half-gramme tablets. Six on Saturdays.'

He took John's arm affectionately and they walked back towards the helicopter.

Lenina came singing into the Changing Room.

'You seem very pleased with yourself,' said Fanny.

'I *am* pleased,' she answered. Zip! 'Bernard rang up half an hour ago.' Zip, zip! She stepped out of her shorts. 'He has an unexpected engagement.' Zip! 'Asked me if I'd take the Savage to the feelies this evening. I must fly.' She hurried away towards the bathroom.

'She's a lucky girl,' Fanny said to herself as she watched Lenina go.

There was no envy in the comment; good-natured Fanny was merely stating a fact. Lenina *was* lucky; lucky in having shared with Bernard a generous portion of the Savage's immense celebrity, lucky in reflecting from her insignificant person the moment's supremely fashionable glory. Had not the Secretary of the Young Women's Fordian Association asked her to give a lecture about her experiences? Had she not been invited to the Annual Dinner of the Aphroditæum Club? Had she not already appeared in the Feelytone News—visibly, audibly and tactually appeared to countless millions all over the planet?

Hardly less flattering had been the attentions paid her by conspicuous individuals. The Resident World Controller's Second Secretary had asked her to dinner and breakfast. She had spent one week-end with the Ford Chief-Justice, and another with the Arch-Community-Songster of Canterbury. The President of the Internal and External Secretions Corporation was perpetually on the phone, and she had been to Deauville with the Deputy-Governor of the Bank of Europe.

'It's wonderful, of course. And yet in a way,' she had confessed to Fanny, 'I feel as though I were getting something on false pretences. Because, of course, the first thing they all want to know is what it's like to make love to a Savage. And I have to say I don't know.' She shook her head. 'Most of the men don't believe me, of course. But it's true. I wish it weren't,' she added sadly, and sighed. 'He's terribly good-looking; don't you think so?'

'But doesn't he like you?' asked Fanny.

'Sometimes I think he does and sometimes I think he doesn't. He always does his best to avoid me; goes out of the room when I come in; won't touch me; won't even look at me. But sometimes if I turn round suddenly, I catch him staring; and then—well, you know how men look when they like you.'

Yes, Fanny knew.

'I can't make it out,' said Lenina.

She couldn't make it out; and not only was bewildered; was also rather upset.

'Because, you see, Fanny, *I* like him.'

Liked him more and more. Well, now there'd be a real chance, she thought, as she scented herself after her bath. Dab, dab, dab —a real chance. Her high spirits overflowed in song.

> 'Hug me .till you drug me, honey;
>   Kiss me till I'm in a coma:
> Hug me, honey, snuggly bunny;
>   Love's as good as *soma*.'

The scent organ was playing a delightfully refreshing Herbal Capriccio—rippling arpeggios of thyme and lavender, of rosemary, basil, myrtle, tarragon; a series of daring modulations through the spice keys into ambergris; and a slow return through sandalwood, camphor, cedar and new-mown hay (with occasional subtle touches of discord—a whiff of kidney pudding, the faintest suspicion of pig's dung) back to the simple aromatics with which the piece began. The final blast of thyme died away; there was a round of applause; the lights went up. In the synthetic music machine the sound-track roll began to unwind. It was a trio for hyper-violin, super-'cello and oboe-surrogate that now filled the air with its agreeable languor. Thirty or forty bars —and then, against this instrumental background, a much more than human voice began to warble; now throaty, now from the head, now hollow as a flute, now charged with yearning harmonics, it effortlessly passed from Gaspard Forster's low record on the very frontiers of musical tone to a trilled bat-note high above the highest C to which (in 1770, at the Ducal opera of Parma, and to the astonishment of Mozart) Lucrezia Ajugari, alone of all the singers in history, once piercingly gave utterance.

Sunk in their pneumatic stalls, Lenina and the Savage sniffed and listened. It was now the turn also for eyes and skin.

The house lights went down; fiery letters stood out solid and as though self-supported in the darkness. THREE WEEKS IN A HELICOPTER. AN ALL-SUPER-SINGING, SYNTHETIC-TALKING, COLOURED, STEREOSCOPIC FEELY. WITH SYNCHRONIZED SCENT-ORGAN ACCOMPANIMENT.

'Take hold of those metal knobs on the arms of your chair,' whispered Lenina. 'Otherwise you won't get any of the feely effects.'

The Savage did as he was told.

Those fiery letters, meanwhile, had disappeared; there were ten seconds of complete darkness; then suddenly, dazzling and incomparably more solid-looking than they would have seemed in actual flesh and blood, far more real than reality, there stood the stereoscopic images, locked in one another's arms, of a gigantic negro and a golden-haired young brachycephalic Beta-Plus female.

The Savage started. That sensation on his lips! He lifted a hand to his mouth; the titillation ceased; let his hand fall back on the metal knob; it began again. The scent organ, meanwhile, breathed pure musk. Expiringly, a sound-track super-dove cooed 'Oo-ooh'; and vibrating only thirty-two times a second, a deeper than African bass made answer: 'Aa-aah.' 'Ooh-ah! Ooh-ah!' the stereoscopic lips came together again, and once more the facial erogenous zones of the six thousand spectators in the Alhambra tingled with almost intolerable galvanic pleasure. 'Ooh . . .'

The plot of the film was extremely simple. A few minutes after the first Ooh's and Aah's (a duet having been sung and a little love made on that famous bearskin, every hair of which— the Assistant Predestinator was perfectly right—could be separately and distinctly felt), the negro had a helicopter accident, fell on his head. Thump! what a twinge through the forehead! A chorus of *ow's* and *aie's* went up from the audience.

The concussion knocked all the negro's conditioning into a cocked hat. He developed for the Beta blonde an exclusive and maniacal passion. She protested. He persisted. There were struggles, pursuits, an assault on a rival, finally a sensational kidnapping. The Beta blonde was ravished away into the sky and kept there, hovering, for three weeks in a wildly anti-social *tête-à-tête* with the black madman. Finally, after a whole series of adventures and much aerial acrobacy, three handsome young Alphas succeeded in rescuing her. The negro was packed off to an Adult Re-conditioning Centre and the film ended happily and decorously, with the Beta blonde becoming the mistress of all her three rescuers. They interrupted themselves for a moment to sing a synthetic quartet, with full super-orchestral accompaniment and gardenias on the scent organ. Then the bearskin made a final appearance and, amid a blare of sexophones, the last stereoscopic kiss faded into darkness, the last electric titillation died on the lips like a dying moth that quivers, quivers, ever more feebly, ever more faintly, and at last is quite, quite still.

But for Lenina the moth did not completely die. Even after the lights had gone up, while they were shuffling slowly along with the crowd towards the lifts, its ghost still fluttered against her lips, still traced fine shuddering roads of anxiety and pleasure across her skin. Her cheeks were flushed, her eyes dewily bright, her breath came deeply. She caught hold of the Savage's arm and pressed it, limp, against her side. He looked down at her for a moment, pale, pained, desiring, and ashamed of his desire. He was not worthy, not . . . Their eyes for a moment met. What treasures hers promised! A queen's ransom of temperament. Hastily he looked away, disengaged his imprisoned arm. He was obscurely terrified lest she should cease to be something he could feel himself unworthy of.

'I don't think you ought to see things like that,' he said, making haste to transfer from Lenina herself to the surrounding circumstances the blame for any past or possible future lapse from perfection.

'Things like what, John?'

'Like this horrible film.'

'Horrible?' Lenina was genuinely astonished. 'But I thought it was lovely.'

'It was base,' he said indignantly, 'it was ignoble.'

She shook her head. 'I don't know what you mean.' Why was he so queer? Why did he go out of his way to spoil things?

In the taxicopter he hardly even looked at her. Bound by strong vows that had never been pronounced, obedient to laws that had long since ceased to run, he sat averted and in silence. Sometimes, as though a finger had plucked at some taut, almost breaking string, his whole body would shake with a sudden nervous start.

The taxicopter landed on the roof of Lenina's apartment house. 'At last,' she thought exultantly as she stepped out of the cab. At last—even though he *had* been so queer just now. Standing under a lamp, she peered into her hand-mirror. At last. Yes, her nose *was* a bit shiny. She shook the loose powder from her puff. While he was paying off the taxi—there would just be time. She rubbed at the shininess, thinking: 'He's terribly good-looking. No need for him to be shy like Bernard. And yet... Any other man would have done it long ago. Well, now at last.' That fragment of a face in the little round mirror suddenly smiled at her.

'Good-night,' said a strangled voice behind her. Lenina wheeled round. He was standing in the doorway of the cab, his eyes fixed, staring; had evidently been staring all this time while she was powdering her nose, waiting—but what for? or hesitating, trying to make up his mind, and all the time thinking, thinking—she could not imagine what extraordinary thoughts. 'Good-night, Lenina,' he repeated, and made a strange grimacing attempt to smile.

'But, John... I thought you were... I mean, aren't you...?'

He shut the door and bent forward to say something to the driver. The cab shot up into the air.

Looking down through the window in the floor, the Savage could see Lenina's upturned face, pale in the bluish light of the lamps. The mouth was open, she was calling. Her foreshortened figure rushed away from him; the diminishing square of the roof seemed to be falling through the darkness.

Five minutes later he was back in his room. From its hiding-place he took out his mouse-nibbled volume, turned with religious care its stained and crumpled pages, and began to read *Othello*. Othello, he remembered, was like the hero of *Three Weeks in a Helicopter*—a black man.

Drying her eyes, Lenina walked across the roof to the lift. On her way down to the twenty-seventh floor she pulled out her *soma* bottle. One gramme, she decided, would not be enough; hers had been more than a one-gramme affliction. But if she took two grammes, she ran the risk of not waking up in time to-morrow morning. She compromised and, into her cupped left palm, shook out three half-gramme tablets.

Chapter XII

BERNARD had to shout through the locked door; the Savage would not open.

'But everybody's there, waiting for you.'

'Let them wait,' came back the muffled voice through the door.

'But you know quite well, John' (how difficult it is to sound persuasive at the top of one's voice!), 'I asked them on purpose to meet you.'

'You ought to have asked *me* first whether I wanted to meet *them*.'

'But you always came before, John.'

'That's precisely why I don't want to come again.'

'Just to please me,' Bernard bellowingly wheedled. 'Won't you come to please me?'

'No.'

'Do you seriously mean it?'

'Yes.'

Despairingly, 'But what shall I do?' Bernard wailed.

'Go to hell!' bawled the exasperated voice from within.

'But the Arch-Community-Songster of Canterbury is there to-night.' Bernard was almost in tears.

'*Ai yaa tákwa!*' It was only in Zuñi that the Savage could adequately express what he felt about the Arch-Community-Songster. '*Háni!*' he added as an afterthought; and then (with what derisive ferocity!): '*Sons éso tse-ná.*' And he spat on the ground, as Popé might have done.

In the end Bernard had to slink back, diminished, to his rooms and inform the impatient assembly that the Savage would not be appearing that evening. The news was received with indignation. The men were furious at having been tricked into behaving politely to this insignificant fellow with the unsavoury reputation

and the heretical opinions. The higher their position in the hierarchy, the deeper their resentment.

'To play such a joke on me,' the Arch-Songster kept repeating,
'on *me!*'

As for the women, they indignantly felt that they had been had
on false pretences—had by a wretched little man who had had
alcohol poured into his bottle by mistake—by a creature with a
Gamma-Minus physique. It was an outrage, and they said so,
more and more loudly. The Head Mistress of Eton was particularly scathing.

Lenina alone said nothing. Pale, her blue eyes clouded with
an unwonted melancholy, she sat in a corner, cut off from those
who surrounded her by an emotion which they did not share.
She had come to the party filled with a strange feeling of anxious
exultation. 'In a few minutes,' she had said to herself, as she
entered the room, 'I shall be seeing him, talking to him, telling
him' (for she had come with her mind made up) 'that I like him
—more than anybody I've ever known. And then perhaps he'll
say . . .'

What would he say? The blood had rushed to her cheeks.

'Why was he so strange the other night, after the feelies? So
queer. And yet I'm absolutely sure he really does rather like me.
I'm sure . . .'

It was at this moment that Bernard had made his announce-
ment; the Savage wasn't coming to the party.

Lenina suddenly felt all the sensations normally experienced
at the beginning of a Violent Passion Surrogate treatment—a
sense of dreadful emptiness, a breathless apprehension, a nausea.
Her heart seemed to stop beating.

'Perhaps it's because he doesn't like me,' she said to herself. And
at once this possibility became an established certainty: John had
refused to come because he didn't like her. He didn't like her. . . .

'It really is a bit *too* thick,' the Head Mistress of Eton was saying to the Director of Crematoria and Phosphorus Reclamation.
'When I think that I actually . . .'

'Yes,' came the voice of Fanny Crowne, 'it's absolutely true about the alcohol. Some one I know knew some one who was working in the Embryo Store at the time. She said to my friend, and my friend said to me . . .'

'Too bad, too bad,' said Henry Foster, sympathizing with the Arch-Community-Songster. 'It may interest you to know that our ex-Director was on the point of transferring him to Iceland.'

Pierced by every word that was spoken, the tight balloon of Bernard's happy self-confidence was leaking from a thousand wounds. Pale, distraught, abject and agitated, he moved among his guests, stammering incoherent apologies, assuring them that next time the Savage would certainly be there, begging them to sit down and take a carotine sandwich, a slice of vitamin A *pâté*, a glass of champagne-surrogate. They duly ate, but ignored him; drank and were either rude to his face or talked to one another about him, loudly and offensively as though he had not been there.

'And now, my friends,' said the Arch-Community-Songster of Canterbury, in that beautiful ringing voice with which he led the proceedings at Ford's Day Celebrations, 'Now, my friends, I think perhaps the time has come . . .' He rose, put down his glass, brushed from his purple viscose waistcoat the crumbs of a considerable collation, and walked towards the door.

Bernard darted forward to intercept him.

'Must you really, Arch-Songster? . . . It's very early still. I'd hoped you would . . .'

Yes, what hadn't he hoped, when Lenina confidentially told him that the Arch-Community-Songster would accept an invitation if it were sent. 'He's really rather sweet, you know.' And she had shown Bernard the little golden zipper-fastening in the form of a T which the Arch-Songster had given her as a memento of the week-end she had spent at the Diocesan Singery. *To meet the Arch-Community-Songster of Canterbury and Mr. Savage.* Bernard had proclaimed his triumph on every invitation card. But the Savage had chosen this evening of all evenings to lock himself up in his room, to shout '*Háni!*' and even (it was lucky that Bernard didn't understand Zuñi) '*Sons éso tse-ná!*' What should have been the crowning moment of Bernard's whole career had turned out to be the moment of his greatest humiliation.

'I'd so much hoped . . .' he stammeringly repeated, looking up at the great dignitary with pleading and distracted eyes.

'My young friend,' said the Arch-Community-Songster in a tone of loud and solemn severity; there was a general silence. 'Let me give you a word of advice.' He wagged his finger at Bernard. 'Before it's too late. A word of good advice.' (His voice became sepulchral.) 'Mend your ways, my young friend, mend your ways.' He made the sign of the T over him and turned away. 'Lenina, my dear,' he called in another tone. 'Come with me.'

Obediently, but unsmiling and (wholly insensible of the honour done to her) without elation, Lenina walked after him, out of the room. The other guests followed at a respectful interval. The last of them slammed the door. Bernard was all alone.

Punctured, utterly deflated, he dropped into a chair and, covering his face with his hands, began to weep. A few minutes later, however, he thought better of it and took four tablets of *soma*.

Upstairs in his room the Savage was reading *Romeo and Juliet*.

Lenina and the Arch-Community-Songster stepped out on to the roof of the Singery. 'Hurry up, my young friend—I mean, Lenina,' called the Arch-Songster impatiently from the lift gates. Lenina, who had lingered for a moment to look at the moon, dropped her eyes and came hurrying across the roof to rejoin him.

'A New Theory of Biology' was the title of the paper which Mustapha Mond had just finished reading. He sat for some time, meditatively frowning, then picked up his pen and wrote across the title-page. 'The author's mathematical treatment of the conception of purpose is novel and highly ingenious, but heretical and, so far as the present social order is concerned, dangerous and potentially subversive. *Not to be published*.' He underlined the words. 'The author will be kept under supervision. His transference to the Marine Biological Station of St. Helena may become necessary.' A pity, he thought, as he signed his name. It was a masterly piece of work. But once you began admitting explanations in terms of purpose—well, you didn't know what the result might be. It was the sort of idea that might easily decondition the more unsettled minds among the higher castes—make them lose their faith in happiness as the Sovereign Good and take to believing, instead, that the goal was somewhere beyond, somewhere outside the present human sphere; that the purpose of life was not the maintenance of well-being, but some intensification and refining of consciousness, some enlargement of knowledge. Which was, the Controller reflected, quite possibly true. But not, in the present circumstances, admissible. He picked up his pen again, and under the words '*Not to be published*' drew a second line, thicker and blacker than the first; then sighed. 'What fun it would be,' he thought, 'if one didn't have to think about happiness!'

With closed eyes, his face shining with rapture, John was softly declaiming to vacancy:

'O, she doth teach the torches to burn bright!
 It seems she hangs upon the cheek of night
 Like a rich jewel in an Ethiop's ear;
 Beauty too rich for use, for earth too dear. . . .'

The golden T lay shining on Lenina's bosom. Sportively, the Arch-Community-Songster caught hold of it, sportively he pulled, pulled. 'I think,' said Lenina suddenly, breaking a long silence, 'I'd better take a couple of grammes of *soma*.'

Bernard, by this time, was fast asleep and smiling at the private paradise of his dreams. Smiling, smiling. But inexorably, every thirty seconds, the minute hand of the electric clock above his bed jumped forward with an almost imperceptible click. Click, click, click, click . . . And it was morning. Bernard was back among the miseries of space and time. It was in the lowest spirits that he taxied across to his work at the Conditioning Centre. The intoxication of success had evaporated; he was soberly his old self; and by contrast with the temporary balloon of these last weeks, the old self seemed unprecedentedly heavier than the surrounding atmosphere.

To this deflated Bernard the Savage showed himself unexpectedly sympathetic.

'You're more like what you were at Malpais,' he said, when Bernard had told him his plaintive story. 'Do you remember when we first talked together? Outside the little house. You're like what you were then.'

'Because I'm unhappy again; that's why.'

'Well, I'd rather be unhappy than have the sort of false, lying happiness you were having here.'

'I like that,' said Bernard bitterly. 'When it's you who were the cause of it all. Refusing to come to my party and so turning them all against me!' He knew that what he was saying was absurd in its injustice; he admitted inwardly, and at last even aloud, the truth of all that the Savage now said about the worthlessness of friends who could be turned upon so slight a provocation into persecuting enemies. But in spite of this knowledge and these admissions, in spite of the fact that his friend's support and sympathy were now his only comfort, Bernard continued perversely to nourish, along with his quite genuine affection, a secret grievance against the Savage, to meditate a campaign of small revenges to be wreaked upon him. Nourishing a grievance against the Arch-Community-Songster was useless; there was no possibility of being revenged on the Chief Bottler or the Assistant Predestinator. As a victim, the Savage possessed, for Bernard, this enormous superiority over the others: that he was accessible. One of the principal functions of a friend is to suffer (in a milder and symbolic form) the punishments that we should like, but are unable, to inflict upon our enemies.

Bernard's other victim-friend was Helmholtz. When, discomfited, he came and asked once more for the friendship which in his prosperity he had not thought it worth his while to preserve, Helmholtz gave it; and gave it without a reproach, without a comment, as though he had forgotten that there had ever been a quarrel. Touched, Bernard felt himself at the same time humiliated by this magnanimity—a magnanimity the more extraordinary and therefore the more humiliating in that it owed nothing to *soma* and everything to Helmholtz's character. It was the Helmholtz of daily life who forgot and forgave, not the Helmholtz of a half-gramme holiday. Bernard was duly grateful (it was an enormous comfort to have his friend again) and also duly resentful (it would be a pleasure to take some revenge on Helmholtz for his generosity).

At their first meeting after the estrangement, Bernard poured out the tale of his miseries and accepted consolation. It was not till some days later that he learned, to his surprise and with a twinge of shame, that he was not the only one who had been in trouble. Helmholtz had also come into conflict with Authority.

'It was over some rhymes,' he explained. 'I was giving my usual course of Advanced Emotional Engineering for Third Year Students. Twelve lectures, of which the seventh is about rhymes. "On the Use of Rhymes in Moral Propaganda and Advertisement," to be precise. I always illustrate my lecture with a lot of technical examples. This time I thought I'd give them one I'd just written myself. Pure madness, of course; but I couldn't resist it.' He laughed. 'I was curious to see what their reactions would be. Besides,' he added more gravely, 'I wanted to do a bit of propaganda; I was trying to engineer them into feeling as I'd felt when I wrote the rhymes. Ford!' He laughed again. 'What an outcry there was! The Principal had me up and threatened to hand me the immediate sack. I'm a marked man.'

'But what were your rhymes?' Bernard asked.

'They were about being alone.'

Bernard's eyebrows went up.

'I'll recite them to you, if you like.' And Helmholtz began:

> 'Yesterday's committee,
> Sticks, but a broken drum,
> Midnight in the City,
> Flutes in a vacuum,
> Shut lips, sleeping faces,
> Every stopped machine,
> The dumb and littered places
> Where crowds have been—
> All silences rejoice,
> Weep (loudly or low),
> Speak—but with the voice
> Of whom, I do not know.
>
> Absence, say, of Susan's,
> Absence of Egeria's
> Arms and respective bosoms,
> Lips and, ah, posteriors,
> Slowly form a presence;
> Whose? and, I ask, of what
> So absurd an essence,
> That something, which is not,
> Nevertheless should populate
> Empty night more solidly
> Than that with which we copulate,
> Why should it seem so squalidly?

Well, I gave them that as an example, and they reported me to the Principal.'

'I'm not surprised,' said Bernard. 'It's flatly against all their sleep-teaching. Remember, they've had at least a quarter of a million warnings against solitude.'

'I know. But I thought I'd like to see what the effect would be.'

'Well, you've seen now.'

Helmholtz only laughed. 'I feel,' he said, after a silence, 'as though I were just beginning to have something to write about. As though I were beginning to be able to use that power I feel I've got inside me—that extra, latent power. Something seems to be coming to me.' In spite of all his troubles, he seemed, Bernard thought, profoundly happy.

Helmholtz and the Savage took to one another at once. So cordially indeed that Bernard felt a sharp pang of jealousy. In all these weeks he had never come to so close an intimacy with the Savage as Helmholtz immediately achieved. Watching them, listening to their talk, he found himself sometimes resentfully wishing that he had never brought them together. He was ashamed of his jealousy and alternately made efforts of will and took *soma* to keep himself from feeling it. But the efforts were not very successful; and between the *soma*-holidays there were, of necessity, intervals. The odious sentiment kept on returning.

At his third meeting with the Savage, Helmholtz recited his rhymes on Solitude.

'What do you think of them?' he asked when he had done.

The Savage shook his head. 'Listen to *this*,' was his answer; and unlocking the drawer in which he kept his mouse-eaten book, he opened and read:

> 'Let the bird of loudest lay,
> On the sole Arabian tree,
> Herald sad and trumpet be . . .'

Helmholtz listened with a growing excitement. At 'sole Arabian tree' he started; at 'thou shrieking harbinger' he smiled

with sudden pleasure; at 'every fowl of tyrant wing' the blood
rushed up into his cheeks; but at 'defunctive music' he turned
pale and trembled with an unprecedented emotion. The Savage
read on:

> 'Property was thus appall'd,
> That the self was not the same;
> Single nature's double name
> Neither two nor one was call'd.
>
> Reason in itself confounded
> Saw division grow together . . .'

'Orgy-porgy!' said Bernard, interrupting the reading with a
loud, unpleasant laugh. 'It's just a Solidarity Service hymn.'
He was revenging himself on his two friends for liking one
another more than they liked him.

In the course of their next two or three meetings he frequently
repeated this little act of vengeance. It was simple and, since
both Helmholtz and the Savage were dreadfully pained by the
shattering and defilement of a favourite poetic crystal, extremely
effective. In the end, Helmholtz threatened to kick him out of
the room if he dared to interrupt again. And yet, strangely
enough, the next interruption, the most disgraceful of all, came
from Helmholtz himself.

The Savage was reading *Romeo and Juliet* aloud—reading (for
all the time he was seeing himself as Romeo and Lenina as Juliet)
with an intense and quivering passion. Helmholtz had listened
to the scene of the lovers' first meeting with a puzzled interest.
The scene in the orchard had delighted him with its poetry; but
the sentiments expressed had made him smile. Getting into such
a state about having a girl—it seemed rather ridiculous. But,
taken detail by verbal detail, what a superb piece of emotional
engineering! 'That old fellow,' he said, 'he makes our best propaganda technicians look absolutely silly.' The Savage smiled
triumphantly and resumed his reading. All went tolerably well
until, in the last scene of the third act, Capulet and Lady Capulet

began to bully Juliet to marry Paris. Helmholtz had been rest-
less throughout the entire scene; but when, pathetically mimed
by the Savage, Juliet cried out:

> 'Is there no pity sitting in the clouds,
> That sees into the bottom of my grief?
> O, sweet my mother, cast me not away!
> Delay this marriage for a month, a week;
> Or, if you do not, make the bridal bed
> In that dim monument where Tybalt lies . . .'

when Juliet said this, Helmholtz broke out in an explosion of
uncontrollable guffawing.

The mother and father (grotesque obscenity) forcing the
daughter to have some one she didn't want! And the idiotic girl not
saying that she was having some one else whom (for the moment,
at any rate) she preferred! In its smutty absurdity the situation
was irresistibly comical. He had managed, with a heroic effort,
to hold down the mounting pressure of his hilarity; but 'sweet
mother' (in the Savage's tremulous tone of anguish) and the reference to Tybalt lying dead, but evidently uncremated and wasting his phosphorus on a dim monument, were too much for him.
He laughed and laughed till the tears streamed down his face—
quenchlessly laughed while, pale with a sense of outrage, the
Savage looked at him over the top of his book and then, as the
laughter still continued, closed it indignantly, got up and, with
the gesture of one who removes his pearl from before swine,
locked it away in its drawer.

'And yet,' said Helmholtz when, having recovered breath
enough to apologize, he had mollified the Savage into listening
to his explanations, 'I know quite well that one needs ridiculous,
mad situations like that; one can't write really well about anything else. Why was that old fellow such a marvellous propaganda technician? Because he had so many insane, excruciating
things to get excited about. You've got to be hurt and upset;
otherwise you can't think of the really good, penetrating, X-

rayish phrases. But fathers and mothers!' He shook his head. 'You can't expect me to keep a straight face about fathers and mothers. And who's going to get excited about a boy having a girl or not having her?' (The Savage winced; but Helmholtz, who was staring pensively at the floor, saw nothing.) 'No,' he concluded, with a sigh, 'it won't do. We need some other kind of madness and violence. But what? What? Where can one find it?' He was silent; then, shaking his head, 'I don't know,' he said at last, 'I don't know.'

Chapter XIII

HENRY FOSTER loomed up through the twilight of the Embryo Store.

'Like to come to a feely this evening?'

Lenina shook her head without speaking.

'Going out with some one else?' It interested him to know which of his friends was being had by which other. 'Is it Benito?' he questioned.

She shook her head again.

Henry detected the weariness in those purple eyes, the pallor beneath that glaze of lupus, the sadness at the corners of the unsmiling crimson mouth. 'You're not feeling ill, are you?' he asked, a trifle anxiously, afraid that she might be suffering from one of the few remaining infectious diseases.

Yet once more Lenina shook her head.

'Anyhow, you ought to go and see the doctor,' said Henry. 'A doctor a day keeps the jim-jams away,' he added heartily, driving home his hypnopædic adage with a clap on the shoulder. 'Perhaps you need a Pregnancy Substitute,' he suggested. 'Or else an extra-strong V.P.S. treatment. Sometimes, you know, the standard passion-surrogate isn't quite . . .'

'Oh, for Ford's sake,' said Lenina, breaking her stubborn silence, 'shut up!' And she turned back to her neglected embryos.

A V.P.S. treatment indeed! She would have laughed, if she hadn't been on the point of crying. As though she hadn't got enough V.P. of her own! She sighed profoundly as she refilled her syringe. 'John,' she murmured to herself, 'John . . .' Then 'My Ford,' she wondered, 'have I given this one its sleeping-sickness injection, or haven't I?' She simply couldn't remember. In the end, she decided not to run the risk of letting it have a second dose, and moved down the line to the next bottle.

Twenty-two years eight months and four days from that moment, a promising young Alpha-Minus administrator at Mwanza-Mwanza was to die of trypanosomiasis—the first case for over half a century. Sighing, Lenina went on with her work.

An hour later, in the Changing Room, Fanny was energetically protesting. 'But it's absurd to let yourself get into a state like this. Simply absurd,' she repeated. 'And what about? A man—*one* man.'

'But he's the one I want.'

'As though there weren't millions of other men in the world.'

'But I don't want them.'

'How can you know till you've tried?'

'I have tried.'

'But how many?' asked Fanny, shrugging her shoulders contemptuously. 'One, two?'

'Dozens. But,' shaking her head, 'it wasn't any good,' she added.

'Well, you must persevere,' said Fanny sententiously. But it was obvious that her confidence in her own prescriptions had been shaken. 'Nothing can be achieved without perseverance.'

'But meanwhile . . .'

'Don't think of him.'

'I can't help it.'

'Take *soma*, then.'

'I do.'

'Well, go on.'

'But in the intervals I still like him. I shall always like him.'

'Well, if that's the case,' said Fanny, with decision, 'why don't you just go and take him. Whether he wants it or no.'

'But if you knew how terribly *queer* he was!'

'All the more reason for taking a firm line.'

'It's all very well to *say* that.'

'Don't stand any nonsense. Act.' Fanny's voice was a trumpet; she might have been a Y.W.F.A. lecturer giving an evening talk to adolescent Beta-Minuses. 'Yes, act—at once. Do it now.'

'I'd be scared,' said Lenina.

'Well, you've only got to take half a gramme of *soma* first. And now I'm going to have my bath.' She marched off, trailing her towel.

The bell rang, and the Savage, who was impatiently hoping that Helmholtz would come that afternoon (for having at last made up his mind to talk to Helmholtz about Lenina, he could not bear to postpone his confidences a moment longer), jumped up and ran to the door.

'I had a premonition it was you, Helmholtz,' he shouted as he opened.

On the threshold, in a white acetate-satin sailor suit, and with a round white cap rakishly tilted over her left ear, stood Lenina.

'Oh!' said the Savage, as though some one had struck him a heavy blow.

Half a gramme had been enough to make Lenina forget her fears and her embarrassments. 'Hullo, John,' she said, smiling, and walked past him into the room. Automatically he closed the door and followed her. Lenina sat down. There was a long silence.

'You don't seem very glad to see me, John,' she said at last.

'Not glad?' The Savage looked at her reproachfully; then suddenly fell on his knees before her and, taking Lenina's hand, reverently kissed it. 'Not glad? Oh, if you only knew,' he whispered, and, venturing to raise his eyes to her face, 'Admired Lenina,' he went on, 'indeed the top of admiration, worth what's dearest in the world.' She smiled at him with a luscious tenderness. 'Oh, you so perfect' (she was leaning towards him with parted lips), 'so perfect and so peerless are created' (nearer and nearer) 'of every creature's best.' Still nearer. The Savage suddenly scrambled to his feet. 'That's why,' he said, speaking with averted face, 'I wanted to *do* something first . . . I mean, to show I was worthy of you. Not that I could ever really be that. But at any rate to show I wasn't absolutely *un*worthy. I wanted to do *something*.'

'Why should you think it necessary . . .' Lenina began, but left the sentence unfinished. There was a note of irritation in her voice. When one has leant forward, nearer and nearer, with parted lips—only to find oneself, quite suddenly, as a clumsy oaf scrambles to his feet, leaning towards nothing at all—well, there is a reason, even with half a gramme of *soma* circulating in one's blood-stream, a genuine reason for annoyance.

'At Malpais,' the Savage was incoherently mumbling, 'you had to bring her the skin of a mountain lion—I mean, when you wanted to marry some one. Or else a wolf.'

'There aren't any lions in England,' Lenina almost snapped.

'And even if there were,' the Savage added, with sudden contemptuous resentment, 'people would kill them out of helicopters, I suppose, with poison gas or something. I wouldn't do *that*, Lenina.' He squared his shoulders, he ventured to look at her and was met with a stare of annoyed incomprehension. Confused, 'I'll do anything,' he went on, more and more incoherently. 'Anything you tell me. There be some sports are painful—you know. But their labour delight in them sets off. That's what I feel. I mean I'd sweep the floor if you wanted.'

'But we've got vacuum cleaners here,' said Lenina in bewilderment. 'It isn't necessary.'

'No, of course it isn't *necessary*. But some kinds of baseness are nobly undergone. I'd like to undergo something nobly. Don't you see?'

'But if there *are* vacuum cleaners . . .'

'That's not the point.'

'And Epsilon Semi-Morons to work them,' she went on, 'well, really, *why?*'

'Why? But for you, for *you*. Just to show that I . . .'

'And what on earth vacuum cleaners have got to do with lions . . .'

'To show how much . . .'

'Or lions with being glad to see *me* . . .' She was getting more and more exasperated.

'How much I love you, Lenina,' he brought out almost desperately.

An emblem of the inner tide of startled elation, the blood rushed up into Lenina's cheeks. 'Do you mean it, John?'

'But I hadn't meant to say so,' cried the Savage, clasping his hands in a kind of agony. 'Not until . . . Listen, Lenina; in Malpais people get married.'

'Get what?' The irritation had begun to creep back into her voice. What was he talking about now?

'For always. They make a promise to live together for always.'

'What a horrible idea!' Lenina was genuinely shocked.

'Outliving beauty's outward, with a mind that doth renew swifter than blood decays.'

'*What?*'

'It's like that in Shakespeare too. "If thou dost break her virgin knot before all sanctimonious ceremonies may with full and holy rite . . ."'

'For Ford's sake, John, talk sense. I can't understand a word you say. First it's vacuum cleaners; then it's knots. You're driving me crazy.' She jumped up and, as though afraid that he might run away from her physically, as well as with his mind, caught him by the wrist. 'Answer me this question: do you really like me, or don't you?'

There was a moment's silence; then, in a very low voice, 'I love you more than anything in the world,' he said.

'Then why on earth didn't you say so?' she cried, and so intense was her exasperation that she drove her sharp nails into the skin of his wrist. 'Instead of drivelling away about knots and vacuum cleaners and lions, and making me miserable for weeks and weeks.'

She released his hand and flung it angrily away from her.

'If I didn't like you so much,' she said, 'I'd be furious with you.'

And suddenly her arms were round his neck; he felt her lips soft against his own. So deliciously soft, so warm and electric that inevitably he found himself thinking of the embraces in *Three Weeks in a Helicopter*. Ooh! ooh! the stereoscopic blonde and aah! the more than real blackamoor. Horror, horror, horror . . . he tried to disengage himself; but Lenina tightened her embrace.

'Why didn't you say so?' she whispered, drawing back her face to look at him. Her eyes were tenderly reproachful.

'The murkiest den, the most opportune place' (the voice of conscience thundered poetically), 'the strongest suggestion our worser genius can, shall never melt mine honour into lust. Never, never!' he resolved.

'You silly boy!' she was saying. 'I wanted you so much. And if you wanted me too, why didn't you . . .?'

'But, Lenina . . .' he began protesting; and as she immediately untwined her arms, as she stepped away from him, he thought, for a moment, that she had taken his unspoken hint. But when she unbuckled her white patent cartridge belt and hung it carefully over the back of a chair, he began to suspect that he had been mistaken.

'Lenina!' he repeated apprehensively.

She put her hand to her neck and gave a long vertical pull; her white sailor's blouse was ripped to the hem; suspicion condensed into a too, too solid certainty. 'Lenina, what *are* you doing?'

Zip, zip! Her answer was wordless. She stepped out of her bell-bottomed trousers. Her zippicamiknicks were a pale shell pink. The Arch-Community-Songster's golden T dangled at her breast.

'For those milk paps that through the window bars bore at men's eyes . . .' The singing, thundering, magical words made her seem doubly dangerous, doubly alluring. Soft, soft, but how piercing! boring and drilling into reason, tunnelling through resolution. 'The strongest oaths are straw to the fire i' the blood. Be more abstemious, or else . . .'

Zip! The rounded pinkness fell apart like a neatly divided apple. A wriggle of the arms, a lifting first of the right foot, then the left: the zippicamiknicks were lying lifeless and as though deflated on the floor.

Still wearing her shoes and socks, and her rakishly tilted round white cap, she advanced towards him. 'Darling. *Darling!* If only you'd said so before!' She held out her arms.

But instead of also saying 'Darling!' and holding out *his* arms, the Savage retreated in terror, flapping his hands at her as though he were trying to scare away some intruding and dangerous animal. Four backward steps, and he was brought to bay against the wall.

'Sweet!' said Lenina and, laying her hands on his shoulders, pressed herself against him. 'Put your arms round me,' she commanded. 'Hug me till you drug me, honey.' She too had poetry at her command, knew words that sang and were spells and beat drums. 'Kiss me'; she closed her eyes, she let her voice sink to a sleepy murmur, 'kiss me till I'm in a coma. Hug me, honey, snuggly . . .'

The Savage caught her by the wrists, tore her hands from his shoulders, thrust her roughly away at arm's length.

'Ow, you're hurting me, you're . . . oh!' She was suddenly silent. Terror had made her forget the pain. Opening her eyes, she had seen his face—no, not *his* face, a ferocious stranger's, pale, distorted, twitching with some insane, inexplicable fury. Aghast, 'But what is it, John?' she whispered. He did not answer, but only stared into her face with those mad eyes. The hands that held her wrists were trembling. He breathed deeply and irregularly. Faint almost to imperceptibility, but appalling, she suddenly heard the grinding of his teeth. 'What is it?' she almost screamed.

And as though awakened by her cry he caught her by the

shoulders and shook her. 'Whore!' he shouted. 'Whore! Impudent strumpet!'

'Oh, don't, do-on't,' she protested in a voice made grotesquely tremulous by his shaking.

'Whore!'

'Plea-ease.'

'Damned whore!'

'A gra-amme is be-etter . . .' she began.

The Savage pushed her away with such force that she staggered and fell. 'Go,' he shouted, standing over her menacingly, 'get out of my sight or I'll kill you.' He clenched his fists.

Lenina raised her arm to cover her face. 'No, please don't, John . . .'

'Hurry up. Quick!'

One arm still raised, and following his every movement with a terrified eye, she scrambled to her feet, and still crouching, still covering her head, made a dash for the bathroom.

The noise of that prodigious slap by which her departure was accelerated was like a pistol-shot.

'Ow!' Lenina bounded forward.

Safely locked into the bathroom, she had leisure to take stock of her injuries. Standing with her back to the mirror, she twisted her head. Looking over her left shoulder she could see the imprint of an open hand standing out distinct and crimson on the pearly flesh. Gingerly she rubbed the wounded spot.

Outside, in the other room, the Savage was striding up and down, marching, marching to the drums and music of magical words. 'The wren goes to't, and the small gilded fly does lecher in my sight.' Maddeningly they rumbled in his ears. 'The fitchew nor the soiled horse goes to't with a more riotous appetite. Down from the waist they are Centaurs, though women all above. But to the girdle do the gods inherit. Beneath is all the fiends'. There's hell, there's darkness, there is the sulphurous pit, burning, scalding, stench, consumption; fie, fie, fie, pah, pah! Give me an ounce of civet, good apothecary, to sweeten my imagination.'

'John!' ventured a small ingratiating voice from the bathroom. 'John!'

'O thou weed, who art so lovely fair and smell'st so sweet that the sense aches at thee. Was this most goodly book made to write "whore" upon? Heaven stops the nose at it . . .'

But her perfume still hung about him, his jacket was white with the powder that had scented her velvety body. 'Impudent strumpet, impudent strumpet, impudent strumpet.' The inexorable rhythm beat itself out. 'Impudent . . .'

'John, do you think I might have my clothes?'

He picked up the bell-bottomed trousers, the blouse, the zippicamiknicks.

'Open!' he ordered, kicking the door.

'No, I won't.' The voice was frightened and defiant.

'Well, how do you expect me to give them to you?'

'Push them through the ventilator over the door.'

He did what she suggested and returned to his uneasy pacing of the room. 'Impudent strumpet, impudent strumpet. The devil Luxury with his fat rump and potato finger . . .'

'John.'

He would not answer. 'Fat rump and potato finger.'

'John.'

'What is it?' he asked gruffly.

'I wonder if you'd mind giving me my Malthusian belt.'

Lenina sat listening to the footsteps in the other room, wondering, as she listened, how long he was likely to go tramping up and down like that; whether she would have to wait until he left the flat; or if it would be safe, after allowing his madness a reasonable time to subside, to open the bathroom door and make a dash for it.

She was interrupted in the midst of these uneasy speculations by the sound of the telephone bell ringing in the other room. Abruptly the tramping ceased. She heard the voice of the Savage parleying with silence.

'Hullo.'

. . . . . .

'Yes.'

. . . . . .

'If I do not usurp myself, I am.'

. . . . . .

'Yes, didn't you hear me say so? Mr. Savage speaking.'

. . . . . .

'What? Who's ill? Of course it interests me.'

. . . . . .

'But is it serious? Is she really bad? I'll go at once. . . .'

. . . . . .

'Not in her rooms any more? Where has she been taken?'

. . . . . .

'Oh, my God! What's the address?'

. . . . . .

'Three Park Lane—is that it? Three? Thanks.'

Lenina heard the click of the replaced receiver, then hurrying steps. A door slammed. There was silence. Was he really gone?

With an infinity of precautions she opened the door a quarter of an inch; peeped through the crack; was encouraged by the view of emptiness; opened a little further, and put her whole head out; finally tiptoed into the room; stood for a few seconds with strongly beating heart, listening, listening; then darted to the front door, opened, slipped through, slammed, ran. It was not till she was in the lift and actually dropping down the well that she began to feel herself secure.

Chapter XIV

THE Park Lane Hospital for the Dying was a sixty-story tower of primrose tiles. As the Savage stepped out of his taxicopter a convoy of gaily-coloured aerial hearses rose whirring from the roof and darted away across the Park, westwards, bound for the Slough Crematorium. At the lift gates the presiding porter gave him the information he required, and he dropped down to Ward 81 (a Galloping Senility ward, the porter explained) on the seventeenth floor.

It was a large room bright with sunshine and yellow paint, and containing twenty beds, all occupied. Linda was dying in company—in company and with all the modern conveniences. The air was continuously alive with gay synthetic melodies. At the foot of every bed, confronting its moribund occupant, was a television box. Television was left on, a running tap, from morning till night. Every quarter of an hour the prevailing perfume of the room was automatically changed. 'We try,' explained the nurse, who had taken charge of the Savage at the door, 'we try to create a thoroughly pleasant atmosphere here—something between a first-class hotel and a feely-palace, if you take my meaning.'

'Where is she?' asked the Savage, ignoring these polite explanations.

The nurse was offended. 'You *are* in a hurry,' she said.

'Is there any hope?' he asked.

'You mean, of her not dying?' (He nodded.) 'No, of course there isn't. When somebody's sent here, there's no ...' Startled by the expression of distress on his pale face, she suddenly broke off. 'Why, whatever is the matter?' she asked. She was not accustomed to this kind of thing in visitors. (Not that there were many visitors anyhow: or any reason why there should be many visitors.) 'You're not feeling ill, are you?'

He shook his head. 'She's my mother,' he said in a scarcely audible voice.

The nurse glanced at him with startled, horrified eyes; then quickly looked away. From throat to temple she was all one hot blush.

'Take me to her,' said the Savage, making an effort to speak in an ordinary tone.

Still blushing, she led the way down the ward. Faces still fresh and unwithered (for senility galloped so hard that it had no time to age the cheeks—only the heart and brain) turned as they passed. Their progress was followed by the blank, incurious eyes of second infancy. The Savage shuddered as he looked.

Linda was lying in the last of the long row of beds, next to the wall. Propped up on pillows, she was watching the Semi-finals of the South American Riemann-Surface Tennis Championship, which were being played in silent and diminished reproduction on the screen of the television box at the foot of the bed. Hither and thither across their square of illumined glass the little figures noiselessly darted, like fish in an aquarium—the silent but agitated inhabitants of another world.

Linda looked on, vaguely and uncomprehendingly smiling. Her pale, bloated face wore an expression of imbecile happiness. Every now and then her eyelids closed, and for a few seconds she seemed to be dozing. Then with a little start she would wake up again—wake up to the aquarium antics of the Tennis Champions, to the Super-Vox-Wurlitzeriana rendering of 'Hug me till you drug me, honey,' to the warm draught of verbena that came blowing through the ventilator above her head—would wake to these things, or rather to a dream of which these things, transformed and embellished by the *soma* in her blood, were the marvellous constituents, and smile once more her broken and discoloured smile of infantile contentment.

'Well, I must go,' said the nurse. 'I've got my batch of children coming. Besides, there's Number 3.' She pointed up the ward. 'Might go off any minute now. Well, make yourself comfortable.' She walked briskly away.

The Savage sat down beside the bed.

'Linda,' he whispered, taking her hand.

At the sound of her name, she turned. Her vague eyes brightened with recognition. She squeezed his hand, she smiled, her lips moved; then quite suddenly her head fell forward. She was asleep. He sat watching her—seeking through the tired flesh, seeking and finding that young, bright face which had stooped over his childhood in Malpais, remembering (and he closed his eyes) her voice, her movements, all the events of their life together. 'Streptocock-Gee to Banbury-T . . .' How beautiful her singing had been! And those childish rhymes, how magically strange and mysterious!

> A, B, C, vitamin D:
> The fat's in the liver, the cod's in the sea.

He felt the hot tears welling up behind his eyelids as he recalled the words and Linda's voice as she repeated them. And then the reading lessons; The tot is in the pot, the cat is on the mat; and the Elementary Instructions for Beta Workers in the Embryo Store. And long evenings by the fire or, in summer time, on the roof of the little house, when she told him those stories about the Other Place, outside the Reservation: that beautiful, beautiful Other Place, whose memory, as of a heaven, a paradise of goodness and loveliness, he still kept whole and intact, undefiled by contact with the reality of this real London, these actual civilized men and women.

A sudden noise of shrill voices made him open his eyes and, after hastily brushing away the tears, look round. What seemed an interminable stream of identical eight-year-old male twins was pouring into the room. Twin after twin, twin after twin, they came—a nightmare. Their faces, their repeated face—for there was only one between the lot of them—puggishly stared, all nostrils and pale goggling eyes. Their uniform was khaki. All their mouths hung open. Squealing and chattering they entered. In a moment, it seemed, the ward was maggoty with them. They swarmed between the beds, clambered over, crawled under, peeped into the television boxes, made faces at the patients.

Linda astonished and rather alarmed them. A group stood clustered at the foot of her bed, staring with the frightened and stupid curiosity of animals suddenly confronted by the unknown.

'Oh, look, look!' They spoke in low, scared voices. 'Whatever is the matter with her? Why is she so fat?'

They had never seen a face like hers before—had never seen a face that was not youthful and taut-skinned, a body that had ceased to be slim and upright. All these moribund sexagenarians had the appearance of childish girls. At forty-four, Linda seemed, by contrast, a monster of flaccid and distorted senility.

'Isn't she awful?' came the whispered comments. 'Look at her teeth!'

Suddenly from under the bed a pug-faced twin popped up between John's chair and the wall, and began peering into Linda's sleeping face.

'I say . . .' he began; but his sentence ended prematurely in a squeal. The Savage had seized him by the collar, lifted him clear over the chair and, with a smart box on the ears, sent him howling away.

His yells brought the Head Nurse hurrying to the rescue.

'What have you been doing to him?' she demanded fiercely. 'I won't have you striking the children.'

'Well, then, keep them away from this bed.' The Savage's voice was trembling with indignation. 'What are these filthy little brats doing here at all? It's disgraceful!'

'Disgraceful? But what do you mean? They're being death-conditioned. And I tell you,' she warned him truculently, 'if I have any more of your interference with their conditioning, I'll send for the porters and have you thrown out.'

The Savage rose to his feet and took a couple of steps towards her. His movements and the expression on his face were so menacing that the nurse fell back in terror. With a great effort he checked himself and, without speaking, turned away and sat down again by the bed.

Reassured, but with a dignity that was a trifle shrill and uncertain, 'I've warned you,' said the nurse, 'so mind.' Still, she led the too inquisitive twins away and made them join in the game of hunt-the-zipper, which had been organized by one of her colleagues at the other end of the room.

'Run along now and have your cup of caffeine solution, dear,' she said to the other nurse. The exercise of authority restored her confidence, made her feel better. 'Now, children!' she called.

Linda had stirred uneasily, had opened her eyes for a moment, looked vaguely around, and then once more dropped off to sleep. Sitting beside her, the Savage tried hard to recapture his mood of a few minutes before. 'A, B, C, vitamin D,' he repeated to himself, as though the words were a spell that would restore the dead past to life. But the spell was ineffective. Obstinately the beautiful memories refused to rise; there was only a hateful resurrection of jealousies and uglinesses and miseries. Popé with the blood trickling down from his cut shoulder; and Linda hideously asleep, and the flies buzzing round the spilt *mescal* on the floor beside the bed; and the boys calling those names as she passed. ... Ah, no, no! He shut his eyes, he shook his head in strenuous denial of these memories. 'A, B, C, vitamin D ...' He tried to think of those times when he sat on her knees and she put her arms about him and sang, over and over again, rocking him, rocking him to sleep. 'A, B, C, vitamin D, vitamin D, vitamin D ...'

The Super-Vox-Wurlitzeriana had risen to a sobbing crescendo; and suddenly the verbena gave place, in the scent-circulating system, to an intense patchouli. Linda stirred, woke up, stared for a few seconds bewilderedly at the Semi-finalists, then, lifting her face, sniffed once or twice at the newly perfumed air and suddenly smiled—a smile of childish ecstasy.

'Popé!' she murmured, and closed her eyes. 'Oh, I do so like it, I do ...' She sighed and let herself sink back into the pillows.

'But, Linda!' The Savage spoke imploringly. 'Don't you know me?' He had tried so hard, had done his very best; why wouldn't she allow him to forget? He squeezed her limp hand almost with violence, as though he would force her to come back from this dream of ignoble pleasures, from these base and hateful memories—back into the present, back into reality; the appalling present, the awful reality—but sublime, but significant, but desperately important precisely because of the imminence of that which made them so fearful. 'Don't you know me, Linda?'

He felt the faint answering pressure of her hand. The tears started into his eyes. He bent over her and kissed her.

Her lips moved. 'Popé!' she whispered again, and it was as though he had had a pailful of ordure thrown in his face.

Anger suddenly boiled up in him. Balked for the second time, the passion of his grief had found another outlet, was transformed into a passion of agonized rage.

'But I'm John!' he shouted. 'I'm John!' And in his furious misery he actually caught her by the shoulder and shook her.

Linda's eyes fluttered open; she saw him, knew him—'John!' —but situated the real face, the real and violent hands, in an imaginary world—among the inward and private equivalents of patchouli and the Super-Wurlitzer, among the transfigured memories and the strangely transposed sensations that constituted the universe of her dream. She knew him for John, her son, but fancied him an intruder into that paradisal Malpais where she had been spending her *soma*-holiday with Popé. He was angry because she liked Popé, he was shaking her because Popé was there in the bed—as though there were something wrong, as though all civilized people didn't do the same? 'Every one belongs to every ...' Her voice suddenly died into an almost inaudible breathless croaking: her mouth fell open: she made a desperate effort to fill her lungs with air. But it was as though she had forgotten how to breathe. She tried to cry out—but no sound came; only the terror of her staring eyes revealed what she was suffering. Her hands went to her throat, then clawed at the air—the air she could no longer breathe, the air that, for her, had ceased to exist.

The Savage was on his feet, bent over her. 'What is it, Linda? What is it?' His voice was imploring; it was as though he were begging to be reassured.

The look she gave him was charged with an unspeakable terror—with terror and, it seemed to him, reproach. She tried to raise herself in bed, but fell back on to the pillows. Her face was horribly distorted, her lips blue.

The Savage turned and ran up the ward.

'Quick, quick!' he shouted. 'Quick!'

Standing in the centre of a ring of zipper-hunting twins, the Head Nurse looked round. The first moment's astonishment gave place almost instantly to disapproval. 'Don't shout! Think of the little ones,' she said, frowning. 'You might decondition . . . But what are you doing?' He had broken through the ring. 'Be careful!' A child was yelling.

'Quick, quick!' He caught her by the sleeve, dragged her after him. 'Quick! Something's happened. I've killed her.'

By the time they were back at the end of the ward Linda was dead.

The Savage stood for a moment in frozen silence, then fell on his knees beside the bed and, covering his face with his hands, sobbed uncontrollably.

The nurse stood irresolute, looking now at the kneeling figure by the bed (the scandalous exhibition!) and now (poor children!) at the twins who had stopped their hunting of the zipper and were staring from the other end of the ward, staring with all their eyes and nostrils at the shocking scene that was being enacted round Bed 20. Should she speak to him? try to bring him back to a sense of decency? remind him of where he was? of what fatal mischief he might do to these poor innocents? Undoing all their wholesome death-conditioning with this disgusting outcry

—as though death were something terrible, as though any one mattered as much as all that! It might give them the most disastrous ideas about the subject, might upset them into reacting in the entirely wrong, the utterly anti-social way.

She stepped forward, she touched him on the shoulder. 'Can't you behave?' she said in a low, angry voice. But, looking round, she saw that half a dozen twins were already on their feet and advancing down the ward. The circle was disintegrating. In another moment . . . No, the risk was too great; the whole Group might be put back six or seven months in its conditioning. She hurried back towards her menaced charges.

'Now, who wants a chocolate éclair?' she asked in a loud, cheerful tone.

'Me!' yelled the entire Bokanovsky Group in chorus. Bed 20 was completely forgotten.

'Oh, God, God, God . . .' the Savage kept repeating to himself. In the chaos of grief and remorse that filled his mind it was the one articulate word. 'God!' he whispered it aloud. 'God . . .'

'Whatever *is* he saying?' said a voice, very near, distinct and shrill through the warblings of the Super-Wurlitzer.

The Savage violently started and, uncovering his face, looked round. Five khaki twins, each with the stump of a long éclair in his right hand, and their identical faces variously smeared with liquid chocolate, were standing in a row, puggily goggling at him.

They met his eyes and simultaneously grinned. One of them pointed with his éclair butt.

'Is she dead?' he asked.

The Savage stared at them for a moment in silence. Then, in silence he rose to his feet, in silence slowly walked towards the door.

'Is she dead?' repeated the inquisitive twin, trotting at his side.

The Savage looked down at him and still without speaking pushed him away. The twin fell on the floor and at once began to howl. The Savage did not even look round.

Chapter XV

THE menial staff of the Park Lane Hospital for the Dying consisted of one hundred and sixty-two Deltas divided into two Bokanovsky Groups of eighty-four red-headed female and seventy-eight dark dolichocephalic male twins, respectively. At six, when their working day was over, the two Groups assembled in the vestibule of the Hospital and were served by the Deputy Sub-Bursar with their *soma* ration.

From the lift the Savage stepped out into the midst of them. But his mind was elsewhere—with death, with his grief, and his remorse; mechanically, without consciousness of what he was doing, he began to shoulder his way through the crowd.

'Who are you pushing? Where do you think you're going?'

High, low, from a multitude of separate throats, only two voices squeaked or growled. Repeated indefinitely, as though by a train of mirrors, two faces, one a hairless and freckled moon haloed in orange, the other a thin, beaked bird-mask, stubbly with two days' beard, turned angrily towards him. Their words and, in his ribs, the sharp nudging of elbows, broke through his unawareness. He woke once more to external reality, looked round him, knew what he saw—knew it, with a sinking sense of horror and disgust, for the recurrent delirium of his days and nights, the nightmare of swarming indistinguishable sameness. Twins, twins. . . . Like maggots they had swarmed defilingly over the mystery of Linda's death. Maggots again, but larger, full grown, they now crawled across his grief and his repentance. He halted and, with bewildered and horrified eyes, stared round him at the khaki mob, in the midst of which, overtopping it by a full head, he stood. 'How many goodly creatures are there here!' The singing words mocked him derisively. 'How beauteous mankind is! O brave new world . . .'

'*Soma* distribution!' shouted a loud voice. 'In good order, please. Hurry up there.'

A door had been opened, a table and chair carried into the vestibule. The voice was that of a jaunty young Alpha, who had entered carrying a black iron cash-box. A murmur of satisfaction went up from the expectant twins. They forgot all about the Savage. Their attention was now focussed on the black cash-box, which the young man had placed on the table, and was now in process of unlocking. The lid was lifted.

'Oo-oh!' said all the hundred and sixty-two simultaneously, as though they were looking at fireworks.

The young man took out a handful of tiny pill-boxes. 'Now,' he said peremptorily, 'step forward, please. One at a time, and no shoving.'

One at a time, with no shoving, the twins stepped forward. First two males, then a female, then another male, then three females, then ...

The Savage stood looking on. 'O brave new world, O brave new world ...' In his mind the singing words seemed to change their tone. They had mocked him through his misery and remorse, mocked him with how hideous a note of cynical derision! Fiendishly laughing, they had insisted on the low squalor, the nauseous ugliness of the nightmare. Now, suddenly, they trumpeted a call to arms. 'O brave new world!' Miranda was proclaiming the possibility of loveliness, the possibility of transforming even the nightmare into something fine and noble. · 'O brave new world!' It was a challenge, a command.

'No shoving there, now!' shouted the Deputy Sub-Bursar in a fury. He slammed down the lid of his cash-box. 'I shall stop the distribution unless I have good behaviour.'

The Deltas muttered, jostled one another a little, and then were still. The threat had been effective. Deprivation of *soma* —appalling thought!

'That's better,' said the young man, and re-opened his cash-box.

Linda had been a slave, Linda had died; others should live in freedom, and the world be made beautiful. A reparation, a duty. And suddenly it was luminously clear to the Savage what he must do; it was as though a shutter had been opened, a curtain drawn back.

'Now,' said the Deputy-Bursar.

Another khaki female stepped forward.

'Stop!' called the Savage in a loud and ringing voice. 'Stop!'

He pushed his way to the table; the Deltas stared at him with astonishment.

'Ford!' said the Deputy Sub-Bursar below his breath. 'It's the Savage.' He felt scared.

'Listen, I beg you,' cried the Savage earnestly. 'Lend me your ears ...' He had never spoken in public before, and found it very difficult to express what he wanted to say. 'Don't take that horrible stuff. It's poison, it's poison.'

'I say, Mr. Savage,' said the Deputy Sub-Bursar, smiling propitiatingly. 'Would you mind letting me ...'

'Poison to soul as well as body.'

'Yes, but let me get on with my distribution, won't you? There's a good fellow.' With the cautious tenderness of one who strokes a notoriously vicious animal, he patted the Savage's arm. 'Just let me ...'

'Never!' cried the Savage.

'But look here, old man ..'

'Throw it all away, that horrible poison.'

The words 'Throw it all away' pierced through the enfolding layers of incomprehension to the quick of the Deltas' consciousness. An angry murmur went up from the crowd.

'I come to bring you freedom,' said the Savage, turning back towards the twins. 'I come ...'

The Deputy Sub-Bursar heard no more; he had slipped out of the vestibule and was looking up a number in the telephone book.

'Not in his own rooms,' Bernard summed up. 'Not in mine, not in yours. Not at the Aphroditæum; not at the Centre or the College. Where can he have got to?'

Helmholtz shrugged his shoulders. They had come back from their work expecting to find the Savage waiting for them at one or other of their usual meeting-places, and there was no sign of the fellow. Which was annoying, as they had meant to nip across to Biarritz in Helmholtz's four-seater sporticopter. They'd be late for dinner if he didn't come soon.

'We'll give him five more minutes,' said Helmholtz. 'If he doesn't turn up by then, we'll . . .'

The ringing of the telephone bell interrupted him. He picked up the receiver. 'Hullo. Speaking.' Then, after a long interval of listening, 'Ford in Flivver!' he swore. 'I'll come at once.'

'What is it?' Bernard asked.

'A fellow I know at the Park Lane Hospital,' said Helmholtz. 'The Savage is there. Seems to have gone mad. Anyhow, it's urgent. Will you come with me?'

Together they hurried along the corridor to the lifts.

'But do you like being slaves?' the Savage was saying as they entered the Hospital. His face was flushed, his eyes bright with ardour and indignation. 'Do you like being babies? Yes, babies. Mewling and puking,' he added, exasperated by their bestial stupidity into throwing insults at those he had come to save. The insults bounced off their carapace of thick stupidity; they stared at him with a blank expression of dull and sullen resentment in their eyes. 'Yes, puking!' he fairly shouted. Grief and remorse, compassion and duty—all were forgotten now and, as it were, absorbed into an intense overpowering hatred of these less than human monsters. 'Don't you want to be free and men? Don't you even understand what manhood and freedom are?' Rage was making him fluent; the words came easily, in a rush. 'Don't you?' he repeated, but got no answer to his question.

'Very well, then,' he went on grimly. 'I'll teach you; I'll *make* you be free whether you want to or not.' And pushing open a window that looked on to the inner court of the Hospital, he began to throw the little pill-boxes of *soma* tablets in handfuls out into the area.

For a moment the khaki mob was silent, petrified, at the spectacle of this wanton sacrilege, with amazement and horror.

'He's mad,' whispered Bernard, staring with wide open eyes. 'They'll kill him. They'll . . .' A great shout suddenly went up from the mob; a wave of movement drove it menacingly towards the Savage. 'Ford help him!' said Bernard, and averted his eyes.

'Ford helps those who help themselves.' And with a laugh, actually a laugh of exultation, Helmholtz Watson pushed his way through the crowd.

'Free, free!' the Savage shouted, and with one hand continued to throw the *soma* into the area while, with the other, he punched the indistinguishable faces of his assailants. 'Free!' And suddenly there was Helmholtz at his side—'Good old Helmholtz!' —also punching—'Men at last!'—and in the interval also throwing the poison out by handfuls through the open window. 'Yes, men! men!' and there was no more poison left. He picked up the cash-box and showed them its black emptiness. 'You're free!'

Howling, the Deltas charged with a redoubled fury.

Hesitant on the fringes of the battle, 'They're done for,' said Bernard and, urged by a sudden impulse, ran forward to help them; then thought better of it and halted; then, ashamed, stepped forward again; then again thought better of it, and was standing in an agony of humiliated indecision—thinking that *they* might be killed if he didn't help them, and that *he* might be killed if he did—when (Ford be praised!), goggle-eyed and swine-snouted in their gas-masks, in ran the police.

Bernard dashed to meet them. He waved his arms; and it was action, he was doing something. He shouted 'Help!' several times, more and more loudly so as to give himself the illusion of helping. 'Help! *Help!* Help!'

The policemen pushed him out of the way and got on with their work. Three men with spraying machines buckled to their shoulders pumped thick clouds of *soma* vapour into the air. Two more were busy round the portable Synthetic Music Box. Carrying water pistols charged with a powerful anæsthetic, four others had pushed their way into the crowd and were methodically laying out, squirt by squirt, the more ferocious of the fighters.

'Quick, quick!' yelled Bernard. 'They'll be killed if you don't hurry. They'll... Oh!' Annoyed by his chatter, one of the policemen had given him a shot from his water pistol. Bernard stood for a second or two wambling unsteadily on legs that seemed to have lost their bones, their tendons, their muscles, to have become mere sticks of jelly, and at last not even jelly—water: he tumbled in a heap on the floor.

Suddenly, from out of the Synthetic Music Box a Voice began to speak. The Voice of Reason, the Voice of Good Feeling. The sound-track roll was unwinding itself in Synthetic Anti-Riot Speech Number Two (Medium Strength). Straight from the depths of a non-existent heart, 'My friends, my friends!' said the Voice so pathetically, with a note of such infinitely tender reproach that, behind their gas-masks, even the policemen's eyes were momentarily dimmed with tears, 'what is the meaning of this? Why aren't you all being happy and good together. Happy and good,' the Voice repeated. 'At peace, at peace.' It trembled, sank into a whisper and momentarily expired. 'Oh, I do want you to be happy,' it began, with a yearning earnestness. 'I do so want you to be good! Please, please be good and...'

Two minutes later the Voice and the *soma* vapour had produced their effect. In tears, the Deltas were kissing and hugging one another—half a dozen twins at a time in a comprehensive embrace. Even Helmholtz and the Savage were almost crying. A fresh supply of pill-boxes was brought in from the Bursary; a new distribution was hastily made and, to the sound of the

Voice's richly affectionate, baritone valedictions, the twins dispersed, blubbering as though their hearts would break. 'Good-bye, my dearest, dearest friends, Ford keep you! Good-bye, my dearest, dearest friends, Ford keep you. Good-bye, my dearest, dearest . . .'

When the last of the Deltas had gone the policeman switched off the current. The angelic Voice fell silent.

'Will you come quietly?' asked the Sergeant, 'or must we anæsthetize?' He pointed his water pistol menacingly.

'Oh, we'll come quietly,' the Savage answered, dabbing alternately a cut lip, a scratched neck, and a bitten left hand.

Still keeping his handkerchief to his bleeding nose, Helmholtz nodded in confirmation.

Awake and having recovered the use of his legs, Bernard had chosen this moment to move as inconspicuously as he could towards the door.

'Hi, you there,' called the Sergeant, and a swine-masked policeman hurried across the room and laid a hand on the young man's shoulder.

Bernard turned with an expression of indignant innocence. Escaping? He hadn't dreamed of such a thing. 'Though what on earth you want *me* for,' he said to the Sergeant, 'I really can't imagine.'

'You're a friend of the prisoners, aren't you?'

'Well . . .' said Bernard, and hesitated. No, he really couldn't deny it. 'Why shouldn't I be?' he asked.

'Come on, then,' said the Sergeant, and led the way towards the door and the waiting police car.

Chapter XVI

THE room into which the three were ushered was the Controller's study.

'His fordship will be down in a moment.' The Gamma butler left them to themselves.

Helmholtz laughed aloud.

'It's more like a caffeine-solution party than a trial,' he said, and let himself fall into the most luxurious of the pneumatic armchairs. 'Cheer up, Bernard,' he added, catching sight of his friend's green unhappy face. But Bernard would not be cheered; without answering, without even looking at Helmholtz, he went and sat down on the most uncomfortable chair in the room, carefully chosen in the obscure hope of somehow deprecating the wrath of the higher powers.

The Savage meanwhile wandered restlessly round the room, peering with a vague superficial inquisitiveness at the books in the shelves, at the sound-track rolls and the reading-machine bobbins in their numbered pigeon-holes. On the table under the window lay a massive volume bound in limp black leather-surrogate, and stamped with large golden T's. He picked it up and opened it. MY LIFE AND WORK, BY OUR FORD. The book had been published at Detroit by the Society for the Propagation of Fordian Knowledge. Idly he turned the pages, read a sentence here, a paragraph there, and had just come to the conclusion that the book didn't interest him, when the door opened, and the Resident World Controller for Western Europe walked briskly into the room.

Mustapha Mond shook hands with all three of them; but it was to the Savage that he addressed himself. 'So you don't much like civilization, Mr. Savage,' he said.

The Savage looked at him. He had been prepared to lie, to bluster, to remain sullenly unresponsive; but, reassured by the good-humoured intelligence of the Controller's face, he decided to tell the truth, straightforwardly. 'No.' He shook his head.

Bernard started and looked horrified. What would the Controller think? To be labelled as the friend of a man who said that he didn't like civilization—said it openly and, of all people, to the Controller—it was terrible. 'But, John,' he began. A look from Mustapha Mond reduced him to an abject silence.

'Of course,' the Savage went on to admit, 'there are some very nice things. All that music in the air, for instance . . .'

'Sometimes a thousand twangling instruments will hum about my ears, and sometimes voices.'

The Savage's face lit up with a sudden pleasure. 'Have you read it too?' he asked. 'I thought nobody knew about that book here, in England.'

'Almost nobody. I'm one of the very few. It's prohibited, you see. But as I make the laws here, I can also break them. With impunity, Mr. Marx,' he added, turning to Bernard. 'Which I'm afraid you *can't* do.'

Bernard sank into a yet more hopeless misery.

'But why is it prohibited?' asked the Savage. In the excitement of meeting a man who had read Shakespeare he had momentarily forgotten everything else.

The Controller shrugged his shoulders. 'Because it's old; that's the chief reason. We haven't any use for old things here.'

'Even when they're beautiful?'

'Particularly when they're beautiful. Beauty's attractive, and we don't want people to be attracted by old things. We want them to like the new ones.'

'But the new ones are so stupid and horrible. Those plays, where there's nothing but helicopters flying about and you *feel* the people kissing.' He made a grimace. 'Goats and monkeys!' Only in Othello's words could he find an adequate vehicle for his contempt and hatred.

'Nice tame animals, anyhow,' the Controller murmured parenthetically.

'Why don't you let them see *Othello* instead?'

'I've told you; it's old. Besides, they couldn't understand it.'

Yes, that was true. He remembered how Helmholtz had laughed at *Romeo and Juliet*. 'Well, then,' he said, after a pause, 'something new that's like *Othello*, and that they could understand.'

'That's what we've all been wanting to write,' said Helmholtz, breaking a long silence.

'And it's what you never will write,' said the Controller. 'Because, if it were really like *Othello* nobody could understand it, however new it might be. And if it were new, it couldn't possibly be like *Othello*.'

'Why not?'

'Yes, why not?' Helmholtz repeated. He too was forgetting the unpleasant realities of the situation. Green with anxiety and apprehension, only Bernard remembered them; the others ignored him. 'Why not?'

'Because our world is not the same as Othello's world. You can't make flivvers without steel—and you can't make tragedies without social instability. The world's stable now. People are happy; they get what they want, and they never want what they can't get. They're well off; they're safe; they're never ill; they're not afraid of death; they're blissfully ignorant of passion and old age; they're plagued with no mothers or fathers; they've got no wives, or children, or lovers to feel strongly about; they're so conditioned that they practically can't help behaving as they ought to behave. And if anything should go wrong, there's *soma*. Which you go and chuck out of the window in the name of liberty, Mr. Savage. *Liberty!*' He laughed. 'Expecting Deltas to know what liberty is! And now expecting them to understand *Othello*! My good boy!'

The Savage was silent for a little. 'All the same,' he insisted obstinately, '*Othello*'s good, *Othello*'s better than those feelies.'

'Of course it is,' the Controller agreed. 'But that's the price we have to pay for stability. You've got to choose between happiness and what people used to call high art. We've sacrificed the high art. We have the feelies and the scent organ instead.'

'But they don't mean anything.'

'They mean themselves; they mean a lot of agreeable sensations to the audience.'

'But they're . . . they're told by an idiot.'

The Controller laughed. 'You're not being very polite to your friend, Mr. Watson. One of our most distinguished Emotional Engineers . . .'

'But he's right,' said Helmholtz gloomily. 'Because it *is* idiotic. Writing when there's nothing to say . . .'

'Precisely. But that requires the most enormous ingenuity. You're making flivvers out of the absolute minimum of steel—works of art out of practically nothing but pure sensation.'

The Savage shook his head. 'It all seems to me quite horrible.'

'Of course it does. Actual happiness always looks pretty squalid in comparison with the over-compensations for misery. And, of course, stability isn't nearly so spectacular as instability. And being contented has none of the glamour of a good fight against misfortune, none of the picturesqueness of a struggle with temptation, or a fatal overthrow by passion or doubt. Happiness is never grand.'

'I suppose not,' said the Savage after a silence. 'But need it be quite so bad as those twins?' He passed his hand over his eyes as though he were trying to wipe away the remembered image of those long rows of identical midgets at the assembling tables, those queued-up twin-herds at the entrance to the Brentford monorail station, those human maggots swarming round Linda's bed of death, the endlessly repeated face of his assailants. He looked at his bandaged left hand and shuddered. 'Horrible!'

'But how useful! I see you don't like our Bokanovsky Groups; but, I assure you, they're the foundation on which everything else is built. They're the gyroscope that stabilizes the rocket plane of state on its unswerving course.' The deep voice thrillingly vibrated; the gesticulating hand implied all space and the onrush of the irresistible machine. Mustapha Mond's oratory was almost up to synthetic standards.

'I was wondering,' said the Savage, 'why you had them at all —seeing that you can get whatever you want out of those bottles. Why don't you make everybody an Alpha Double Plus while you're about it?'

Mustapha Mond laughed. 'Because we have no wish to have our throats cut,' he answered. 'We believe in happiness and stability. A society of Alphas couldn't fail to be unstable and miserable. Imagine a factory staffed by Alphas—that is to say by separate and unrelated individuals of good heredity and conditioned so as to be capable (within limits) of making a free choice and assuming responsibilities. Imagine it!' he repeated.

The Savage tried to imagine it, not very successfully.

'It's an absurdity. An Alpha-decanted, Alpha-conditioned man would go mad if he had to do Epsilon Semi-Moron work— go mad, or start smashing things up. Alphas can be completely socialized—but only on condition that you make them do Alpha work. Only an Epsilon can be expected to make Epsilon sacrifices, for the good reason that for him they aren't sacrifices; they're the line of least resistance. His conditioning has laid down rails along which he's got to run. He can't help himself; he's foredoomed. Even after decanting, he's still inside a bottle —an invisible bottle of infantile and embryonic fixations. Each one of us, of course,' the Controller meditatively continued, 'goes through life inside a bottle. But if we happen to be Alphas, our bottles are, relatively speaking, enormous. We should suffer acutely if we were confined in a narrower space. You cannot pour upper-caste champagne-surrogate into lower-caste bottles. It's obvious theoretically. But it has also been proved in actual practice. The result of the Cyprus experiment was convincing.'

'What was that?' asked the Savage.

Mustapha Mond smiled. 'Well, you can call it an experiment in rebottling if you like. It began in A.F. 473. The Controllers had the island of Cyprus cleared of all its existing inhabitants and re-colonized with a specially prepared batch of twenty-two thousand Alphas. All agricultural and industrial equipment was handed over to them and they were left to manage their own affairs. The result exactly fulfilled all the theoretical predictions. The land wasn't properly worked; there were strikes in all the factories; the laws were set at naught, orders disobeyed; all the people detailed for a spell of low-grade work were perpetually intriguing for high-grade jobs, and all the people with high-grade jobs were counter-intriguing at all costs to stay where they were. Within six years they were having a first-class civil war. When nineteen out of the twenty-two thousand had been killed, the survivors unanimously petitioned the World Controllers to resume the government of the island. Which they did. And that was the end of the only society of Alphas that the world has ever seen.'

The Savage sighed, profoundly.

'The optimum population,' said Mustapha Mond, 'is modelled on the iceberg—eight-ninths below the water line, one-ninth above.'

'And they're happy below the water line?'

'Happier than above it. Happier than your friends here, for example.' He pointed.

'In spite of that awful work?'

'Awful? *They* don't find it so. On the contrary, they like it. It's light, it's childishly simple. No strain on the mind or the muscles. Seven and a half hours of mild, unexhausting labour, and then the *soma* ration and games and unrestricted copulation and the feelies. What more can they ask for? True,' he added, 'they might ask for shorter hours. And of course we could give them shorter hours. Technically, it would be perfectly simple to reduce all lower-caste working hours to three or four a day. But would they be any the happier for that? No, they wouldn't. The experiment was tried, more than a century and a half ago. The whole of Ireland was put on to the four-hour day. What was the result? Unrest and a large increase in the consumption of *soma*; that was all. Those three and a half hours of extra leisure were so far from being a source of happiness, that people felt constrained to take a holiday from them. The Inventions Office is stuffed with plans for labour-saving processes. Thousands of them.' Mustapha Mond made a lavish gesture. 'And why don't we put them into execution? For the sake of the labourers; it would be sheer cruelty to afflict them with excessive leisure. It's the same with agriculture. We could synthesize every morsel of food, if we wanted to. But we don't. We prefer to keep a third of the population on the land. For their own sakes—because it takes *longer* to get food out of the land than out of a factory. Besides, we have our stability to think of. We don't want to change. Every change is a menace to stability. That's another reason why we're so chary of applying new inventions. Every discovery in pure science is potentially subversive; even science must sometimes be treated as a possible enemy. Yes, even science.'

Science? The Savage frowned. He knew the word. But what it exactly signified he could not say. Shakespeare and the old men of the pueblo had never mentioned science, and from Linda he had only gathered the vaguest hints: science was something you made helicopters with, something that caused you to laugh at the Corn Dances, something that prevented you from being wrinkled and losing your teeth. He made a desperate effort to take the Controller's meaning.

'Yes,' Mustapha Mond was saying, 'that's another item in the cost of stability. It isn't only art that's incompatible with happiness; it's also science. Science is dangerous; we have to keep it most carefully chained and muzzled.'

'What?' said Helmholtz, in astonishment. 'But we're always saying that science is everything. It's a hypnopædic platitude.'

'Three times a week between thirteen and seventeen,' put in Bernard.

'And all the science propaganda we do at the College . . .'

'Yes; but what sort of science?' asked Mustapha Mond sarcastically. 'You've had no scientific training, so you can't judge. I was a pretty good physicist in my time. Too good—good enough to realize that all our science is just a cookery book, with an orthodox theory of cooking that nobody's allowed to question, and a list of recipes that mustn't be added to except by special permission from the head cook. I'm the head cook now. But I was an inquisitive young scullion once. I started doing a bit of cooking on my own. Unorthodox cooking, illicit cooking. A bit of real science, in fact.' He was silent.

'What happened?' asked Helmholtz Watson.

The Controller sighed. 'Very nearly what's going to happen to you young men. I was on the point of being sent to an island.'

The words galvanized Bernard into a violent and unseemly activity. 'Send *me* to an island?' He jumped up, ran across the room, and stood gesticulating in front of the Controller. 'You can't send *me*. I haven't done anything. It was the others. I swear it was the others.' He pointed accusingly to Helmholtz and the Savage. 'Oh, please don't send me to Iceland. I promise I'll do what I ought to do. Give me another chance. Please give me another chance.' The tears began to flow. 'I tell you, it's their fault,' he sobbed. 'And not to Iceland. Oh, please, your fordship, please . . .' And in a paroxysm of abjection he threw himself on his knees before the Controller. Mustapha Mond tried to make him get up; but Bernard persisted in his grovelling; the stream of words poured out inexhaustibly. In the end the Controller had to ring for his fourth secretary.

'Bring three men,' he ordered, 'and take Mr. Marx into a bedroom. Give him a good *soma* vaporization and then put him to bed and leave him.'

The fourth secretary went out and returned with three green-uniformed twin footmen. Still shouting and sobbing, Bernard was carried out.

'One would think he was going to have his throat cut,' said

the Controller, as the door closed. 'Whereas, if he had the smallest sense, he'd understand that his punishment is really a reward. He's being sent to an island. That's to say, he's being sent to a place where he'll meet the most interesting set of men and women to be found anywhere in the world. All the people who, for one reason or another, have got too self-consciously individual to fit into community-life. All the people who aren't satisfied with orthodoxy, who've got independent ideas of their own. Every one, in a word, who's any one. I almost envy you, Mr. Watson.'

Helmholtz laughed. 'Then why aren't you on an island your-self?'

'Because, finally, I preferred this,' the Controller answered. 'I was given the choice: to be sent to an island, where I could have got on with my pure science, or to be taken on to the Controllers' Council with the prospect of succeeding in due course to an actual Controllership. I chose this and let the science go.' After a little silence, 'Sometimes,' he added, 'I rather regret the science. Happiness is a hard master—particularly other people's happiness. A much harder master, if one isn't conditioned to accept it unquestionably, than truth.' He sighed, fell silent again, then continued in a brisker tone. 'Well, duty's duty. One can't consult one's own preferences. I'm interested in truth, I like science. But truth's a menace, science is a public danger. As dangerous as it's been beneficent. It has given us the stablest equilibrium in history. China's was hopelessly insecure by comparison; even the primitive matriarchies weren't steadier than we are. Thanks, I repeat, to science. But we can't allow science to undo its own good work. That's why we so carefully limit the scope of its researches—that's why I almost got sent to an island. We don't allow it to deal with any but the most immediate problems of the moment. All other enquiries are most sedulously discouraged. It's curious,' he went on after a little pause, 'to read what people in the time of Our Ford used to write about scientific progress. They seemed to have imagined that it could be allowed to go on indefinitely, regardless of every-thing else. Knowledge was the highest good, truth the supreme value; all the rest was secondary and subordinate. True, ideas were beginning to change even then. Our Ford himself did a great deal to shift the emphasis from truth and beauty to comfort and happiness. Mass production demanded the shift. Universal happiness keeps the wheels steadily turning; truth and beauty can't. And, of course, whenever the masses seized political power, then it was happiness rather than truth and beauty that mattered. Still, in spite of everything, unrestricted scientific research was still permitted. People still went on talking about truth and beauty as though they were the sovereign goods. Right up to the time of the Nine Years' War. *That* made them change their tune all right. What's the point of truth or beauty or knowledge when the anthrax bombs are popping all around you? That was when science first began to be controlled—after the Nine Years' War. People were ready to have even their appetites controlled then. Anything for a quiet life. We've gone on con-trolling ever since. It hasn't been very good for truth, of course. But it's been very good for happiness. One can't have something for nothing. Happiness has got to be paid for. You're paying for it, Mr. Watson—paying because you happen to be too much interested in beauty. I was too much interested in truth; I paid too.'

'But *you* didn't go to an island,' said the Savage, breaking a long silence.

The Controller smiled. 'That's how I paid. By choosing to serve happiness. Other people's—not mine. It's lucky,' he added, after a pause, 'that there are such a lot of islands in the world. I don't know what we should do without them. Put you all in the lethal chamber, I suppose. By the way, Mr. Watson, would you like a tropical climate? The Marquesas, for example; or Samoa? Or something rather more bracing?'

Helmholtz rose from his pneumatic chair. 'I should like a thoroughly bad climate,' he answered. 'I believe one would write better if the climate were bad. If there were a lot of wind and storms, for example . . .'

The Controller nodded his approbation. 'I like your spirit, Mr. Watson. I like it very much indeed. As much as I officially disapprove of it.' He smiled. 'What about the Falkland Islands?'

'Yes, I think that will do,' Helmholtz answered. 'And now, if you don't mind, I'll go and see how poor Bernard's getting on.'

Chapter XVII

'ART, science—you seem to have paid a fairly high price for
your happiness,' said the Savage, when they were alone.
'Anything else?'

'Well, religion, of course,' replied the Controller. 'There
used to be something called God—before the Nine Years' War.
But I was forgetting; you know all about God, I suppose.'

'Well . . .' The Savage hesitated. He would have liked to say
something about solitude, about night, about the mesa lying pale
under the moon, about the precipice, the plunge into shadowy
darkness, about death. He would have liked to speak; but there
were no words. Not even in Shakespeare.

The Controller, meanwhile, had crossed to the other side of
the room and was unlocking a large safe let into the wall between
the bookshelves. The heavy door swung open. Rummaging
in the darkness within, 'It's a subject,' he said, 'that has always
had a great interest for me.' He pulled out a thick black volume.
'You've never read this, for example.'

The Savage took it. '*The Holy Bible, containing the Old and
New Testaments*,' he read aloud from the title-page.

'Nor this.' It was a small book and had lost its cover.

'*The Imitation of Christ.*'

'Nor this.' He handed out another volume.

'*The Varieties of Religious Experience.* By William James.'

'And I've got plenty more,' Mustapha Mond continued, re-
suming his seat. 'A whole collection of pornographic old books.
God in the safe and Ford on the shelves.' He pointed with a
laugh to his avowed library—to shelves of books, the racks full
of reading-machine bobbins and sound-track rolls.

'But if you know about God, why don't you tell them?' asked
the Savage indignantly. 'Why don't you give them these books
about God?'

'For the same reason as we don't give them *Othello*: they're old; they're about God hundreds of years ago. Not about God now.'

'But God doesn't change.'

'Men do, though.'

'What difference does that make?'

'All the difference in the world,' said Mustapha Mond. He got up again and walked to the safe. 'There was a man called Cardinal Newman,' he said. 'A cardinal,' he exclaimed parenthetically, 'was a kind of Arch-Community-Songster.'

'"I, Pandulph, of fair Milan cardinal." I've read about them in Shakespeare.'

'Of course you have. Well, as I was saying, there was a man called Cardinal Newman. Ah, here's the book.' He pulled it out. 'And while I'm about it I'll take this one too. It's by a man called Maine de Biran. He was a philosopher, if you know what that was.'

'A man who dreams of fewer things than there are in heaven and earth,' said the Savage promptly.

'Quite so. I'll read you one of the things he *did* dream of in a moment. Meanwhile, listen to what this old Arch-Community-Songster said.' He opened the book at the place marked by a slip of paper and began to read. '"We are not our own any more than what we possess is our own. We did not make ourselves, we cannot be supreme over ourselves. We are not our own masters. We are God's property. Is it not our happiness thus to view the matter? Is it any happiness, or any comfort, to consider that we *are* our own? It may be thought so by the young and prosperous. These may think it a great thing to have everything, as they suppose, their own way—to depend on no one—to have to think of nothing out of sight, to be without the irksomeness of continual acknowledgment, continual prayer, continual reference of what they do to the will of another. But as time goes on, they, as all men, will find that independence was not made for man—that it is an unnatural state—will do for a

while, but will not carry us on safely to the end ...'' Mustapha
Mond paused, put down the first book and, picking up the other,
turned over the pages. 'Take this, for example,' he said, and in
his deep voice once more began to read: '"A man grows old;
he feels in himself that radical sense of weakness, of listlessness,
of discomfort, which accompanies the advance of age; and, feeling thus, imagines himself merely sick, lulling his fears with the
notion that this distressing condition is due to some particular
cause, from which, as from an illness, he hopes to recover. Vain
imaginings! That sickness is old age; and a horrible disease it
is. They say that it is the fear of death and of what comes after
death that makes men turn to religion as they advance in years.
But my own experience has given me the conviction that, quite
apart from any such terrors or imaginings, the religious sentiment
tends to develop as we grow older; to develop because, as the
passions grow calm, as the fancy and sensibilities are less excited
and less excitable, our reason becomes less troubled in its working, less obscured by the images, desires and distractions, in
which it used to be absorbed; whereupon God emerges as from
behind a cloud; our soul feels, sees, turns towards the source of
all light; turns naturally and inevitably; for now that all that
gave to the world of sensations its life and charm has begun to
leak away from us, now that phenomenal existence is no more
bolstered up by impressions from within or from without, we
feel the need to lean on something that abides, something that
will never play us false—a reality, an absolute and everlasting
truth. Yes, we inevitably turn to God; for this religious sentiment is of its nature so pure, so delightful to the soul that experiences it, that it makes up to us for all our other losses."'
Mustapha Mond shut the book and leaned back in his chair. 'One
of the numerous things in heaven and earth that these philosophers didn't dream about was this' (he waved his hand), 'us,
the modern world. "You can only be independent of God while
you've got youth and prosperity; independence won't take you
safely to the end." Well, we've now got youth and prosperity

right up to the end. What follows? Evidently, that we can be independent of God. "The religious sentiment will compensate us for all our losses." But there aren't any losses for us to compensate; religious sentiment is superfluous. And why should we go hunting for a substitute for youthful desires, when youthful desires never fail? A substitute for distractions, when we go on enjoying all the old fooleries to the very last? What need have we of repose when our minds and bodies continue to delight in activity? of consolation, when we have *soma*? of something immovable, when there is the social order?'

'Then you think there is no God?'

'No, I think there quite probably is one.'

'Then why . . .?'

Mustapha Mond checked him. 'But he manifests himself in different ways to different men. In pre-modern times he manifested himself as the being that's described in these books. Now...'

'How does he manifest himself now?' asked the Savage.

'Well, he manifests himself as an absence; as though he weren't there at all.'

'That's your fault.'

'Call it the fault of civilization. God isn't compatible with machinery and scientific medicine and universal happiness. You must make your choice. Our civilization has chosen machinery and medicine and happiness. That's why I have to keep these books locked up in the safe. They're smut. People would be shocked if . . .'

The Savage interrupted him. 'But isn't it *natural* to feel there's a God?'

'You might as well ask if it's natural to do up one's trousers with zippers,' said the Controller sarcastically. 'You remind me of another of those old fellows called Bradley. He defined philosophy as the finding of bad reason for what one believes by instinct. As if one believed anything by instinct! One believes things because one has been conditioned to believe them. Finding bad reasons for what one believes for other bad reasons—

that's philosophy. People believe in God because they've been conditioned to believe in God.'

'But all the same,' insisted the Savage, 'it is natural to believe in God when you're alone—quite alone, in the night, thinking about death . . .'

'But people never are alone now,' said Mustapha Mond. 'We make them hate solitude; and we arrange their lives so that it's almost impossible for them ever to have it.'

The Savage nodded gloomily. At Malpais he had suffered because they had shut him out from the communal activities of the pueblo, in civilized London he was suffering because he could never escape from those communal activities, never be quietly alone.

'Do you remember that bit in *King Lear*?' said the Savage at last: '"The gods are just, and of our pleasant vices make instruments to plague us; the dark and vicious place where thee he got cost him his eyes," and Edmund answers—you remember, he's wounded, he's dying—"Thou hast spoken right; 'tis true. The wheel is come full circle; I am here." What about that, now? Doesn't there seem to be a God managing things, punishing, rewarding?'

'Well, does there?' questioned the Controller in his turn. 'You can indulge in any number of pleasant vices with a free-martin and run no risks of having your eyes put out by your son's mistress. "The wheel is come full circle; I am here." But where would Edmund be nowadays? Sitting in a pneumatic chair, with his arm round a girl's waist, sucking away at his sex-hormone chewing-gum and looking at the feelies. The gods are just. No doubt. But their code of law is dictated, in the last resort, by the people who organize society; Providence takes its cue from men.'

'Are you sure?' asked the Savage. 'Are you quite sure that the Edmund in that pneumatic chair hasn't been just as heavily punished as the Edmund who's wounded and bleeding to death? The gods are just. Haven't they used his pleasant vices as an instrument to degrade him?'

'Degrade him from what position? As a happy, hard-working, goods-consuming citizen he's perfect. Of course, if you choose some other standard than ours, then perhaps you might say he was degraded. But you've got to stick to one set of postulates. You can't play Electro-magnetic Golf according to the rules of Centrifugal Bumble-puppy.'

'But value dwells not in particular will,' said the Savage. 'It holds his estimate and dignity as well wherein 'tis precious of itself as in the prizer.'

'Come, come,' protested Mustapha Mond, 'that's going rather far, isn't it?'

'If you allowed yourselves to think of God, you wouldn't allow yourselves to be degraded by pleasant vices. You'd have a reason for bearing things patiently, for doing things with courage. I've seen it with the Indians.'

'I'm sure you have,' said Mustapha Mond. 'But then we aren't Indians. There isn't any need for a civilized man to bear anything that's seriously unpleasant. And as for doing things—Ford forbid that he should get the idea into his head. It would upset the whole social order if men started doing things on their own.'

'What about self-denial, then? If you had a God, you'd have a reason for self-denial.'

'But industrial civilization is only possible when there's no self-denial. Self-indulgence up to the very limits imposed by hygiene and economics. Otherwise the wheels stop turning.'

'You'd have a reason for chastity!' said the Savage, blushing a little as he spoke the words.

'But chastity means passion, chastity means neurasthenia. And passion and neurasthenia mean instability. And instability means the end of civilization. You can't have a lasting civilization without plenty of pleasant vices.'

'But God's the reason for everything noble and fine and heroic. If you had a God...'

'My dear young friend,' said Mustapha Mond, 'civilization has absolutely no need of nobility or heroism. These things are symptoms of political inefficiency. In a properly organized society like ours, nobody has any opportunities for being noble or heroic. Conditions have got to be thoroughly unstable before the occasion can arise. Where there are wars, where there are divided allegiances, where there are temptations to be resisted, objects of love to be fought for or defended—there, obviously, nobility and heroism have some sense. But there aren't any wars nowadays. The greatest care is taken to prevent you from loving any one too much. There's no such thing as a divided allegiance; you're so conditioned that you can't help doing what you ought to do. And what you ought to do is on the whole so pleasant, so many of the natural impulses are allowed free play, that there really aren't any temptations to resist. And if ever, by some unlucky chance, anything unpleasant should somehow happen, why, there's always *soma* to give you a holiday from the facts. And there's always *soma* to calm your anger, to reconcile you to your enemies, to make you patient and long-suffering. In the past you could only accomplish these things by making a great effort and after years of hard moral training. Now, you swallow two or three half-gramme tablets, and there you are. Anybody can be virtuous now. You can carry at least half your morality about in a bottle. Christianity without tears—that's what *soma* is.'

'But the tears are necessary. Don't you remember what Othello said? "If after every tempest come such calms, may the winds blow till they have wakened death." There's a story one of the old Indians used to tell us, about the Girl of Mátsaki. The young men who wanted to marry her had to do a morning's hoeing in her garden. It seemed easy; but there were flies and mosquitoes, magic ones. Most of the young men simply couldn't stand the biting and stinging. But the one that could—he got the girl.'

'Charming! But in civilized countries,' said the Controller, 'you can have girls without hoeing for them; and there aren't any flies or mosquitoes to sting you. We got rid of them all centuries ago.'

The Savage nodded, frowning. 'You got rid of them. Yes, that's just like you. Getting rid of everything unpleasant instead of learning to put up with it. Whether 'tis nobler in the mind to suffer the slings and arrows of outrageous fortune, or to take arms against a sea of troubles and by opposing end them. . . . But you don't do either. Neither suffer nor oppose. You just abolish the slings and arrows. It's too easy.'

He was suddenly silent, thinking of his mother. In her room on the thirty-seventh floor, Linda had floated in a sea of singing lights and perfumed caresses—floated away, out of space, out of time, out of the prison of her memories, her habits, her aged and bloated body. And Tomakin, ex-Director of Hatcheries and Conditioning, Tomakin was still on holiday—on holiday from humiliation and pain, in a world where he could not hear those words, that derisive laughter, could not see that hideous face, feel those moist and flabby arms round his neck, in a beautiful world . . .

'What you need,' the Savage went on, 'is something *with* tears for a change. Nothing costs enough here.'

('Twelve and a half million dollars,' Henry Foster had protested when the Savage told him that. 'Twelve and a half million—that's what the new Conditioning Centre cost. Not a cent less.')

'Exposing what is mortal and unsure to all that fortune, death and danger dare, even for an egg-shell. Isn't there something in that?' he asked, looking up at Mustapha Mond. 'Quite apart from God—though of course God would be a reason for it. Isn't there something in living dangerously?'

'There's a great deal in it,' the Controller replied. 'Men and women must have their adrenals stimulated from time to time.'

'What?' questioned the Savage, uncomprehending.

'It's one of the conditions of perfect health. That's why we've made the V.P.S. treatments compulsory.'

'V.P.S.?'

'Violent Passion Surrogate. Regularly once a month. We flood the whole system with adrenin. It's the complete physiological equivalent of fear and rage. All the tonic effects of murdering Desdemona and being murdered by Othello, without any of the inconveniences.'

'But I like the inconveniences.'

'We don't,' said the Controller. 'We prefer to do things comfortably.'

'But I don't want comfort. I want God, I want poetry, I want real danger, I want freedom, I want goodness. I want sin.'

'In fact,' said Mustapha Mond, 'you're claiming the right to be unhappy.'

'All right, then,' said the Savage defiantly, 'I'm claiming the right to be unhappy.'

'Not to mention the right to grow old and ugly and impotent; the right to have syphilis and cancer; the right to have too little to eat; the right to be lousy; the right to live in constant apprehension of what may happen to-morrow; the right to catch typhoid; the right to be tortured by unspeakable pains of every kind.'

There was a long silence.

'I claim them all,' said the Savage at last.

Mustapha Mond shrugged his shoulders. 'You're welcome,' he said.

Chapter XVIII

THE door was ajar; they entered.

'John!'

From the bathroom came an unpleasant and characteristic sound.

'Is there anything the matter?' Helmholtz called.

There was no answer. The unpleasant sound was repeated, twice; there was silence. Then, with a click, the bathroom door opened and, very pale, the Savage emerged.

'I say,' Helmholtz exclaimed solicitously, 'you *do* look ill, John!'

'Did you eat something that didn't agree with you?' asked Bernard.

The Savage nodded. 'I ate civilization.'

'What?'

'It poisoned me; I was defiled. And then,' he added, in a lower tone, 'I ate my own wickedness.'

'Yes, but what exactly . . .? I mean, just now you were . . .'

'Now I am purified,' said the Savage. 'I drank some mustard and warm water.'

The others stared at him in astonishment. 'Do you mean to say that you were doing it on purpose?' asked Bernard.

'That's how the Indians always purify themselves.' He sat down and, sighing, passed his hand across his forehead. 'I shall rest for a few minutes,' he said. 'I'm rather tired.'

'Well, I'm not surprised,' said Helmholtz. After a silence, 'We've come to say good-bye,' he went on in another tone. 'We're off to-morrow morning.'

'Yes, we're off to-morrow,' said Bernard, on whose face the Savage remarked a new expression of determined resignation. 'And by the way, John,' he continued, leaning forward in his chair and laying a hand on the Savage's knee, 'I want to say how

198

sorry I am about everything that happened yesterday.' He blushed. 'How ashamed,' he went on, in spite of the unsteadiness of his voice, 'how really . . .'

The Savage cut him short and, taking his hand, affectionately pressed it.

'Helmholtz was wonderful to me,' Bernard resumed, after a little pause. 'If it hadn't been for him, I should . . .'

'Now, now,' Helmholtz protested.

There was a silence. In spite of their sadness—because of it, even; for their sadness was the symptom of their love for one another—the three young men were happy.

'I went to see the Controller this morning,' said the Savage at last.

'What for?'

'To ask if I mightn't go to the islands with you.'

'And what did he say?' asked Helmholtz eagerly.

The Savage shook his head. 'He wouldn't let me.'

'Why not?'

'He said he wanted to go on with the experiment. But I'm damned,' the Savage added, with sudden fury, 'I'm damned if I'll go on being experimented with. Not for all the Controllers in the world. I shall go away to-morrow too.'

'But where?' the others asked in unison.

The Savage shrugged his shoulders. 'Anywhere. I don't care. So long as I can be alone.'

From Guildford the down-line followed the Wey valley to Godalming, then, over Milford and Witley, proceeded to Haslemere and on through Petersfield towards Portsmouth. Roughly parallel to it, the up-line passed over Worplesden, Tongham, Puttenham, Elstead and Grayshott. Between the Hog's Back and Hindhead there were points where the two lines were not more than six or seven kilometres apart. The distance was too small for careless flyers—particularly at night and when they had taken half a gramme too much. There had been accidents. Serious ones. It had been decided to deflect the up-line a few kilometres to the west. Between Grayshott and Tongham four abandoned air-lighthouses marked the course of the old Portsmouth-to-London road. The skies above them were silent and deserted. It was over Selborne, Borden and Farnham that the helicopters now ceaselessly hummed and roared.

The Savage had chosen as his hermitage the old lighthouse which stood on the crest of the hill between Puttenham and Elstead. The building was of ferro-concrete and in excellent condition—almost too comfortable, the Savage had thought when he first explored the place, almost too civilizedly luxurious. He pacified his conscience by promising himself a compensatingly harder self-discipline, purifications the more complete and thorough. His first night in the hermitage was, deliberately, a sleepless one. He spent the hours on his knees praying, now to that Heaven from which the guilty Claudius had begged forgiveness, now in Zuñi to Awonawilona, now to Jesus and Pookong, now to his own guardian animal, the eagle. From time to time he stretched out his arms as though he were on the cross, and held them thus through long minutes of an ache that gradually increased till it became a tremulous and excruciating agony; held them, in voluntary crucifixion, while he repeated, through clenched teeth (the sweat, meanwhile, pouring down his face), 'Oh, forgive me! Oh, make me pure! Oh, help me to be good!' again and again, till he was on the point of fainting from the pain.

When morning came, he felt he had earned the right to inhabit the lighthouse; yes, even though there still *was* glass in most of the windows, even though the view from the platform *was* so fine. For the very reason why he had chosen the lighthouse had become almost instantly a reason for going somewhere else. He had decided to live there because the view was so beautiful, because, from his vantage point, he seemed to be looking out on to the incarnation of a divine being. But who was he to be pampered with the daily and hourly sight of loveliness? Who was he to be living in the visible presence of God? All he deserved to live in was some filthy sty, some blind hole in the ground. Stiff and still aching after his long night of pain, but for that very reason inwardly reassured, he climbed up to the platform of his tower, he looked out over the bright sunrise world which he had regained the right to inhabit. On the north the view was bounded by the long chalk ridge of the Hog's Back, from behind whose eastern extremity rose the towers of the seven skyscrapers which constituted Guildford. Seeing them, the Savage made a grimace; but he was to become reconciled to them in course of time; for at night they twinkled gaily with geometrical constellations, or else, flood-lighted, pointed their luminous fingers (with a gesture whose significance nobody in England but the Savage now understood) solemnly towards the plumbless mysteries of heaven.

In the valley which separated the Hog's Back from the sandy hill on which the lighthouse stood, Puttenham was a modest little village nine stories high, with silos, a poultry farm, and a small vitamin-D factory. On the other side of the lighthouse, towards the south, the ground fell away in long slopes of heather to a chain of ponds.

Beyond them, above the intervening woods, rose the fourteen-story tower of Elstead. Dim in the hazy English air, Hindhead and Selborne invited the eye into a blue romantic distance. But it was not alone the distance that had attracted the Savage to his lighthouse; the near was as seductive as the far. The woods, the open stretches of heather and yellow gorse, the clumps of Scotch firs, the shining ponds with their overhanging birch trees, their water lilies, their beds of rushes—these were beautiful and, to an eye accustomed to the aridities of the American desert, astonishing. And then the solitude! Whole days passed during which he never saw a human being. The lighthouse was only a quarter of an hour's flight from the Charing-T Tower; but the hills of Malpais were hardly more deserted than this Surrey heath. The crowds that daily left London left it only to play Electro-magnetic Golf or Tennis. Puttenham possessed no links; the nearest Riemann-surfaces were at Guildford. Flowers and a landscape were the only attractions here. And so, as there was no good reason for coming, nobody came. During the first days the Savage lived alone and undisturbed.

Of the money which, on his first arrival, John had received for his personal expenses, most had been spent on his equipment. Before leaving London he had bought four viscose-woollen blankets, rope and string, nails, glue, a few tools, matches (though he intended in due course to make a fire drill), some pots and pans, two dozen packets of seeds, and ten kilogrammes of wheat flour. 'No, *not* synthetic starch and cotton-waste flour-substitute,' he had insisted. 'Even though it is more nourishing.' But when it came to pan-glandular biscuits and vitaminized beef-surrogate, he had not been able to resist the shopman's persuasion. Looking at the tins now, he bitterly reproached himself for his weakness. Loathsome civilized stuff! He had made up his mind that he would never eat it, even if he were starving. 'That'll teach them,' he thought vindictively. It would also teach him.

He counted his money. The little that remained would be enough, he hoped, to tide him over the winter. By next spring, his garden would be producing enough to make him independent of the outside world. Meanwhile, there would always be game. He had seen plenty of rabbits, and there were water-fowl on the ponds. He set to work at once to make a bow and arrows.

There were ash trees near the lighthouse and, for arrow shafts, a whole copse full of beautifully straight hazel saplings. He began by felling a young ash, cut out six feet of unbranched stem, stripped off the bark and, paring by paring, shaved away the white wood, as old Mitsima had taught him, until he had a stave of his own height, stiff at the thickened centre, lively and quick at the slender tips. The work gave him an intense pleasure. After those weeks of idleness in London, with nothing to do, whenever he wanted anything, but to press a switch or turn a handle, it was pure delight to be doing something that demanded skill and patience.

He had almost finished whittling the stave into shape, when he realized with a start that he was singing—*singing!* It was as though, stumbling upon himself from the outside, he had suddenly caught himself out, taken himself flagrantly at fault. Guiltily he blushed. After all, it was not to sing and enjoy himself that he had come here. It was to escape further contamination by the filth of civilized life; it was to be purified and made good; it was actively to make amends. He realized to his dismay that, absorbed in the whittling of his bow, he had forgotten what he had sworn to himself he would constantly remember—poor Linda, and his own murderous unkindness to her, and those loathsome twins, swarming like lice across the mystery of her death, insulting, with their presence, not merely his own grief and repentance, but the very gods themselves. He had sworn to remember, he had sworn unceasingly to make amends. And here was he, sitting happily over his bow-stave, singing, actually singing. . . .

He went indoors, opened the box of mustard, and put some water to boil on the fire.

Half an hour later, three Delta-Minus landworkers from one of the Puttenham Bokanovsky Groups happened to be driving to Elstead and, at the top of the hill, were astonished to see a young man standing outside the abandoned lighthouse stripped to the waist and hitting himself with a whip of knotted cords. His back was horizontally streaked with crimson, and from weal to weal ran thin trickles of blood. The driver of the lorry pulled up at the side of the road and, with his two companions, stared open-mouthed at the extraordinary spectacle. One, two, three —they counted the strokes. After the eighth, the young man interrupted his self-punishment to run to the wood's edge and there be violently sick. When he had finished, he picked up the whip and began hitting himself again. Nine, ten, eleven, twelve . . .

'Ford!' whispered the driver. And his twins were of the same opinion.

'Fordey!' they said.

Three days later, like turkey buzzards settling on a corpse, the reporters came.

Dried and hardened over a slow fire of green wood, the bow was ready. The Savage was busy on his arrows. Thirty hazel sticks had been whittled and dried, tipped with sharp nails, carefully nocked. He had made a raid one night on the Puttenham poultry farm, and now had feathers enough to equip a whole armoury. It was at work upon the feathering of his shafts that the first of the reporters found him. Noiseless on his pneumatic shoes, the man came up behind him.

'Good-morning, Mr. Savage,' he said. 'I am the representative of *The Hourly Radio*.'

Startled as though by the bite of a snake, the Savage sprang to his feet, scattering arrows, feathers, glue-pot and brush in all directions.

'I beg your pardon,' said the reporter, with genuine compunction. 'I had no intention . . .' He touched his hat—the aluminium stove-pipe hat in which he carried his wireless receiver and transmitter. 'Excuse my not taking it off,' he said. 'It's a bit heavy. Well, as I was saying, I am the representative of *The Hourly* . . .'

'What do you want?' asked the Savage, scowling. The reporter returned his most ingratiating smile.

'Well, of course, our readers would be profoundly interested . . .' He put his head on one side, his smile became almost coquettish. 'Just a few words from you, Mr. Savage.' And rapidly, with a series of ritual gestures, he uncoiled two wires connected to the portable battery buckled round his waist; plugged them simultaneously into the sides of his aluminium hat; touched a spring on the crown—and antennæ shot up into the air; touched another spring on the peak of the brim—and, like a jack-in-the-box, out jumped a microphone and hung there, quivering, six inches in front of his nose; pulled down a pair of receivers over his ears; pressed a switch on the left side of the hat—and from within came a faint waspy buzzing; turned a knob on the right—and the buzzing was interrupted by a stethoscopic wheeze and crackle, by hiccoughs and sudden squeaks. 'Hullo,' he said to the microphone, 'hullo, hullo . . .' A bell suddenly rang inside his hat. 'Is that you, Edzel? Primo Mellon speaking. Yes, I've got hold of him. Mr. Savage will now take the microphone and say a few words. Won't you, Mr. Savage?' He looked up at the Savage with another of those winning smiles of his. 'Just tell our readers why you came here. What made you leave London (hold on, Edzel!) so very suddenly. And, of course, that whip.' (The Savage started. How did they know about the whip?) 'We're all crazy to know about the whip. And then something about Civilization. You know the sort of stuff. "What I think of the Civilized Girl." Just a few words, a very few . . .'

The Savage obeyed with a disconcerting literalness. Five words he uttered and no more—five words, the same as those he had said to Bernard about the Arch-Community-Songster of Canterbury. '*Háni! Sons éso tse-ná!*' And seizing the reporter by the shoulder, he spun him round (the young man revealed himself invitingly well-covered), aimed and, with all the force and accuracy of a champion foot-and-mouth-baller, delivered a most prodigious kick.

Eight minutes later, a new edition of *The Hourly Radio* was on sale in the streets of London. 'HOURLY RADIO REPORTER HAS COCCYX KICKED BY MYSTERY SAVAGE,' ran the headlines on the front page. 'SENSATION IN SURREY.'

'Sensation even in London,' thought the reporter when, on his return, he read the words. And a very painful sensation, what was more. He sat down gingerly to his luncheon.

Undeterred by that cautionary bruise on their colleague's coccyx, four other reporters, representing the New York *Times*, the Frankfurt *Four-Dimensional Continuum*, *The Fordian Science*

Monitor, and *The Delta Mirror*, called that afternoon at the lighthouse and met with receptions of progressively increasing violence.

From a safe distance and still rubbing his buttocks, 'Benighted fool!' shouted the man from *The Fordian Science Monitor*, 'why don't you take *soma*?'

'Get away!' The Savage shook his fist.

The other retreated a few steps, then turned round again. 'Evil's an unreality if you take a couple of grammes.'

'*Kohakwa iyathtokyai!*' The tone was menacingly derisive. 'Pain's a delusion.'

'Oh, is it?' said the Savage and, picking up a thick hazel switch, strode forward.

The man from *The Fordian Science Monitor* made a dash for his helicopter.

After that the Savage was left for a time in peace. A few helicopters came and hovered inquisitively round the tower. He shot an arrow into the importunately nearest of them. It pierced the aluminium floor of the cabin; there was a shrill yell, and the machine went rocketing up into the air with all the acceleration that its super-charger could give it. The others, in future, kept their distance respectfully. Ignoring their tiresome humming (he likened himself in his imagination to one of the suitors of the Maiden of Mátsaki, unmoved and persistent among the winged vermin), the Savage dug at what was to be his garden. After a time the vermin evidently became bored and flew away; for hours at a stretch the sky above his head was empty and, but for the larks, silent.

The weather was breathlessly hot, there was thunder in the air. He had dug all the morning and was resting, stretched out along the floor. And suddenly the thought of Lenina was a real presence, naked and tangible, saying 'Sweet!' and 'Put your arms round me!'—in shoes and socks, perfumed. Impudent strumpet! But oh, oh, her arms round his neck, the lifting of her breasts, her mouth! Eternity was in our lips and eyes. Lenina

'... No, no, no, no! He sprang to his feet and, half naked as he was, ran out of the house. At the edge of the heath stood a clump of hoary juniper bushes. He flung himself against them, he embraced, not the smooth body of his desires, but an armful of green spikes. Sharp, with a thousand points, they pricked him. He tried to think of poor Linda, breathless and dumb, with her clutching hands and the unutterable terror in her eyes. Poor Linda whom he had sworn to remember. But it was still the presence of Lenina that haunted him. Lenina whom he had promised to forget. Even through the stab and sting of the juniper needles, his wincing flesh was aware of her, unescapably real. 'Sweet, sweet ... And if you wanted me too, why didn't you ...'

The whip was hanging on a nail by the door, ready to hand against the arrival of reporters. In a frenzy the Savage ran back to the house, seized it, whirled it. The knotted cords bit into his flesh.

'Strumpet! Strumpet!' he shouted at every blow as though it were Lenina (and how frantically, without knowing it, he wished it were!), white, warm, scented, infamous Lenina that he was flogging thus. 'Strumpet!' And then, in a voice of despair, 'Oh, Linda, forgive me. Forgive me, God. I'm bad. I'm wicked. I'm ... No, no, you strumpet, you strumpet!'

From his carefully constructed hide in the wood three hundred metres away, Darwin Bonaparte, the Feely Corporation's most expert big-game photographer, had watched the whole proceedings. Patience and skill had been rewarded. He had spent three days sitting inside the bole of an artificial oak tree, three nights crawling on his belly through the heather, hiding microphones in gorse bushes, burying wires in the soft grey sand. Seventy-two hours of profound discomfort. But now the great moment had come—the greatest, Darwin Bonaparte had time to reflect, as he moved among his instruments, the greatest since his taking of the famous all-howling stereoscopic feely of the gorillas' wedding. 'Splendid,' he said to himself, as the Savage started his astonishing performance. 'Splendid!' He kept his telescopic cameras carefully aimed—glued to their moving objective; clapped on a higher power to get a close-up of the frantic and distorted face (admirable!); switched over, for half a minute, to slow motion (an exquisitely comical effect, he promised himself); listened in, meanwhile, to the blows, the groans, the wild and raving words that were being recorded on the sound-track at the edge of his film, tried the effect of a little amplification (yes, that was decidedly better); was delighted to hear, in a momentary lull, the shrill singing of a lark; wished the Savage would turn round so that he could get a good close-up of the blood on his back—and almost instantly (what astonishing luck!) the accommodating fellow did turn round, and he was able to take a perfect close-up.

'Well, that was grand!' he said to himself when it was all over. 'Really grand!' He mopped his face. When they had put in the feely effects at the studio, it would be a wonderful film. Almost as good, thought Darwin Bonaparte, as the *Sperm Whale's Love-Life*—and that, by Ford, was saying a good deal!

Twelve days later *The Savage of Surrey* had been released and could be seen, heard and felt in every first-class feely-palace in Western Europe.

The effect of Darwin Bonaparte's film was immediate and enormous. On the afternoon which followed the evening of its release, John's rustic solitude was suddenly broken by the arrival overhead of a great swarm of helicopters.

He was digging in his garden—digging, too, in his own mind, laboriously turning up the substance of his thought. Death—and he drove in his spade once, and again, and yet again. And all our yesterdays have lighted fools the way to dusty death. A convincing thunder rumbled through the words. He lifted another spadeful of earth. Why had Linda died? Why had she been allowed to become gradually less than human and at last . . . He shuddered. A good kissing carrion. He planted his foot on his spade and stamped it fiercely into the tough ground. As flies to wanton boys are we to the gods; they kill us for their sport.

Thunder again; words that proclaimed themselves true—truer somehow than truth itself. And yet that same Gloucester had called them ever-gentle gods. Besides, thy best of rest is sleep, and that thou oft provok'st; yet grossly fear'st thy death which is no more. No more than sleep. Sleep. Perchance to dream. His spade struck against a stone; he stooped to pick it up. For in that sleep of death, what dreams . . . ?

A humming overhead had become a roar; and suddenly he was in shadow, there was something between the sun and him. He looked up, startled, from his digging, from his thoughts; looked up in a dazzled bewilderment, his mind still wandering in that other world of truer-than-truth, still focussed on the immensities of death and deity; looked up and saw, close above him, the swarm of hovering machines. Like locusts they came, hung poised, descended all around him on the heather. And from out of the bellies of these giant grasshoppers stepped men in white viscose-flannels, women (for the weather was hot) in acetate-shantung pyjamas or velveteen shorts and sleeveless, half-unzippered singlets—one couple from each. In a few minutes there were dozens of them, standing in a wide circle round the lighthouse, staring, laughing, clicking their cameras, throwing (as to an ape) pea-nuts, packets of sex-hormone chewing-gum, pan-glandular *petits beurres*. And every moment—for across the Hog's Back the stream of traffic now flowed unceasingly—their numbers increased. As in a nightmare, the dozens became scores, the scores hundreds.

The Savage had retreated towards cover, and now, in the posture of an animal at bay, stood with his back to the wall of the lighthouse, staring from face to face in speechless horror, like a man out of his senses.

From this stupor he was aroused to a more immediate sense of reality by the impact on his cheek of a well-aimed packet of chewing-gum. A shock of startling pain—and he was broad awake, awake and fiercely angry.

'Go away!' he shouted.

The ape had spoken; there was a burst of laughter and hand-clapping. 'Good old Savage! Hurrah, hurrah!' And through the babel he heard cries of: 'Whip, whip, the whip!'

Acting on the word's suggestion, he seized the bunch of knotted cords from its nail behind the door and shook it at his tormentors.

There was a yell of ironical applause.

Menacingly he advanced towards them. A woman cried out in fear. The line wavered at its most immediately threatened point, then stiffened again, stood firm. The consciousness of being in overwhelming force had given these sightseers a courage which the Savage had not expected of them. Taken aback, he halted and looked round.

'Why don't you leave me alone?' There was an almost plaintive note in his anger.

'Have a few magnesium-salted almonds!' said the man who, if the Savage were to advance, would be the first to be attacked. He held out a packet. 'They're really very good, you know,' he added, with a rather nervous smile of propitiation. 'And the magnesium salts will help to keep you young.'

The Savage ignored his offer. 'What do you want with me?' he asked, turning from one grinning face to another. 'What do you want with me?'

'The whip,' answered a hundred voices confusedly. 'Do the whipping stunt. Let's see the whipping stunt.'

Then, in unison and on a slow, heavy rhythm, 'We—want—the whip,' shouted a group at the end of the line. 'We—want—the whip.'

Others at once took up the cry, and the phrase was repeated, parrot-fashion, again and again, with an ever-growing volume of sound, until, by the seventh or eighth reiteration, no other word was being spoken. 'We—want—the whip.'

They were all crying together; and, intoxicated by the noise, the unanimity, the sense of rhythmical atonement, they might, it seemed, have gone on for hours—almost indefinitely. But at about the twenty-fifth repetition the proceedings were startlingly interrupted. Yet another helicopter had arrived from across the Hog's Back, hung poised above the crowd, then dropped within a few yards of where the Savage was standing, in the open space between the line of sightseers and the lighthouse. The roar of the air screws momentarily drowned the shouting; then, as the machine touched the ground and the engines were turned off: 'We—want—the whip; we—want—the whip,' broke out again in the same loud, insistent monotone.

The door of the helicopter opened, and out stepped, first a fair and ruddy-faced young man, then, in green velveteen shorts, white shirt, and jockey cap, a young woman.

At the sight of the young woman, the Savage started, recoiled, turned pale.

The young woman stood, smiling at him—an uncertain, imploring, almost abject smile. The seconds passed. Her lips moved, she was saying something; but the sound of her voice was covered by the loud reiterated refrain of the sightseers.

'We—want—the whip! We—want—the whip!'

The young woman pressed both hands to her left side, and on that peach-bright, doll-beautiful face of hers appeared a strangely incongruous expression of yearning distress. Her blue eyes seemed to grow larger, brighter; and suddenly two tears rolled down her cheeks. Inaudibly, she spoke again; then, with a quick, impassioned gesture, stretched out her arms towards the Savage, stepped forward.

'We—want—the whip! We—want . . .'

And all of a sudden they had what they wanted.

'Strumpet!' The Savage had rushed at her like a madman. 'Fitchew!' Like a madman, he was slashing at her with his whip of small cords.

Terrified, she had turned to flee, had tripped and fallen in the heather. 'Henry, Henry!' she shouted. But her ruddy-faced companion had bolted out of harm's way behind the helicopter.

With a whoop of delighted excitement the line broke; there

was a convergent stampede towards that magnetic centre of attraction. Pain was a fascinating horror.

'Fry, lechery, fry!' Frenzied, the Savage slashed again.

Hungrily they gathered round, pushing and scrambling like swine about the trough.

'Oh, the flesh!' The Savage ground his teeth. This time it was on his shoulders that the whip descended. 'Kill it, kill it!'

Drawn by the fascination of the horror of pain and, from within, impelled by that habit of co-operation, that desire for unanimity and atonement, which their conditioning had so ineradicably implanted in them, they began to mime the frenzy of his gestures, striking at one another as the Savage struck at his own rebellious flesh, or at that plump incarnation of turpitude writhing in the heather at his feet.

'Kill it, kill it, kill it . . .' the Savage went on shouting.

Then suddenly somebody started singing 'Orgy-porgy,' and in a moment they had all caught up the refrain and, singing, had begun to dance. Orgy-porgy, round and round and round, beating one another in six-eight time. Orgy-porgy . . .

It was after midnight when the last of the helicopters took its flight. Stupefied by *soma*, and exhausted by a long-drawn frenzy of sensuality, the Savage lay sleeping in the heather. The sun was already high when he awoke. He lay for a moment, blinking in owlish incomprehension at the light; then suddenly remembered—everything.

'Oh, my God, my God!' He covered his eyes with his hand.

That evening the swarm of helicopters that came buzzing across the Hog's Back was a dark cloud ten kilometres long. The description of last night's orgy of atonement had been in all the papers.

'Savage!' called the first arrivals, as they alighted from their machine. 'Mr. Savage!'

There was no answer.

The door of the lighthouse was ajar. They pushed it open and walked into a shuttered twilight. Through an archway on the further side of the room they could see the bottom of the staircase that led up to the higher floors. Just under the crown of the arch dangled a pair of feet.

'Mr. Savage!'

Slowly, very slowly, like two unhurried compass needles, the feet turned towards the right; north, north-east, east, south-east, south, south-south-west; then paused, and, after a few seconds, turned as unhurriedly back towards the left. South-south-west, south, south-east, east . . .

Notes

The notes in this edition are intended to serve the needs of overseas students as well as those of British-born users.

> *Brave New World:* the title is taken from *The Tempest*, Act V, Scene I. For a discussion of Huxley's use of literary sources see *Introduction*, pages xii–xv. As there are about fifty more Shakespearean quotations in the book these notes will usually only give references. (Any work for which no writer is mentioned is a play by Shakespeare.)

xxiv *Nicholas Berdiaeff:* (1874–1948), Russian revolutionary, agitator and student of Marx, elected to the Chair of Philosophy at Moscow University in 1917, but was expelled from the country in 1922. He is principally remembered for putting forward a religious interpretation of social developments.

> It seems that utopias are much more easily achieved than we once thought. In our time we have to face a far more agonizing question: How can we prevent them from being finally achieved? ... Utopias can be achieved. Life moves on towards Utopia. And perhaps a new age is beginning, an age when intellectuals and men of education will try to devise some means of steering clear of utopias, and returning to a society that is not utopian, with less 'perfection' and more freedom.

Foreword

Points in the 1946 Foreword are only dealt with if they are not covered by the notes on the main body of the novel.

xxv *Utopia:* most famous work of Sir Thomas More (1478–1535), published in 1516. The subject is the search for the best form of government. The book takes the form of a description of the land of Utopia, 'Nowhere land', by a traveller, Raphael Hythloday. The word has come to mean any ideal state of affairs.

xxvi *Pyrrhonic:* sceptical. Pyrrho of Elis (lived about 300 BC) was the founder of the first school of Greek sceptic philosophy, the doctrine of the impossibility of attaining certainty of knowledge.

aesthete: one who pretends to have a great love of the arts and is not interested in practical affairs.

having compiled an anthology . . . : The Perennial Philosophy, published in 1945.

Pantheon: usually a building for the worship of all the gods revered in a certain area, but in this context a place where famous men are buried.

ossuary: vault for the bones of the dead, a charnel-house.

SI MONUMENTUM REQUIRIS CIRCUMSPICE: 'If you would see his monument, look around.' The epitaph of Sir Christopher Wren (1632–1723), inscribed over the interior of the north door of St Paul's Cathedral in London – his most famous work.

xxvii *Henry-Georgian:* the fundamental doctrine of Henry George (1839–97) was the equal right of all men to the use of the earth. This was not original but his proposition of the *Single Tax*, a practical enforcement of his ideas, was new. He suggested that there should be no private ownership of land, and that a system of ground rent should be the basic form of taxation.

Kropotkinesque: Prince Peter Alexeivich Kropotkin (1842–1921) championed a system of government based on a level of cooperation which makes it unnecessary for laws to be enforced from above.

immanent: inherent, indwelling.

Tao: universal cosmic energy behind the visible order of

nature, upon which the religion of Taoism is based.

Logos: Greek word meaning 'word' or 'reason' which is used in Christian theology to signify God from eternity who became incarnate in the man, Jesus Christ of Nazareth.

Brahman: universal or supreme soul in Hinduism.

Higher Utilitarianism: form of ethical doctrine which teaches that conduct is morally good as long as it promotes the greatest happiness of the greatest number of people. This philosophy was developed by Jeremy Bentham (1748–1832) and John Stuart Mill (1806–73).

xxviii *Robert Nichols:* (1893–1944), contemporary of Huxley's. The play is *Wings over Europe*, first presented in New York in 1928 and in London in 1932.

Marquis de Sade: notorious French writer (1740–1814) whose activities and writings gave rise to the term 'sadism', a form of sexual perversion marked by a love of cruelty.

Robespierre: Isidore Maximilien de Robespierre (1758–94) was one of the leaders of the Reign of Terror during the French Revolution, but was himself overthrown and executed.

Babeuf: François Noel Babeuf (1760–97), contemporary of Robespierre, whose importance lies in his being the first to propound socialism as a practical policy.

xxx *Bolshevism:* doctrine of the extreme left wing of the Russian Social Democratic Party during the Russian Revolution.

Fascism: originally the doctrine of the nationalist Fascist party which came into power in Italy under Mussolini in 1922. However, it became a general term describing the regimes of Hitler in Germany, Franco in Spain and Mussolini in Italy.

Hiroshima: on 6 August 1945 the first atomic bomb to be used in war was dropped on the Japanese city of Hiroshima.

Magdeburg: in 1631, during the Thirty Years War, the

whole of the German town of Magdeburg, except for the cathedral and about 140 houses, was burned to the ground, and most of the inhabitants were killed.

Procrustes: according to the Greek legend the robber Procrustes used to tie travellers to a bed and stretch or mutilate them until they were of the right size.

xxxi *statism:* subservience of all personal considerations to the interests of the state.

Voltaire: name assumed by François Marie Arouet (1694–1778), and by which he is generally known. At the age of ten he was sent to the Collège Louis-le-Grand which was run by the Jesuits, but in his writings he was violently opposed to the Roman Catholic Church.

'iron curtain': phrase which has been used since at least 1920 to describe the borders of the Soviet Union or countries under its direct influence.

Manhattan Projects: in June 1942 the United States War Department organized a new district in the corps of engineers to develop the work on the atomic bomb. This was known as the Manhattan District, and its work was known as the Manhattan Project.

xxxii *scopolamine:* used in combination with morphine for an anaesthetic, or as a hypnotic in delirium or to produce twilight sleep. It is popularly known as a 'truth drug'.

eugenics: the science adapted to the production of first-rate offspring, especially in human beings.

Chapter I

1 *COMMUNITY, IDENTITY, STABILITY:* compare *Liberté! Egalité! Fraternité,* (Liberty! Equality! Brotherhood!) – the slogan of the French Revolution.

2 *fret-sawyers:* fret-saws have a narrow blade and fine teeth, and are used for shaping ornamental carved wood.

AF *632:* in Chapter III it is explained that the introduction of the first T-Model Ford was chosen as the opening of the new era. The commercial launch of the T-Model was in 1908, so the year After Ford 632 is AD 2540.

ova: eggs in the female reproductive cells.

gametes: reproductive cells which unite at fertilization.

thermogene: device for keeping blood warm.

3 *salinity:* degree to which something is composed of salt.

viscosity: quality of being between solid and fluid.

bouillon: broth or soup.

Alphas and Betas ... Gammas, Deltas and Epsilons: first five letters of the Greek alphabet.

Bokanovsky's Process: Maurice Bokanowski (1879–1928), French politician who was an expert on economic and financial matters. He was killed in an air crash soon after being appointed Minister for Commerce. Huxley may have used his name because Bokanovsky's Process has economic rather than human considerations behind it.

4 *burgeoned:* put out shoots or buds.

viviparous: producing living young that have reached an advanced stage of development.

5 *Podsnap's Technique:* Mr Podsnap is a self-satisfied character in Charles Dickens's novel *Our Mutual Friend.*

Mr Foster: Sir Michael Foster (1836–1907), friend of T H Huxley, Aldous' grandfather. Foster succeeded T H Huxley as Fullerian Professor of Physiology at the Royal Institution, and in 1870 left London for Cambridge where he had a very large share in the organization and development of the Biological School. Mr Foster's first name, Henry, which we discover at the end of the chapter, is of course borrowed from Henry Ford.

Mombasa: in 1931 the chief port of Kenya Colony, East Africa.

6 *pituitary:* small gland at the base of the brain which is very important in controlling many bodily functions such as growth. It secretes hormones, the chemical communica-

tors which regulate many physiological processes of the body.

peritoneum: membrane which lines the cavity of the abdomen.

morula: state of development of an ovum at which it has become completely segmented.

7 *lupus:* ulcerous disease of the skin which can either eat it away or cause excessive growth.

8 *demijohn:* large two-handled bottle containing as much as fifteen gallons (68 litres); the standard size holds about five gallons (22.7 litres).

placentin: extract from the placenta, the organ to which the foetus is attached and through which it is nourished.

thyroxin: hormone extract from the thyroid gland which has great influence on growth of body.

'corpus luteum': structure which forms in the ovary after the egg has been released. It produces the hormone progesterone, which maintains the uterine lining in readiness for fertilization and implantation of the embryo. If fertilization does not take place the *corpus luteum* degenerates.

blood-surrogate: substitute for the blood of the mother.

9 *freemartin*: hermaphrodite, looking like a woman but incapable of producing children. The term was originally used of cattle.

10 *Consider the horse:* this is the first direct allusion to Dickens' *Hard Times*. In Chapter 2, Sissy Jupe, whose father works in a travelling circus, cannot provide a factual definition of a horse for Mr Gradgrind, the owner of a 'model school'. Mr Gradgrind's world is too narrow and factual to understand the wonder and fantasy a circus horse might inspire in a child. Later in the same chapter the children are told that they should never paper a room with pictures of horses because they never see horses walking up and down the sides of rooms in reality.

11 *endocrine:* glands without ducts, such as the thyroid or

pituitary. They secrete the hormones directly into the blood.

Pilkington: the glassmaking company of Pilkington at St Helens near Liverpool was technically one of the most advanced plate-glassmakers in the world. It had generated publicity in the late 1920s through its new product vitaglass which Huxley has made into one of the main building materials in evidence at Eton (see note to page 131).

12 *acetate:* form of artificial silk.

Lenina: Vladimir Ilyich Ulyanov (1870–1924) adopted the name Lenin in 1901. He founded the Communist Party in Russia, led the October Revolution in 1917, and ruled the country until his death.

Chapter II

14 *NEO-PAVLOVIAN:* Ivan Petrovich Pavlov (1849–1936) is most widely known for his work with dogs, which led to discovery of the 'conditioned reflex' or acquired automatic response. This is a basis of the behaviourist school of psychology which analyzes behaviour through our conditioned responses rather than heredity.

viscose: special form of cotton pulp, normally applied to various industrial purposes.

aseptically: so as to avoid causing infection.

Aryan: originally meaning coming from a large group of Indo-European peoples; but in this context, having white or pink skin.

apoplectic: red-faced.

posthumous: after death.

quartos: large books; the usual size of the quarto page is about 30 cm by 20 cm.

dumb-waiter: movable table for serving food at meals.

17 *gratuitous:* provided freely.

18 *Bernard Shaw:* (1856–1950), Irish playwright and critic with a great reputation for abrasiveness in public debate.

19 *T-Model:* see note to page 2.
20 *sibilant:* hissing consonant sounds, as in *s* and *z*.
    categorical imperative: term first used in the writings of the philosopher Immanuel Kant (1724–1804), meaning the absolute unconditional command of the moral law.
21 *asafoetida:* gum, smelling strongly like garlic and onions, which is used in medicine as an anti-spasmodic.

Chapter III

23 *boskage:* old-fashioned poetical word meaning wooded undergrowth.
    Centrifugal Bumble-puppy: Bumble-puppy is first recorded at the beginning of the nineteenth century as an outdoor game resembling bagatelle. More recently the name has been applied to a game played with a tennis ball attached by elastic to a fixed post.
24 *'What's your name?':* another echo of the second chapter of *Hard Times*, when Mr Gradgrind rebukes Sissy Jupe for saying her name is Sissy. 'Sissy is not a name,' said Mr Gradgrind. 'Don't call yourself Sissy. Call yourself Cecilia.'
    Polly Trotsky: Lev Davidovich Trotsky (1879–1940) was Lenin's chief partner in organizing the Russian Revolution. By the time *Brave New World* was written he had been expelled from the Communist Party and from Russia.
25 *auto-eroticism:* masturbation.
    Mustapha Mond: Mustapha Kemal Atatürk (1880–1938), reviver of Turkish Nationalism after the First World War. Ludwig Mond (1839–1909), co-founder of the great chemical manufacturing firm of Brunner, Mond and Co which was one of the first companies in Britain to adopt an eight-hour day and to provide model dwellings and playing fields for their workers.
26 *Discarnate:* disembodied.
    Bernard Marx: the first name may be taken from Bernard

Shaw (see note to page 18), or from Claude Bernard (1813–78), French physiologist, founder of experimental medicine.

The major work of Karl Marx (1818–83) was *Das Kapital*. In it he analyzes the free enterprise system and criticizes it severely. Together with Friedrich Engels (see note to page 66), who edited the second and third volumes of *Das Kapital* after Marx's death, he wrote the *Manifesto of the Communist Party* in 1848.

Lenina Crowne: the seventeenth-century dramatist John Crowne was well known for his easy living. Perhaps Lenina's character is rather like his.

History is bunk: remark made by Henry Ford in the witness box during a libel suit against the *Chicago Tribune* in July 1919.

Harappa...Mycenae: sites of some of the most famous archaeological discoveries where remains of great empires and civilizations have been found. Excavations begun in the 1920s showed Harappa in the Punjab to have been one of the capitals of the people of the Indus civilization. Sir Leonard Wooley's book *Ur of the Chaldees*, a popular account of his discoveries at this Sumerian site south of Babylon and the reputed early home of Abraham, was published in 1929. *Thebes* was the Greek name for the capital of Upper Egypt, the civilization which left such spectacular remains as the tomb of Tutankhamen. The city of Thebes in Greece played an important part in Greek history and was the scene of the story of Oedipus. However the link of all these names being important archaeological sites suggests that Huxley is referring to the Egyptian Thebes. *Babylon* was one of the centres of the ancient Assyrian Empire. The palace of *Cnossos* (sometimes spelled Knossos), in Crete, is a remarkable monument of early Mediterranean civilization. At almost the same time as Cnossos flourished so did *Mycenae*, site of some amazing finds from bronze-age Greece, and the home of Agamemnon.

Odysseus: the wanderings of Odysseus, King of Ithaca, after the Trojan War are the subject of Homer's *Odyssey.* His twenty-year absence from his home makes his sufferings a classical parallel to those of the biblical Job.

Job: the main subject of the Book of Job is the problem of innocent suffering, illustrated in the figure of Job himself.

27 *Jupiter:* originally the elemental god of the Romans. He came to be identified with the Greek Zeus.

Gotama: (sometimes spelled Gautama) the Buddah.

Middle Kingdom: period of Egyptian history dated as 1991 –1786 BC. This was Dynasty XII under which Egypt flourished politically and culturally.

Pascal: Blaise Pascal (1623–62), French religious philosopher who in his *Pensées* (Thoughts), hoped to demonstrate the truth of Christianity by the presentation of facts and fulfilment of prophecy, and by an appeal to people's innermost emotions.

Alhambra: popular name for cinemas, taken from the Palace of the Moorish kings at Granada.

There's a love scene on a bearskin rug: reference to Elinor Glyn's *Three Weeks*, a popular novel published in 1907 containing several scenes of passionate love, most of which take place on a tiger skin.

Huxley's contempt for her novels is seen in a letter to his father, Leonard Huxley, in November 1915, when he reflected on how odd it was that D H Lawrence's *The Rainbow* should have been suppressed: 'It is always the serious books that get sat on – how much better to suppress Mrs Glyn.'

29 *eau-de-Cologne:* perfume first made at Cologne, West Germany, in 1709.

chypre: exotic perfume from Cyprus.

midden: dunghill, refuse dump.

30 *Dr Wells:* see *Introduction*, page xiv, for some remarks about the novelist H G Wells (1886–1946).

OVARIN: extract from the ovary.

Our Freud: Sigmund Freud (1856–1939), known as the inventor of psychoanalysis. One of his conclusions was that there is an unconscious element in the mind which influences consciousness.

Samoa: Pacific island to the north east of Fiji.

hibiscus: tropical species of hibiscus are evergreen shrubs with large exotic flowers.

31 *Trobriands:* group of islands near Papua New Guinea in the south west Pacific. The islanders are divided into four matrilineal clans, each with its own chief.

35 *Ford's in his flivver . . . All's well with the world:* The DHC's version of Browning's lines from *Pippa Passes:* 'God's in his heaven – All's right with the world!' *Flivver* was slang for a cheap car or aeroplane, but it was also used to mean a failure or disaster. Presumably this second meaning had died out by the year AF 623, though Huxley's readers could be expected to know it.

Wonderfully pneumatic: this use of pneumatic may have been suggested by a verse in T S Eliot's poem *Whispers of Immortality*, published in 1920:

> Grishkin is nice: her Russian eye
> Is underlined for emphasis;
> Uncorseted, her friendly bust
> Gives promise of pneumatic bliss.

More than half of the instances of 'pneumatic' in the novel are appreciative remarks about female charms.

37 *Ectogenesis:* producing babies outside the mother.

Pfitzner: Hans Pfitzner (1869–1949), musician whose works have never been well received outside German-speaking countries; his music is often considered unoriginal in style.

Kawaguchi: in *On The Margin*, published in 1923, Huxley wrote an essay reviewing a book called *Three Years in Tibet* by the Shramana Ekai Kawaguchi, Late Rector of

Gohyakurakan Monastery, Japan. Huxley mocks the appalling backwardness and corruption of Tibetan society which the Japanese monk described, though saying of the writer: 'a more charming and sympathetic character never revealed himself in a book'.

38 *Phosgene . . . dichlorethyl sulphide:* all are poisonous gases which would revive horrific memories of gas warfare for Huxley's early readers. Two hundred parts per million in the air of *phosgene*, carbonyl chloride, constitute a fatal dose within two minutes. *Chloropicrin* is also an acute lung irritant introduced in 1916 and used by both sides in the First World War. *Ethyl iodoacetate* induces tears and makes vision impossible by its irritant action on the eyes. *Diphenylcyanarsine* attacks the eyes, nose and chest, and *trichlormethl chloroformate* the lungs. *Dichlorethyl sulphide* is more widely known as mustard gas, primarily an incapacitating agent and called 'king of gases' for its effectiveness in causing casualties.

hydrocyanic acid: immediately fatal in a concentration of one part to two thousand parts air.

Kurfurstendamm: one of the chief streets in the fashionable south west quarter of Berlin.

Eighth Arrondissement: in Paris, the Eighth Arrondissement, the Élysée, covers the fashionable central part of the city including the Champs Élysées.

39 *anthrax bombs:* although it is a distortion of the book to read *Brave New World* as a series of prophecies and to award Huxley metaphorical points for accurate predictions, his projection of anthrax bombs is remarkable as an informed scientific guess for 1931. In the BBC television programme *Newsnight* in May 1981 it was revealed that British military planners were ready in certain circumstances to use two thousand seven hundred aircraft to bomb Germany with anthrax weapons in 1945. It was estimated that three million Germans would have died in Berlin, Hamburg, Stuttgart, Frankfurt, Wilhelmshafen and

Aachen, the chosen targets, and that these areas would still be uninhabitable after thirty-six years.

To most bacteriologists who had considered the idea of using germs as a weapon, anthrax was the logical first choice: its spores are strong enough to withstand being dispersed in the air by an explosion, and they can be manufactured with relative ease. Huxley was even right in projecting that the noise of the bombs exploding would be 'hardly louder than the popping of a paper bag'.

$CH_3C_6H_2(NO_2)_3$ + $Hg(CNO)_2$: TNT (Trinitrotoluene) and mercury fulminate, its detonator. Probably the most powerful chemical explosion known at the time.

41 *Golders Green:* area of north London.

42 *morocco-surrogate:* substitute for goat- or sheep-skin leather.

Malthusian belt: Rev Thomas Malthus (1766–1834) influenced public opinion in the first half of the nineteenth century with his views on population control. His essay *The Principle of Population* held war, disease and moral restraint as the possible controls on population growth. In the 1920s, when the spectre of over-population began once more to concern people, his reputation started to rise again.

bandolier: broad belt worn over the shoulder and across the breast.

43 *T-Model:* see note to page 2.

45 *'soma':* intoxicating drink holding a prominent place in the ritual and religion of Vedic India.

46 *Gonadal:* gonads is the general term for the sex organs, either the ovary or testes.

stigmata: marks of disgrace.

Chapter IV

48 *George Edzel:* Edsel B Ford (1893–1943), President of the

Ford Company from 1919 to 1943, was Henry Ford's only son.

parathyroid: small endocrine (see note to page 11) organ, embedded in the thyroid, which controls the calcium and phosphorus levels in the body.

Benito Hoover: Benito Mussolini (1883–1945), Fascist Italian dictator who came to power in 1922. Herbert Clark Hoover (1974–1964), elected thirty-first President of the USA in 1928. At the time Huxley was writing *Brave New World*, Hoover's popularity had declined as a result of the Stock Exchange crash of 1929, and his Republican Party had suffered enormous reverses in the Congressional elections of 1930.

49 *Charing-T:* Charing Cross in central London is traditionally the place from which all distances to the capital are measured.

Hampstead: area of north London where Huxley and his wife lived for the first eighteen months of their marriage.

simian: ape-like.

52 *Shepherd's Bush ... Notting Hill ... Willesden ... Ealing ... Hounslow ... Brentford:* areas of west London which would be visible on such a helicopter journey as described.

Riemann-surface: Georg Friedrich Riemann (1826–66), one of the most creative mathematicians of the nineteenth century whose bold theories concerning the geometry of space led to the idea of the Riemann surface. In mathematical terms this is a multi-layered surface on which a multi-valued function of a complex variable can be interpreted as a single-valued variable. Such a surface would be saddle-shaped.

Escalator Fives Courts: fives is a game which is played by striking a ball with the hands against the walls of a special court.

revitrifying: re-covering with a molten glassy surface.

incandescence: glow of heat.

aphides: greenflies.

Stoke Poges: village in Buckinghamshire. Thomas Gray the poet is buried in the churchyard, which is the setting for his *Elegy Written in a Country Churchyard.*

55 *Fleet Street:* centre of London's newspaper industry.

Helmholtz Watson: Hermann Ludwig Ferdinand von Helmholtz (1821–94), German philosopher and man of science who denied the doctrine of innate ideas and held that all knowledge is founded on experience, hereditarily transmitted or acquired.

John Broadus Watson (1878–1958), American psychologist, known as the leading exponent in his day of behaviourism. (See note to page 14 on *Neo-Pavlovian.*) Some of his experimental work on conditioning human emotional reaction, such as linking loud noise with a loss of support, is disturbingly similar to the events at the beginning of Chapter II.

56 *Exmoor:* area of outstanding natural beauty on the borders of Somerset and Devon.

57 *asceticism:* rigorous self-discipline.

Chapter V

60 *By eight o'clock . . . Farnham Royal:* the loudspeaker and the cattle are the equivalent of the curfew and the 'lowing herd' in the first verse of Thomas Gray's *Elegy Written in a Country Churchyard.*

Farnham Royal . . . Burnham Beeches: two famous golf courses.

pullulation: teeming, swarming – not a word usually applied to human activity.

Slough: town eighteen miles (29 km) west of London.

61 *P_2O_5:* phosphorus pentoxide, from which phosphoric acid and numerous commercial phosphates are prepared.

63 *CALVIN STOPES:* John Calvin (1509–64) preached a rigorously protestant form of Christianity which held to

Scripture as the only rule of faith and asserted absolute predestination. Marie Stopes (1880–1958), co-founder with her husband H V Rose of the Mothers' Clinic for constructive birth control. She became President of the Society for Constructive Birth Control and Racial Progress.

ambergris and sandalwood: ambergris is a waxlike substance of marbled ashy colour, used in perfumery; sandalwood is a scented wood used for the same purposes.

deturgescence: progressive decrease in volume.

'*diminuendo*': musical term for a passage in which there is a gradual decrease in force or loudness of tone.

65 *Aphroditaeum:* Aprodite was the Greek goddess of love and beauty. In 1921 Huxley had been elected to the Athenaeum Club in London.

Carrara: Italian town in Tuscany, famous for its marble quarries which have been worked for over two thousand years. The best marble from Carrara is peculiarly white and flawless.

Ludgate Hill: site of St Paul's Cathedral in the City of London.

66 *Morgana Rothschild:* John Pierpont Morgan (1837–1913) and his son, John Pierpont Morgan, Junior (1867–1945) became symbols of enormous financial power in America. Thomas Hunt Morgan (1866–1945), was an American biologist whose work on heredity and mutation won a Nobel Prize in 1933.

The bewitching effect Morgana Rothschild has on Bernard Marx suggests that Huxley may have had in mind Morgan le Fay, known as Morgana Fata, one of King Arthur's sisters who possessed magic powers and who tried to kill Arthur in several versions of the Arthurian legend.

Rothschild is the name of a Jewish family whose financial businesses in Vienna, London, Paris and Naples flourished in the nineteenth century, and led to their name coming to symbolize vast wealth.

Fifi Bradlaugh: Charles Bradlaugh (1833–91), famous for his protracted battle over taking his seat in the House of Commons after being elected MP in 1880 for Northampton. The issue was whether an atheist, as Bradlaugh was, should be allowed to swear an oath of loyalty. The matter was not resolved until 1886 when a new Speaker insisted on Bradlaugh's being allowed to take the oath. His name being borrowed for *Brave New World* probably owes more to his work with the Malthusian League, and his prosecution in 1877 for selling a pamphlet by Dr Charles Knowlton, called *The Fruits of Philisophy* – an action which gave enormous publicity to birth control methods.

Joanna Diesel: Rudolf Diesel (1858–1913), German engineer whose principal achievement was the invention of the diesel engine, though he did not live to see its possibilities fully exploited. Between 1926 and 1929 there was a rapid advance in the use of the diesel engine.

Clara Deterding: in 1887 Henry Ford married Clara Bryant. Sir Henri Wilhelm August Deterding (1886–1939) gives a fair summary of his own significance in the title of his book *An International Oilman*, published in 1934. He had been Director General of the Royal Dutch Petroleum Company and was a director of Shell.

Tom Kawaguchi: see note to page 37.

Sarojini Engels: in a letter to his brother Julian, dated 4 October 1925, Huxley describes meeting in Bombay Mrs Sarojini Naidu, 'who seems to be one of the most important political leaders in the country, after Ghandi and Nehru'.

Friedrich Engels (1820–95), close associate of Karl Marx. He was the son of a wealthy cotton spinner and came to live in England where his father's firm had a factory near Manchester. His most famous publication is *The Condition of the Working Classes in 1844*.

Herbert Bakunin: Herbert Spencer (1820–1903), pioneer of sociology. The major concern of his writings was the application of the doctrine of evolution to man in society. In *Brave New World Revisited*, published in 1959, Huxley is scathing about Spencer's claims.

Herbert was also the first name of President Hoover (see note to page 48).

Mikhail Bakunin (1814–76), Russian anarchist, but a particularly autocratic organizer of anarchist groups. His chief principles are set out in *God and the State*, published in 1882, and in his letters. He was an atheist who saw violent uprising as the only possible liberation from the oppression of the State.

plangently: with a resounding sound such as the breaking of waves on the shore.

67 *yearning bowels of compassion:* deliberate use of the language of committed religious passion. The phrase occurs in the First Epistle General of John, Chapter 3, verse 17: 'But whoso hath this world's good, and seeth his brother have need, and shutteth up his bowels of compassion from him, how dwelleth the love of God in him?'

Come, Greater Being...: based on the hymn by Bishop J Cosin (1594–1672), the first verse of which is:

Come, Holy Ghost, our souls inspire,
And lighten with celestial fire;
Thou the anointing spirit art,
Who dost thy sevenfold gifts impart.

70 *Orgy-porgy...:* the original version of the nursery rhyme is:

Georgie Porgie, pudding and pie,
Kissed the girls and made them cry;

When the boys came out to play
Georgie Porgie ran away.

Chapter VI

72 *Jean-Jacques Habibullah:* the most popular teaching of Jean-Jacques Rousseau (1712–78) was the superiority of the 'noble savage' to civilized man. Habibullah Khan (1872–1919) succeeded his father Abd-er-Rahman as Amir of Afghanistan in 1901, a title he held until his assassination. He was a loyal friend of Britain and an enthusiast for Western civilization. He played golf and insisted on his courtiers wearing European dress.

73 *Torquay:* holiday resort in Devon on the south west coast of England.

Oxford Union: distinguished social and debating club in the University at Oxford.

St Andrews: perhaps the most famous golf course in the world, on the east coast of Scotland.

Skiddaw: mountain overlooking Derwentwater and the town of Keswick in the English Lake District.

79 *solecism:* flagrant breaking of the rules of good taste and conduct.

82 *Santa Fé:* state capital of New Mexico since 1912 when it was admitted to the United States of America.

Aurora Bora Palace: the hotel at the North Pole takes its name from the Aurora Borealis, a phenomenon of the atmosphere which can take the form of great waves of light crossing the sky.

hot contraceptives: Huxley's jokes should not always be taken literally.

83 *brachycephalic:* short-headed. Technically the term is used of a skull of which the breadth is at least four-fifths of the length.

Grand Canyon: spectacular gorge of the Colorado river in Arizona, USA.

85 *Zuñi:* name of a tribe and their language and homeland among the Pueblo Indians of New Mexico. (See the introductory note for Chapter VII.)

Athapascan: (sometimes spelled Athabascan), group of tribes of North American Indians, whose languages were closely related to one another. None of them developed a significant degree of cultural advancement beyond efficient hunting techniques.

86 *octoroon:* person having one-eighth Negro blood.

pueblos: permanent Indian towns or villages, usually sited at the foot of a hill or mountain, but sometimes perched on cliff edges.

Malpais: in New Mexico, nearly 300 miles (480 km) south of Santa Fé, and close to the Mexican border.

mesa: high tableland.

fulminated: literally, struck with lightning.

87 *Taos . . . Ojo Caliente:* settlements or tribal areas of New Mexico's Pueblo Indians. Some of them such as *Laguna* and *Acoma*, were still important centres when Huxley was writing, but some, like *Pojoaque*, had been abandoned. This is not a route, or if it is, it is more of a roundabout tour, as a southward flight from *Taos* would cross *Nambe* and *Picuris* before reaching *Tesuque*.

Chapter VII

In this and the following chapter, Huxley shows considerable knowledge about the world of the Pueblo Indians, but it is important to realize that his portrait of the Savage's home is a deliberate distortion of Pueblo culture and not an accurate description.

The setting of the mesa and the pueblo is convincingly detailed, and a study of photographs of New Mexico pueblos such as the magnificent collection in *Pueblo Mountain, Village, Dance* by Vincent Scully (published by

233

Thames and Hudson 1975) will give the reader a vivid picture of the scenery.

Huxley had not visited this part of the United States before writing *Brave New World*, but his experience of editing D H Lawrence's letters for publication and his friendship with the writer would have ensured that he had received a clear impression of New Mexico. Lawrence and his wife had lived for a time at Taos and at a nearby ranch, and Huxley's description of the Indians' ceremonies contains echoes of Lawrence's essay *The Hopi Snake Dance*. Indeed, the powerful emotional and religious feelings of the Savage bear comparison with Lawrence's statement from a letter in 1928 that: 'Curious as it may sound, it was New Mexico that liberated me from the present era of civilization, the great era of material and mechanical development.'

The available literature on Pueblo Indians is rather formidable and sometimes contradictory, and these notes rely on three works in particular. M C Stevenson's *The Zuñi Indians* was published in 1904 as the Annual Report of the Bureau of American Ethnology, and was the first full-scale study made of these people. Chapter 4 of Ruth Benedict's *Patterns of Culture* (1935) is a thorough investigation into the Pueblos of New Mexico. In 1935 the University of Chicago Press published E C Parsons' magisterial two-volume work, *Pueblo Indian Religion*. A less scholarly and more anecdotal note is struck by Leo Crane's study, *Desert Drums*, published in 1928.

The ceremony which so terrifies Lenina has elements of the Corn Dance, the Snake Dance and a complicated occasional ceremony at Zuñi known as the Whipping of Children. There is clearly a mixture of tribal and Roman Catholic faiths in the beliefs of the Pueblo Indians, but anthropologists disagree about the extent of this mingling. Similarly, the degree to which the Penitentes of New Mexico (whose customs are illustrated in an Eton Geography lesson in Chapter XI) are separate from the Pueblo Indians is not at all certain. Benedict says that they are the last surviving sect of the Flagellants of mediaeval Spain, but Parsons suggests that the many Pueblo ceremonies which involve whipping rites may trace some of their developments to imitation of the Spanish. Crane cheerfully dismisses the flagellants as 'crack-brained' and sees no connection between them and the Indians, saying that they form 'a curious commentary on the state of civilization among the lower-class Mexicans in certain backwaters of New Mexico'.

The *peyotl*, to which Linda becomes practically addicted, is not a characteristic drink of the Pueblo Indians, most of whom regard with horror deliberately induced hallucinations. On the other hand, the attack on her by the jealous wives is recorded as normal Zuñi behaviour in such circumstances.

89 *ochre:* clay which varies in colour from light yellow to deep orange or brown.

90 *obsidian:* dark volcanic glass.

91 *magnesium-calcium ratio:* balance which affects the nervous transmission and therefore muscular co-ordination.

92 *ophthalmia:* inflammation of the eye.

goitre: morbid and often enormously developed enlargement of the thyroid gland of the neck.

95 *A most unhappy gentleman:* although 'most unhappy' and 'gentleman' frequently occur in Shakespeare's works, there is no place where this precise phrase can be found. In *Richard II*, Act III, Scene I, the King is referred to as 'a happy gentleman in blood and lineaments'.

Do you see that damned spot?: Macbeth, Act V, Scene I.

96 *The multitudinous seas incarnadine: Macbeth*, Act II, Scene II.

The disliked me for my complexion: The Merchant of Venice, Act II, Scene I. The Prince of Morocco's opening words are: 'Mislike me not for my complexion'.

Pookong: perhaps an invention of Huxley's, although the name does bear some resemblance to Pe′kwin, the Zuñi

235

sun-priest. In Chapter XI Pookong is represented by an eagle image which is presumably the same as that described earlier in this chapter. In the Pueblos eagles are kept for a year then killed to be sent to the gods to report on the world of men.

98 *'mescal'*: strong intoxicating drink distilled from the fermented juice of the American aloe.

Popé: Popé of San Juan was the leader of the Great Rebellion of the Pueblo Indians against the Spanish in 1680. It took over fourteen years for the Spanish to re-establish their control.

'peyotl': species of cactus, and a drink – made from the cactus buttons – which can induce hallucinations.

Chelsea: fashionable part of south west London.

99 *aseptic*: not liable to decay.

Streptock-Gee: streptococcus is of bacteria which causes sore throats. It was a streptococcus which destroyed the cornea of one of Huxley's eyes when he was sixteen.

100 *Waihusiwa*: Zuñi name. Parsons describes a meeting with Waihu'siwa of Zuñi, chief of the rain society of the East.

Chapter VIII

101 *tortillas*: thin round cake made out of maize flour.

Bye, Baby Banting: Banting was the name of a nineteenth-century cabinet-maker who devised a system for losing weight. His name was used for a time as popular slang for slimming.

The original form of the nursery rhyme is

Bye, baby bunting,
Daddy's gone a-hunting,
Gone to get a rabbit skin
To wrap the baby bunting in.

102 *gourd*: 'shell' or rind of a large fleshy fruit, dried and used as a bottle.

105 *Awonawilona:* literally 'keepers of the roads of life'. Awonawilona was thought by Stevenson to be a single god
who was the first creator in Zuñi legend, but Parsons suggests that the word applies to a more diffuse sort of life
force.

Ahaiyuta and Marsailema: according to Stevenson the twin
gods of Laughing Water both bore the name A'hayuta in
times of peace, but when associated with war the elder is
always referred to as U'yuyeni and the younger as Ma†sai
'lema.

108 *Kiva:* chamber built wholly or partly underground,
though the word is a corruption of the Pueblo term ki-he
which means a building of any kind.

Nay, but to live...: Hamlet, Act III, Scene IV.

A man can smile...: Hamlet, Act I, Scene V.

109 *When he is drunk asleep...:* Hamlet, Act III, Scene III.

110 *Ahaiyuta:* see note to page 105. Here, presumably, the
term refers to the god in wartime.

113 *To-morrow and to-morrow and to-morrow....* Macbeth, Act V,
Scene V.

114 *Miranda:* see *Introduction*, page xii.

Chapter IX

116 *agaves:* plants such as the American aloe whose flower-
stem can grow to forty feet (12m).

Whitehall: street where most of the important government
ministeries are situated in London.

117 *electrolytic:* breaking up a compound by the action of elec-
tricity.

118 *He crammed up his thieveries:* Troilus and Cressida, Act IV,
Scene IV: 'Injurious Time now with a robber's haste /
Crams his rich thievery up, he knows not how.'

119 *Her eyes, her hair...:* Triolus and Cressida, Act I, Scene I.

may seize...: Romeo and Juliet, Act III, Scene III.

Dare to profane...: Romeo and Juliet, Act I, Scene V.

If I profane with my unworthiest hand
This holy shrine, the gentle sin is this,
My lips, two blushing pilgrims, ready stand
To smooth that rough touch with a tender kiss.

Chapter X

120 *Bloomsbury Centre:* the British Museum is in Bloomsbury,
West Central London.
aeons: immeasurable periods of time, ages of the universe.

124 *scatalogical:* filthy. Scatology is the branch of science which
deals with diagnosis by means of an examination of faeces.

Chapter XI

125 *Dr Shaw:* see note to page 18 for Bernard Shaw.

126 *Eternity was in our lips: Antony and Cleopatra,* Act I, Scene
III.
patchouli: penetrating and lasting perfume.

129 *Dravidian:* from southern India or the northern half of
Ceylon. Strictly, the word should only be applied to the
languages of the area.
Ariel could put a girdle . . .: Ariel was the spirit who was
Prospero's servant in *The Tempest.* It was Puck in *A Mid-
summer Night's Dream,* Act II, Scene I, who promised his
master Oberon: 'I'll put a girdle round about the earth /
In forty minutes.'

130 *prognathous:* having prominent projecting jaws.

131 *Eton:* Huxley was at Eton College for two and a half years
until the serious deterioration of his eyesight (see *Introduction,* page vii) and he spent nearly two years as a master
there from September 1917.
Lupton's Tower: named after Provost Lupton who in 1504
left a bequest to seventy scholars and a hundred Oppidans
(fee-paying pupils). The Tower is one of the most easily
recognized pieces of Eton architecture. It is not 'gleaming

white', but brick-faced. In front of it stands a statue of King Henry VI, the founder of the College.

School Community Singery: Eton College Chapel is one of the most distinguished and famous of its buildings.

vita-glass: variety of glass which allows ultra-violet rays to pass through it. (See note to page 11 on *Pilkington*.)

Dr Gaffney: Mr Gaffney was the School Clerk at Eton who retired in 1910.

Miss Keate: John Keate (1773–1852) was Headmaster of Eton from 1809 until 1834. His character has inspired many legends, and while it is clear that he was highly regarded, it is for such feats as his flogging of eighty boys in one day that he is chiefly remembered.

132 *elementary relativity:* Einstein's Theory of Relativity, that time and space are not absolute but merely relative to the observer, had been widely acclaimed in scientific circles about ten years before the writing of *Brave New World*.

133 *selenium:* one of the rarer elements, whose electrical resistance is greatly increased by exposure to light.

134 *Savoy:* Savoy Hotel in the Strand, London, completed in 1891. It became a byword for luxury.

What's in those . . . caskets?: scenes in *The Merchant of Venice* when Portia's suitors open the caskets are: Act II, Scene VII; Act II, Scene IX; Act III, Scene II.

135 *Young Women's Fordian Association:* the object of the Young Women's Christian Association, founded in 1855, is to win young women and girls for Christ by uniting them in fellowship through activities designed to develop their powers of body, mind and spirit.

Feelytone News: the first British sound newsreel was British Movietone, released in June 1929.

Deauville: seaside resort in northern France. It was popular for visits by the British, for whom the town acquired the reputation of being rather stylish and mildly sinful.

136 *Capriccio:* musical composition of lively character and more or less free in form.

arpeggios: playing the notes of a chord in rapid succession instead of simultaneously.

Gaspard Forster: Kaspar Forster (1617–73), German singer and composer. His powerful bass voice went down to a full-sounding A (fifty-five cycles per second).

Lucrezia Ajugari: Italian opera singer who indeed surprised Mozart by singing the note described.

137 *THREE WEEKS IN A HELICOPTER:* see note to page 27 for a reference to Elinor Glyn's *Three Weeks*.

erogenous zones: portions of the skin which yield a feeling of pleasure when stimulated.

138 *gardenias:* tropical plants with beautiful and fragrant flowers.

Chapter XII

143 *carotine:* carotene is a red crystalline compound contained in carrots and tomatoes.

145 *St Helena:* small island in the South Atlantic where Napoleon Bonaparte was held prisoner from 1815 until his death in 1821.

O, she doth teach . . .: Romeo and Juliet, Act I, Scene V.

147 *discomfited:* defeated, utterly dejected.

148 *Yesterday's committee:* although there is no single source for Helmholtz's poem, there are distinct echoes in it of T S Eliot's *Rhapsody on a Windy Night*, published in 1915.

Egeria: it is not easy to explain why the name of an Italian goddess of fountains should have survived into the brave new world; perhaps the rhyme demanded it.

149 *Let the bird . . .:* opening of Shakespeare's poem *The Phoenix and the Turtle*.

151 *Is there no pity . . .: Romeo and Juliet,* Act III, Scene V.

Chapter XIII

153 *adage:* proverb.

154 *Mwanza-Mwanza:* large town on the south shore of Lake

Victoria in what was Tanganyika Territory. It is now the fourth town of Tanzania.

trypanosomiasis: sleeping-sickness.

155 *Admired Lenina: The Tempest*, Act III, Scene I. Ferdinand's words to Miranda are:

> Admired Miranda!
> Indeed the top of admiration! worth
> What's dearest to the world! . . . but you, O you,
> So perfect and so peerless, are created
> Of every creature's best.

156 *There be some sports . . . : The Tempest*, Act III, Scene I.

157 *Outliving beauty's outward . . . : Troilus and Cressida*, Act III, Scene III.

If thou dost break . . . : The Tempest, Act IV, Scene I.

158 *The murkiest den . . . : The Tempest*, Act IV, Scene I.

For those milk paps . . . : Timon of Athens, Act IV, Scene III.

159 *The strongest oaths . . . : The Tempest*, Act IV, Scene I.

160 *Impudent strumpet!: Othello*, Act IV, Scene II.

The wren goes to't . . . : King Lear, Act IV, Scene VI.

161 *O thou weed . . . : Othello*, Act IV, Scene II.

The devil Luxury . . . : Troilus and Cressida, Act V, Scene II.

162 *If I do not usurp myself, I am: Twelfth Night*, Act I, Scene V.

Park Lane: extremely fashionable and expensive part of the West End of London.

Chapter XIV

164 *Super-Vox-Wurlitzeriana:* the Wurlitzer 'Electronic' piano was particularly popular as a cinema organ.

verbena: lemon-scented plant.

169 *Bed 20:* In Chapter 2 of *Hard Times* Sissy Jupe is known as girl number twenty.

Chapter XV

171 *dolichocephalic:* long-headed. Technically the term is used

of a skull of which the breadth is less than four-fifths of the length.

173 *Lend me your ears: Julius Caesar*, Act III, Scene II.

174 *Biarritz:* holiday resort in south west France, well known for luxurious and expensive living.

Mewling and puking: As You Like It, Act II, Scene VII.

carapace: upper body-shell of tortoises and of crustaceans.

176 *wambling:* tottering.

177 *valedictions:* farewells.

Chapter XVI

Mustapha Mond's explanation of his responsibilities here and in Chapter XVII is based on 'The Grand Inquisitor', a chapter in *The Brothers Karamazov* by Fyodor Dostoyevsky (1821–81).

During the time of the Spanish Inquisition, Christ visits Seville the day after a hundred heretics had been burnt on the orders of the Cardinal, the Grand Inquisitor. He is recognized by the people, but they make no move to save him when the soldiers arrest him. At night the Grand Inquisitor, an old man of nearly ninety, comes to visit the prisoner, and is the only one to speak at their meeting.

The central point of what he says is that men do not want the freedom which Christ came to give them; men do not want to be faced with moral choice, they prefer to abdicate all authority to others, in this case the Church. Men wish to be led like sheep: 'for what man seeks is not so much God as miracles'. Freedom of choice leads inevitably to anarchy and misery.

Mustapha Mond's account of the Cyprus experiment pursues the same theme, as does his assertion that it is absurd to expect Deltas to know what liberty is. His reflection that 'Happiness is a hard master – particularly other people's happiness', is explained in more detail by the Grand Inquisitor. He is talking about the enormous responsibil-

ity borne by those who have removed the burden of freedom from the mass of people.

> And they will all be happy, all the millions of creatures,
> except the hundred thousand who rule over them. For
> we alone, we who guard the mystery, we alone shall be
> unhappy. There will be thousands of millions of happy
> infants and one hundred thousand sufferers who have
> taken on themselves the curse of knowledge of good and
> evil.
>
> (*The Brothers Karamazov*, translated by David
> Magarshack)

178 *Detroit:* centre of the American automobile industry and of
the Ford Company.
Society for the Propagation of Fordian Knowledge: the society
for the Propagation of Christian Knowledge applies itself
to educational and missionary work.

179 *Sometimes a thousand. . . .: The Tempest,* Act III, Scene II.
Goats and monkeys!: Othello, Act IV, Scene I.

181 *told by an idiot: Macbeth,* Act V, Scene V.
gyroscope: instrument in which a rotating wheel mounted
in a ring can be used for keeping a compass needle pointing in the same direction when fitted in a ship or aircraft.

187 *The Marquesas:* islands situated roughly in the middle of
the Pacific Ocean.

188 *Falkland Islands:* group of two main islands with about a
hundred smaller ones clustered around them, off the tip of
South America in the South Atlantic.

Chapter XVII

189 *'The Imitation of Christ':* the purpose of this famous manual
of spiritual devotion is to instruct the Christian how to
seek perfection by following Christ as his model. The

authorship has traditionally been assigned to Thomas à Kempis (lived about 1380–1471).

'The Varieties of Religious Experience': the principal conclusion of this book, by the philosopher and psychologist William James (1842–1910), is that in times of trouble we can make specific contact with various reservoirs of consciousness-like energies. James' work was seen as a possible bridge over what appeared to be a widening gap between the claims of religion and of science.

190   *Cardinal Newman:* John Henry Newman (1801–90), leader of the Oxford – or Tracterian – Movement in the Church of England, which based its search for spirituality on a systematic study of the Fathers of the early Church. Between 1833 and 1841 he wrote twenty-four *Tracts for the Times*, but in 1845 was received into the Roman Catholic Church.

exclaimed: it is hard to believe that Huxley had not intended to write 'explained' here.

I, Pandulph . . .: King John, Act III, Scene I.

Maine de Biran: Marie-François-Pierre Gonthier de Biran (1766–1824), writer in whose works Huxley took a particular interest. Maine de Biran, as he was known, is one of the most important figures in the history of nineteenth-century French philosophy. Although he was initially a sceptic, his final view of humans was that we are reflective beings, free to exercise intellectual and moral choice in spite of the pressures of external circumstances, and that our best path to an understanding of the truth lies in observation and study of our own personalities. His *Journal Intime*, not published for a hundred years after his death, is the best illustration of his principles. In *Themes and Variations*, published in 1950, Huxley devotes over half of the book to a study of Maine de Biran, liberally illustrated with quotations from the *Journal*.

A man who dreams . . .: Hamlet, Act I, Scene V. When Hamlet says to Horatio: 'There are more things in heaven and

earth, Horatio, / Than are dreamt of in your philosophy',
he is not talking about Horatio's personal beliefs, but of
all philosophy; 'your' is impersonal in this context.

We are not our own...: this passage is taken from Sermon 6
in Volume 5 of Newman's *Parochial and Plain Sermons*. The
title of the sermon, for the Second Sunday after Christ-
mas, is *Remembrance of Past Mercies*, and in it Newman
dwells on three figures, Jacob, David and St Paul, 'the
three great patterns of thankfulness which are set before
us in the Scripture'. The extract, with one or two significant differences from the version in *Brave New World*, was
included in *A Newman Synthesis*, arranged by Erich Przy-
wara S J and published in 1930. It seems probable that
Huxley imagined Mustapha Mond taking this single
volume from his safe rather than his having room in it for
a shelf-full of Newman's collected works.

The passage appears in *A Newman Synthesis* as follows:

We are not our own, any more than what we possess is
our own. We did not make ourselves; we cannot be supreme over ourselves. We cannot be our own masters.
We are God's property by creation, by redemption, by
regeneration. He has a triple claim upon us. Is it not
our happiness thus to view the matter? Is it any happiness, or any comfort, to consider that we *are* our own? It
may be thought so by the young and prosperous. These
may think it a great thing to have everything, as they
suppose, their own way – to depend on no one, – to have
to think of nothing out of sight, to be without the
irksomeness of continual acknowledgement, continual
prayer, continual reference of what they do to the will of
another. But as time goes on, they, as all men, will find
that independence was not made for man – that it is an
unnatural state – may do for a while, but will not carry
us on safely to the end. No, we are creatures; and as
being such, we have two duties, to be resigned and to be
thankful.

Apart from minor changes, such as 'we are not our own masters' for 'we cannot be our own masters', and '– will do for a while, but will not carry us...' for '– may do for a while, but will not carry us...', the major alterations Huxley has made have the effect of avoiding the impact of specifically Christian teaching. Creation, redemption, regeneration and man's duties to God are all omitted.

What Huxley appears to have done is to alter Newman's words until they approach more closely to his own views, and then pass them off as what was originally written.

191 *A man grows old...*: translation, presumably by Huxley himself, of the entry in Maine de Biran's *Journal* under the date *6 et 7 juin 1818*. As with the Newman passage there are significant differences between the original and what appears in *Brave New World*, as can be seen by comparing Huxley's translation with a modern one by Janet M Ferrier.

> ...Growing old is inevitably associated with feelings of weakness, lethargy and discomfort inseparable from increasing age; and we declare that we are sick, deluding ourselves with the idea that this distressing condition results from some particular cause from which we may hope to recover, as from a sickness. Vain *imaginings!* The sickness is old age, and it is incurable; we have to *resign* ourselves to it. The feeling of distress can only diminish, to a greater or lesser degree, as sensations of our youth recede into the distance and are lost to our memory. For it is precisely this contrast which makes us so unhappy, as we pass from one age to another, this feeling that we are *growing old*; when we are indeed old, in other words *dead to our youth*, we are no longer so unhappy.
>
> It is said that men become religious or devout as they grow older because they fear death and what must follow in another life; but speaking for myself I realize

that without any such fear or any working of the imagination, religious feelings may develop as we advance in years, at first because once our passions are stilled and our imagination and sensibility less often or less easily stimulated, *reason* has less difficulty in exerting its sway, is less clouded by the images or affections that used to preoccupy it. Then God, the sovereign good, appears as from a cloud; our soul feels him, sees him, as it turns towards him, the source of all light, because, as all the world of the senses slips away and phenomenal existence is no longer supported by sensations from within and without, we feel the need to rely upon something enduring, an end to deception, a reality, a truth that is absolute and eternal; because in the end religious feeling, so pure and gentle an experience, can make up for all the other things we have lost. The fear of death and hell has nothing to do with this feeling, and indeed is directly opposed to it.

The alterations and omissions made by Huxley subtly alter the thought of the original. He implies that the religious impulse is a second best because the joys and intense feelings of youth have vanished. Maine de Biran, on the contrary, says that we cease to regret these things because we find a greater good.

192 *Bradley:* F H Bradley (1846–1924), whose view that all human judgments can never be entirely free from error or potential error is of particular relevance here.

193 *The gods are just . . .: King Lear*, Act V, Scene III.

194 *But value dwells not . . .: Troilus and Cressida*, Act II, Scene II.
neurasthenia: nervous debility.

195 *If after every tempest . . .: Othello*, Act II, Scene I.
Mátsaki: Ma⁺sakia, village less than two miles from Zuñi. The word originally means salt.

196 *Whether 'tis nobler . . .: Hamlet*, Act III, Scene I.
Exposing what is mortal . . .: Hamlet, Act IV, Scene IV.
adrenals: glands above the kidneys which produce adrena-

line, a substance which increases blood pressure and creates a state of high excitement in human beings.

197 *adrenin:* substance from the adrenals.

Chapter XVIII

199 *Guildford ... Wey valley ...:* the setting for the last chapter is that part of England with particular ties for Huxley as it is where he was brought up. He was born at Laleham, near *Godalming*, and went to preparatory school near the town. This area of Surrey was where he used to roam on foot and on bicycle when he was a child; his cousin, Gervas Huxley, remembered him riding down the Devil's Punch-bowl into *Milford* at terrific speeds. When he was very young he was taken to concerts at *Haslemere*. *The Hog's Back* is a narrow part of the Surrey North Downs between *Guildford* and *Farnham*, with splendid views of the surrounding countryside, and *Hindhead* is known as one of southern England's finest viewpoints. *Selborne* was made famous by Gilbert White's *The Natural History of Selborne*, published in 1789. Farnham, though famous for its golf course, was also where Jonathan Swift wrote two of his satires, *Tale of a Tub* and *Battle of the Books* in 1696 and 1697.

The sense of personal involvement for the writer is increased by the setting for the Savage's suicide being close to where Huxley's brother Trevenan hanged himself at the age of twenty-four. (See *Introduction*, page viii and ix.)

200 *Claudius: Hamlet*, Act III, Scene III.

201 *plumbless:* beyond measurement.

205 *Primo Mellon:* the name Primo may have been suggested by the Italian heavyweight boxer Primo Carnera, but he did not become world champion until 1933, two years after the book was written. Andrew Mellon (1855–1937) was President of the Mellon National Bank, USA, a position from which he resigned in 1921 in order to become

Secretary of the Treasury for President Harding, and later for President Coolidge.

coccyx: small triangular bone at the lower end of the spinal column.

206 *importunately:* in a persistently troublesome fashion.

207 *Darwin Bonaparte:* Charles Robert Darwin (1809–82) published *On the Origin of Species by Means of Natural Selection* in 1859. His theory of evolution through natural selection caused a revolution in biological science. Napoleon Bonaparte (1769–1821) crowned himself Emperor of the French in 1804, and was one of the greatest military geniuses of his time. He died in exile on the island of St Helena (see note to page 145).

bole: round trunk of a tree.

208 *And all our yesterdays . . . : Macbeth,* Act V, Scene V.

A good kissing carrion: Hamlet, Act II, Scene II.

As flies to wanton boys . . . : King Lear, Act IV, Scene I.

209 *ever-gentle gods: King Lear,* Act IV, Scene VI.

thy best of rest . . . : Measure for Measure, Act III, Scene I.

Perchance to dream: Hamlet, Act III, Scene I.

shantung: soft Chinese silk.

'petits beurres': small sweetened biscuits.

211 *Fitchew!:* polecat. Used as a contemptuous term for a prostitute in *Othello,* Act IV, Scene II.

212 *Fry, lechery, fry!: Troilus and Cressida,* Act V, Scene II.

Further reading

To offer yet more books for further reading after notes which suggest over fifty works which could be useful to the student studying *Brave New World* might signal the final overwhelming of one's interest. However, there are particular areas where selective reading can help to develop more informed critical responses, and some of the following books may prove helpful:

Other works by Aldous Huxley

Crome Yellow (1921)
Antic Hay (1923)
Those Barren Leaves (1925)
Point Counter Point (1928)
All published by Chatto and Windus.

These four novels were all written before *Brave New World* and show the development of Huxley's style and principal concerns. His further thoughts on the issues raised in the book can be seen in:
Ape and Essence (1948)
Brave New World Revisited (1959)
Island (1962)
All published by Chatto and Windus.

Aldous Huxley's life

SYBILLE BEDFORD *Aldous Huxley: a biography* 2 vols, William Collins and Chatto and Windus 1973.

GROVER SMITH (ed.) *Letters of Aldous Huxley*, Chatto and Windus 1969.

DONALD WATTS (ed.) *Aldous Huxley: the critical heritage*, Routledge and Kegan Paul 1975 – which contains some fascinating contemporary reviews of Huxley's writings.

Discussion points

There are other books which provide useful comparisons with *Brave New World*. A list of 'Utopian' literature could stretch for several pages, but I shall limit it in this case to three works:

THOMAS MORE *Utopia*, now available in a modern English translation by P Turner, Oxford University Press 1965.
GEORGE ORWELL *Nineteen Eighty Four*, Longman Study Texts. – frequently compared with *Brave New World*. (See *Introduction*, page xxi.)
ANTHONY BURGESS *A Clockwork Orange*, Heinemann 1962.

Perhaps the most vigorous critical responses to *Brave New World* will be provoked by comparing the way we react to advances in technology today with that in which they are received in the novel. For example, there are two aspects of modern life, one a remote but distinct possibility and the other seen all around us, which might be put forward to stimulate argument. It may eventually be possible to clone human beings, reproducing the same person, not just someone similar but a version as identical as two members of a Bokanovsky group. Is our response fascination or horror? It comforts us to imagine that it is horror, but is that the principal response reflected in newspaper or television speculation on the subject? The other example is the staggering increase in the number of electronic toys and games. Electro-magnetic golf may seem silly, but how does it differ essentially from the equally popular Space Invaders? The games in *Brave New World* were designed to kill time, to stave off boredom rather than to stimulate the imagination; do the complicated and inviting video games of the 1980s create a 'boredom trap' in which the imagination is stifled and boredom can only be kept at bay by yet more new toys?

Recent history suggests that the attractions of the hippy culture of the 1960s – plenty of sex, lots of drugs, and freedom from responsibility – are very like the good life to be enjoyed in Huxley's book: promiscuity is encouraged, *soma* provides instant holidays, and no one has to worry about moral decisions. Have the ideals of the hippies turned into the dissatisfaction of a Bernard Marx or a Helmholtz Watson?

Simply keeping eyes and ears open should provide perceptive students with plenty of material by which to measure the present age against the values shown in *Brave New World*.